Dorothy L. Sayers

WHOSE BODY?

Dorothy L. Sayers (1893–1957) was an English poet, writer, and student of classical languages. She was one of the first women to be awarded a degree by Oxford University and later worked as a copywriter at an advertising agency. She was best known for her mystery novels, many of them featuring the amateur sleuth Lord Peter Wimsey, and for her translation of Dante's *Divine Comedy*.

D0110766

WHOSE BODY?

WHOSE BODY?

A LORD PETER WIMSEY MYSTERY

Dorothy L. Sayers

VINTAGE BOOKS

A Division of Penguin Random House LLC

New York

FIRST VINTAGE BOOKS EDITION, MAY 2019

All rights reserved. Published in the United States by Vintage Books,
a division of Penguin Random House LLC, New York, and distributed
in Canada by Random House of Canada, a division of Penguin Random
House Canada Limited, Toronto. Originally published in Great
Britain by T. Fisher Unwin, London, and in the United States by
Harper & Row Publishers, Inc., New York, in 1923.

Vintage and colophon are registered trademarks of
Penguin Random House LLC.

This is a work of fiction. Names, characters, places, and incidents
either are the product of the author's imagination or are used
fictitiously. Any resemblance to actual persons, living or dead, events,
or locales is entirely coincidental.

Library of Congress Cataloging-in-Publication Data
Names: Sayers, Dorothy L. (Dorothy Leigh), 1893–1957.
Title: Whose body? : a Lord Peter Wimsey novel / Dorothy L. Sayers.
Description: 1st HarperPerennial ed. |
New York : HarperPerennial, 1993. | Identifiers: LCCN 92042525
Subjects: LCSH: Wimsey, Peter, Lord (Fictitious character),
1890—Fiction. | Private investigators—England—Fiction. |
GSAFD: Detective and mystery stories.
Classification: LCC PR6037.A95 W4 1993 | DDC 823/.912—dc23
LC record available at https://lccn.loc.gov/92042525

Vintage Books Trade Paperback ISBN: 978-0-525-56511-6

www.vintagebooks.com

Printed in the United States of America

The Singular Adventure of the

MAN WITH THE GOLDEN PINCE-NEZ

To M. J.

Dear Jim:
This book is your fault. If it had not been for your brutal insistence, Lord Peter would never have staggered through to the end of this enquiry. Pray consider that he thanks you with his accustomed suavity.

Yours ever,
D. L. S.

WHOSE BODY?

WHOSE BODY?

I

"Oh, damn!" said Lord Peter Wimsey at Piccadilly Circus. "Hi, driver!"

The taxi man, irritated at receiving this appeal while negotiating the intricacies of turning into Lower Regent Street across the route of a 19 'bus, a 38-B and a bicycle, bent an unwilling ear.

"I've left the catalogue behind," said Lord Peter deprecatingly. "Uncommonly careless of me. D'you mind puttin' back to where we came from?"

"To the Savile Club, sir?"

"No—110 Piccadilly—just beyond—thank you."

"Thought you was in a hurry," said the man, overcome with a sense of injury.

"I'm afraid it's an awkward place to turn in," said Lord Peter, answering the thought rather than the words. His long, amiable face looked as if it had generated spontaneously from his top hat, as white maggots breed from Gorgonzola.

The taxi, under the severe eye of a policeman, revolved by slow jerks, with a noise like the grinding of teeth.

The block of new, perfect and expensive flats in which Lord Peter dwelt upon the second floor, stood directly opposite the Green Park, in a spot for many years occupied by the skeleton of a frustrate commercial enterprise. As Lord Peter let himself in he heard his man's voice in the library, uplifted in that throttled stridency peculiar to well-trained persons using the telephone.

"I believe that's his lordship just coming in again—if your Grace would kindly hold the line a moment."

"What is it, Bunter?"

"Her Grace has just called up from Denver, my lord. I was just saying your lordship had gone to the sale when I heard your lordship's latchkey."

"Thanks," said Lord Peter; "and you might find me my catalogue, would you? I think I must have left it in my bedroom, or on the desk."

He sat down to the telephone with an air of leisurely courtesy, as though it were an acquaintance dropped in for a chat.

"Hullo, Mother—that you?"

"Oh, there you are, dear," replied the voice of the Dowager Duchess. "I was afraid I'd just missed you."

"Well, you had, as a matter of fact. I'd just started off to Brocklebury's sale to pick up a book or two, but I had to come back for the catalogue. What's up?"

"Such a quaint thing," said the Duchess. "I thought I'd tell you. You know little Mr. Thipps?"

"Thipps?" said Lord Peter. "Thipps? Oh, yes, the little architect man who's doing the church roof. Yes. What about him?"

"Mrs. Throgmorton's just been in, in quite a state of mind."

"Sorry, Mother, I can't hear. Mrs. Who?"

"Throgmorton—Throgmorton—the vicar's wife."

"Oh, Throgmorton, yes?"

"Mr. Thipps rang them up this morning. It was his day to come down, you know."

"Yes?"

"He rang them up to say he couldn't. He was so upset, poor little man. He'd found a dead body in his bath."

"Sorry, Mother, I can't hear; found what, where?"

"A dead body, dear, in his bath."

"What?—no, no, we haven't finished. Please don't cut us off. Hullo! Hullo! Is that you, Mother? Hullo!—Mother!—Oh, yes—sorry, the girl was trying to cut us off. What sort of body?"

"A dead man, dear, with nothing on but a pair of pince-nez. Mrs. Throgmorton positively blushed when she was telling me. I'm afraid people do get a little narrow-minded in country vicarages."

"Well, it sounds a bit unusual. Was it anybody he knew?"

"No, dear, I don't think so, but, of course, he couldn't give her many details. She said he sounded quite distracted. He's such a respectable little man—and having the police in the house and so on, really worried him."

"Poor little Thipps! Uncommonly awkward for him. Let's see, he lives in Battersea, doesn't he?"

"Yes, dear; 59, Queen Caroline Mansions; opposite the Park. That big block just round the corner from the Hospital. I thought perhaps you'd like to run round and see him and ask if there's anything we can do. I always thought him a nice little man."

"Oh, quite," said Lord Peter, grinning at the telephone. The Duchess was always of the greatest assistance to his hobby of criminal investigation, though she never alluded to it, and maintained a polite fiction of its non-existence.

"What time did it happen, Mother?"

"I think he found it early this morning, but, of course, he didn't think of telling the Throgmortons just at first. She came up to me just before lunch—so tiresome, I had to ask her to stay. Fortunately, I was alone. I don't mind being bored myself, but I hate having my guests bored."

"Poor old Mother! Well, thanks awfully for tellin' me. I think

I'll send Bunter to the sale and toddle round to Battersea now an' try and console the poor little beast. So-long."

"Good-bye, dear."

"Bunter!"

"Yes, my lord."

"Her Grace tells me that a respectable Battersea architect has discovered a dead man in his bath."

"Indeed, my lord? That's very gratifying."

"Very, Bunter. Your choice of words is unerring. I wish Eton and Balliol had done as much for me. Have you found the catalogue?"

"Here it is, my lord."

"Thanks. I am going to Battersea at once. I want you to attend the sale for me. Don't lose time—I don't want to miss the Folio Dante[*] nor the de Voragine—here you are—see? 'Golden Legend'—Wynkyn de Worde, 1493—got that?—and, I say, make a special effort for the Caxton folio of the 'Four Sons of Aymon'—it's the 1489 folio and unique. Look! I've marked the lots I want, and put my outside offer against each. Do your best for me. I shall be back to dinner."

"Very good, my lord."

"Take my cab and tell him to hurry. He may for you; he doesn't like me very much. Can I," said Lord Peter, looking at himself in the eighteenth-century mirror over the mantelpiece, "can I have the heart to fluster the flustered Thipps further—that's very difficult to say quickly—by appearing in a top-hat

---

[*] This is the first Florence edition, 1481, by Niccolo di Lorenzo. Lord Peter's collection of printed Dantes is worth inspection. It includes, besides the famous Aldine 8vo. of 1502, the Naples folio of 1477—"edizione rarissima," according to Colomb. This copy has no history, and Mr. Parker's private belief is that its present owner conveyed it away by stealth from somewhere or other. Lord Peter's own account is that he "picked it up in a little place in the hills," when making a walking-tour through Italy.

and frock-coat? I think not. Ten to one he will overlook my trousers and mistake me for the undertaker. A grey suit, I fancy, neat but not gaudy, with a hat to tone, suits my other self better. Exit the amateur of first editions; new motive introduced by solo bassoon; enter Sherlock Holmes, disguised as a walking gentleman. There goes Bunter. Invaluable fellow—never offers to do his job when you've told him to do somethin' else. Hope he doesn't miss the 'Four Sons of Aymon.' Still, there *is* another copy of that—in the Vatican.* It might become available, you never know—if the Church of Rome went to pot or Switzerland invaded Italy—whereas a strange corpse doesn't turn up in a suburban bathroom more than once in a lifetime—at least, I should think not—at any rate, the number of times it's happened, *with* a pince-nez, might be counted on the fingers of one hand, I imagine. Dear me! it's a dreadful mistake to ride two hobbies at once."

He had drifted across the passage into his bedroom, and was changing with a rapidity one might not have expected from a man of his mannerisms. He selected a dark-green tie to match his socks and tied it accurately without hesitation or the slightest compression of his lips; substituted a pair of brown shoes for his black ones, slipped a monocle into a breast pocket, and took up a beautiful Malacca walking-stick with a heavy silver knob.

"That's all, I think," he murmured to himself. "Stay—I may as well have you—you may come in useful—one never knows." He added a flat silver matchbox to his equipment, glanced at his watch, and seeing that it was already a quarter to three, ran briskly downstairs, and, hailing a taxi, was carried to Battersea Park.

---

* Lord Peter's wits were wool-gathering. The book is in the possession of Earl Spencer. The Brocklebury copy is incomplete, the last five signatures being altogether missing, but is unique in possessing the colophon.

Mr. Alfred Thipps was a small, nervous man, whose flaxen hair was beginning to abandon the unequal struggle with destiny. One might say that his only really marked feature was a large bruise over the left eyebrow, which gave him a faintly dissipated air incongruous with the rest of his appearance. Almost in the same breath with his first greeting, he made a self-conscious apology for it, murmuring something about having run against the dining-room door in the dark. He was touched almost to tears by Lord Peter's thoughtfulness and condescension in calling.

"I'm sure it's most kind of your lordship," he repeated for the dozenth time, rapidly blinking his weak little eyelids. "I appreciate it very deeply, very deeply, indeed, and so would Mother, only she's so deaf, I don't like to trouble you with making her understand. It's been very hard all day," he added, "with the policemen in the house and all this commotion. It's what Mother and me have never been used to, always living very retired, and it's most distressing to a man of regular habits, my lord, and reely, I'm almost thankful Mother doesn't understand, for I'm sure it would worry her terribly if she was to know about it. She was upset at first, but she's made up some idea of her own about it now, and I'm sure it's all for the best."

The old lady who sat knitting by the fire nodded grimly in response to a look from her son.

"I always said as you ought to complain about that bath, Alfred," she said suddenly, in the high, piping voice peculiar to the deaf, "and it's to be 'oped the landlord'll see about it now; not but what I think you might have managed without having the police in, but there! you always were one to make a fuss about a little thing, from chicken-pox up."

"There now," said Mr. Thipps apologetically, "you see how it is. Not but what it's just as well she's settled on that, because she understands we've locked up the bathroom and don't try to go in there. But it's been a terrible shock to me, sir—my lord, I should say, but there! my nerves are all to pieces. Such a thing has never 'appened—happened to me in all my born days. Such a state I was in this morning—I didn't know if I was on my head or my heels—I reely didn't, and my heart not being too strong, I hardly knew how to get out of that horrid room and telephone for the police. It's affected me, sir, it's affected me, it reely has—I couldn't touch a bit of breakfast, nor lunch neither, and what with telephoning and putting off clients and interviewing people all morning, I've hardly known what to do with myself."

"I'm sure it must have been uncommonly distressin'," said Lord Peter, sympathetically, "especially comin' like that before breakfast. Hate anything tiresome happenin' before breakfast. Takes a man at such a confounded disadvantage, what?"

"That's just it, that's just it," said Mr. Thipps, eagerly. "When I saw that dreadful thing lying there in my bath, mother-naked, too, except for a pair of eyeglasses, I assure you, my lord, it regularly turned my stomach, if you'll excuse the expression. I'm not very strong, sir, and I get that sinking feeling sometimes in the morning, and what with one thing and another I 'ad—had to send the girl for a stiff brandy, or I don't know *what* mightn't have happened. I felt so queer, though I'm anything but partial to spirits as a rule. Still, I make it a rule never to be without brandy in the house, in case of emergency, you know?"

"Very wise of you," said Lord Peter, cheerfully. "You're a very far-seein' man, Mr. Thipps. Wonderful what a little nip'll do in case of need, and the less you're used to it the more good it does you. Hope your girl is a sensible young woman, what? Nuisance to have women faintin' and shriekin' all over the place."

"Oh, Gladys is a good girl," said Mr. Thipps, "very reasonable indeed. She was shocked, of course; that's very understandable. I was shocked myself, and it wouldn't be proper in a young woman not to be shocked under the circumstances, but she is reely a helpful, energetic girl in a crisis, if you understand me. I consider myself very fortunate these days to have got a good, decent girl to do for me and Mother, even though she is a bit careless and forgetful about little things, but that's only natural. She was very sorry indeed about having left the bathroom window open, she reely was, and though I was angry at first, seeing what's come of it, it wasn't anything to speak of, not in the ordinary way, as you might say. Girls will forget things, you know, my lord, and reely she was so distressed I didn't like to say too much to her. All I said was: 'It might have been burglars,' I said, 'remember that, next time you leave a window open all night; this time it was a dead man,' I said, 'and that's unpleasant enough, but next time it might be burglars,' I said, 'and all of us murdered in our beds.' But the police inspector—Inspector Sugg, they called him, from the Yard—he was very sharp with her, poor girl. Quite frightened her, and made her think he suspected her of something, though what good a body could be to her, poor girl, I can't imagine, and so I told the inspector. He was quite rude to me, my lord—I may say I didn't like his manner at all. 'If you've got anything definite to accuse Gladys or me of, Inspector,' I said to him, 'bring it forward, that's what you have to do,' I said, 'but I've yet to learn that you're paid to be rude to a gentleman in his own 'ouse—house.' Reely," said Mr. Thipps, growing quite pink on the top of his head, "he regularly roused me, regularly roused me, my lord, and I'm a mild man as a rule."

"Sugg all over," said Lord Peter. "I know him. When he don't know what else to say, he's rude. Stands to reason you and the girl wouldn't go collectin' bodies. Who'd want to saddle himself with a body? Difficulty's usually to get rid of 'em. Have you got rid of this one yet, by the way?"

"It's still in the bathroom," said Mr. Thipps. "Inspector Sugg said nothing was to be touched till his men came in to move it.

I'm expecting them at any time. If it would interest your lordship to have a look at it—"

"Thanks awfully," said Lord Peter. "I'd like to very much, if
I'm not puttin' you out."

"Not at all," said Mr. Thipps. His manner as he led the way
along the passage convinced Lord Peter of two things—first,
that, gruesome as his exhibit was, he rejoiced in the importance
it reflected upon himself and his flat, and secondly, that Inspector Sugg had forbidden him to exhibit it to anyone. The latter
supposition was confirmed by the action of Mr. Thipps, who
stopped to fetch the door-key from his bedroom, saying that the
police had the other, but that he made it a rule to have two keys
to every door, in case of accident.

The bathroom was in no way remarkable. It was long and narrow, the window being exactly over the head of the bath. The
panes were of frosted glass; the frame wide enough to admit a
man's body. Lord Peter stepped rapidly across to it, opened it
and looked out.

The flat was the top one of the building and situated about
the middle of the block. The bathroom window looked out
upon the back-yards of the flats, which were occupied by various small outbuildings, coal-holes, garages, and the like. Beyond
these were the back gardens of a parallel line of houses. On the
right rose the extensive edifice of St. Luke's Hospital, Battersea,
with its grounds, and, connected with it by a covered way, the
residence of the famous surgeon, Sir Julian Freke, who directed
the surgical side of the great new hospital, and was, in addition,
known in Harley Street as a distinguished neurologist with a
highly individual point of view.

This information was poured into Lord Peter's ear at considerable length by Mr. Thipps, who seemed to feel that the
neighbourhood of anybody so distinguished shed a kind of halo
of glory over Queen Caroline Mansions.

"We had him round here himself this morning," he said, "about this horrid business. Inspector Sugg thought one of the young medical gentlemen at the hospital might have brought the corpse round for a joke, as you might say, they always having bodies in the dissecting-room. So Inspector Sugg went round to see Sir Julian this morning to ask if there was a body missing. He was very kind, was Sir Julian, very kind indeed, though he was at work when they got there, in the dissecting-room. He looked up the books to see that all the bodies were accounted for, and then very obligingly came round here to look at this"—he indicated the bath—"and said he was afraid he couldn't help us—there was no corpse missing from the hospital, and this one didn't answer to the description of any they'd had."

"Nor to the description of any of the patients, I hope," suggested Lord Peter casually.

At this grisly hint Mr. Thipps turned pale.

"I didn't hear Inspector Sugg inquire," he said, with some agitation. "What a very horrid thing that would be—God bless my soul, my lord, I never thought of it."

"Well, if they had missed a patient they'd probably have discovered it by now," said Lord Peter. "Let's have a look at this one."

He screwed his monocle into his eye, adding: "I see you're troubled here with the soot blowing in. Beastly nuisance, ain't it? I get it, too—spoils all my books, you know. Here, don't you trouble, if you don't care about lookin' at it."

He took from Mr. Thipps's hesitating hand the sheet which had been flung over the bath, and turned it back.

The body which lay in the bath was that of a tall, stout man of about fifty. The hair, which was thick and black and naturally curly, had been cut and parted by a master hand, and exuded a faint violet perfume, perfectly recognisable in the close air of the bathroom. The features were thick, fleshy and strongly marked, with prominent dark eyes, and a long nose curving down to a heavy chin. The clean-shaven lips were full and sensual, and the dropped jaw showed teeth stained with tobacco. On the dead face the handsome pair of gold pince-nez mocked death with grotesque elegance; the fine gold chain curved over the naked breast. The legs lay stiffly stretched out side by side; the arms reposed close to the body; the fingers were flexed naturally. Lord Peter lifted one arm, and looked at the hand with a little frown.

"Bit of a dandy, your visitor, what?" he murmured. "Parma violet and manicure." He bent again, slipping his hand beneath the head. The absurd eyeglasses slipped off, clattering into the bath, and the noise put the last touch to Mr. Thipps's growing nervousness.

"If you'll excuse me," he murmured, "it makes me feel quite faint, it reely does."

He slipped outside, and he had no sooner done so than Lord Peter, lifting the body quickly and cautiously, turned it over and inspected it with his head on one side, bringing his monocle into play with the air of the late Joseph Chamberlain approving a rare orchid. He then laid the head over his arm, and bringing out the silver matchbox from his pocket, slipped it into the open mouth. Then making the noise usually written "Tut-tut," he laid the body down, picked up the mysterious pince-nez, looked at it, put it on his nose and looked through it, made the same noise again, readjusted the pince-nez upon the nose of the corpse, so as to leave no traces of interference for the irritation of Inspector Sugg; rearranged the body; returned to the window and, leaning out, reached upwards and sideways with his walking-stick, which he had somewhat incongruously brought along with him. Nothing appearing to come of these investigations, he withdrew his head, closed the window, and rejoined Mr. Thipps in the passage.

Mr. Thipps, touched by this sympathetic interest in the younger son of a duke, took the liberty, on their return to the sitting-room, of offering him a cup of tea. Lord Peter, who had strolled over to the window and was admiring the outlook on Battersea Park, was about to accept, when an ambulance came into view at the end of Prince of Wales Road. Its appearance reminded Lord Peter of an important engagement, and with a hurried "By Jove!" he took his leave of Mr. Thipps.

"My mother sent kind regards and all that," he said, shaking hands fervently; "hopes you'll soon be down at Denver again. Good-bye, Mrs. Thipps," he bawled kindly into the ear of the old lady. "Oh, no, my dear sir, please don't trouble to come down."

He was none too soon. As he stepped out of the door and turned towards the station, the ambulance drew up from the other direction, and Inspector Sugg emerged from it with two constables. The inspector spoke to the officer on duty at the Mansions, and turned a suspicious gaze on Lord Peter's retreating back.

"Dear old Sugg," said that nobleman, fondly, "dear, dear old bird! How he does hate me, to be sure."

II

"Excellent, Bunter," said Lord Peter, sinking with a sigh into a luxurious armchair. "I couldn't have done better myself. The thought of the Dante makes my mouth water—and the 'Four Sons of Aymon.' And you've saved me £60—that's glorious. What shall we spend it on, Bunter? Think of it—all ours, to do as we like with, for as Harold Skimpole so rightly observes, £60 saved is £60 gained, and I'd reckoned on spending it all. It's your saving, Bunter, and properly speaking, your £60. What do we want? Anything in your department? Would you like anything altered in the flat?"

"Well, my lord, as your lordship is so good"—the man-servant paused, about to pour an old brandy into a liqueur glass.

"Well, out with it, my Bunter, you imperturbable old hypocrite. It's no good talking as if you were announcing dinner—you're spilling the brandy. The voice is Jacob's voice, but the hands are the hands of Esau. What does that blessed darkroom of yours want now?"

"There's a Double Anastigmat with a set of supplementary lenses, my lord," said Bunter, with a note almost of religious fervour. "If it was a case of forgery now—or footprints—I could enlarge them right up on the plate. Or the wide-angled lens would be useful. It's as though the camera had eyes at the back of its head, my lord. Look—I've got it here."

He pulled a catalogue from his pocket, and submitted it, quivering, to his employer's gaze.

Lord Peter perused the description slowly, the corners of his long mouth lifted into a faint smile.

"It's Greek to me," he said, "and £50 seems a ridiculous price for a few bits of glass. I suppose, Bunter, you'd say £750 was a bit out of the way for a dirty old book in a dead language, wouldn't you?"

"It wouldn't be my place to say so, my lord."

"No, Bunter, I pay you £200 a year to keep your thoughts to yourself. Tell me, Bunter, in these democratic days, don't you think that's unfair?"

"No, my lord."

"You don't. D'you mind telling me frankly why you don't think it unfair?"

"Frankly, my lord, your lordship is paid a nobleman's income to take Lady Worthington in to dinner and refrain from exercising your lordship's undoubted powers of repartee."

Lord Peter considered this.

"That's your idea, is it, Bunter? Noblesse oblige—for a consideration. I daresay you're right. Then you're better off than I am, because I'd have to behave myself to Lady Worthington if I hadn't a penny. Bunter, if I sacked you here and now, would you tell me what you think of me?"

"No, my lord."

"You'd have a perfect right to, my Bunter, and if I sacked you on top of drinking the kind of coffee you make, I'd deserve everything you could say of me. You're a demon for coffee, Bunter—I don't want to know how you do it, because I believe it to be witchcraft, and I don't want to burn eternally. You can buy your cross-eyed lens."

"Thank you, my lord."

"Have you finished in the dining-room?"

"Not quite, my lord."

"Well, come back when you have. I have many things to tell you. Hullo! who's that?"

The doorbell had rung sharply.

"Unless it's anybody interestin' I'm not at home."

"Very good, my lord."

Lord Peter's library was one of the most delightful bachelor rooms in London. Its scheme was black and primrose; its walls were lined with rare editions, and its chairs and Chesterfield sofa suggested the embraces of the houris. In one corner stood a black baby grand, a wood fire leaped on a wide old-fashioned hearth, and the Sèvres vases on the chimneypiece were filled with ruddy and gold chrysanthemums. To the eyes of the young man who was ushered in from the raw November fog it seemed not only rare and unattainable, but friendly and familiar, like a colourful and gilded paradise in a mediaeval painting.

"Mr. Parker, my lord."

Lord Peter jumped up with genuine eagerness.

"My dear man, I'm delighted to see you. What a beastly foggy night, ain't it? Bunter, some more of that admirable coffee and another glass and the cigars. Parker, I hope you're full of crime—nothing less than arson or murder will do for us tonight. 'On such a night as this—' Bunter and I were just sitting down to carouse. I've got a Dante, and a Caxton folio that is practically unique, at Sir Ralph Brocklebury's sale. Bunter, who did the bargaining, is going to have a lens which does all kinds of wonderful things with its eyes shut, and

We both have got a body in a bath,
We both have got a body in a bath—
* For in spite of all temptations*

> *To go in for cheap sensations*
> *We insist upon a body in a bath—*

Nothing less will do for us, Parker. It's mine at present, but we're going shares in it. Property of the firm. Won't you join us? You really must put *something* in the jack-pot. Perhaps you have a body. Oh, do have a body. Every body welcome.

> *Gin a body meet a body*
> *Hauled before the beak,*
> *Gin a body jolly well knows who murdered a*
> *body and that old Sugg is on the wrong tack,*
> *Need a body speak?*

Not a bit of it. He tips a glassy wink to yours truly and yours truly reads the truth."

"Ah," said Parker, "I knew you'd been round to Queen Caroline Mansions. So've I, and met Sugg, and he told me he'd seen you. He was cross, too. Unwarrantable interference, he calls it."

"I knew he would," said Lord Peter. "I love taking a rise out of dear old Sugg, he's always so rude. I see by the *Star* that he has excelled himself by taking the girl, Gladys What's-her-name, into custody. Sugg of the evening, beautiful Sugg! But what were *you* doing there?"

"To tell you the truth," said Parker, "I went round to see if the Semitic-looking stranger in Mr. Thipps's bath was by any extraordinary chance Sir Reuben Levy. But he isn't."

"Sir Reuben Levy? Wait a minute, I saw something about that. I know! A headline: 'Mysterious disappearance of famous financier.' What's it all about? I didn't read it carefully."

"Well, it's a bit odd, though I daresay it's nothing really—old chap may have cleared for some reason best known to himself. It only happened this morning, and nobody would have thought anything about it, only it happened to be the day on which he had arranged to attend a most important financial meeting and do some deal involving millions—I haven't got all the details. But I know he's got enemies who'd just as soon the deal didn't come off, so when I got wind of this fellow in the bath, I buzzed round to have a look at him. It didn't seem likely, of course, but unlikelier things do happen in our profession. The funny thing is, old Sugg had got bitten with the idea it *is* him, and is wildly telegraphing to Lady Levy to come and identify him. But as a matter of fact, the man in the bath is no more Sir Reuben Levy than Adolf Beck, poor devil, was John Smith. Oddly enough, though, he would be really extraordinarily like Sir Reuben if he had a beard, and as Lady Levy is abroad with the family, some-body may say it's him, and Sugg will build up a lovely theory, like the Tower of Babel, and destined so to perish."

"Sugg's a beautiful, braying ass," said Lord Peter. "He's like a detective in a novel. Well, I don't know anything about Levy, but I've seen the body, and I should say the idea was preposter-ous upon the face of it. What do you think of the brandy?"

"Unbelievable, Wimsey—sort of thing makes one believe in heaven. But I want your yarn."

"D'you mind if Bunter hears it, too? Invaluable man, Bunter—amazin' fellow with a camera. And the odd thing is, he's always on the spot when I want my bath or my boots. I don't know when he develops things—I believe he does 'em in his sleep. Bunter!"

"Yes, my lord."

"Stop fiddling about in there, and get yourself the proper things to drink and join the merry throng."

"Certainly, my lord."

"Mr. Parker has a new trick: The Vanishing Financier. Abso-lutely no deception. Hey, presto, pass! and where is he? Will some gentleman from the audience kindly step upon the platform and inspect the cabinet? Thank you, sir. The quickness of the 'and deceives the heye."

"I'm afraid mine isn't much of a story," said Parker. "It's just one of those simple things that offer no handle. Sir Reuben Levy dined last night with three friends at the Ritz. After dinner the friends went to the theatre. He refused to go with them on account of an appointment. I haven't yet been able to trace the appointment, but anyhow, he returned home to his house— 9a Park Lane—at twelve o'clock."

"Who saw him?"

"The cook, who had just gone up to bed, saw him on the doorstep and heard him let himself in. He walked upstairs, leaving his greatcoat on the hall peg and his umbrella in the stand— you remember how it rained last night. He undressed and went to bed. Next morning he wasn't there. That's all," said Parker abruptly, with a wave of the hand.

"It isn't all, it isn't all. Daddy, go on, that's not *half* a story," pleaded Lord Peter.

"But it *is* all. When his man came to call him he wasn't there. The bed had been slept in. His pyjamas and all his clothes were there, the only odd thing being that they were thrown rather untidily on the ottoman at the foot of the bed, instead of being neatly folded on a chair, as is Sir Reuben's custom—looking as though he had been rather agitated or unwell. No clean clothes were missing, no suit, no boots—nothing. The boots he had worn were in his dressing-room as usual. He had washed and cleaned his teeth and done all the usual things. The housemaid was down cleaning the hall at half-past six, and can swear that nobody came in or out after that. So one is forced to suppose that a respectable middle-aged Hebrew financier either went mad between twelve and six a.m. and walked quietly out of the house in his birthday suit on a November night, or else was spirited away like the lady in the 'Ingoldsby Legends,' body and bones, leaving only a heap of crumpled clothes behind him."

"Was the front door bolted?"

"That's the sort of question you *would* ask, straight off; it took me an hour to think of it. No; contrary to custom, there was only the Yale lock on the door. On the other hand, some of the maids had been given leave to go to the theatre, and Sir Reuben may quite conceivably have left the door open under the impression they had not come in. Such a thing has happened before."

"And that's really all?"

"Really all. Except for one very trifling circumstance."

"I love trifling circumstances," said Lord Peter, with childish delight; "so many men have been hanged by trifling circumstances. What was it?"

"Sir Reuben and Lady Levy, who are a most devoted couple, always share the same room. Lady Levy, as I said before, is in Mentonne at the moment for her health. In her absence, Sir Reuben sleeps in the double bed as usual, and invariably on his own side—the outside—of the bed. Last night he put the two pillows together and slept in the middle, or, if anything, rather closer to the wall than otherwise. The housemaid, who is a most intelligent girl, noticed this when she went up to make the bed, and, with really admirable detective instinct, refused to touch the bed or let anybody else touch it, though it wasn't till later that they actually sent for the police."

"Was nobody in the house but Sir Reuben and the servants?"

"No; Lady Levy was away with her daughter and her maid. The valet, cook, parlourmaid, housemaid and kitchen-maid were the only people in the house, and naturally wasted an hour or two squawking and gossiping. I got there about ten."

"What have you been doing since?"

"Trying to get on the track of Sir Reuben's appointment last night, since, with the exception of the cook, his 'appointer' was the last person who saw him before his disappearance. There may be some quite simple explanation, though I'm dashed if I can think of one for the moment. Hang it all, a man doesn't come in and go to bed and walk away again 'mid nodings on' in the middle of the night."

"He may have been disguised."

"I thought of that—in fact, it seems the only possible explanation. But it's deuced odd, Wimsey. An important city man, on the eve of an important transaction, without a word of warning to anybody, slips off in the middle of the night, disguised down to his skin, leaving behind his watch, purse, chequebook, and— most mysterious and important of all—his spectacles, without which he can't see a step, as he is extremely short-sighted. He—"

"That *is* important," interrupted Wimsey. "You are sure he didn't take a second pair?"

"His man vouches for it that he had only two pairs, one of which was found on his dressing-table, and the other in the drawer where it is always kept."

Lord Peter whistled.

"You've got me there, Parker. Even if he'd gone out to commit suicide he'd have taken those."

"So you'd think—or the suicide would have happened the first time he started to cross the road. However, I didn't overlook the possibility. I've got particulars of all today's street accidents, and I can lay my hand on my heart and say that none of them is Sir Reuben. Besides, he took his latchkey with him, which looks as though he'd meant to come back."

"Have you seen the men he dined with?"

"I found two of them at the club. They said that he seemed in the best of health and spirits, spoke of looking forward to joining Lady Levy later on—perhaps at Christmas—and referred with great satisfaction to this morning's business transaction, in which one of them—a man called Anderson of Wyndham's—was himself concerned."

"Then up till about nine o'clock, anyhow, he had no apparent intention or expectation of disappearing."

"None—unless he was a most consummate actor. Whatever happened to change his mind must have happened either at the mysterious appointment which he kept after dinner, or while he was in bed between midnight and 5.30 a.m."

"Well, Bunter," said Lord Peter, "what do you make of it?"

"Not in my department, my lord. Except that it is odd that a gentleman who was too flurried or unwell to fold his clothes as usual should remember to clean his teeth and put his boots out. Those are two things that quite frequently get overlooked, my lord."

"If you mean anything personal, Bunter," said Lord Peter, "I can only say that I think the speech an unworthy one. It's a sweet little problem, Parker mine. Look here, I don't want to butt in, but I should dearly love to see that bedroom tomorrow. 'Tis not that I mistrust thee, dear, but I should uncommonly like to see it. Say me not nay—take another drop of brandy and a Villar Villar, but say not, say not nay!"

"Of course you can come and see it—you'll probably find lots of things I've overlooked," said the other, equally, accepting the proffered hospitality.

"Parker, acushla, you're an honour to Scotland Yard. I look at you, and Sugg appears a myth, a fable, an idiot-boy, spawned in a moonlight hour by some fantastic poet's brain. Sugg is too perfect to be possible. What does he make of the body, by the way?"

"Sugg says," replied Parker, with precision, "that the body died from a blow on the back of the neck. The doctor told him that. He says it's been dead a day or two. The doctor told him that, too. He says it's the body of a well-to-do Hebrew of about fifty. Anybody could have told him that. He says it's ridicu-

lous to suppose it came in through the window without anybody knowing anything about it. He says it probably walked
in through the front door and was murdered by the household.
He's arrested the girl because she's short and frail-looking and
quite unequal to downing a tall and sturdy Semite with a poker.
He'd arrest Thipps, only Thipps was away in Manchester all
yesterday and the day before and didn't come back till late last
night—in fact, he wanted to arrest him till I reminded him that
if the body had been a day or two dead, little Thipps couldn't
have done him in at 10.30 last night. But he'll arrest him tomorrow as an accessory—and the old lady with the knitting, too, I
shouldn't wonder."

"Well, I'm glad the little man has so much of an alibi," said
Lord Peter, "though if you're only glueing your faith to cadav-
eric lividity, rigidity, and all the other quiddities, you must be
prepared to have some sceptical beast of a prosecuting counsel walk slap-bang through the medical evidence. Remember
Impey Biggs defending in that Chelsea tea-shop affair? Six
bloomin' medicos contradictin' each other in the box, an' old
Impey elocutin' abnormal cases from Glaister and Dixon Mann
till the eyes of the jury reeled in their heads! 'Are you prepared to
swear, Dr. Thingumtight, that the onset of rigor mortis indicates
the hour of death without the possibility of error?' 'So far as my
experience goes, in the majority of cases,' says the doctor, all stiff.
'Ah!' says Biggs, 'but this is a Court of Justice, Doctor, not a Par-
liamentary election. We can't get on without a minority report.
The law, Dr. Thingumtight, respects the rights of the minority,
alive or dead.' Some ass laughs, and old Biggs sticks his chest out
and gets impressive. 'Gentlemen, this is no laughing matter. My
client—an upright and honourable gentleman—is being tried
for his life—for his life, gentlemen—and it is the business of the
prosecution to show his guilt—if they can—without a shadow
of doubt. Now, Dr. Thingumtight, I ask you again, can you sol-

emnly swear, without the least shadow of doubt,—probable, possible shadow of doubt—that this unhappy woman met her death neither sooner nor later than Thursday evening? A probable opinion? Gentlemen, we are not Jesuits, we are straightforward Englishmen. You cannot ask a British-born jury to convict any man on the authority of a probable opinion.' Hum of applause."

"Biggs's man was guilty all the same," said Parker.

"Of course he was. But he was acquitted all the same, an' what you've just said is libel." Wimsey walked over to the bookshelf and took down a volume of Medical Jurisprudence. "'Rigor mortis—can only be stated in a very general way—many factors determine the result.' Cautious brute. 'On the average, however, stiffening will have begun—neck and jaw—5 to 6 hours after death'—'m—'in all likelihood have passed off in the bulk of cases by the end of 36 hours. Under certain circumstances, however, it may appear unusually early, or be retarded unusually long!'" Helpful, ain't it, Parker? 'Brown-Séquard states ... 3½ minutes after death.... In certain cases not until lapse of 16 hours after death ... present as long as 21 days thereafter.' Lord! 'Modifying factors—age—muscular state—or febrile diseases—or where temperature of environment is high'—and so on and so on—any bloomin' thing. Never mind. You can run the argument for what it's worth to Sugg. *He* won't know any better." He tossed the book away. "Come back to facts. What did *you* make of the body?"

"Well," said the detective, "not very much—I was puzzled—frankly. I should say he had been a rich man, but self-made, and that his good fortune had come to him fairly recently."

"Ah, you noticed the calluses on the hands—I thought you wouldn't miss that."

"Both his feet were badly blistered—he had been wearing tight shoes."

"Walking a long way in them, too," said Lord Peter, "to get

such blisters as that. Didn't that strike you as odd, in a person evidently well off?"

"Well, I don't know. The blisters were two or three days old. He might have got stuck in the suburbs one night, perhaps—last train gone and no taxi—and had to walk home."

"Possibly."

"There were some little red marks all over his back and one leg I couldn't quite account for."

"I saw them."

"What did you make of them?"

"I'll tell you afterwards. Go on."

"He was very long-sighted—oddly long-sighted for a man in the prime of life; the glasses were like a very old man's. By the way, they had a very beautiful and remarkable chain of flat links chased with a pattern. It struck me he might be traced through it."

"I've just put an advertisement in the *Times* about it," said Lord Peter. "Go on."

"He had had the glasses some time—they had been mended twice."

"Beautiful, Parker, beautiful. Did you realize the importance of that?"

"Not specially, I'm afraid—why?"

"Never mind—go on."

"He was probably a sullen, ill-tempered man—his nails were filed down to the quick as though he habitually bit them, and his fingers were bitten as well. He smoked quantities of cigarettes without a holder. He was particular about his personal appearance."

"Did you examine the room at all? I didn't get a chance."

"I couldn't find much in the way of footprints. Sugg & Co. had tramped all over the place, to say nothing of little Thipps and the maid, but I noticed a very indefinite patch just behind the head of the bath, as though something damp might have stood there. You could hardly call it a print."

"It rained hard all last night, of course."

"Yes; did you notice that the soot on the window-sill was vaguely marked?"

"I did," said Wimsey, "and I examined it hard with this little fellow, but I could make nothing of it except that something or other had rested on the sill." He drew out his monocle and handed it to Parker.

"My word, that's a powerful lens."

"It is," said Wimsey, "and jolly useful when you want to take a good squint at somethin' and look like a bally fool all the time. Only it don't do to wear it permanently—if people see you full-face they say: 'Dear me! how weak the sight of that eye must be!' Still, it's useful."

"Sugg and I explored the ground at the back of the building," went on Parker, "but there wasn't a trace."

"That's interestin'. Did you try the roof?"

"No."

"We'll go over it tomorrow. The gutter's only a couple of feet off the top of the window. I measured it with my stick—the gentleman-scout's vademecum, I call it—it's marked off in inches. Uncommonly handy companion at times. There's a sword inside and a compass in the head. Got it made specially. Anything more?"

"Afraid not. Let's hear your version, Wimsey."

"Well, I think you've got most of the points. There are just one or two little contradictions. For instance, here's a man wears expensive gold-rimmed pince-nez and has had them long enough to be mended twice. Yet his teeth are not merely dis-coloured, but badly decayed and look as if he'd never cleaned them in his life. There are four molars missing on one side and three on the other and one front tooth broken right across. He's a man careful of his personal appearance, as witness his hair and his hands. What do you say to that?"

"Oh, these self-made men of low origin don't think much about teeth, and are terrified of dentists."

"True; but one of the molars has a broken edge so rough that it had made a sore place on the tongue. Nothing's more painful. D'you mean to tell me a man would put up with that if he could afford to get the tooth filed?"

"Well, people are queer. I've known servants endure agonies rather than step over a dentist's doormat. How did you see that, Wimsey?"

"Had a look inside; electric torch," said Lord Peter. "Handy little gadget. Looks like a matchbox. Well—I daresay it's all right, but I just draw your attention to it. Second point: Gentleman with hair smellin' of Parma violet and manicured hands and all the rest of it, never washes the inside of his ears. Full of wax. Nasty."

"You've got me there, Wimsey; I never noticed it. Still—old bad habits die hard."

"Right oh! Put it down at that. Third point: Gentleman with the manicure and the brilliantine and all the rest of it suffers from fleas."

"By Jove, you're right! Flea-bites. It never occurred to me."

"No doubt about it, old son. The marks were faint and old, but unmistakable."

"Of course, now you mention it. Still, that might happen to anybody. I loosed a whopper in the best hotel in Lincoln the week before last. I hope it bit the next occupier!"

"Oh, all these things *might* happen to anybody—separately. Fourth point: Gentleman who uses Parma violet for his hair, etc., etc., washes his body in strong carbolic soap—so strong that the smell hangs about twenty-four hours later."

"Carbolic to get rid of the fleas."

"I will say for you, Parker, you've an answer for everything. Fifth point: Carefully got-up gentleman, with manicured, though masticated, finger-nails, has filthy black toe-nails which look as if they hadn't been cut for years."

"All of a piece with habits as indicated."

"Yes, I know, but such habits! Now, sixth and last point: This gentleman with the intermittently gentlemanly habits arrives in the middle of a pouring wet night, and apparently through the window, when he has already been twenty-four hours dead, and lies down quietly in Mr. Thipps's bath, unseasonably dressed in a pair of pince-nez. Not a hair on his head is ruffled—the hair has been cut so recently that there are quite a number of little short hairs stuck on his neck and the sides of the bath—and he has shaved so recently that there is a line of dried soap on his cheek—"

"Wimsey!"

"Wait a minute—and *dried soap in his mouth*."

Bunter got up and appeared suddenly at the detective's elbow, the respectful man-servant all over.

"A little more brandy, sir?" he murmured.

"Wimsey," said Parker, "you are making me feel cold all over." He emptied his glass—stared at it as though he were surprised to find it empty, set it down, got up, walked across to the bookcase, turned round, stood with his back against it and said:

"Look here, Wimsey—you've been reading detective stories; you're talking nonsense."

"No, I ain't," said Lord Peter, sleepily, "uncommon good incident for a detective story, though, what? Bunter, we'll write one, and you shall illustrate it with photographs."

"Soap in his—Rubbish!" said Parker. "It was something else— some discoloration—"

"No," said Lord Peter, "there were hairs as well. Bristly ones. He had a beard."

He took his watch from his pocket, and drew out a couple of longish, stiff hairs, which he had imprisoned between the inner and the outer case.

Parker turned them over once or twice in his fingers, looked at them close to the light, examined them with a lens, handed them to the impassible Bunter, and said:

"Do you mean to tell me, Wimsey, that any man alive would"—he laughed harshly—"shave off his beard with his mouth open, and then go and get killed with his mouth full of hairs? You're mad."

"I don't tell you so," said Wimsey. "You policemen are all alike—only one idea in your skulls. Blest if I can make out why you're ever appointed. He was shaved after he was dead. Pretty, ain't it? Uncommonly jolly little job for the barber, what? Here, sit down, man, and don't be an ass, stumpin' about the room like that. Worse things happen in war. This is only a blinkin' old shillin' shocker. But I'll tell you what, Parker, we're up against a criminal—*the* criminal—the real artist and blighter with imagination—real, artistic, finished stuff. I'm enjoyin' this, Parker."

III

Lord Peter finished a Scarlatti sonata, and sat looking thoughtfully at his own hands. The fingers were long and muscular, with wide, flat joints and square tips. When he was playing, his rather hard grey eyes softened, and his long, indeterminate mouth hardened in compensation. At no other time had he any pretensions to good looks, and at all times he was spoilt by a long, narrow chin, and a long, receding forehead, accentuated by the brushed-back sleekness of his tow-coloured hair. Labour papers, softening down the chin, caricatured him as a typical aristocrat.

"That's a wonderful instrument," said Parker.

"It ain't so bad," said Lord Peter, "but Scarlatti wants a harpsichord. Piano's too modern—all thrills and overtones. No good for our job, Parker. Have you come to any conclusion?"

"The man in the bath," said Parker, methodically, "was *not* a well-off man careful of his personal appearance. He was a labouring man, unemployed, but who had only recently lost his employment. He had been tramping about looking for a job when he met with his end. Somebody killed him and washed him and scented him and shaved him in order to disguise him, and put him into Thipps's bath without leaving a trace. Conclusion: the murderer was a powerful man, since he killed him with a single blow on the neck, a man of cool head and masterly intellect, since he did all that ghastly business without leaving a mark, a man of wealth and refinement, since he had all the apparatus of an elegant toilet handy, and a man of bizarre, and almost perverted imagination, as is shown in the two horrible touches of putting the body in the bath and of adorning it with a pair of pince-nez."

"He is a poet of crime," said Wimsey. "By the way, your difficulty about the pince-nez is cleared up. Obviously, the pince-nez never belonged to the body."

"That only makes a fresh puzzle. One can't suppose the murderer left them in that obliging manner as a clue to his own identity."

"We can hardly suppose that; I'm afraid this man possessed what most criminals lack—a sense of humour."

"Rather macabre humour."

"True. But a man who can afford to be humorous at all in such circumstances is a terrible fellow. I wonder what he did with the body between the murder and depositing it chez Thipps. Then there are more questions. How did he get it there? And why? Was it brought in at the door, as Sugg of our heart suggests? or through the window, as we think, on the not very adequate testimony of a smudge on the window-sill? Had the murderer accomplices? Is little Thipps really in it, or the girl? It don't do to put the notion out of court merely because Sugg inclines to it. Even idiots occasionally speak the truth accidentally. If not, why was Thipps selected for such an abominable practical joke? Has anybody got a grudge against Thipps? Who are the people in the other flats? We must find out that. Does Thipps play the piano at midnight over their heads or damage the reputation of the staircase by bringing home dubiously respectable ladies? Are there unsuccessful architects thirsting for his blood? Damn it all, Parker, there must be a motive somewhere. Can't have a crime without a motive, you know."

"A madman—" suggested Parker, doubtfully.

"With a deuced lot of method in his madness. He hasn't made a mistake—not one, unless leaving hairs in the corpse's mouth can be called a mistake. Well, anyhow, it's not Levy—you're right there. I say, old thing, neither your man nor mine has left much clue to go upon, has he? And there don't seem to be any motives knockin' about, either. And we seem to be two suits of clothes short in last night's work. Sir Reuben makes tracks without so much as a fig-leaf, and a mysterious individual turns up with a pince-nez, which is quite useless for purposes of decency. Dash it all! If only I had some good excuse for takin' up this body case officially—"

The telephone bell rang. The silent Bunter, whom the other two had almost forgotten, padded across to it.

"It's an elderly lady, my lord," he said. "I think she's deaf—I can't make her hear anything, but she's asking for your lordship."

Lord Peter seized the receiver, and yelled into it a "Hullo!" that might have cracked the vulcanite. He listened for some minutes with an incredulous smile, which gradually broadened into a grin of delight. At length he screamed: "All right! all right!" several times, and rang off.

"By Jove!" he announced, beaming, "sportin' old bird! It's old Mrs. Thipps. Deaf as a post. Never used the 'phone before. But determined. Perfect Napoleon. The incomparable Sugg has made a discovery and arrested little Thipps. Old lady abandoned in the flat. Thipps's last shriek to her: 'Tell Lord Peter Wimsey.' Old girl undaunted. Wrestles with telephone book. Wakes up the people at the exchange. Won't take no for an answer (not bein' able to hear it), gets through, says: 'Will I do what I can?' Says she would feel safe in the hands of a real gentleman. Oh, Parker,

Parker! I could kiss her, I reely could, as Thipps says. I'll write to her instead—no, hang it, Parker, we'll go round. Bunter, get your infernal machine and the magnesium. I say, we'll all go into partnership—pool the two cases and work 'em out together. You shall see my body tonight, Parker, and I'll look for your wandering Jew tomorrow. I feel so happy, I shall explode. O Sugg, Sugg, how art thou suggified! Bunter, my shoes. I say, Parker, I suppose yours are rubber-soled. Not? Tut, tut, you mustn't go out like that. We'll lend you a pair. Gloves? Here. My stick, my torch, the lampblack, the forceps, knife, pill-boxes—all complete?"

"Certainly, my lord."

"Oh, Bunter, don't look so offended. I mean no harm. I believe in you, I trust you—what money have I got? That'll do. I knew a man once, Parker, who let a world-famous poisoner slip through his fingers because the machine on the Underground took nothing but pennies. There was a queue at the booking office and the man at the barrier stopped him, and while they were arguing about accepting a five-pound note (which was all he had) for a two-penny ride to Baker Street, the criminal had sprung into a Circle train, and was next heard of in Constantinople, disguised as an elderly Church of England clergyman touring with his niece. Are we all ready? Go!"

They stepped out, Bunter carefully switching off the lights behind them.

As they emerged into the gloom and gleam of Piccadilly, Wimsey stopped short with a little exclamation.

"Wait a second," he said. "I've thought of something. If Sugg's there he'll make trouble. I must short-circuit him."

He ran back, and the other two men employed the few minutes of his absence in capturing a taxi.

Inspector Sugg and a subordinate Cerberus were on guard at 59, Queen Caroline Mansions, and showed no disposition to admit unofficial inquirers. Parker, indeed, they could not easily turn away, but Lord Peter found himself confronted with a surly manner and what Lord Beaconsfield described as a masterly inactivity. It was in vain that Lord Peter pleaded that he had been retained by Mrs. Thipps on behalf of her son.

"Retained!" said Inspector Sugg, with a snort. "*She'll* be retained if she doesn't look out. Shouldn't wonder if she wasn't in it herself, only she's so deaf, she's no good for anything at all."

"Look here, Inspector," said Lord Peter, "what's the use of bein' so bally obstructive? You'd much better let me in—you know I'll get there in the end. Dash it all, it's not as if I was takin' the bread out of your children's mouths. Nobody paid me for finding Lord Attenbury's emeralds for you."

"It's my duty to keep out the public," said Inspector Sugg, morosely, "and it's going to stay out."

"I never said anything about your keeping out of the public," said Lord Peter, easily, sitting down on the staircase to thrash the matter out comfortably, "though I've no doubt pussyfoot's a good thing, on principle, if not exaggerated. The golden mean, Sugg, as Aristotle says, keeps you from bein' a golden ass. Ever been a golden ass, Sugg? I have. It would take a whole rose-garden to cure me, Sugg—

"*'You are my garden of beautiful roses,*
My own rose, my one rose, that's you!'"

"I'm not going to stay any longer talking to you," said the harassed Sugg, "it's bad enough—Hullo, drat that telephone. Here, Cawthorn, go and see what it is, if that old catamaran will let you into the room. Shutting herself up there and screaming," said the inspector, "it's enough to make a man give up crime and take to hedging and ditching."

The constable came back:

"It's from the Yard, sir," he said, coughing apologetically; "the Chief says every facility is to be given to Lord Peter Wimsey, sir. Um!" He stood apart noncommittally, glazing his eyes.

"Five aces," said Lord Peter, cheerfully. "The Chief's a dear friend of my mother's. No go, Sugg, it's no good buckin'; you've got a full house. I'm goin' to make it a bit fuller."

He walked in with his followers.

The body had been removed a few hours previously, and when the bathroom and the whole flat had been explored by the naked eye and the camera of the competent Bunter, it became evident that the real problem of the household was old Mrs. Thipps. Her son and servant had both been removed, and it appeared that they had no friends in town, beyond a few business acquaintances of Thipps's, whose very addresses the old lady did not know. The other flats in the building were occupied respectively by a family of seven, at present departed to winter abroad, an elderly Indian colonel of ferocious manners, who lived alone with an Indian man-servant, and a highly respectable family on the third floor, whom the disturbance over their heads had outraged to the last degree. The husband, indeed, when appealed to by Lord Peter, showed a little human weakness, but Mrs. Appledore, appearing suddenly in a warm dressing-gown, extricated him from the difficulties into which he was carelessly wandering.

"I am sorry," she said, "I'm afraid we can't interfere in any way. This is a very unpleasant business, Mr.—I'm afraid I didn't catch your name, and we have always found it better not to be mixed up with the police. Of course, *if* the Thippses are innocent, and I am sure I hope they are, it is very unfortunate for them, but I must say that the circumstances seem to me most suspicious, and to Theophilus too, and I should not like to have it said that we had assisted murderers. We might even be supposed to be accessories. Of course you are young, Mr.—"

"This is Lord Peter Wimsey, my dear," said Theophilus mildly.

She was unimpressed.

"Ah, yes," she said, "I believe you are distantly related to my late cousin, the Bishop of Carisbrooke. Poor man! He was always being taken in by impostors; he died without ever learning any better. I imagine you take after him, Lord Peter."

"I doubt it," said Lord Peter. "So far as I know he is only a connection, though it's a wise child that knows its own father. I congratulate you, dear lady, on takin' after the other side of the family. You'll forgive my buttin' in upon you like this in the middle of the night, though, as you say, it's all in the family, and I'm sure I'm very much obliged to you, and for permittin' me to admire that awfully fetchin' thing you've got on. Now, don't you worry, Mr. Appledore. I'm thinkin' the best thing I can do is to trundle the old lady down to my mother and take her out of your way, otherwise you might be findin' your Christian feelin's gettin' the better of you some fine day, and there's nothin' like Christian feelin's for upsettin' a man's domestic comfort. Goodnight, sir—good-night, dear lady—it's simply rippin' of you to let me drop in like this."

"Well!" said Mrs. Appledore, as the door closed behind him. And—

"I thank the goodness and the grace
That on my birth have smiled,"

said Lord Peter, "and taught me to be bestially impertinent when I choose. Cat!"

Two a.m. saw Lord Peter Wimsey arrive in a friend's car at

the Dower House, Denver Castle, in company with a deaf and aged lady and an antique portmanteau.

"It's very nice to see you, dear," said the Dowager Duchess, placidly. She was a small, plump woman, with perfectly white hair and exquisite hands. In feature she was as unlike her second son as she was like him in character; her black eyes twinkled cheerfully, and her manners and movements were marked with a neat and rapid decision. She wore a charming wrap from Liberty's, and sat watching Lord Peter eat cold beef and cheese as though his arrival in such incongruous circumstances and company were the most ordinary event possible, which with him, indeed, it was.

"Have you got the old lady to bed?" asked Lord Peter.

"Oh, yes, dear. Such a striking old person, isn't she? And very courageous. She tells me she has never been in a motor-car before. But she thinks you a very nice lad, dear—that careful of her, you remind her of her own son. Poor little Mr. Thipps— whatever made your friend the inspector think he could have murdered anybody?"

"My friend the inspector—no, no more, thank you, Mother— is determined to prove that the intrusive person in Thipps's bath is Sir Reuben Levy, who disappeared mysteriously from his house last night. His line of reasoning is: We've lost a middle-aged gentleman without any clothes on in Park Lane; we've found a middle-aged gentleman without any clothes on in Battersea. Therefore they're one and the same person, Q.E.D., and put little Thipps in quod."

"You're very elliptical, dear," said the Duchess, mildly. "Why should Mr. Thipps be arrested even if they are the same?"

"Sugg must arrest somebody," said Lord Peter, "but there is one odd little bit of evidence come out which goes a long way

to support Sugg's theory, only that I know it to be no go by
the evidence of my own eyes. Last night at about 9:15 a young
woman was strollin' up the Battersea Park Road for purposes
best known to herself, when she saw a gentleman in a fur coat
and top-hat saunterin' along under an umbrella, lookin' at the
names of all the streets. He looked a bit out of place, so, not
bein' a shy girl, you see, she walked up to him, and said: 'Good-
evening.' 'Can you tell me, please,' says the mysterious stranger,
'whether this street leads into Prince of Wales Road?' She said
it did, and further asked him in a jocular manner what he was
doing with himself and all the rest of it, only she wasn't altogether so explicit about that part of the conversation, because
she was unburdenin' her heart to Sugg, d'you see, and he's paid
by a grateful country to have very pure, high-minded ideals,
what? Anyway, the old boy said he couldn't attend to her just
then as he had an appointment. 'I've got to go and see a man,
my dear,' was how she said he put it, and he walked on up Alex-
andra Avenue towards Prince of Wales Road. She was starin'
after him, still rather surprised, when she was joined by a friend
of hers, who said: 'It's no good wasting your time with him—
that's Levy—I knew him when I lived in the West End, and the
girls used to call him Peagreen Incorruptible'—friend's name
suppressed, owing to implications of story, but girl vouches for
what was said. She thought no more about it till the milkman
brought news this morning of the excitement at Queen Caroline Mansions; then she went round, though not likin' the police
as a rule, and asked the man there whether the dead gentleman had a beard and glasses. Told he had glasses but no beard,
she incautiously said: 'Oh, then, it isn't him,' and the man said:
'Isn't who?' and collared her. That's her story. Sugg's delighted,
of course, and quodded Thipps on the strength of it."

"Dear me," said the Duchess, "I hope the poor girl won't get
into trouble."

"Shouldn't think so," said Lord Peter. "Thipps is the one that's going to get it in the neck. Besides, he's done a silly thing. I got that out of Sugg, too, though he was sittin' tight on the information. Seems Thipps got into a confusion about the train he took back from Manchester. Said first he got home at 10.30. Then they pumped Gladys Horrocks, who let out he wasn't back till after 11.45. Then Thipps, bein' asked to explain the discrepancy, stammers and bungles and says, first that he missed the train. Then Sugg makes inquiries at St. Pancras and discovers that he left a bag in the cloakroom there at ten. Thipps, again asked to explain, stammers worse an' says he walked about for a few hours—met a friend—can't say who—didn't meet a friend—can't say what he did with his time—can't explain why he didn't go back for his bag—can't say what time he *did* get in—can't explain how he got a bruise on his forehead. In fact, can't explain himself at all. Gladys Horrocks interrogated again. Says, this time, Thipps came in at 10.30. Then admits she didn't hear him come in. Can't say why she didn't hear him come in. Can't say why she said first of all that she *did* hear him. Bursts into tears. Contradicts herself. Everybody's suspicion roused. Quod 'em both."

"As you put it, dear," said the Duchess, "it all sounds very confusing, and not quite respectable. Poor little Mr. Thipps would be terribly upset by anything that wasn't respectable."

"I wonder what he did with himself," said Lord Peter thoughtfully. "I really don't think he was committing a murder. Besides, I believe the fellow has been dead a day or two, though it don't do to build too much on doctors' evidence. It's an entertainin' little problem."

"Very curious, dear. But so sad about poor Sir Reuben. I must write a few lines to Lady Levy; I used to know her quite well, you know, dear, down in Hampshire, when she was a girl. Christine Ford, she was then, and I remember so well the dreadful trouble there was about her marrying a Jew. That was before he made his money, of course, in that oil business out in America. The family wanted her to marry Julian Freke, who did so well afterwards and was connected with the family, but she fell in love with this Mr. Levy and eloped with him. He was very handsome, then, you know, dear, in a foreign-looking way, but he hadn't any means, and the Fords didn't like his religion. Of course we're all Jews nowadays and they wouldn't have minded so much if he'd pretended to be something else, like that Mr. Simons we met at Mrs. Porchester's, who always tells everybody that he got his nose in Italy at the Renaissance, and claims to be descended somehow or other from La Bella Simonetta—so foolish, you know, dear—as if anybody believed it; and I'm sure some Jews are very good people, and personally I'd much rather they believed something, though of course it must be very inconvenient, what with not working on Saturdays and circumcising the poor little babies and everything depending on the new moon and that funny kind of meat they have with such a slang-sounding name, and never being able to have bacon for breakfast. Still, there it was, and it was much better for the girl to marry him if she was really fond of him, though I believe young Freke was really devoted to her, and they're still great friends. Not that there was ever a real engagement, only a sort of understanding with her father, but he's never married, you know, and lives all by himself in that big house next to the hospital, though he's very rich and distinguished now, and I know ever so many people have tried to get hold of him—there was Lady Mainwaring wanted him for that eldest girl of hers, though I remember saying at the time it was no use expecting a surgeon to be taken in by a figure that was all padding—they have so many opportunities of judging, you know, dear."

"Lady Levy seems to have had the knack of makin' people devoted to her," said Peter. "Look at the pea-green incorruptible Levy."

"That's quite true, dear; she was a most delightful girl, and they say her daughter is just like her. I rather lost sight of them when she married, and you know your father didn't care much about business people, but I know everybody always said they were a model couple. In fact it was a proverb that Sir Reuben was as well loved at home as he was hated abroad. I don't mean in foreign countries, you know, dear—just the proverbial way of putting things—like 'a saint abroad and a devil at home'—only the other way on, reminding one of the *Pilgrim's Progress*."

"Yes," said Peter, "I daresay the old man made one or two enemies."

"Dozens, dear—such a dreadful place, the City, isn't it? Everybody Ishmaels together—though I don't suppose Sir Reuben would like to be called that, would he? Doesn't it mean illegitimate, or not a proper Jew, anyway? I always did get confused with those Old Testament characters."

Lord Peter laughed and yawned.

"I think I'll turn in for an hour or two," he said. "I must be back in town at eight—Parker's coming to breakfast."

The Duchess looked at the clock, which marked five minutes to three.

"I'll send up your breakfast at half-past six, dear," she said. "I hope you'll find everything all right. I told them just to slip a hot-water bottle in; those linen sheets are so chilly; you can put it out if it's in your way."

IV

"So there it is, Parker," said Lord Peter, pushing his coffee-cup aside and lighting his after-breakfast pipe; "you may find it leads you to something, though it don't seem to get me any further with my bathroom problem. Did you do anything more at that after I left?"

"No; but I've been on the roof this morning."

"The deuce you have—what an energetic devil you are! I say, Parker, I think this co-operative scheme is an uncommonly good one. It's much easier to work on someone else's job than one's own—gives one that delightful feelin' of interferin' and bossin' about, combined with the glorious sensation that another fellow is takin' all one's own work off one's hands. You scratch my back and I'll scratch yours, what? Did you find anything?"

"Not very much. I looked for any footmarks of course, but naturally, with all this rain, there wasn't a sign. Of course, if this were a detective story, there'd have been a convenient shower exactly an hour before the crime and a beautiful set of marks which could only have come there between two and three in the morning, but this being real life in a London November, you might as well expect footprints in Niagara. I searched the roofs right along—and came to the jolly conclusion that any person in any blessed flat in the blessed row might have done it. All the staircases open on to the roof and the leads are quite flat; you can walk along as easy as along Shaftesbury Avenue. Still, I've got some evidence that the body did walk along there."

"What's that?"

Parker brought out his pocketbook and extracted a few shreds of material, which he laid before his friend.

"One was caught in the gutter just above Thipps's bathroom window, another in a crack of the stone parapet just over it, and the rest came from the chimney-stack behind, where they had caught in an iron stanchion. What do you make of them?"

Lord Peter scrutinized them very carefully through his lens.

"Interesting," he said, "damned interesting. Have you developed those plates, Bunter?" he added, as that discreet assistant came in with the post.

"Yes, my lord."

"Caught anything?"

"I don't know whether to call it anything or not, my lord," said Bunter, dubiously. "I'll bring the prints in."

"Do," said Wimsey. "Hallo! here's our advertisement about the gold chain in the *Times*—very nice it looks: 'Write, 'phone or call 110, Piccadilly.' Perhaps it would have been safer to put a box number, though I always think that the franker you are with people, the more you're likely to deceive 'em; so unused is the modern world to the open hand and the guileless heart, what?"

"But you don't think the fellow who left that chain on the body is going to give himself away by coming here and inquiring about it?"

"I don't, fathead," said Lord Peter, with the easy politeness of the real aristocracy; "that's why I've tried to get hold of the jeweller who originally sold the chain. See?" He pointed to the paragraph. "It's not an old chain—hardly worn at all. Oh, thanks, Bunter. Now, see here, Parker, these are the fingermarks you noticed yesterday on the window-sash and on the far edge of the bath. I'd overlooked them; I give you full credit for the discovery, I crawl, I grovel, my name is Watson, and you need not say what you were just going to say, because I admit it all. Now we shall—Hullo, hullo, hullo!"

The three men stared at the photographs.

"The criminal," said Lord Peter, bitterly, "climbed over the roofs in the wet and not unnaturally got soot on his fingers. He arranged the body in the bath, and wiped away all traces of himself except two, which he obligingly left to show us how to do our job. We learn from a smudge on the floor that he wore India rubber boots, and from this admirable set of finger-prints on the edge of the bath that he had the usual number of fingers and wore rubber gloves. That's the kind of man he is. Take the fool away, gentlemen."

He put the prints aside, and returned to an examination of the shreds of material in his hand. Suddenly he whistled softly.

"Do you make anything of these, Parker?"

"They seemed to me to be ravellings of some coarse cotton stuff—a sheet, perhaps, or an improvised rope."

"Yes," said Lord Peter—"yes. It may be a mistake—it may be *our* mistake. I wonder. Tell me, d'you think these tiny threads are long enough and strong enough to hang a man?"

He was silent, his long eyes narrowing into slits behind the smoke of his pipe.

"What do you suggest doing this morning?" asked Parker.

"Well," said Lord Peter, "it seems to me it's about time I took a hand in your job. Let's go round to Park Lane and see what larks Sir Reuben Levy was up to in bed last night."

"And now, Mrs. Pemming, if you would be so kind as to give me a blanket," said Mr. Bunter, coming down into the kitchen, "and permit of me hanging a sheet across the lower part of this window, and drawing the screen across here, so—so as to shut off any reflections, if you understand me, we'll get to work."

Sir Reuben Levy's cook, with her eye upon Mr. Bunter's gentlemanly and well-tailored appearance, hastened to produce what was necessary. Her visitor placed on the table a basket, containing a water-bottle, a silver-backed hair-brush, a pair of boots, a small roll of linoleum, and the "Letters of a Self-made Merchant to His Son," bound in polished morocco. He drew an umbrella from beneath his arm and added it to the collection. He then advanced a ponderous photographic machine and set it up in the neighbourhood of the kitchen range; then, spreading a newspaper over the fair, scrubbed surface of the table, he began to roll up his sleeves and insinuate himself into a pair of surgical gloves. Sir Reuben Levy's valet, entering at the moment and finding him thus engaged, put aside the kitchen-maid, who was staring from a front-row position, and inspected the apparatus critically. Mr. Bunter nodded brightly to him, and uncorked a small bottle of grey powder.

"Odd sort of fish, your employer, isn't he?" said the valet, carelessly.

"Very singular, indeed," said Mr. Bunter. "Now, my dear," he added, ingratiatingly, to the kitchen-maid, "I wonder if you'd just pour a little of this grey powder over the edge of the bottle while I'm holding it—and the same with this boot—here, at the top—thank you, Miss—what is your name? Price? Oh, but you've got another name besides Price, haven't you? Mabel, eh? That's a name I'm uncommonly partial to—that's very nicely done, you've a steady hand, Miss Mabel—see that? That's the fingermarks—three there, and two here, and smudged over in both places. No, don't you touch 'em, my dear, or you'll rub the bloom off. We'll stand 'em up here till they're ready to have their portraits taken. Now then. Let's take the hair-brush next.

Perhaps, Mrs. Pemming, you'd like to lift him up very carefully by the bristles."

"By the bristles, Mr. Bunter?"

"If you please, Mrs. Pemming—and lay him here. Now, Miss Mabel, another little exhibition of your skill, *if* you please. No—we'll try lampblack this time. Perfect. Couldn't have done it better myself. Ah! there's a beautiful set. No smudges this time. That'll interest his lordship. Now the little book—no, I'll pick that up myself—with these gloves, you see, and by the edges—I'm a careful criminal, Mrs. Pemming, I don't want to leave any traces. Dust the cover all over, Miss Mabel; now this side—that's the way to do it. Lots of prints and no smudges. All according to plan. Oh, please, Mr. Graves, you mustn't touch it—it's as much as my place is worth to have it touched."

"D'you have to do much of this sort of thing?" inquired Mr. Graves, from a superior standpoint.

"Any amount," replied Mr. Bunter, with a groan calculated to appeal to Mr. Graves's heart and unlock his confidence. "If you'd kindly hold one end of this bit of linoleum, Mrs. Pemming, I'll hold up this end while Miss Mabel operates. Yes, Mr. Graves, it's a hard life, valeting by day and developing by night—morning tea at any time from 6.30 to 11, and criminal investigation at all hours. It's wonderful, the ideas these rich men with nothing to do get into their heads."

"I wonder you stand it," said Mr. Graves. "Now there's none of that here. A quiet, orderly, domestic life, Mr. Bunter, has much to be said for it. Meals at regular hours; decent, respectable families to dinner—none of your painted women—and no valeting at night, there's *much* to be said for it. I don't hold with Hebrews as a rule, Mr. Bunter, and of course I understand that you may find it to your advantage to be in a titled family, but there's less thought of that these days, and I will say, for a self-

made man, no one could call Sir Reuben vulgar, and my lady at
any rate is county—Miss Ford, she was, one of the Hampshire
Fords, and both of them always most considerate."

"I agree with you, Mr. Graves—his lordship and me have
never held with being narrow-minded—why, yes, my dear, of
course it's a footmark, this is the washstand linoleum. A good
Jew can be a good man, that's what I've always said. And regular
hours and considerate habits have a great deal to recommend
them. Very simple in his tastes, now, Sir Reuben, isn't he? for
such a rich man, I mean."

"Very simple indeed," said the cook; "the meals he and her
ladyship have when they're by themselves with Miss Rachel—
well, there now—if it wasn't for the dinners, which is always
good when there's company, I'd be wastin' my talents and education here, if you understand me, Mr. Bunter."

Mr. Bunter added the handle of the umbrella to his collection, and began to pin a sheet across the window, aided by the
housemaid.

"Admirable," said he. "Now, if I might have this blanket on the
table and another on a towel-horse or something of that kind by
way of a background—you're very kind, Mrs. Pemming.... Ah!
I wish his lordship never wanted valeting at night. Many's the
time I've sat up till three and four, and up again to call him early
to go off Sherlocking at the other end of the country. And the
mud he gets on his clothes and his boots!"

"I'm sure it's a shame, Mr. Bunter," said Mrs. Pemming,
warmly. "Low, I calls it. In my opinion, policework ain't no fit
occupation for a gentleman, let alone a lordship."

"Everything made so difficult, too," said Mr. Bunter, nobly
sacrificing his employer's character and his own feelings in a
good cause; "boots chucked into a corner, clothes hung up on
the floor, as they say—"

"That's often the case with these men as are born with a silver spoon in their mouths," said Mr. Graves. "Now, Sir Reuben, he's never lost his good old-fashioned habits. Clothes folded up neat, boots put out in his dressing-room, so as a man could get them in the morning, everything made easy."

"He forgot them the night before last, though."

"The clothes, not the boots. Always thoughtful for others, is Sir Reuben. Ah! I hope nothing's happened to him."

"Indeed, no, poor gentleman," chimed in the cook, "and as for what they're sayin', that he'd 'ave gone out surrepshous-like to do something he didn't ought, well, I'd never believe it of him, Mr. Bunter, not if I was to take my dying oath upon it."

"Ah!" said Mr. Bunter, adjusting his arc-lamps and connecting them with the nearest electric light, "and that's more than most of us could say of them as pays us."

"Five foot ten," said Lord Peter, "and not an inch more." He peered dubiously at the depression in the bed clothes, and measured it a second time with the gentleman-scout's vademecum. Parker entered this particular in a neat pocketbook.

"I suppose," he said, "a six-foot-two man *might* leave a five-foot-ten depression if he curled himself up."

"Have you any Scotch blood in you, Parker?" inquired his colleague, bitterly.

"Not that I know of," replied Parker. "Why?"

"Because of all the cautious, ungenerous, deliberate and cold-blooded devils I know," said Lord Peter, "you are the most cautious, ungenerous, deliberate and cold-blooded. Here am I, sweating my brains out to introduce a really sensational incident into your dull and disreputable little police investigation, and you refuse to show a single spark of enthusiasm."

"Well, it's no good jumping at conclusions."

"Jump? You don't even crawl distantly within sight of a conclusion. I believe if you caught the cat with her head in the cream-jug you'd say it was conceivable that the jug was empty when she got there."

"Well, it would be conceivable, wouldn't it?"

"Curse you," said Lord Peter. He screwed his monocle into his eye, and bent over the pillow, breathing hard and tightly through his nose. "Here, give me the tweezers," he said presently. "Good heavens, man, don't blow like that, you might be a whale." He nipped up an almost invisible object from the linen.

"What is it?" asked Parker.

"It's a hair," said Wimsey grimly, his hard eyes growing harder. "Let's go and look at Levy's hats, shall we? And you might just ring for that fellow with the churchyard name, do you mind?"

Mr. Graves, when summoned, found Lord Peter Wimsey squatting on the floor of the dressing-room before a row of hats arranged upside down before him.

"Here you are," said that nobleman cheerfully. "Now, Graves, this is a guessin' competition—a sort of three-hat trick, to mix metaphors. Here are nine hats, including three top-hats. Do you identify all these hats as belonging to Sir Reuben Levy? You do? Very good. Now I have three guesses as to which hat he wore the night he disappeared, and if I guess right, I win; if I don't, you win. See? Ready? Go. I suppose you know the answer yourself, by the way?"

"Do I understand your lordship to be asking which hat Sir Reuben wore when he went out on Monday night, your lordship?"

"No, you don't understand a bit," said Lord Peter. "I'm asking if *you* know—don't tell me, I'm going to guess."

"I do know, your lordship," said Mr. Graves, reprovingly.

"Well," said Lord Peter, "as he was dinin' at the Ritz he wore a topper. Here are three toppers. In three guesses I'd be bound to hit the right one, wouldn't I? That don't seem very sportin'. I'll take one guess. It was this one."

He indicated the hat next the window.

"Am I right, Graves—have I got the prize?"

"That *is* the hat in question, my lord," said Mr. Graves, without excitement.

"Thanks," said Lord Peter, "that's all I wanted to know. Ask Bunter to step up, would you?"

Mr. Bunter stepped up with an aggrieved air, and his usually smooth hair ruffled by the focussing cloth.

"Oh, there you are, Bunter," said Lord Peter; "look here—"

"Here I am, my lord," said Mr. Bunter, with respectful reproach, "but if you'll excuse me saying so, downstairs is where I ought to be, with all those young women about—they'll be fingering the evidence, my lord."

"I cry your mercy," said Lord Peter, "but I've quarrelled hopelessly with Mr. Parker and distracted the estimable Graves, and I want you to tell me what fingerprints you have found. I shan't be happy till I get it, so don't be harsh with me, Bunter."

"Well, my lord, your lordship understands I haven't photographed them yet, but I won't deny that their appearance is interesting, my lord. The little book off the night table, my lord, has only the marks of one set of fingers—there's a little scar on the right thumb which makes them easy recognised. The hair-brush, too, my lord, has only the same set of marks. The umbrella, the toothglass and the boots all have two sets: the hand with the scarred thumb, which I take to be Sir Reuben's, my lord, and a set of smudges superimposed upon them, if I may put it that way, my lord, which may or may not be the same hand in rubber gloves. I could tell you better when I've got the photographs made, to measure them, my lord. The linoleum in front of the washstand is very gratifying indeed, my lord, if you will excuse my mentioning it. Besides the marks of Sir Reuben's boots which your lordship pointed out, there's the print of a man's naked foot—a much smaller one, my lord, not much more than a ten-inch sock, I should say if you asked me."

Lord Peter's face became irradiated with almost a dim, religious light.

"A mistake," he breathed, "a mistake, a little one, but he can't afford it. When was the linoleum washed last, Bunter?"

"Monday morning, my lord. The housemaid did it and remembered to mention it. Only remark she's made yet, and it's to the point. The other domestics—"

His features expressed disdain.

"What did I say, Parker? Five-foot-ten and not an inch longer. And he didn't dare to use the hair-brush. Beautiful. But he *had* to risk the top-hat. Gentleman can't walk home in the rain late at night without a hat, you know, Parker. Look! what do you make of it? Two sets of fingerprints on everything but the book and the brush, two sets of feet on the linoleum; and two kinds of hair in the hat!"

He lifted the top-hat to the light, and extracted the evidence with tweezers.

"Think of it, Parker—to remember the hair-brush and forget the hat—to remember his fingers all the time, and to make that one careless step on the tell-tale linoleum. Here they are, you see, black hair and tan hair—black hair in the bowler and the panama, and black and tan in last night's topper. And then, just to make certain that we're on the right track, just one little auburn hair on the pillow, on this pillow, Parker, which isn't quite in the right place. It almost brings tears to my eyes."

"Do you mean to say—" said the detective, slowly.

"I mean to say," said Lord Peter, "that it was not Sir Reuben Levy whom the cook saw last night on the doorstep. I say that it was another man, perhaps a couple of inches shorter, who came here in Levy's clothes and let himself in with Levy's latchkey.

Oh, he was a bold, cunning devil, Parker. He had on Levy's boots, and every stitch of Levy's clothing down to the skin. He had rubber gloves on his hands which he never took off, and he did everything he could to make us think that Levy slept here last night. He took his chances, and won. He walked upstairs, he undressed, he even washed and cleaned his teeth, though he didn't use the hair-brush for fear of leaving red hairs in it. He had to guess what Levy did with boots and clothes; one guess was wrong and the other right, as it happened. The bed must look as if it had been slept in, so he gets in, and lies there in his victim's very pyjamas. Then, in the morning sometime, probably in the deadest hour between two and three, he gets up, dresses himself in his own clothes that he has brought with him in a bag, and creeps downstairs. If anybody wakes, he is lost, but he is a bold man, and he takes his chance. He knows that people do not wake as a rule—and they don't wake. He opens the street door which he left on the latch when he came in—he listens for the stray passer-by or the policeman on his beat. He slips out. He pulls the door quietly to with the latchkey. He walks briskly away in rubber-soled shoes—he's the kind of criminal who isn't complete without rubber-soled shoes. In a few minutes he is at Hyde Park Corner. After that—"

He paused, and added:

"He did all that, and unless he had nothing at stake, he had everything at stake. Either Sir Reuben Levy has been spirited away for some silly practical joke, or the man with the auburn hair has the guilt of murder upon his soul."

"Dear me!" ejaculated the detective, "you're very dramatic about it."

Lord Peter passed his hand rather wearily over his hair.

"My true friend," he murmured in a voice surcharged with emotion, "you recall me to the nursery rhymes of my youth—the sacred duty of flippancy:

"There was an old man of Whitehaven
Who danced a quadrille with a raven,
  But they said: It's absurd
To encourage that bird—
  So they smashed that old man of Whitehaven.

"That's the correct attitude, Parker. Here's a poor old buffer spirited away—such a joke—and I don't believe he'd hurt a fly himself—that makes it funnier. D'you know, Parker, I don't care frightfully about this case after all."

"Which, this or yours?"

"Both. I say, Parker, shall we go quietly home and have lunch and go to the Coliseum?"

"You can if you like," replied the detective; "but you forget I do this for my bread and butter."

"And I haven't even that excuse," said Lord Peter; "well, what's the next move? What would you do in my case?"

"I'd do some good, hard grind," said Parker. "I'd distrust every bit of work Sugg ever did, and I'd get the family history of every tenant of every flat in Queen Caroline Mansions. I'd examine all their box-rooms and roof-traps, and I would inveigle them into conversations and suddenly bring in the words 'body' and 'pince-nez,' and see if they wriggled, like those modern psyo-what's-his-names."

"You would, would you?" said Lord Peter with a grin. "Well, we've exchanged cases, you know, so just you toddle off and do it. I'm going to have a jolly time at Wyndham's."

Parker made a grimace.

"Well," he said, "I don't suppose you'd ever do it, so I'd better. You'll never become a professional till you learn to do a little work, Wimsey. How about lunch?"

"I'm invited out," said Lord Peter, magnificently. "I'll run

around and change at the club. Can't feed with Freddy Arbuthnot in these bags; Bunter!"

"Yes, my lord."

"Pack up if you're ready, and come round and wash my face
and hands for me at the club."

"Work here for another two hours, my lord. Can't do with less
than thirty minutes' exposure. The current's none too strong."

"You see how I'm bullied by my own man, Parker? Well, I
must bear it, I suppose. Ta-ta!"

He whistled his way downstairs.

The conscientious Mr. Parker, with a groan, settled down to
a systematic search through Sir Reuben Levy's papers, with the
assistance of a plate of ham sandwiches and a bottle of Bass.

Lord Peter and the Honourable Freddy Arbuthnot, looking
together like an advertisement for gents' trouserings, strolled
into the dining-room at Wyndham's.

"Haven't seen you for an age," said the Honourable Freddy.
"What have you been doin' with yourself?"

"Oh, foolin' about," said Lord Peter, languidly.

"Thick or clear, sir?" inquired the waiter of the Honourable
Freddy.

"Which'll you have, Wimsey?" said that gentleman, transfer-
ring the burden of selection to his guest. "They're both equally
poisonous."

"Well, clear's less trouble to lick out of the spoon," said Lord
Peter.

"Clear," said the Honourable Freddy.

"Consommé Polonais," agreed the waiter. "Very nice, sir."

Conversation languished until the Honourable Freddy found
a bone in the filleted sole, and sent for the head waiter to explain

its presence. When this matter had been adjusted Lord Peter found energy to say:

"Sorry to hear about your gov'nor, old man."

"Yes, poor old buffer," said the Honourable Freddy; "they say he can't last long now. What? Oh! the Montrachet '08. There's nothing fit to drink in this place," he added gloomily.

After this deliberate insult to a noble vintage there was a further pause, till Lord Peter said: "'How's 'Change?"

"Rotten," said the Honourable Freddy.

He helped himself gloomily to salmis of game.

"Can I do anything?" asked Lord Peter.

"Oh, no, thanks—very decent of you, but it'll pan out all right in time."

"This isn't a bad salmis," said Lord Peter.

"I've eaten worse," admitted his friend.

"What about those Argentines?" inquired Lord Peter. "Here, waiter, there's a bit of cork in my glass."

"Cork?" cried the Honourable Freddy, with something approaching animation; "you'll hear about this, waiter. It's an amazing thing a fellow who's paid to do the job can't manage to take a cork out of a bottle. What you say? Argentines? Gone all to hell. Old Levy bunkin' off like that's knocked the bottom out of the market."

"You don't say so," said Lord Peter. "What d'you suppose has happened to the old man?"

"Cursed if I know," said the Honourable Freddy; "knocked on the head by the bears, I should think."

"P'r'aps he's gone off on his own," suggested Lord Peter. "Double life, you know. Giddy old blighters, some of these City men."

"Oh, no," said the Honourable Freddy, faintly roused; "no, hang it all, Wimsey, I wouldn't care to say that. He's a decent old domestic bird, and his daughter's a charmin' girl. Besides, he's straight enough—he'd *do* you down fast enough, but he wouldn't *let* you down. Old Anderson is badly cut up about it."

"Who's Anderson?"

"Chap with property out there. He belongs here. He was goin' to meet Levy on Tuesday. He's afraid those railway people will get in now, and then it'll be all U. P."

"Who's runnin' the railway people over here?" inquired Lord Peter.

"Yankee blighter, John P. Milligan. He's got an option, or says he has. You can't trust these brutes."

"Can't Anderson hold on?"

"Anderson isn't Levy. Hasn't got the shekels. Besides, he's only one. Levy covers the ground—he could boycott Milligan's beastly railway if he liked. That's where he's got the pull, you see."

"B'lieve I met the Milligan man somewhere," said Lord Peter, thoughtfully. "Ain't he a hulking brute with black hair and a beard?"

"You're thinkin' of somebody else," said the Honourable Freddy. "Milligan don't stand any higher than I do, unless you call five-feet-ten hulking—and he's bald, anyway."

Lord Peter considered this over the Gorgonzola. Then he said: "Didn't know Levy had a charmin' daughter."

"Oh, yes," said the Honourable Freddy, with an elaborate detachment. "Met her and Mamma last year abroad. That's how I got to know the old man. He's been very decent. Let me into this Argentine business on the ground floor, don't you know?"

"Well," said Lord Peter, "you might do worse. Money's money, ain't it? And Lady Levy is quite a redeemin' point. At least, my mother knew her people."

"Oh, *she's* all right," said the Honourable Freddy, "and the old man's nothing to be ashamed of nowadays. He's self-made, of course, but he don't pretend to be anything else. No side. Toddles off to business on a 96 'bus every morning. 'Can't make up my mind to taxis, my boy,' he says. 'I had to look at every half-penny when I was a young man, and I can't get out of the way of it now.' Though, if he's takin' his family out, nothing's too good. Rachel—that's the girl—always laughs at the old man's little economies."

"I suppose they've sent for Lady Levy," said Lord Peter.

"I suppose so," agreed the other. "I'd better pop round and express sympathy or somethin', what? Wouldn't look well not to, d'you think? But it's deuced awkward. What am I to say?"

"I don't think it matters much what you say," said Lord Peter, helpfully. "I should ask if you can do anything."

"Thanks," said the lover, "I will. Energetic young man. Count on me. Always at your service. Ring me up any time of the day or night. That's the line to take, don't you think?"

"That's the idea," said Lord Peter.

Mr. John P. Milligan, the London representative of the great Milligan railroad and shipping company, was dictating code cables to his secretary in an office in Lombard Street, when a card was brought up to him, bearing the simple legend:

LORD PETER WIMSEY
Marlborough Club

Mr. Milligan was annoyed at the interruption, but, like many of his nation, if he had a weak point, it was the British aristocracy. He postponed for a few minutes the elimination from the map of a modest but promising farm, and directed that the visitor should be shown up.

"Good-afternoon," said that nobleman, ambling genially in, "it's most uncommonly good of you to let me come round wastin' your time like this. I'll try not to be too long about it, though I'm not awfully good at comin' to the point. My brother never would let me stand for the county, y'know—said I wandered on so nobody'd know what I was talkin' about."

"Pleased to meet you, Lord Wimsey," said Mr. Milligan. "Won't you take a seat?"

"Thanks," said Lord Peter, "but I'm not a peer, you know—that's my brother Denver. My name's Peter. It's a silly name, I always think, so old-world and full of homely virtue and that sort of thing, but my godfathers and godmothers in my baptism are responsible for that, I suppose, officially—which is rather hard on them, you know, as they didn't actually choose it. But we always have a Peter, after the third duke, who betrayed five kings somewhere about the Wars of the Roses, though come to think of it, it ain't anything to be proud of. Still, one has to make the best of it."

Mr. Milligan, thus ingeniously placed at that disadvantage which attends ignorance, manoeuvred for position, and offered his interrupter a Corona Corona.

"Thanks, awfully," said Lord Peter, "though you really mustn't tempt me to stay here burblin' all afternoon. By Jove, Mr. Milligan, if you offer people such comfortable chairs and cigars like these, I wonder they don't come an' live in your office." He added mentally: "I wish to goodness I could get those long-toed boots off you. How's a man to know the size of your feet? And a head like a potato. It's enough to make one swear."

"Say now, Lord Peter," said Mr. Milligan, "can I do anything for you?"

"Well, d'you know," said Lord Peter, "I'm wonderin' if you would. It's damned cheek to ask you, but fact is, it's my mother, you know. Wonderful woman, but don't realize what it means, demands on the time of a busy man like you. We don't understand hustle over here, you know, Mr. Milligan."

"Now don't you mention that," said Mr. Milligan; "I'd be surely charmed to do anything to oblige the Duchess."

He felt a momentary qualm as to whether a duke's mother were also a duchess, but breathed more freely as Lord Peter went on:

"Thanks—that's uncommonly good of you. Well, now, it's like this. My mother—most energetic, self-sacrificin' woman, don't you see, is thinkin' of gettin' up a sort of a charity bazaar down at Denver this winter, in aid of the church roof, y'know. Very sad case, Mr. Milligan—fine old antique—early English windows and decorated angel roof, and all that—all tumblin' to pieces, rain pourin' in and so on—vicar catchin' rheumatism at early service, owin' to the draught blowin' in over the altar— you know the sort of thing. They've got a man down startin' on it—little beggar called Thipps—lives with an aged mother in Battersea—vulgar little beast, but quite good on angel roofs and things, I'm told."

At this point, Lord Peter watched his interlocutor narrowly, but finding that this rigmarole produced in him no reaction more startling than polite interest tinged with faint bewilderment, he abandoned this line of investigation, and proceeded:

"I say, I beg your pardon, frightfully—I'm afraid I'm bein' beastly long-winded. Fact is, my mother is gettin' up this bazaar, and she thought it'd be an awfully interestin' side-show to have some lectures—sort of little talks, y'know—by eminent business men of all nations. 'How I Did It' kind of touch, y'know—'A Drop of Oil with a Kerosene King'—'Cash Conscience and Cocoa' and so on. It would interest people down there no end. You see, all my mother's friends will be there, and we've none of us any money—not what you'd call money, I mean—I expect our incomes wouldn't pay your telephone calls, would they?—but we like awfully to hear about the people who can make money. Gives us a sort of uplifted feelin', don't you know. Well, anyway, I mean, my mother'd be frightfully pleased and grateful to you, Mr. Milligan, if you'd come down and give us a few words as a representative American. It needn't take more than ten minutes or so, y'know, because the local people can't understand much beyond shootin' and huntin', and my mother's crowd can't keep their minds on anythin' more than ten minutes together, but we'd really appreciate it very much if you'd come and stay a day or two and just give us a little breezy word on the almighty dollar."

"Why, yes," said Mr. Milligan, "I'd like to, Lord Peter. It's kind of the Duchess to suggest it. It's a very sad thing when these fine old antiques begin to wear out. I'll come with great pleasure. And perhaps you'd be kind enough to accept a little donation to the Restoration Fund."

This unexpected development nearly brought Lord Peter up all standing. To pump, by means of an ingenious lie, a hospitable gentleman whom you are inclined to suspect of a peculiarly malicious murder, and to accept from him in the course of the proceedings a large cheque for a charitable object, has something about it unpalatable to any but the hardened Secret Service agent. Lord Peter temporized.

"That's awfully decent of you," he said. "I'm sure they'd be no end grateful. But you'd better not give it to me, you know. I might spend it, or lose it. I'm not very reliable, I'm afraid. The vicar's the right person—the Rev. Constantine Throgmorton, St. John-before-the-Latin-Gate Vicarage, Duke's Denver, if you'd like to send it there."

"I will," said Mr. Milligan. "Will you write it out now for a thousand pounds, Scoot, in case it slips my mind later?"

The secretary, a sandy-haired young man with a long chin and no eyebrows, silently did as he was requested. Lord Peter looked from the bald head of Mr. Milligan to the red head of the secretary, hardened his heart and tried again.

"Well, I'm no end grateful to you, Mr. Milligan, and so'll my mother be when I tell her. I'll let you know the date of the bazaar—it's not quite settled yet, and I've got to see some other business men, don't you know. I thought of askin' someone from one of the big newspaper combines to represent British advertisin' talent, what?—and a friend of mine promises me a leadin' German financier—very interestin' if there ain't too much feelin' against it down in the country, and I'll have to find somebody or other to do the Hebrew point of view. I thought of askin' Levy, y'know, only he's floated off in this inconvenient way."

"Yes," said Mr. Milligan, "that's a very curious thing, though I don't mind saying, Lord Peter, that it's a convenience to me. He had a cinch on my railroad combine, but I'd nothing against him personally, and if he turns up after I've brought off a little deal I've got on, I'll be happy to give him the right hand of welcome."

A vision passed through Lord Peter's mind of Sir Reuben kept somewhere in custody till a financial crisis was over. This was exceedingly possible, and far more agreeable than his earlier conjecture; it also agreed better with the impression he was forming of Mr. Milligan.

"Well, it's a rum go," said Lord Peter, "but I daresay he had his reasons. Much better not to inquire into people's reasons, y'know, what? Specially as a police friend of mine who's connected with the case says the old johnnie dyed his hair before he went."

Out of the tail of his eye, Lord Peter saw the red-headed secretary add up five columns of figures simultaneously and jot down the answer.

"Dyed his hair, did he?" said Mr. Milligan.

"Dyed it red," said Lord Peter. The secretary looked up. "Odd thing is," continued Wimsey, "they can't lay hands on the bottle. Somethin' fishy there, don't you think, what?"

The secretary's interest seemed to have evaporated. He inserted a fresh sheet into his looseleaf ledger, and carried forward a row of digits from the preceding page.

"I daresay there's nothin' in it," said Lord Peter, rising to go. "Well, it's uncommonly good of you to be bothered with me like this, Mr. Milligan—my mother'll be no end pleased. She'll write you about the date."

"I'm charmed," said Mr. Milligan. "Very pleased to have met you."

Mr. Scoot rose silently to open the door, uncoiling as he did so a portentous length of thin leg, hitherto hidden by the desk. With a mental sigh Lord Peter estimated him at six-foot-four.

"It's a pity I can't put Scoot's head on Milligan's shoulders," said Lord Peter, emerging into the swirl of the city. "And what *will* my mother say?"

V

Mr. Parker was a bachelor, and occupied a Georgian but inconvenient flat at No. 12A Great Ormond Street, for which he paid
a pound a week. His exertions in the cause of civilization were
rewarded, not by the gift of diamond rings from empresses
or munificent cheques from grateful Prime Ministers, but by
a modest, though sufficient, salary, drawn from the pockets of
the British taxpayer. He awoke, after a long day of arduous and
inconclusive labour, to the smell of burnt porridge. Through
his bedroom window, hygienically open top and bottom, a raw
fog was rolling slowly in, and the sight of a pair of winter pants,
flung hastily over a chair the previous night, fretted him with a
sense of the sordid absurdity of the human form. The telephone
bell rang, and he crawled wretchedly out of bed and into the
sitting-room, where Mrs. Munns, who did for him by the day,
was laying the table, sneezing as she went.

Mr. Bunter was speaking.

"His lordship says he'd be very glad, sir, if you could make it
convenient to step round to breakfast."

If the odour of kidneys and bacon had been wafted along the
wire, Mr. Parker could not have experienced a more vivid sense
of consolation.

"Tell his lordship I'll be with him in half an hour," he said, thankfully, and plunging into the bathroom, which was also the kitchen, he informed Mrs. Munns, who was just making tea from a kettle which had gone off the boil, that he should be out to breakfast.

"You can take the porridge home for the family," he added, viciously, and flung off his dressing-gown with such determination that Mrs. Munns could only scuttle away with a snort.

A 19 'bus deposited him in Piccadilly only fifteen minutes later than his rather sanguine impulse had prompted him to suggest, and Mr. Bunter served him with glorious food, incomparable coffee, and the *Daily Mail* before a blazing fire of wood and coal. A distant voice singing the "et iterum venturus est" from Bach's Mass in B minor proclaimed that for the owner of the flat cleanliness and godliness met at least once a day, and presently Lord Peter roamed in, moist and verbena-scented, in a bathrobe cheerfully patterned with unnaturally variegated peacocks.

"Mornin', old dear," said that gentleman. "Beast of a day, ain't it? Very good of you to trundle out in it, but I had a letter I wanted you to see, and I hadn't the energy to come round to your place. Bunter and I've been makin' a night of it."

"What's the letter?" asked Parker.

"Never talk business with your mouth full," said Lord Peter, reprovingly; "have some Oxford marmalade—and then I'll show you my Dante; they brought it round last night. What ought I to read this morning, Bunter?"

"Lord Erith's collection is going to be sold, my lord. There is a column about it in the *Morning Post.* I think your lordship should look at this review of Sir Julian Freke's new book on 'The Physiological Bases of the Conscience' in the *Times Literary Supplement.* Then there is a very singular little burglary in the *Chronicle,* my lord, and an attack on titled families in the *Herald*—rather ill-written, if I may say so, but not without unconscious humour which your lordship will appreciate."

"All right, give me that and the burglary," said his lordship.

"I have looked over the other papers," pursued Mr. Bunter, indicating a formidable pile, "and marked your lordship's after-breakfast reading."

"Oh, pray don't allude to it," said Lord Peter; "you take my appetite away."

There was silence, but for the crunching of toast and the crackling of paper.

"I see they adjourned the inquest," said Parker presently.

"Nothing else to do," said Lord Peter; "but Lady Levy arrived last night, and will have to go and fail to identify the body this morning for Sugg's benefit."

"Time, too," said Mr. Parker shortly.

Silence fell again.

"I don't think much of your burglary, Bunter," said Lord Peter. "Competent, of course, but no imagination. I want imagination in a criminal. Where's the *Morning Post*?"

After a further silence, Lord Peter said: "You might send for the catalogue, Bunter, that Apollonios Rhodios* might be worth looking at. No, I'm damned if I'm going to stodge through that review, but you can stick the book on the library list if you like. His book on Crime was entertainin' enough as far as it went, but the fellow's got a bee in his bonnet. Thinks God's a secretion of the liver—all right once in a way, but there's no need to keep on about it. There's nothing you can't prove if your outlook is only sufficiently limited. Look at Sugg."

"I beg your pardon," said Parker; "I wasn't attending. Argentines are steadying a little, I see."

---

* Apollonios Rhodios. Lorenzobodi Alopa. Firenze. 1496. (4to.) The excitement attendant on the solution of the Battersea Mystery did not prevent Lord Peter from securing this rare work before his departure for Corsica.

"Milligan," said Lord Peter.

"Oil's in a bad way. Levy's made a difference there. That funny little boom in Peruvians that came on just before he disappeared has died away again. I wonder if he was concerned in it. D'you know at all?"

"I'll find out," said Lord Peter. "What was it?"

"Oh, an absolutely dud enterprise that hadn't been heard of for years. It suddenly took a little lease of life last week. I happened to notice it because my mother got let in for a couple of hundred shares a long time ago. It never paid a dividend. Now it's petered out again."

Wimsey pushed his plate aside and lit a pipe.

"Having finished, I don't mind doing some work," he said. "How did you get on yesterday?"

"I didn't," replied Parker. "I sleuthed up and down those flats in my own bodily shape and two different disguises. I was a gas-meter man and a collector for a Home for Lost Doggies, and I didn't get a thing to go on, except a servant in the top flat at the Battersea Bridge Road end of the row who said she thought she heard a bump on the roof one night. Asked which night, she couldn't rightly say. Asked if it was Monday night, she thought it very likely. Asked if it mightn't have been in that high wind on Saturday night that blew my chimney-pot off, she couldn't say but what it might have been. Asked if she was sure it was on the roof and not inside the flat, said to be sure they did find a picture tumbled down next morning. Very suggestible girl. I saw your friends, Mr. and Mrs. Appledore, who received me coldly, but could make no definite complaint about Thipps except that his mother dropped her h's, and that he once called on them uninvited, armed with a pamphlet about anti-vivisection. The Indian Colonel on the first floor was loud, but unexpectedly friendly. He gave me Indian curry for supper and some very good whisky, but he's a sort of hermit, and all *he* could tell me was that he couldn't stand Mrs. Appledore."

"Did you get nothing at the house?"

"Only Levy's private diary. I brought it away with me. Here it is. It doesn't tell one much, though. It's full of entries like: 'Tom and Annie to dinner'; and 'My dear wife's birthday; gave her an old opal ring'; 'Mr. Arbuthnot dropped in to tea; he wants to marry Rachel, but I should like someone steadier for my treasure.' Still, I thought it would show who came to the house and so on. He evidently wrote it up at night. There's no entry for Monday."

"I expect it'll be useful," said Lord Peter, turning over the pages. "Poor old buffer. I say, I'm not so certain now he was done away with."

He detailed to Mr. Parker his day's work.

"Arbuthnot?" said Parker. "Is that the Arbuthnot of the diary?"

"I suppose so. I hunted him up because I knew he was fond of fooling round the Stock Exchange. As for Milligan, he *looks* all right, but I believe he's pretty ruthless in business and you never can tell. Then there's the red-haired secretary—lightnin' calculator man with a face like a fish, keeps on sayin' nuthin'— got the Tar baby in his family tree, I should think. Milligan's got a jolly good motive for, at any rate, suspendin' Levy for a few days. Then there's the new man."

"What new man?"

"Ah, that's the letter I mentioned to you. Where did I put it? Here we are. Good parchment paper, printed address of solicitor's office in Salisbury, and postmark to correspond. Very precisely written with a fine nib by an elderly business man of old-fashioned habits."

Parker took the letter and read:

CRIMPLESHAM AND WICKS,
SOLICITORS,
MILFORD HILL, SALISBURY

17 November, 192—.

Sir,

With reference to your advertisement today in the personal column of The Times, *I am disposed to believe that the eyeglasses and chain in question may be those I lost on the L. B. & S. C. Electric Railway while visiting London last Monday. I left Victoria by the 5.45 train, and did not notice my loss till I arrived at Balham. This indication and the optician's specification of the glasses, which I enclose, should suffice at once as an identification and a guarantee of my bona fides. If the glasses should prove to be mine, I should be greatly obliged to you if you would kindly forward them to me by registered post, as the chain was a present from my daughter, and is one of my dearest possessions.*

Thanking you in advance for this kindness, and regretting the trouble to which I shall be putting you, I am,

Yours very truly,
Thos. Crimplesham

Lord Peter Wimsey,
110, Piccadilly, W.
(Encl.)

"Dear me," said Parker, "this is what you might call unexpected."

"Either it is some extraordinary misunderstanding," said Lord Peter, "or Mr. Crimplesham is a very bold and cunning villain. Or possibly, of course, they are the wrong glasses. We may as well get a ruling on that point at once. I suppose the glasses are at the Yard. I wish you'd just ring 'em up and ask 'em to send round an optician's description of them at once—and you might ask at the same time whether it's a very common prescription."

"Right you are," said Parker, and took the receiver off its hook.

"And now," said his friend, when the message was delivered, "just come into the library for a minute."

On the library table, Lord Peter had spread out a series of bromide prints, some dry, some damp, and some but half-washed.

"These little ones are the originals of the photos we've been taking," said Lord Peter, "and these big ones are enlargements all made to precisely the same scale. This one here is the footmark on the linoleum; we'll put that by itself at present. Now these finger-prints can be divided into five lots. I've numbered 'em on the prints—see?—and made a list:

"A. The finger-prints of Levy himself, off his little bedside book and his hair-brush—this and this—you can't mistake the little scar on the thumb.

"B. The smudges made by the gloved fingers of the man who slept in Levy's room on Monday night. They show clearly on the water-bottle and on the boots—superimposed on Levy's. They are very distinct on the boots—surprisingly so for gloved hands, and I deduce that the gloves were rubber ones and had recently been in water.

"Here's another interestin' point. Levy walked in the rain on Monday night, as we know, and these dark marks are mud-splashes. You see they lie *over* Levy's finger-prints in every case. Now see: on this left boot we find the stranger's thumb-mark *over* the mud on the leather above the heel. That's a funny place to find a thumb-mark on a boot, isn't it? That is, if Levy took off his own boots. But it's the place where you'd expect to see it if somebody forcibly removed his boots for him. Again, most of the stranger's fingermarks come *over* the mud-marks, but here is one splash of mud which comes on top of them again. Which makes me infer that the stranger came back to Park Lane, wearing Levy's boots, in a cab, carriage or car, but that at some point or other he walked a little way—just enough to tread in a puddle and get a splash on the boots. What do you say?"

"Very pretty," said Parker. "A bit intricate, though, and the marks are not all that I could wish a finger-print to be."

"Well, I won't lay too much stress on it. But it fits in with our previous ideas. Now let's turn to:

"C. The prints obligingly left by my own particular villain on the further edge of Thipps's bath, where you spotted them, and I ought to be scourged for not having spotted them. The left hand, you notice, the base of the palm and the fingers, but not the tips, looking as though he had steadied himself on the edge of the bath while leaning down to adjust something at the bottom, the pince-nez perhaps. Gloved, you see, but showing no ridge or seam of any kind—I say rubber, you say rubber. That's that. Now see here:

"D and E come off a visiting-card of mine. There's this thing at the corner, marked F, but that you can disregard; in the original document it's a sticky mark left by the thumb of the youth who took it from me, after first removing a piece of chewing-gum from his teeth with his finger to tell me that Mr. Milligan might or might not be disengaged. D and E are the thumb-marks of Mr. Milligan and his red-haired secretary. I'm not clear which is which, but I saw the youth with the chewing-gum hand the card to the secretary, and when I got into the inner shrine I saw John P. Milligan standing with it in his hand, so it's one or the other, and for the moment it's immaterial to our purpose which is which. I boned the card from the table when I left.

"Well, now, Parker, here's what's been keeping Bunter and me up till the small hours. I've measured and measured every way backwards and forwards till my head's spinnin', and I've stared till I'm nearly blind, but I'm hanged if I can make my mind up.

Question 1. Is C identical with B? Question 2. Is D or E identical with B? There's nothing to go on but the size and shape, of course, and the marks are so faint—what do you think?"

Parker shook his head doubtfully.

"I think E might almost be put out of the question," he said; "it seems such an excessively long and narrow thumb. But I think there is a decided resemblance between the span of B on the water-bottle and C on the bath. And I don't see any reason why D shouldn't be the same as B, only there's so little to judge from."

"Your untutored judgment and my measurements have brought us both to the same conclusion—if you can call it a conclusion," said Lord Peter, bitterly.

"Another thing," said Parker. "Why on earth should we try to connect B with C? The fact that you and I happen to be friends doesn't make it necessary to conclude that the two cases we happen to be interested in have any organic connection with one another. Why should they? The only person who thinks they have is Sugg, and he's nothing to go by. It would be different if there were any truth in the suggestion that the man in the bath was Levy, but we know for a certainty he wasn't. It's ridiculous to suppose that the same man was employed in committing two totally distinct crimes on the same night, one in Battersea and the other in Park Lane."

"I know," said Wimsey, "though of course we mustn't forget that Levy *was* in Battersea at the time, and now we know he didn't return home at twelve as was supposed, we've no reason to think he ever left Battersea at all."

"True. But there are other places in Battersea besides Thipps's bathroom. And he *wasn't* in Thipps's bathroom. In fact, come to think of it, that's the one place in the universe where we know definitely that he wasn't. So what's Thipps's bath got to do with it?"

"I don't know," said Lord Peter. "Well, perhaps we shall get something better to go on today."

He leaned back in his chair and smoked thoughtfully for some time over the papers which Bunter had marked for him.

"They've got you out in the limelight," he said. "Thank Heaven, Sugg hates me too much to give me any publicity. What a dull Agony Column! 'Darling Pipsey—Come back soon to your distracted Popsey'—and the usual young man in need of financial assistance, and the usual injunction to 'Remember thy Creator in the days of thy youth.' Hullo! there's the bell. Oh, it's our answer from Scotland Yard."

The note from Scotland Yard enclosed an optician's specification identical with that sent by Mr. Crimplesham, and added that it was an unusual one, owing to the peculiar strength of the lenses and the marked difference between the sight of the two eyes.

"That's good enough," said Parker.

"Yes," said Wimsey. "Then Possibility No. 3 is knocked on the head. There remain Possibility No. 1: Accident or Misunderstanding, and No. 2: Deliberate Villainy, of a remarkably bold and calculating kind—of a kind, in fact, characteristic of the author or authors of our two problems. Following the methods inculcated at that University of which I have the honour to be a member, we will now examine severally the various suggestions afforded by Possibility No. 2. This Possibility may be again subdivided into two or more Hypotheses. On Hypothesis 1 (strongly advocated by my distinguished colleague Professor Snupshed), the criminal, whom we may designate as X, is not identical with Crimplesham, but is using the name of Crimplesham as his shield, or aegis. This hypothesis may be further subdivided into two alternatives. Alternative A: Crimplesham is an innocent and unconscious accomplice, and X is in his employment. X writes in Crimplesham's name on Crimplesham's office-paper and obtains that the object in question, i.e., the eyeglasses, be despatched to Crimplesham's address. He is in a position to intercept the parcel before it reaches Crimplesham. The presumption is that X is Crimplesham's charwoman, office-boy, clerk, secretary or porter. This offers a wide field of investigation. The method of inquiry will be to interview Crimplesham and discover whether he sent the letter, and if not, who has access to his correspondence. Alternative B: Crimplesham is under X's influence or in his power, and has been induced to write the letter by (*a*) bribery, (*b*) misrepresentation or (*c*) threats. X may in that case be a persuasive relation or friend, or else a creditor, blackmailer or assassin; Crimplesham, on the other hand, is obviously venal or a fool. The method of inquiry in this case, I would tentatively suggest, is again to interview Crimplesham, put the facts of the case strongly before him, and assure him in the most intimidating terms that he is liable to a prolonged term of penal servitude as an accessory after the fact in the crime of murder—Ah-hem! Trusting, gentlemen, that you have followed me thus far, we will pass to the consideration of Hypothesis No. 2, to which I personally incline, and according to which X is identical with Crimplesham.

"In this case, Crimplesham, who is, in the words of an English classic, a man-of-infinite-resource-and-sagacity, correctly deduces that, of all people, the last whom we shall expect to find answering our advertisement is the criminal himself. Accordingly, he plays a bold game of bluff. He invents an occasion on which the glasses may very easily have been lost or stolen, and applies for them. If confronted, nobody will be more astonished than he to learn where they were found. He will produce witnesses to prove that he left Victoria at 5.45 and emerged from the train at Balham at the scheduled time, and sat up all Monday night playing chess with a respectable gentleman well known in Balham. In this case, the method of inquiry will be to pump the respectable gentleman in Balham, and if he should happen to be a single gentleman with a deaf housekeeper, it may be no easy matter to impugn the alibi, since, outside detective romances, few ticket-collectors and 'bus-conductors keep an exact remembrance of all the passengers passing between Balham and London on any and every evening of the week.

"Finally, gentlemen, I will frankly point out the weak point of all these hypotheses, namely: that none of them offers any explanation as to why the incriminating article was left so conspicuously on the body in the first instance."

Mr. Parker had listened with commendable patience to this academic exposition.

"Might not X," he suggested, "be an enemy of Crimplesham's, who designed to throw suspicion upon him?"

"He might. In that case he should be easy to discover, since he obviously lives in close proximity to Crimplesham and his glasses, and Crimplesham in fear of his life will then be a valuable ally for the prosecution."

"How about the first possibility of all, misunderstanding or accident?"

"Well! Well, for purposes of discussion, nothing, because it really doesn't afford any data for discussion."

"In any case," said Parker, "the obvious course appears to be to go to Salisbury."

"That seems indicated," said Lord Peter.

"Very well," said the detective, "is it to be you or me or both of us?"

"It is to be me," said Lord Peter, "and that for two reasons. First, because, if (by Possibility No. 2, Hypothesis 1, Alternative A) Crimplesham is an innocent catspaw, the person who put in the advertisement is the proper person to hand over the property. Secondly, because, if we are to adopt Hypothesis 2, we must not overlook the sinister possibility that Crimplesham-X is laying a careful trap to rid himself of the person who so unwarily advertised in the daily press his interest in the solution of the Battersea Park mystery."

"That appears to me to be an argument for our both going," objected the detective.

"Far from it," said Lord Peter. "Why play into the hands of Crimplesham-X by delivering over to him the only two men in London with the evidence, such as it is, and shall I say the wits, to connect him with the Battersea body?"

"But if we told the Yard where we were going, and we both got nobbled," said Mr. Parker, "it would afford strong presumptive evidence of Crimplesham's guilt, and anyhow, if he didn't get hanged for murdering the man in the bath he'd at least get hanged for murdering us."

"Well," said Lord Peter, "if he only murdered me you could still hang him—what's the good of wasting a sound, marriageable young male like yourself? Besides, how about old Levy? If you're incapacitated, do you think anybody else is going to find him?"

"But we could frighten Crimplesham by threatening him with the Yard."

"Well, dash it all, if it comes to that, *I* can frighten him by threatening him with *you*, which, seeing you hold what evidence there is, is much more to the point. And, then, suppose it's a wild-goose chase after all, you'll have wasted time when you might have been getting on with the case. There are several things that need doing."

"Well," said Parker, silenced but reluctant, "why can't I go, in that case?"

"Bosh!" said Lord Peter. "I am retained (by old Mrs. Thipps, for whom I entertain the greatest respect) to deal with this case, and it's only by courtesy I allow you to have anything to do with it."

Mr. Parker groaned.

"Will you at least take Bunter?" he said.

"In deference to your feelings," replied Lord Peter, "I will take Bunter, though he could be far more usefully employed taking photographs or overhauling my wardrobe. When is there a good train to Salisbury, Bunter?"

"There is an excellent train at 10.50, my lord."

"Kindly make arrangements to catch it," said Lord Peter, throwing off his bathrobe and trailing away with it into his bedroom. "And Parker—if you have nothing else to do you might get hold of Levy's secretary and look into that little matter of the Peruvian Oil."

Lord Peter took with him, for light reading in the train, Sir Reuben Levy's diary. It was a simple, and in the light of recent facts, rather a pathetic document. The terrible fighter of the Stock Exchange, who could with one nod set the surly bear dancing, or bring the savage bull to feed out of his hand, whose breath devastated whole districts with famine or swept financial potentates from their seats, was revealed in private life as kindly, domestic, innocently proud of himself and his belongings, confiding, generous and a little dull. His own small economies were duly chronicled side by side with extravagant presents to his wife and daughter. Small incidents of household routine appeared, such as: "Man came to mend the conservatory roof," or "The new butler (Simpson) has arrived, recommended by the Goldbergs. I think he will be satisfactory." All visitors and entertainments were duly entered, from a very magnificent lunch to Lord Dewsbury, the Minister for Foreign Affairs, and Dr. Jabez K. Wort, the American plenipotentiary, through a series of diplomatic dinners to eminent financiers, down to intimate family gatherings of persons designated by Christian names or nicknames. About May there came a mention of Lady Levy's nerves, and further reference was made to the subject in subsequent months. In September it was stated that "Freke came to see my dear wife and advised complete rest and change of scene. She thinks of going abroad with Rachel." The name of the famous nerve-specialist occurred as a diner or luncher about once a month, and it came into Lord Peter's mind that Freke would be a good person to consult about Levy himself. "People sometimes tell things to the doctor," he murmured to himself. "And, by Jove! if Levy was simply going round to see Freke on Monday night, that rather disposes of the Battersea incident, doesn't it?" He made a note to look up Sir Julian and turned on further. On September 18th, Lady Levy and her daughter had left for the south of France. Then suddenly, under the date October 5th, Lord Peter found what he was looking for: "Goldberg, Skriner and Milligan to dinner."

There was the evidence that Milligan had been in that house. There had been a formal entertainment—a meeting as of two duellists shaking hands before the fight. Skriner was a well-known picture-dealer; Lord Peter imagined an after-dinner excursion upstairs to see the two Corots in the drawing-room, and the portrait of the eldest Levy girl, who had died at the age of sixteen. It was by Augustus John, and hung in the bedroom. The name of the red-haired secretary was nowhere mentioned, unless the initial S., occurring in another entry, referred to him. Throughout September and October, Anderson (of Wyndham's) had been a frequent visitor.

Lord Peter shook his head over the diary, and turned to the consideration of the Battersea Park mystery. Whereas in the Levy affair it was easy enough to supply a motive for the crime, if crime it were, and the difficulty was to discover the method of its carrying out and the whereabouts of the victim, in the other case the chief obstacle to inquiry was the entire absence of any imaginable motive. It was odd that, although the papers had carried news of the affair from one end of the country to the other and a description of the body had been sent to every police station in the country, nobody had as yet come forward to identify the mysterious occupant of Mr. Thipps's bath. It was true that the description, which mentioned the clean-shaven chin, elegantly cut hair and the pince-nez, was rather misleading but on the other hand, the police had managed to discover the number of molars missing, and the height, complexion and other data were correctly enough stated, as also the date at which death had presumably occurred. It seemed, however, as though the man had melted out of society without leaving a gap or so much as a ripple. Assigning a motive for the murder of a person without relations or antecedents or even clothes is like trying to visualize the fourth dimension—admirable exercise for the imagination, but arduous and inconclusive. Even if the day's interview should disclose black spots in the past or present of Mr. Crimplesham, how were they to be brought into connection with a person apparently without a past, and whose present was confined to the narrow limits of a bath and a police mortuary?

"Bunter," said Lord Peter, "I beg that in the future you will restrain me from starting two hares at once. These cases are gettin' to be a strain on my constitution. One hare has nowhere to run from, and the other has nowhere to run to. It's a kind of mental D.T., Bunter. When this is over I shall turn pussyfoot, forswear the police news, and take to an emollient diet of the works of the late Charles Garvice."

It was its comparative proximity to Milford Hill that induced Lord Peter to lunch at the Minster Hotel rather than at the White Hart or some other more picturesquely situated hostel. It was not a lunch calculated to cheer his mind; as in all

Cathedral cities, the atmosphere of the Close pervades every nook and corner of Salisbury, and no food in that city but seems faintly flavoured with prayer-books. As he sat sadly consuming that impassive pale substance known to the English as "cheese" unqualified (for there are cheeses which go openly by their names, as Stilton, Camembert, Gruyère, Wensleydale or Gorgonzola, but "cheese" is cheese and everywhere the same), he inquired of the waiter the whereabouts of Mr. Crimplesham's office.

The waiter directed him to a house rather further up the street on the opposite side, adding, "But anybody'll tell you, sir; Mr. Crimplesham's very well known hereabouts."

"He's a good solicitor, I suppose?" said Lord Peter.

"Oh, yes, sir," said the waiter, "you couldn't do better than trust to Mr. Crimplesham, sir. There's folk say he's old-fashioned, but I'd rather have my little bits of business done by Mr. Crimplesham than by one of these flyaway young men. Not but what Mr. Crimplesham'll be retiring soon, sir, I don't doubt, for he must be close on eighty, sir, if he's a day, but then there's young Mr. Wicks to carry on the business, and he's a very nice, steady-like young gentleman."

"Is Mr. Crimplesham really as old as that?" said Lord Peter. "Dear me! He must be very active for his years. A friend of mine was doing business with him in town last week."

"Wonderful active, sir," agreed the waiter, "and with his game leg, too, you'd be surprised. But there, sir, I often think when a man's once past a certain age, the older he grows the tougher he gets, and women the same or more so."

"Very likely," said Lord Peter, calling up and dismissing the mental picture of a gentleman of eighty with a game leg carrying a dead body over the roof of a Battersea flat at midnight. " 'He's tough, sir, tough, is old Joey Bagstock, tough and devilish sly,' " he added, thoughtlessly.

"Indeed, sir?" said the waiter. "I couldn't say, I'm sure."

"I beg your pardon," said Lord Peter; "I was quoting poetry. Very silly of me. I got the habit at my mother's knee and I can't break myself of it."

"No, sir," said the waiter, pocketing a liberal tip. "Thank you very much, sir. You'll find the house easy. Just afore you come to Penny-farthing Street, sir, about two turnings off, on the right-hand side opposite."

"Afraid that disposes of Crimplesham-X," said Lord Peter. "I'm rather sorry; he was a fine sinister figure as I had pictured him. Still, his may yet be the brain behind the hands—the aged spider sitting invisible in the centre of the vibrating web, you know, Bunter."

"Yes, my lord," said Bunter. They were walking up the street together.

"There is the office over the way," pursued Lord Peter. "I think, Bunter, you might step into this little shop and purchase a sporting paper, and if I do not emerge from the villain's lair—say within three-quarters of an hour, you may take such steps as your perspicuity may suggest."

Mr. Bunter turned into the shop as desired, and Lord Peter walked across and rang the lawyer's bell with decision.

"The truth, the whole truth and nothing but the truth is my long suit here, I fancy," he murmured, and when the door was opened by a clerk he delivered over his card with an unflinching air.

He was ushered immediately into a confidential-looking office, obviously furnished in the early years of Queen Victoria's reign, and never altered since. A lean, frail-looking old gentleman rose briskly from his chair as he entered and limped forward to meet him.

"My dear sir," exclaimed the lawyer, "how extremely good of you to come in person! Indeed, I am ashamed to have given you so much trouble. I trust you were passing this way, and that my glasses have not put you to any great inconvenience. Pray take a seat, Lord Peter." He peered gratefully at the young man over a pince-nez obviously the fellow of that now adorning a dossier in Scotland Yard.

Lord Peter sat down. The lawyer sat down. Lord Peter picked up a glass paper-weight from the desk and weighed it thoughtfully in his hand. Subconsciously he noted what an admirable set of finger-prints he was leaving upon it. He replaced it with precision on the exact centre of a pile of letters.

"It's quite all right," said Lord Peter. "I was here on business. Very happy to be of service to you. Very awkward to lose one's glasses, Mr. Crimplesham."

"Yes," said the lawyer, "I assure you I feel quite lost without them. I have this pair, but they do not fit my nose so well—besides, that chain has a great sentimental value for me. I was terribly distressed on arriving at Balham to find that I had lost them. I made inquiries of the railway, but to no purpose. I feared they had been stolen. There were such crowds at Victoria, and the carriage was packed with people all the way to Balham. Did you come across them in the train?"

"Well, no," said Lord Peter, "I found them in rather an unexpected place. Do you mind telling me if you recognized any of your fellow-travellers on that occasion?"

The lawyer stared at him.

"Not a soul," he answered. "Why do you ask?"

"Well," said Lord Peter, "I thought perhaps the—the person with whom I found them might have taken them for a joke."

The lawyer looked puzzled.

"Did the person claim to be an acquaintance of mine?" he inquired. "I know practically nobody in London, except the friend with whom I was staying in Balham, Dr. Philpots, and I should be very greatly surprised at his practising a jest upon me. He knew very well how distressed I was at the loss of the glasses. My business was to attend a meeting of shareholders in Medlicott's Bank, but the other gentlemen present were all personally unknown to me, and I cannot think that any of them would take so great a liberty. In any case," he added, "as the glasses are here, I will not inquire too closely into the manner of their restoration. I am deeply obliged to you for your trouble."

Lord Peter hesitated.

"Pray forgive my seeming inquisitiveness," he said, "but I must ask you another question. It sounds rather melodramatic, I'm afraid, but it's this. Are you aware that you have any enemy— anyone, I mean, who would profit by your—er—decease or disgrace?"

Mr. Crimplesham sat frozen into stony surprise and disapproval.

"May I ask the meaning of this extraordinary question?" he inquired stiffly.

"Well," said Lord Peter, "the circumstances are a little unusual. You may recollect that my advertisement was addressed to the jeweller who sold the chain."

"That surprised me at the time," said Mr. Crimplesham, "but I begin to think your advertisement and your behaviour are all of a piece."

"They are," said Lord Peter. "As a matter of fact I did not expect the owner of the glasses to answer my advertisement. Mr. Crimplesham, you have no doubt read what the papers have to say about the Battersea Park mystery. Your glasses are the pair that was found on the body, and they are now in the possession of the police at Scotland Yard, as you may see by this." He placed the specification of the glasses and the official note before Crimplesham.

"Good God!" exclaimed the lawyer. He glanced at the paper, and then looked narrowly at Lord Peter.

"Are you yourself connected with the police?" he inquired.

"Not officially," said Lord Peter. "I am investigating the matter privately, in the interests of one of the parties."

Mr. Crimplesham rose to his feet.

"My good man," he said, "this is a very impudent attempt, but blackmail is an indictable offence, and I advise you to leave my office before you commit yourself." He rang the bell.

"I was afraid you'd take it like that," said Lord Peter. "It looks as though this ought to have been my friend Detective Parker's job, after all." He laid Parker's card on the table beside the specification, and added: "If you should wish to see me again, Mr. Crimplesham, before tomorrow morning, you will find me at the Minster Hotel."

Mr. Crimplesham disdained to reply further than to direct the clerk who entered to "show this person out."

In the entrance Lord Peter brushed against a tall young man who was just coming in, and who stared at him with surprised recognition. His face, however, aroused no memories in Lord Peter's mind, and that baffled nobleman, calling out Bunter from the newspaper shop, departed to his hotel to get a trunk-call through to Parker.

Meanwhile, in the office, the meditations of the indignant Mr. Crimplesham were interrupted by the entrance of his junior partner.

"I say," said the latter gentleman, "has somebody done something really wicked at last? Whatever brings such a distinguished amateur of crime on our sober doorstep?"

"I have been the victim of a vulgar attempt at blackmail,"

said the lawyer; "an individual passing himself off as Lord Peter Wimsey—"

"But that *is* Lord Peter Wimsey," said Mr. Wicks, "there's no mistaking him. I saw him give evidence in the Attenbury emerald case. He's a big little pot in his way, you know, and goes fishing with the head of Scotland Yard."

"Oh, dear," said Mr. Crimplesham.

Fate arranged that the nerves of Mr. Crimplesham should be tried that afternoon. When, escorted by Mr. Wicks, he arrived at the Minster Hotel, he was informed by the porter that Lord Peter Wimsey had strolled out, mentioning that he thought of attending Evensong. "But his man is here, sir," he added, "if you'd like to leave a message."

Mr. Wicks thought that on the whole it would be well to leave a message. Mr. Bunter, on inquiry, was found to be sitting by the telephone, waiting for a trunk-call. As Mr. Wicks addressed him the bell rang, and Mr. Bunter, politely excusing himself, took down the receiver.

"Hullo!" he said. "Is that Mr. Parker? Oh, thanks! Exchange! Exchange! Sorry, can you put me through to Scotland Yard? Excuse me, gentlemen, keeping you waiting.—Exchange! all right—Scotland Yard—Hullo! Is that Scotland Yard?—Is Detective Parker round there?—Can I speak to him?—I shall have done in a moment, gentlemen.—Hullo! is that you, Mr. Parker? Lord Peter would be much obliged if you could find it convenient to step down to Salisbury, sir. Oh, no, sir, he's in excellent health, sir—just stepped round to hear Evensong, sir—oh, no, I think tomorrow morning would do excellently, sir, thank you, sir."

VI

It was, in fact, inconvenient for Mr. Parker to leave London. He had had to go and see Lady Levy towards the end of the morning, and subsequently his plans for the day had been thrown out of gear and his movements delayed by the discovery that the adjourned inquest of Mr. Thipps's unknown visitor was to be held that afternoon, since nothing very definite seemed forthcoming from Inspector Sugg's inquiries. Jury and witnesses had been convened accordingly for three o'clock. Mr. Parker might altogether have missed the event, had he not run against Sugg that morning at the Yard and extracted the information from him as one would a reluctant tooth. Inspector Sugg, indeed, considered Mr. Parker rather interfering; moreover, he was hand-in-glove with Lord Peter Wimsey, and Inspector Sugg had no words for the interferingness of Lord Peter. He could not, however, when directly questioned, deny that there was to be an inquest that afternoon, nor could he prevent Mr. Parker from enjoying the inalienable right of any interested British citizen to be present. At a little before three, therefore, Mr. Parker was in his place, and amusing himself with watching the efforts of those persons who arrived after the room was packed to insinuate, bribe or bully themselves into a position of vantage. The coroner, a medical man of precise habits and unimaginative aspect, arrived punctually, and looking peevishly round at the crowded assembly, directed all the windows to be opened, thus letting in a stream of drizzling fog upon the heads of the unfortunates on that side of the room. This caused a commotion and some expressions of disapproval, checked sternly by the coroner, who said that with the influenza about again an unventilated room was a death-trap; that anybody who chose to object to open windows had the obvious remedy of leaving the court, and further, that if any disturbance was made he would clear the court. He then took a Formamint lozenge, and proceeded, after the usual preliminaries, to call up fourteen good and lawful persons and swear them diligently to inquire and a true presentment make of all matters touching the death of the gentleman with the pince-nez and to give a true verdict according to the evidence, so help them God. When an expostulation by a woman juror—an elderly lady in spectacles who kept a sweetshop, and appeared to wish she was back there—had been summarily quashed by the coroner, the jury departed to view the body. Mr. Parker gazed round again and identified the unhappy Mr. Thipps and the girl Gladys led into an adjoining room under the grim guard of the police. They were soon followed by a gaunt old lady in a bonnet and mantle. With her, in a wonderful fur coat and a motor bonnet of fascinating construction, came the Dowager Duchess of Denver, her quick, dark eyes darting hither and thither about the crowd. The next moment they had lighted on Mr. Parker, who had several times visited the Dower House, and she nodded to him, and spoke to a policeman. Before long, a way opened magically through the press, and Mr. Parker found himself accommodated with a front seat just behind the Duchess, who greeted him charmingly, and said: "What's happened to poor Peter?" Parker began to explain, and the coroner glanced irritably in their direction. Somebody went up and whispered in his ear, at which he coughed, and took another Formamint.

"We came up by car," said the Duchess—"so tiresome—such bad roads between Denver and Gunbury St. Walters—and there were people coming to lunch—I had to put them off—I couldn't let the old lady go alone, could I? By the way, such an odd thing's happened about the Church Restoration Fund—the vicar—oh, dear, here are these people coming back again; well, I'll tell you afterwards—do look at that woman looking shocked, and the girl in tweeds trying to look as if she sat on undraped gentlemen every day of her life—I don't mean that—corpses of course—but one finds oneself being so Elizabethan nowadays—what an awful little man the coroner is, isn't he? He's looking daggers at me—do you think he'll dare to clear me out of the court or commit me for what-you-may-call-it?"

The first part of the evidence was not of great interest to Mr. Parker. The wretched Mr. Thipps, who had caught cold in gaol, deposed in an unhappy croak to having discovered the body when he went in to take his bath at eight o'clock. He had had such a shock, he had to sit down and send the girl for brandy. He had never seen the deceased before. He had no idea how he came there.

Yes, he had been in Manchester the day before. He had arrived at St. Pancras at ten o'clock. He had cloak-roomed his bag. At this point Mr. Thipps became very red, unhappy and confused, and glanced nervously about the court.

"Now, Mr. Thipps," said the Coroner, briskly, "we must have your movements quite clear. You must appreciate the importance of the matter. You have chosen to give evidence, which you need not have done, but having done so, you will find it best to be perfectly explicit."

"Yes," said Mr. Thipps faintly.

"Have you cautioned this witness, officer?" inquired the Coroner, turning sharply to Inspector Sugg.

The inspector replied that he had told Mr. Thipps that anything he said might be used again' him at his trial. Mr. Thipps became ashy, and said in a bleating voice that he 'adn't—hadn't meant to do anything that wasn't right.

This remark produced a mild sensation, and the Coroner became even more acidulated in manner than before.

"Is anybody representing Mr. Thipps?" he asked, irritably. "No? Did you not explain to him that he could—that he *ought* to be represented? You did not? Really, Inspector! Did you not know, Mr. Thipps, that you had a right to be legally represented?"

Mr. Thipps clung to a chair-back for support, and said, "No," in a voice barely audible.

"It is incredible," said the Coroner, "that so-called educated people should be so ignorant of the legal procedure of their own country. This places us in a very awkward position. I doubt, Inspector, whether I should permit the prisoner—Mr. Thipps—to give evidence at all. It is a delicate position."

The perspiration stood on Mr. Thipps's forehead.

"Save us from our friends," whispered the Duchess to Parker. "If that cough-drop-devouring creature had openly instructed those fourteen people—and what unfinished-looking faces they have—so characteristic, I always think, of the lower middle-class, rather like sheep, or calves' head (boiled, I mean), to bring in wilful murder against the poor little man, he couldn't have made himself plainer."

"He can't let him incriminate himself, you know," said Parker.

"Stuff!" said the Duchess. "How could the man incriminate himself when he never did anything in his life? You men never think of anything but your red tape."

Meanwhile Mr. Thipps, wiping his brow with a handkerchief, had summoned up courage. He stood up with a kind of weak dignity, like a small white rabbit brought to bay.

"I would rather tell you," he said, "though it's reelly very unpleasant for a man in my position. But I really couldn't have it thought for a moment that I'd committed this dreadful crime. I assure you, gentlemen, I *couldn't bear* that. No. I'd rather tell you the truth, though I'm afraid it places me in rather a—well, I'll tell you."

"You fully understand the gravity of making such a statement, Mr. Thipps," said the Coroner.

"Quite," said Mr. Thipps. "It's all right—I—might I have a drink of water?"

"Take your time," said the Coroner, at the same time robbing his remark of all conviction by an impatient glance at his watch.

"Thank you, sir," said Mr. Thipps. "Well, then, it's true I got to St. Pancras at ten. But there was a man in the carriage with me. He'd got in at Leicester. I didn't recognise him at first, but he turned out to be an old school-fellow of mine."

"What was this gentleman's name?" inquired the Coroner, his pencil poised.

Mr. Thipps shrank together visibly.

"I'm afraid I can't tell you that," he said. "You see—that is, you *will* see—it would get him into trouble, and I couldn't do that—no, I reelly couldn't do that, not if my life depended on it. No!" he added, as the ominous pertinence of the last phrase smote upon him, "I'm sure I couldn't do that."

"Well, well," said the Coroner.

The Duchess leaned over to Parker again. "I'm beginning quite to admire the little man," she said.

Mr. Thipps resumed.

"When we got to St. Pancras I was going home, but my friend said no. We hadn't met for a long time and we ought to—to make a night of it, was his expression. I fear I was weak, and let him overpersuade me to accompany him to one of his haunts. I use the word advisedly," said Mr. Thipps, "and I assure you, sir, that if I had known beforehand where we were going I never would have set foot in the place.

"I cloak-roomed my bag, for he did not like the notion of our being encumbered with it, and we got into a taxicab and drove to the corner of Tottenham Court Road and Oxford Street. We then walked a little way, and turned into a side street (I do not recollect which) where there was an open door, with the light shining out. There was a man at a counter, and my friend bought some tickets, and I heard the man at the counter say something to him about 'Your friend,' meaning me, and my friend said, 'Oh, yes, he's been here before, haven't you, Alf?' (which was what they called me at school), though I assure you, sir"—here Mr. Thipps grew very earnest—"I never had, and nothing in the world should induce me to go to such a place again.

"Well, we went down into a room underneath, where there were drinks, and my friend had several, and made me take one or two—though I am an abstemious man as a rule—and he talked to some other men and girls who were there—a very vulgar set of people, I thought them, though I wouldn't say but what some of the young ladies were nice-looking enough. One of them sat on my friend's knee and called him a slow old thing, and told him to come on—so we went into another room, where there were a lot of people dancing all these up-to-date dances. My friend went and danced, and I sat on a sofa. One of the young ladies came up to me and said, didn't I dance, and I said 'No,' so she said wouldn't I stand her a drink then. 'You'll stand us a drink then, darling,' that was what she said, and I said, 'Wasn't it after hours?' and she said that didn't matter. So I ordered the drink—a gin and bitters it was—for I didn't like not to, the young lady seemed to expect it of me and I felt it wouldn't be gentlemanly to refuse when she asked. But it went against my conscience—such a young girl as she was—and she put her arm round my neck afterwards and kissed me just like as if she was paying for the drink—and it reely went to my 'eart," said Mr. Thipps, a little ambiguously, but with uncommon emphasis.

Here somebody at the back said, "Cheer-oh!" and a sound was heard as of the noisy smacking of lips.

"Remove the person who made that improper noise," said the Coroner, with great indignation. "Go on, please, Mr. Thipps."

"Well," said Mr. Thipps, "about half-past twelve, as I should reckon, things began to get a bit lively, and I was looking for my friend to say good-night, not wishing to stay longer, as you will understand, when I saw him with one of the young ladies, and they seemed to be getting on altogether too well, if you follow me, my friend pulling the ribbons off her shoulder and the young lady laughing—and so on," said Mr. Thipps, hurriedly, "so I thought I'd just slip quietly out, when I heard a scuffle and a shout—and before I knew what was happening there were half-a-dozen policemen in, and the lights went out, and everybody stampeding and shouting—quite horrid, it was. I was knocked down in the rush, and hit my head a nasty knock on a chair—that was where I got that bruise they asked me about—and I was dreadfully afraid I'd never get away and it would all come out, and perhaps my photograph in the papers, when someone caught hold of me—I think it was the young lady I'd given the gin and bitters to—and she said, 'This way,' and pushed me along a passage and out at the back somewhere. So I ran through some streets, and found myself in Goodge Street, and there I got a taxi and came home. I saw the account of the raid afterwards in the papers, and saw my friend had escaped, and so, as it wasn't the sort of thing I wanted made public, and I didn't want to get him into difficulties, I just said nothing. But that's the truth."

"Well, Mr. Thipps," said the Coroner, "we shall be able to substantiate a certain amount of this story. Your friend's name—"

"No," said Mr. Thipps, stoutly, "not on any account."

"Very good," said the Coroner. "Now, can you tell us what time you did get in?"

"About half-past one, I should think. Though reelly, I was so upset—"

"Quite so. Did you go straight to bed?"

"Yes, I took my sandwich and glass of milk first. I thought it might settle my inside, so to speak," added the witness, apologetically, "not being accustomed to alcohol so late at night and on an empty stomach, as you may say."

"Quite so. Nobody sat up for you?"

"Nobody."

"How long did you take getting to bed first and last?"

Mr. Thipps thought it might have been half-an-hour.

"Did you visit the bathroom before turning in?"

"No."

"And you heard nothing in the night?"

"No. I fell fast asleep. I was rather agitated, so I took a little dose to make me sleep, and what with being so tired and the milk and the dose, I just tumbled right off and didn't wake till Gladys called me."

Further questioning elicited little from Mr. Thipps. Yes, the bathroom window had been open when he went in in the morning, he was sure of that, and he had spoken very sharply to the girl about it. He was ready to answer any questions; he would be only too 'appy—happy to have this dreadful affair sifted to the bottom.

Gladys Horrocks stated that she had been in Mr. Thipps's employment about three months. Her previous employers would speak to her character. It was her duty to make the round of the flat at night, when she had seen Mrs. Thipps to bed at ten. Yes, she remembered doing so on Monday evening. She had looked into all the rooms. Did she recollect shutting the bathroom window that night? Well, no, she couldn't swear to it, not in particular, but when Mr. Thipps called her into the bathroom in the morning it certainly *was* open. She had not been into the bathroom before Mr. Thipps went in. Well, yes, it had happened that she had left that window open before, when anyone had been 'aving a bath in the evening and 'ad left the blind down. Mrs. Thipps 'ad 'ad a bath on Monday evening, Mondays was one of her regular bath nights. She was very much afraid she 'adn't shut the window on Monday night, though she wished her 'ead 'ad been cut off afore she'd been so forgetful.

Here the witness burst into tears and was given some water, while the Coroner refreshed himself with a third lozenge.

Recovering, witness stated that she had certainly looked into all the rooms before going to bed. No, it was quite impossible for a body to be 'idden in the flat without her seeing of it. She 'ad been in the kitchen all evening, and there wasn't 'ardly room to keep the best dinner service there, let alone a body. Old Mrs. Thipps sat in the drawing-room. Yes, she was sure she'd been into the dining-room. How? Because she put Mr. Thipps's milk and sandwiches there ready for him. There had been nothing in there—that she could swear to. Nor yet in her own bedroom, nor in the 'all. Had she searched the bedroom cupboard and the box-room? Well, no, not to say searched; she wasn't use to searchin' people's 'ouses for skelintons every night. So that a man might have concealed himself in the box-room or a wardrobe? She supposed he might.

In reply to a woman juror—well, yes, she was walking out with a young man. Williams was his name, Bill Williams,—well, yes, William Williams, if they insisted. He was a glazier by profession. Well, yes, he 'ad been in the flat sometimes. Well, she supposed you might say he was acquainted with the flat. Had she ever—no, she 'adn't, and if she'd thought such a question was going to be put to a respectable girl she wouldn't 'ave offered to give evidence. The vicar of St. Mary's would speak to her character and to Mr. Williams's. Last time Mr. Williams was at the flat was a fortnight ago.

Well, no, it wasn't exactly the last time she 'ad seen Mr. Williams. Well, yes, the last time was Monday—well, yes, Monday night. Well, if she must tell the truth, she must. Yes, the officer had cautioned her, but there wasn't any 'arm in it, and it was better to lose her place than to be 'ung, though it was a cruel shame a girl couldn't 'ave a bit of fun without a nasty corpse comin' in through the window to get 'er into difficulties. After she 'ad put Mrs. Thipps to bed, she 'ad slipped out to go to the Plumbers' and Glaziers' Ball at the "Black Faced Ram." Mr. Williams 'ad met 'er and brought 'er back. 'E could testify to where she'd been and that there wasn't no 'arm in it. She'd left before the end of the ball. It might 'ave been two o'clock when she got back. She'd got the keys of the flat from Mrs. Thipps's drawer when Mrs. Thipps wasn't looking. She 'ad asked leave to go, but couldn't get it, along of Mr. Thipps bein' away that night. She was bitterly sorry she 'ad be'aved so, and she was sure she'd been punished for it. She had 'eard nothing suspicious when she came in. She had gone straight to bed without looking round the flat. She wished she were dead.

No, Mr. and Mrs. Thipps didn't 'ardly ever 'ave any visitors; they kep' themselves very retired. She had found the outside door bolted that morning as usual. She wouldn't never believe any 'arm of Mr. Thipps. Thank you, Miss Horrocks. Call Georgiana Thipps, and the Coroner thought we had better light the gas.

The examination of Mrs. Thipps provided more entertainment than enlightenment, affording as it did an excellent example of the game called "cross questions and crooked answers." After fifteen minutes' suffering, both in voice and temper, the Coroner abandoned the struggle, leaving the lady with the last word.

"You needn't try to bully me, young man," said that octo-
genarian with spirit, "settin' there spoilin' your stomach with
them nasty jujubes."

At this point a young man arose in court and demanded
to give evidence. Having explained that he was William Williams, glazier, he was sworn, and corroborated the evidence of
Gladys Horrocks in the matter of her presence at the "Black
Faced Ram" on the Monday night. They had returned to the
flat rather before two, he thought, but certainly later than 1.30.
He was sorry that he had persuaded Miss Horrocks to come out
with him when she didn't ought. He had observed nothing of a
suspicious nature in Prince of Wales Road at either visit.

Inspector Sugg gave evidence of having been called in at
about half-past eight on Monday morning. He had considered
the girl's manner to be suspicious and had arrested her. On later
information, leading him to suspect that the deceased might
have been murdered that night, he had arrested Mr. Thipps. He
had found no trace of breaking into the flat. There were marks
on the bathroom window-sill which pointed to somebody having got in that way. There were no ladder marks or footmarks
in the yard; the yard was paved with asphalt. He had examined
the roof, but found nothing on the roof. In his opinion the body
had been brought into the flat previously and concealed till the
evening by someone who had then gone out during the night
by the bathroom window, with the connivance of the girl. In
that case, why should not the girl have let the person out by
the door? Well, it might have been so. Had he found traces of a
body or a man or both having been hidden in the flat? He found
nothing to show that they might *not* have been so concealed.
What was the evidence that led him to suppose that the death
had occurred that night?

At this point Inspector Sugg appeared uneasy, and endeav-
oured to retire upon his professional dignity. On being pressed,

however, he admitted that the evidence in question had come to nothing.

> ONE OF THE JURORS: Was it the case that any fingermarks had been left by the criminal?
>
> Some marks had been found on the bath, but the criminal had worn gloves.
>
> THE CORONER: Do you draw any conclusion from this fact as to the experience of the criminal?
>
> INSPECTOR SUGG: Looks as if he was an old hand, sir.
>
> THE JUROR: Is that very consistent with the charge against Alfred Thipps, Inspector?

The inspector was silent.

> THE CORONER: In the light of the evidence which you have just heard, do you still press the charge against Alfred Thipps and Gladys Horrocks?
>
> INSPECTOR SUGG: I consider the whole set-out highly suspicious. Thipps's story isn't corroborated, and as for the girl Horrocks, how do we know this Williams ain't in it as well?
>
> WILLIAM WILLIAMS: Now, you drop that. I can bring a 'undred witnesses—
>
> THE CORONER: Silence, if you please. I am surprised, Inspector, that you should make this suggestion in that manner. It is highly improper. By the way, can you tell us whether a police raid was actually carried out on the Monday night on any Night Club in the neighbourhood of St. Giles's Circus?
>
> INSPECTOR SUGG (sulkily): I believe there was something of the sort.
>
> THE CORONER: You will, no doubt, inquire into the mat-

ter. I seem to recollect having seen some mention of it in the newspapers. Thank you, Inspector, that will do.

Several witnesses having appeared and testified to the characters of Mr. Thipps and Gladys Horrocks, the Coroner stated his intention of proceeding to the medical evidence.

"Sir Julian Freke."

There was considerable stir in the court as the great specialist walked up to give evidence. He was not only a distinguished man, but a striking figure, with his wide shoulders, upright carriage and leonine head. His manner as he kissed the Book presented to him with the usual deprecatory mumble by the Coroner's officer, was that of a St. Paul condescending to humour the timid mumbo-jumbo of superstitious Corinthians.

"So handsome, I always think," whispered the Duchess to Mr. Parker; "just exactly like William Morris, with that bush of hair and beard and those exciting eyes looking out of it—so splendid, these dear men always devoted to something or other—not but what I think socialism is a mistake—of course it works with all those nice people, so good and happy in art linen and the weather always perfect—Morris, I mean, you know—but so difficult in real life. Science is different—I'm sure if I had nerves I should go to Sir Julian just to look at him—eyes like that give one something to think about, and that's what most of these people want, only I never had any—nerves, I mean. Don't you think so?"

"You are Sir Julian Freke," said the Coroner, "and live at St. Luke's House, Prince of Wales Road, Battersea, where you exercise a general direction over the surgical side of St. Luke's Hospital?"

Sir Julian assented briefly to this definition of his personality.

"You were the first medical man to see the deceased?"

"I was."

"And you have since conducted an examination in collaboration with Dr. Grimbold of Scotland Yard?"

"I have."

"You are in agreement as to the cause of death?"

"Generally speaking, yes."

"Will you communicate your impressions to the jury?"

"I was engaged in research work in the dissecting room at St. Luke's Hospital at about nine o'clock on Monday morning, when I was informed that Inspector Sugg wished to see me. He told me that the dead body of a man had been discovered under mysterious circumstances at 59 Queen Caroline Mansions. He asked me whether it could be supposed to be a joke perpetrated by any of the medical students at the hospital. I was able to assure him, by an examination of the hospital's books, that there was no subject missing from the dissecting room."

"Who would be in charge of such bodies?"

"William Watts, the dissecting-room attendant."

"Is William Watts present?" inquired the Coroner of the officer.

William Watts was present, and could be called if the Coroner thought it necessary.

"I suppose no dead body would be delivered to the hospital without your knowledge, Sir Julian?"

"Certainly not."

"Thank you. Will you proceed with your statement?"

"Inspector Sugg then asked me whether I would send a medical man round to view the body. I said that I would go myself."

"Why did you do that?"

"I confess to my share of ordinary human curiosity, Mr. Coroner."

Laughter from a medical student at the back of the room.

"On arriving at the flat I found the deceased lying on his back in the bath. I examined him, and came to the conclusion that death had been caused by a blow on the back of the neck, dislocating the fourth and fifth cervical vertebrae, bruising the spinal cord and producing internal haemorrhage and partial paralysis of the brain. I judged the deceased to have been dead at least twelve hours, possibly more. I observed no other sign of violence of any kind upon the body. Deceased was a strong, well-nourished man of about fifty to fifty-five years of age."

"In your opinion, could the blow have been self-inflicted?"

"Certainly not. It had been made with a heavy, blunt instrument from behind, with great force and considerable judgment. It is quite impossible that it was self-inflicted."

"Could it have been the result of an accident?"

"That is possible, of course."

"If, for example, the deceased had been looking out of the window, and the sash had shut violently down upon him?"

"No; in that case there would have been signs of strangulation and a bruise upon the throat as well."

"But deceased might have been killed through a heavy weight accidentally falling upon him?"

"He might."

"Was death instantaneous, in your opinion?"

"It is difficult to say. Such a blow might very well cause death instantaneously, or the patient might linger in a partially paralyzed condition for some time. In the present case I should be disposed to think that deceased might have lingered for some hours. I base my decision upon the condition of the brain revealed at the autopsy. I may say, however, that Dr. Grimbold and I are not in complete agreement on the point."

"I understand that a suggestion has been made as to the identification of the deceased. *You* are not in a position to identify him?"

"Certainly not. I never saw him before. The suggestion to which you refer is a preposterous one, and ought never to have been made. I was not aware until this morning that it had been made; had it been made to me earlier, I should have known how to deal with it, and I should like to express my strong disapproval of the unnecessary shock and distress inflicted upon a lady with whom I have the honour to be acquainted."

THE CORONER: It was not my fault, Sir Julian; I had nothing to do with it; I agree with you that it was unfortunate you were not consulted.

The reporters scribbled busily, and the court asked each other what was meant, while the jury tried to look as if they knew already.

"In the matter of the eyeglasses found upon the body, Sir Julian. Do these give any indication to a medical man?"

"They are somewhat unusual lenses; an oculist would be able to speak more definitely, but I will say for myself that I should have expected them to belong to an older man than the deceased."

"Speaking as a physician, who has had many opportunities of observing the human body, did you gather anything from the appearance of the deceased as to his personal habits?"

"I should say that he was a man in easy circumstances, but who had only recently come into money. His teeth are in a bad state, and his hands show signs of recent manual labour."

"An Australian colonist, for instance, who had made money?"

"Something of that sort; of course, I could not say positively."

"Of course not. Thank you, Sir Julian."

Dr. Grimbold, called, corroborated his distinguished colleague in every particular, except that, in his opinion, death had not occurred for several days after the blow. It was with the greatest hesitancy that he ventured to differ from Sir Julian Freke, and he might be wrong. It was difficult to tell in any case, and when he saw the body, deceased had been dead at least twenty-four hours, in his opinion.

Inspector Sugg, recalled. Would he tell the jury what steps had been taken to identify the deceased?

A description had been sent to every police station and had been inserted in all the newspapers. In view of the suggestion made by Sir Julian Freke, had inquiries been made at all the seaports? They had. And with no results? With no results at all. No one had come forward to identify the body? Plenty of people had come forward; but nobody had succeeded in identifying it. Had any effort been made to follow up the clue afforded by the eyeglasses? Inspector Sugg submitted that, having regard to the interests of justice, he would beg to be excused from answering that question. Might the jury see the eyeglasses? The eyeglasses were handed to the jury.

William Watts, called, confirmed the evidence of Sir Julian Freke with regard to dissecting-room subjects. He explained the system by which they were entered. They usually were supplied by the work-houses and free hospitals. They were under his sole charge. The young gentlemen could not possibly get the keys. Had Sir Julian Freke, or any of the house surgeons, the keys? No, not even Sir Julian Freke. The keys had remained in his possession on Monday night? They had. And, in any case, the inquiry was irrelevant, as there was no body missing, nor ever had been? That was the case.

The Coroner then addressed the jury, reminding them with some asperity that they were not there to gossip about who the deceased could or could not have been, but to give their opinion as to the cause of death. He reminded them that they should consider whether, according to the medical evidence, death could have been accidental or self-inflicted, or whether it was deliberate murder, or homicide. If they considered the evidence on this point insufficient, they could return an open verdict. In any case, their verdict could not prejudice any person; if they brought it in "murder," all the whole evidence would have to be gone through again before the magistrate. He then dismissed them, with the unspoken adjuration to be quick about it.

Sir Julian Freke, after giving his evidence, had caught the eye of the Duchess, and now came over and greeted her.

"I haven't seen you for an age," said that lady. "How are you?"

"Hard at work," said the specialist. "Just got my new book out. This kind of thing wastes time. Have you seen Lady Levy yet?"

"No, poor dear," said the Duchess. "I only came up this morning, for this. Mrs. Thipps is staying with me—one of Peter's eccentricities, you know. Poor Christine! I must run round and see her. This is Mr. Parker," she added, "who is investigating that case."

"Oh," said Sir Julian, and paused. "Do you know," he said in a low voice to Parker, "I am very glad to meet you. Have you seen Lady Levy yet?"

"I saw her this morning."

"Did she ask you to go on with the inquiry?"

"Yes," said Parker; "she thinks," he added, "that Sir Reuben may be detained in the hands of some financial rival or that perhaps some scoundrels are holding him to ransom."

"And is that *your* opinion?" asked Sir Julian.

"I think it very likely," said Parker, frankly.

Sir Julian hesitated again.

"I wish you would walk back with me when this is over," he said.

"I should be delighted," said Parker.

At this moment the jury returned and took their places, and there was a little rustle and hush. The Coroner addressed the foreman and inquired if they were agreed upon their verdict.

"We are agreed, Mr. Coroner, that deceased died of the effects of a blow upon the spine, but how that injury was inflicted we consider that there is not sufficient evidence to show."

Mr. Parker and Sir Julian Freke walked up the road together.

"I had absolutely no idea until I saw Lady Levy this morning," said the doctor, "that there was any idea of connecting this matter with the disappearance of Sir Reuben. The suggestion was perfectly monstrous, and could only have grown up in the mind of that ridiculous police officer. If I had had any idea what was in his mind I could have disabused him and avoided all this."

"I did my best to do so," said Parker, "as soon as I was called in to the Levy case—"

"Who called you in, if I may ask?" inquired Sir Julian.

"Well, the household first of all, and then Sir Reuben's uncle, Mr. Levy of Portman Square, wrote to me to go on with the investigation."

"And now Lady Levy has confirmed those instructions?"

"Certainly," said Parker in some surprise.

Sir Julian was silent for a little time.

"I'm afraid I was the first person to put the idea into Sugg's head," said Parker, rather penitently. "When Sir Reuben disappeared, my first step, almost, was to hunt up all the street accidents and suicides and so on that had turned up during the day, and I went down to see this Battersea Park body as a matter of routine. Of course, I saw that the thing was ridiculous as soon as I got there, but Sugg froze on to the idea—and it's true there was a good deal of resemblance between the dead man and the portraits I've seen of Sir Reuben."

"A strong superficial likeness," said Sir Julian. "The upper part of the face is a not uncommon type, and as Sir Reuben wore a heavy beard and there was no opportunity of comparing the mouths and chins, I can understand the idea occurring to anybody. But only to be dismissed at once. I am sorry," he added, "as the whole matter has been painful to Lady Levy. You may know, Mr. Parker, that I am an old, though I should not call myself an intimate, friend of the Levys."

"I understood something of the sort."

"Yes. When I was a young man I—in short, Mr. Parker, I hoped once to marry Lady Levy." (Mr. Parker gave the usual sympathetic groan.) "I have never married, as you know," pursued Sir Julian. "We have remained good friends. I have always done what I could to spare her pain."

"Believe me, Sir Julian," said Parker, "that I sympathize very much with you and with Lady Levy, and that I did all I could to disabuse Inspector Sugg of this notion. Unhappily, the coincidence of Sir Reuben's being seen that evening in the Battersea Park Road—"

"Ah, yes," said Sir Julian. "Dear me, here we are at home. Perhaps you would come in for a moment, Mr. Parker, and have tea or a whisky-and-soda or something."

Parker promptly accepted this invitation, feeling that there were other things to be said.

The two men stepped into a square, finely furnished hall with a fireplace on the same side as the door, and a staircase opposite. The dining-room door stood open on their right, and as Sir Julian rang the bell a man-servant appeared at the far end of the hall.

"What will you take?" asked the doctor.

"After that dreadfully cold place," said Parker, "what I really want is gallons of hot tea, if you, as a nerve specialist, can bear the thought of it."

"Provided you allow of a judicious blend of China in it," replied Sir Julian in the same tone, "I have no objection to make.

Tea in the library at once," he added to the servant, and led the way upstairs.

"I don't use the downstairs rooms much, except the dining-room," he explained as he ushered his guest into a small but cheerful library on the first floor. "This room leads out of my bedroom and is more convenient. I only live part of my time here, but it's very handy for my research work at the hospital. That's what I do there, mostly. It's a fatal thing for a theorist, Mr. Parker, to let the practical work get behindhand. Dissection is the basis of all good theory and all correct diagnosis. One must keep one's hand and eye in training. This place is far more important to me than Harley Street, and some day I shall abandon my consulting practice altogether and settle down here to cut up my subjects and write my books in peace. So many things in this life are a waste of time, Mr. Parker."

Mr. Parker assented to this.

"Very often," said Sir Julian, "the only time I get for any research work—necessitating as it does the keenest observation and the faculties at their acutest—has to be at night, after a long day's work and by artificial light, which, magnificent as the lighting of the dissecting room here is, is always more trying to the eyes than daylight. Doubtless your own work has to be carried on under even more trying conditions."

"Yes, sometimes," said Parker; "but then you see," he added, "the conditions are, so to speak, part of the work."

"Quite so, quite so," said Sir Julian; "you mean that the burglar, for example, does not demonstrate his methods in the light of day, or plant the perfect footmark in the middle of a damp patch of sand for you to analyze."

"Not as a rule," said the detective, "but I have no doubt many of your diseases work quite as insidiously as any burglar."

"They do, they do," said Sir Julian, laughing, "and it is my pride, as it is yours, to track them down for the good of society.

The neuroses, you know, are particularly clever criminals—
they break out into as many disguises as—"

"As Leon Kestrel, the Master-Mummer," suggested Parker,
who read railway-stall detective stories on the principle of the
'busman's holiday.

"No doubt," said Sir Julian, who did not, "and they cover up
their tracks wonderfully. But when you can really investigate,
Mr. Parker, and break up the dead, or for preference the living body with the scalpel, you always find the footmarks—the
little trail of ruin or disorder left by madness or disease or drink
or any other similar pest. But the difficulty is to trace them
back, merely by observing the surface symptoms—the hysteria,
crime, religion, fear, shyness, conscience, or whatever it may be;
just as you observe a theft or a murder and look for the footsteps
of the criminal, so I observe a fit of hysterics or an outburst
of piety and hunt for the little mechanical irritation which has
produced it."

"You regard all these things as physical?"

"Undoubtedly. I am not ignorant of the rise of another school
of thought, Mr. Parker, but its exponents are mostly charlatans
or self-deceivers. 'Sie haben sich so weit darin eingeheimnisst' that,
like Sludge the Medium, they are beginning to believe their
own nonsense. I should like to have the exploring of some of
their brains, Mr. Parker; I would show you the little faults and
landslips in the cells—the misfiring and short-circuiting of the
nerves, which produce these notions and these books. At least,"
he added, gazing sombrely at his guest, "at least, if I could not
quite show you today, I shall be able to do so tomorrow—or in
a year's time—or before I die."

He sat for some minutes gazing into the fire, while the red
light played upon his tawny beard and struck out answering
gleams from his compelling eyes.

Parker drank tea in silence, watching him. On the whole, however, he remained but little interested in the causes of nervous phenomena and his mind strayed to Lord Peter, coping with the redoubtable Crimplesham down in Salisbury. Lord Peter had wanted him to come: that meant, either that Crimplesham was proving recalcitrant or that a clue wanted following. But Bunter had said that tomorrow would do, and it was just as well. After all, the Battersea affair was not Parker's case; he had already wasted valuable time attending an inconclusive inquest, and he really ought to get on with his legitimate work. There was still Levy's secretary to see and the little matter of the Peruvian Oil to be looked into. He looked at his watch.

"I am very much afraid—if you will excuse me—" he murmured.

Sir Julian came back with a start to the consideration of actuality.

"Your work calls you?" he said, smiling. "Well, I can understand that. I won't keep you. But I wanted to say something to you in connection with your present enquiry—only I hardly know—I hardly like—"

Parker sat down again, and banished every indication of hurry from his face and attitude.

"I shall be very grateful for any help you can give me," he said.

"I'm afraid it's more in the nature of hindrance," said Sir Julian, with a short laugh. "It's a case of destroying a clue for you, and a breach of professional confidence on my side. But since—accidentally—a certain amount has come out, perhaps the whole had better do so."

Mr. Parker made the encouraging noise which, among laymen, supplies the place of the priest's insinuating, "Yes, my son?"

"Sir Reuben Levy's visit on Monday night was to me," said Sir Julian.

"Yes?" said Mr. Parker, without expression.

"He found cause for certain grave suspicions concerning his health," said Sir Julian, slowly, as though weighing how much he could in honour disclose to a stranger. "He came to me, in preference to his own medical man, as he was particularly anxious that the matter should be kept from his wife. As I told you, he knew me fairly well, and Lady Levy had consulted me about a nervous disorder in the summer."

"Did he make an appointment with you?" asked Parker.

"I beg your pardon," said the other, absently.

"Did he make an appointment?"

"An appointment? Oh, no! He turned up suddenly in the evening after dinner when I wasn't expecting him. I took him up here and examined him, and he left me somewhere about ten o'clock, I should think."

"May I ask what was the result of your examination?"

"Why do you want to know?"

"It might illuminate—well, conjecture as to his subsequent conduct," said Parker, cautiously. This story seemed to have little coherence with the rest of the business, and he wondered whether coincidence was alone responsible for Sir Reuben's disappearance on the same night that he visited the doctor.

"I see," said Sir Julian. "Yes. Well, I will tell you in confidence that I saw grave grounds of suspicion, but as yet, no absolute certainty of mischief."

"Thank you. Sir Reuben left you at ten o'clock?"

"Then or thereabouts. I did not at first mention the matter as it was so very much Sir Reuben's wish to keep his visit to me secret, and there was no question of accident in the street or anything of that kind, since he reached home safely at midnight."

"Quite so," said Parker.

"It would have been, and is, a breach of confidence," said Sir Julian, "and I only tell you now because Sir Reuben was accidentally seen, and because I would rather tell you in private than have you ferreting round here and questioning my servants, Mr. Parker. You will excuse my frankness."

"Certainly," said Parker. "I hold no brief for the pleasantness of my profession, Sir Julian. I am very much obliged to you for telling me this. I might otherwise have wasted valuable time following up a false trail."

"I am sure I need not ask you, in your turn, to respect this confidence," said the doctor. "To publish the matter abroad could only harm Sir Reuben and pain his wife, besides placing me in no favourable light with my patients."

"I promise to keep the thing to myself," said Parker, "except of course," he added hastily, "that I must inform my colleague."

"You have a colleague in the case?"

"I have."

"What sort of person is he?"

"He will be perfectly discreet, Sir Julian."

"Is he a police officer?"

"You need not be afraid of your confidence getting into the records at Scotland Yard."

"I see that you know how to be discreet, Mr. Parker."

"We also have our professional etiquette, Sir Julian."

On returning to Great Ormond Street, Mr. Parker found a wire awaiting him, which said: "Do not trouble to come. All well. Returning tomorrow. Wimsey."

VII

On returning to the flat just before lunch-time on the following morning, after a few confirmatory researches in Balham and the neighbourhood of Victoria Station, Lord Peter was greeted at the door by Mr. Bunter (who had gone straight home from Waterloo) with a telephone message and a severe and nursemaid-like eye.

"Lady Swaffham rang up, my lord, and said she hoped your lordship had not forgotten you were lunching with her."

"I have forgotten, Bunter, and I mean to forget. I trust you told her I had succumbed to lethargic encephalitis suddenly, no flowers by request."

"Lady Swaffham said, my lord, she was counting on you. She met the Duchess of Denver yesterday—"

"If my sister-in-law's there I won't go, that's flat," said Lord Peter.

"I beg your pardon, my lord, the Dowager Duchess."

"What's she doing in town?"

"I imagine she came up for the inquest, my lord."

"Oh, yes—we missed that, Bunter."

"Yes, my lord. Her Grace is lunching with Lady Swaffham."

"Bunter, I can't. I can't, really. Say I'm in bed with whooping cough, and ask my mother to come round after lunch."

"Very well, my lord. Mrs. Tommy Frayle will be at Lady Swaffham's, my lord, and Mr. Milligan—"

"Mr. Who?"

"Mr. John P. Milligan, my lord, and—"

"Good God, Bunter, why didn't you say so before? Have I time to get there before he does? All right. I'm off. With a taxi I can just—"

"Not in those trousers, my lord," said Mr. Bunter, blocking the way to the door with deferential firmness.

"Oh, Bunter," pleaded his lordship, "do let me—just this once. You don't know how important it is."

"Not on any account, my lord. It would be as much as my place is worth."

"The trousers are all right, Bunter."

"Not for Lady Swaffham's, my lord. Besides, your lordship forgets the man that ran against you with a milk-can at Salisbury."

And Mr. Bunter laid an accusing finger on a slight stain of grease showing across the light cloth.

"I wish to God I'd never let you grow into a privileged family retainer, Bunter," said Lord Peter, bitterly, dashing his walking-stick into the umbrella-stand. "You've no conception of the mistakes my mother may be making."

Mr. Bunter smiled grimly and led his victim away.

When an immaculate Lord Peter was ushered, rather late for lunch, into Lady Swaffham's drawing-room, the Dowager Duchess of Denver was seated on a sofa, plunged in intimate conversation with Mr. John P. Milligan of Chicago.

"I'm vurry pleased to meet you, Duchess," had been that financier's opening remark, "to thank you for your exceedingly kind invitation. I assure you it's a compliment I deeply appreciate."

The Duchess beamed at him, while conducting a rapid rally of all her intellectual forces.

"Do come and sit down and talk to me, Mr. Milligan," she said. "I do so love talking to you great business men—let me see, is it a railway king you are or something about puss-in-the-corner—at least, I don't mean that exactly, but that game one used to play with cards, all about wheat and oats, and there was a bull and a bear, too—or was it a horse?—no, a bear, because I remember one always had to try and get rid of it and it used to get so dreadfully crumpled and torn, poor thing, always being handed about, one got to recognise it, and then one had to buy a new pack—so foolish it must seem to you, knowing the real thing, and dreadfully noisy, but really excellent for breaking the ice with rather stiff people who didn't know each other—I'm quite sorry it's gone out."

Mr. Milligan sat down.

"Wal, now," he said, "I guess it's as interesting for us business men to meet British aristocrats as it is for Britishers to meet American railway kings, Duchess. And I guess I'll make as many mistakes talking your kind of talk as you would make if you were tryin' to run a corner in wheat in Chicago. Fancy now, I called that fine lad of yours Lord Wimsey the other day, and he thought I'd mistaken him for his brother. That made me feel rather green."

This was an unhoped-for lead. The Duchess walked warily.

"Dear boy," she said, "I am so glad you met him, Mr. Milligan. *Both* my sons are a *great* comfort to me, you know, though, of course, Gerald is more conventional—just the right kind of person for the House of Lords, you know, and a splendid farmer. I can't see Peter down at Denver half so well, though he is always going to all the right things in town, and very amusing sometimes, poor boy."

"I was vurry much gratified by Lord Peter's suggestion," pursued Mr. Milligan, "for which I understand you are responsible, and I'll surely be very pleased to come any day you like, though I think you're flattering me too much."

"Ah, well," said the Duchess, "I don't know if you're the best judge of that, Mr. Milligan. Not that I know anything about business myself," she added. "I'm rather old-fashioned for these days, you know, and I can't pretend to do more than know a nice *man* when I see him; for the other things I rely on my son."

The accent of this speech was so flattering that Mr. Milligan purred almost audibly, and said:

"Wal, Duchess, I guess that's where a lady with a real, beautiful, old-fashioned soul has the advantage of these modern young blatherskites—there aren't many men who wouldn't be nice—to her, and even then, if they aren't rock-bottom she can see through them."

"But that leaves me where I was," thought the Duchess. "I believe," she said aloud, "that I ought to be thanking you in the name of the vicar of Duke's Denver for a very munificent cheque which reached him yesterday for the Church Restoration Fund. He was so delighted and astonished, poor dear man."

"Oh, that's nothing," said Mr. Milligan, "we haven't any fine old crusted buildings like yours over on our side, so it's a privilege to be allowed to drop a little kerosene into the worm-holes when we hear of one in the old country suffering from senile decay. So when your lad told me about Duke's Denver I took the liberty to subscribe without waiting for the Bazaar."

"I'm sure it was very kind of you," said the Duchess. "You are coming to the Bazaar, then?" she continued, gazing into his face appealingly.

"Sure thing," said Mr. Milligan, with great promptness. "Lord Peter said you'd let me know for sure about the date, but we can always make time for a little bit of good work anyway. Of course I'm hoping to be able to avail myself of your kind invitation to stop, but if I'm rushed, I'll manage anyhow to pop over and speak my piece and pop back again."

"I hope so very much," said the Duchess. "I must see what can be done about the date—of course, I can't promise—"

"No, no," said Mr. Milligan heartily. "I know what these things are to fix up. And then there's not only me—there's all the real big men of European eminence your son mentioned, to be consulted."

The Duchess turned pale at the thought that any one of these illustrious persons might some time turn up in somebody's drawing-room, but by this time she had dug herself in comfortably, and was even beginning to find her range.

"I can't say how grateful we are to you," she said; "it will be such a treat. Do tell me what you think of saying."

"Wal—" began Mr. Milligan.

Suddenly everybody was standing up and a penitent voice was heard to say:

"Really, most awfully sorry, y'know—hope you'll forgive me, Lady Swaffham, what? Dear lady, could I possibly forget an invitation from you? Fact is, I had to go an' see a man down in Salisbury—absolutely true, 'pon my word, and the fellow wouldn't let me get away. I'm simply grovellin' before you, Lady Swaffham. Shall I go an' eat my lunch in the corner?"

Lady Swaffham gracefully forgave the culprit.

"Your dear mother is here," she said.

"How do, Mother?" said Lord Peter, uneasily.

"How are you, dear?" replied the Duchess. "You really oughtn't to have turned up just yet. Mr. Milligan was just going to tell me what a thrilling speech he's preparing for the Bazaar, when you came and interrupted us."

Conversation at lunch turned, not unnaturally, on the Battersea inquest, the Duchess giving a vivid impersonation of Mrs. Thipps being interrogated by the Coroner.

" 'Did you hear anything unusual in the night?' says the little man, leaning forward and screaming at her, and so crimson in the face and his ears sticking out so—just like a cherubim in that poem of Tennyson's—or is a cherub blue?—perhaps it's seraphim I mean—anyway, you know what I mean, all eyes, with little wings on its head. And dear old Mrs. Thipps saying, 'Of course I have, any time these eighty years,' and *such* a sensation in court till they found out she thought he'd said, 'Do you sleep without a light?' and everybody laughing, and then the Coroner said quite loudly, 'Damn the woman,' and she heard that, I can't think why, and said: 'Don't you get swearing, young man, sitting there in the presence of Providence, as you may say. I don't know what young people are coming to nowadays'—and he's sixty if he's a day, you know," said the Duchess.

By a natural transition, Mrs. Tommy Frayle referred to the man who was hanged for murdering three brides in a bath.

"I always thought that was so ingenious," she said, gazing soulfully at Lord Peter, "and do you know, as it happened, Tommy had just made me insure my life, and I got so frightened, I gave up my morning bath and took to having it in the afternoon when he was in the House—I mean, when he was *not* in the house—not at home, I mean."

"Dear lady," said Lord Peter, reproachfully, "I have a distinct recollection that all those brides were thoroughly unattractive. But it was an uncommonly ingenious plan—the first time of askin'—only he shouldn't have repeated himself."

"One demands a little originality in these days, even from murderers," said Lady Swaffham. "Like dramatists, you know—so much easier in Shakespeare's time, wasn't it? Always the same girl dressed up as a man, and even that borrowed from Boccaccio or Dante or somebody. I'm sure if I'd been a Shakespeare hero, the very minute I saw a slim-legged young page-boy I'd have said: 'Odsbodikins! There's that girl again!'"

"That's just what happened, as a matter of fact," said Lord Peter. "You see, Lady Swaffham, if ever you want to commit a murder, the thing you've got to do is to prevent people from associatin' their ideas. Most people don't associate anythin'— their ideas just roll about like so many dry peas on a tray, makin' a lot of noise and goin' nowhere, but once you begin lettin' 'em string their peas into a necklace, it's goin' to be strong enough to hang you, what?"

"Dear me!" said Mrs. Tommy Frayle, with a little scream, "what a blessing it is none of my friends have any ideas at all!"

"Y'see," said Lord Peter, balancing a piece of duck on his fork and frowning, "it's only in Sherlock Holmes and stories like that, that people think things out logically. Or'nar'ly, if somebody tells you somethin' out of the way, you just say, 'By Jove!' or 'How sad!' an' leave it at that, an' half the time you forget about it, 'nless somethin' turns up afterwards to drive it home. F'r instance, Lady Swaffham, I told you when I came in that I'd been down to Salisbury, 'n' that's true, only I don't suppose it impressed you much; 'n' I don't suppose it'd impress you much if you read in the paper tomorrow of a tragic discovery of a dead lawyer down in Salisbury, but if I went to Salisbury again next week 'n' there was a Salisbury doctor found dead the day after, you might begin to think I was a bird of ill omen for Salisbury residents; and if I went there again the week after, 'n' you heard next day that the see of Salisbury had fallen vacant suddenly, you might begin to wonder what took me to Salisbury, an' why I'd never mentioned before that I had friends down there, don't you see, an' you might think of goin' down to Salisbury yourself, an' askin' all kinds of people if they'd happened to see a young man in plum-coloured socks hangin' round the Bishop's Palace."

"I daresay I should," said Lady Swaffham.

"Quite. An' if you found that the lawyer and the doctor had once upon a time been in business at Poggleton-on-the-Marsh when the Bishop had been vicar there, you'd begin to remember you'd once heard of me payin' a visit to Poggleton-on-the-Marsh a long time ago, an' you'd begin to look up the parish registers there an' discover I'd been married under an assumed name by the vicar to the widow of a wealthy farmer, who'd died suddenly of peritonitis, as certified by the doctor, after the lawyer'd made a will leavin' me all her money, and *then* you'd begin to think I might have very good reasons for gettin' rid of such promisin' blackmailers as the lawyer, the doctor an' the bishop. Only, if I hadn't started an association in your mind by gettin' rid of 'em all in the same place, you'd never have thought of goin' to Poggleton-on-the-Marsh, 'n' you wouldn't even have remembered I'd ever been there."

"*Were* you ever there, Lord Peter?" inquired Mrs. Tommy, anxiously.

"I don't think so," said Lord Peter; "the name threads no beads in my mind. But it might, any day, you know."

"But if you were investigating a crime," said Lady Swaffham, "you'd have to begin by the usual things, I suppose—finding out what the person had been doing, and who'd been to call, and looking for a motive, wouldn't you?"

"Oh, yes," said Lord Peter, "but most of us have such dozens of motives for murderin' all sorts of inoffensive people. There's lots of people I'd like to murder, wouldn't you?"

"Heaps," said Lady Swaffham. "There's that dreadful— perhaps I'd better not say it, though, for fear you should remember it later on."

"Well, I wouldn't if I were you," said Peter, amiably. "You never know. It'd be beastly awkward if the person died suddenly tomorrow."

"The difficulty with this Battersea case, I guess," said Mr.

Milligan, "is that nobody seems to have any associations with the gentleman in the bath."

"So hard on poor Inspector Sugg," said the Duchess. "I quite felt for the man, having to stand up there and answer a lot of questions when he had nothing at all to say."

Lord Peter applied himself to the duck, having got a little behindhand. Presently he heard somebody ask the Duchess if she had seen Lady Levy.

"She is in great distress," said the woman who had spoken, a Mrs. Freemantle, "though she clings to the hope that he will turn up. I suppose you knew him, Mr. Milligan—know him, I should say, for I hope he's still alive somewhere."

Mrs. Freemantle was the wife of an eminent railway director, and celebrated for her ignorance of the world of finance. Her *faux pas* in this connection enlivened the tea parties of City men's wives.

"Wal, I've dined with him," said Mr. Milligan, good-naturedly. "I think he and I've done our best to ruin each other, Mrs. Freemantle. If this were the States," he added, "I'd be much inclined to suspect myself of having put Sir Reuben in a safe place. But we can't do business that way in your old country; no, ma'am."

"It must be exciting work doing business in America," said Lord Peter.

"It is," said Mr. Milligan. "I guess my brothers are having a good time there now. I'll be joining them again before long, as soon as I've fixed up a little bit of work for them on this side."

"Well, you mustn't go till after my bazaar," said the Duchess.

Lord Peter spent the afternoon in a vain hunt for Mr. Parker. He ran him down eventually after dinner in Great Ormond Street.

Parker was sitting in an elderly but affectionate armchair, with his feet on the mantelpiece, relaxing his mind with a modern commentary on the Epistle to the Galatians. He received

Lord Peter with quiet pleasure, though without rapturous enthusiasm, and mixed him a whisky-and-soda. Peter took up the book his friend had laid down and glanced over the pages.

"All these men work with a bias in their minds, one way or other," he said; "they find what they are looking for."

"Oh, they do," agreed the detective, "but one learns to discount that almost automatically, you know. When I was at college, I was all on the other side—Conybeare and Robertson and Drews and those people, you know, till I found they were all so busy looking for a burglar whom nobody had ever seen, that they couldn't recognise the footprints of the household, so to speak. Then I spent two years learning to be cautious."

"Hum," said Lord Peter, "theology must be good exercise for the brain then, for you're easily the most cautious devil I know. But I say, do go on reading—it's a shame for me to come and root you up in your off-time like this."

"It's all right, old man," said Parker.

The two men sat silent for a little, and then Lord Peter said: "D'you like your job?"

The detective considered the question, and replied:

"Yes—yes, I do. I know it to be useful, and I am fitted to it. I do it quite well—not with inspiration, perhaps, but sufficiently well to take a pride in it. It is full of variety and it forces one to keep up to the mark and not get slack. And there's a future to it. Yes, I like it. Why?"

"Oh, nothing," said Peter. "It's a hobby to me, you see. I took it up when the bottom of things was rather knocked out for me, because it was so damned exciting, and the worst of it is, I enjoy it—up to a point. If it was all on paper I'd enjoy every bit of it. I love the beginning of a job—when one doesn't know any of the people and it's just exciting and amusing. But if it comes to really running down a live person and getting him hanged, or even quodded, poor devil, there don't seem as if there was any excuse for me buttin' in, since I don't have to make my livin' by it. And I feel as if I oughtn't ever to find it amusin'. But I do."

Parker gave this speech his careful attention.

"I see what you mean," he said.

"There's old Milligan, f'r instance," said Lord Peter. "On paper, nothin' would be funnier than to catch old Milligan out. But he's rather a decent old bird to talk to. Mother likes him. He's taken a fancy to me. It's awfully entertainin' goin' and pumpin' him with stuff about a bazaar for church expenses, but when he's so jolly pleased about it and that, I feel a worm. S'pose old Milligan has cut Levy's throat and plugged him into the Thames. It ain't my business."

"It's as much yours as anybody's," said Parker; "it's no better to do it for money than to do it for nothing."

"Yes, it is," said Peter stubbornly. "Havin' to live is the only excuse there is for doin' that kind of thing."

"Well, but look here!" said Parker. "If Milligan has cut poor old Levy's throat for no reason except to make himself richer, I don't see why he should buy himself off by giving £1,000 to Duke's Denver church roof, or why he should be forgiven just because he's childishly vain, or childishly snobbish."

"That's a nasty one," said Lord Peter.

"Well, if you like, even because he has taken a fancy to you."

"No, but—"

"Look here, Wimsey—do you think he *has* murdered Levy?"

"Well, he may have."

"But do you think he has?"

"I don't want to think so."

"Because he has taken a fancy to you?"

"Well, that biases me, of course—"

"I daresay it's quite a legitimate bias. You don't think a callous murderer would be likely to take a fancy to you?"

"Well—besides, I've taken rather a fancy to him."

"I daresay that's quite legitimate, too. You've observed him and made a subconscious deduction from your observations, and the result is, you don't think he did it. Well, why not? You're entitled to take that into account."

"But perhaps I'm wrong and he did do it."

"Then why let your vainglorious conceit in your own power of estimating character stand in the way of unmasking the singularly cold-blooded murder of an innocent and lovable man?"

"I know—but I don't feel I'm playing the game somehow."

"Look here, Peter," said the other with some earnestness, "suppose you get this playing-fields-of-Eton complex out of your system once and for all. There doesn't seem to be much doubt that something unpleasant has happened to Sir Reuben Levy. Call it murder, to strengthen the argument. If Sir Reuben has been murdered, is it a game? and is it fair to treat it as a game?"

"That's what I'm ashamed of, really," said Lord Peter. "It *is* a game to me, to begin with, and I go on cheerfully, and then I suddenly see that somebody is going to be hurt, and I want to get out of it."

"Yes, yes, I know," said the detective, "but that's because you're thinking about your attitude. You want to be consistent, you want to look pretty, you want to swagger debonairly through a comedy of puppets or else to stalk magnificently through a tragedy of human sorrows and things. But that's childish. If you've any duty to society in the way of finding out the truth about murders, you must do it in any attitude that comes handy. You want to be elegant and detached? That's all right, if you find the truth out that way, but it hasn't any value in itself, you know. You want to look dignified and consistent—what's that got to do with it? You want to hunt down a murderer for the sport of the thing and then shake hands with him and say, 'Well played—hard luck—you shall have your revenge tomorrow!' Well, you can't do it like that. Life's not a football match. You want to be a sportsman. You can't be a sportsman. You're a responsible person."

"I don't think you ought to read so much theology," said Lord Peter. "It has a brutalizing influence."

He got up and paced about the room, looking idly over the bookshelves. Then he sat down again, filled and lit his pipe, and said:

"Well, I'd better tell you about the ferocious and hardened Crimplesham."

He detailed his visit to Salisbury. Once assured of his bona fides, Mr. Crimplesham had given him the fullest details of his visit to town.

"And I've substantiated it all," groaned Lord Peter, "and unless he's corrupted half Balham, there's no doubt he spent the night there. And the afternoon was really spent with the bank people. And half the residents of Salisbury seem to have seen him off on Monday before lunch. And nobody but his own family or young Wicks seems to have anything to gain by his death. And even if young Wicks wanted to make away with him, it's rather far-fetched to go and murder an unknown man in Thipps's place in order to stick Crimplesham's eyeglasses on his nose."

"Where was young Wicks on Monday?" asked Parker.

"At a dance given by the Precentor," said Lord Peter, wildly. "David—his name is David—dancing before the ark of the Lord in the face of the whole Cathedral Close."

There was a pause.

"Tell me about the inquest," said Wimsey.

Parker obliged with a summary of the evidence.

"Do you believe the body could have been concealed in the flat after all?" he asked. "I know we looked, but I suppose we might have missed something."

"We might. But Sugg looked as well."

"Sugg!"

"You do Sugg an injustice," said Lord Peter; "if there had been any signs of Thipps's complicity in the crime, Sugg would have found them."

"Why?"

"Why? Because he was looking for them. He's like your commentators on Galatians. He thinks that either Thipps, or Gladys Horrocks, or Gladys Horrocks's young man did it. Therefore he found marks on the window-sill where Gladys Horrocks's young man might have come in or handed something in to Gladys Horrocks. He didn't find any signs on the roof, because he wasn't looking for them."

"But he went over the roof before me."

"Yes, but only in order to prove that there were no marks there. He reasons like this: Gladys Horrocks's young man is a glazier. Glaziers come on ladders. Glaziers have ready access to ladders. Therefore Gladys Horrocks's young man had ready access to a ladder. Therefore Gladys Horrocks's young man came on a ladder. Therefore there will be marks on the window-sill and none on the roof. Therefore he finds marks on the window-sill but none on the roof. He finds no marks on the ground, but he thinks he would have found them if the yard didn't happen to be paved with asphalt. Similarly, he thinks Mr. Thipps may have concealed the body in the box-room or elsewhere. Therefore you may be sure he searched the box-room and all the other places for signs of occupation. If they had been there he would have found them, because he was looking for them. Therefore, if he didn't find them it's because they weren't there."

"All right," said Parker, "stop talking. I believe you."

He went on to detail the medical evidence.

"By the way," said Lord Peter, "to skip across for a moment to the other case, has it occurred to you that perhaps Levy was going out to see Freke on Monday night?"

"He was; he did," said Parker, rather unexpectedly, and proceeded to recount his interview with the nerve-specialist.

"Humph!" said Lord Peter. "I say, Parker, these are funny cases, ain't they? Every line of inquiry seems to peter out. It's awfully exciting up to a point, you know, and then nothing comes of it. It's like rivers getting lost in the sand."

"Yes," said Parker. "And there's another one I lost this morning."

"What's that?"

"Oh, I was pumping Levy's secretary about his business. I couldn't get much that seemed important except further details about the Argentine and so on. Then I thought I'd just ask round in the City about those Peruvian Oil shares, but Levy hadn't even heard of them so far as I could make out. I routed out the brokers, and found a lot of mystery and concealment, as one always does, you know, when somebody's been rigging the market, and at last I found one name at the back of it. But it wasn't Levy's."

"No? Whose was it?"

"Oddly enough, Freke's. It seems mysterious. He bought a lot of shares last week, in a secret kind of way, a few of them in his own name, and then quietly sold 'em out on Tuesday at a small profit—a few hundreds, not worth going to all that trouble about, you wouldn't think."

"Shouldn't have thought he ever went in for that kind of gamble."

"He doesn't as a rule. That's the funny part of it."

"Well, you never know," said Lord Peter; "people do these things just to prove to themselves or somebody else that they could make a fortune that way if they liked. I've done it myself in a small way."

He knocked out his pipe and rose to go.

"I say, old man," he said suddenly, as Parker was letting him out, "does it occur to you that Freke's story doesn't fit in awfully well with what Anderson said about the old boy having been so jolly at dinner on Monday night? Would you be, if you thought you'd got anything of that sort?"

"No, I shouldn't," said Parker; "but," he added with his habitual caution, "some men will jest in the dentist's waiting-room. You, for one."

"Well, that's true," said Lord Peter, and went downstairs.

VIII

Lord Peter reached home about midnight, feeling extraordinarily wakeful and alert. Something was jigging and worrying in his brain; it felt like a hive of bees, stirred up by a stick. He felt as though he were looking at a complicated riddle, of which he had once been told the answer but had forgotten it and was always on the point of remembering.

"Somewhere," said Lord Peter to himself, "somewhere I've got the key to these two things. I know I've got it, only I can't remember what it is. Somebody said it. Perhaps I said it. I can't remember where, but I know I've got it. Go to bed, Bunter, I shall sit up a little. I'll just slip on a dressing-gown."

Before the fire he sat down with his pipe in his mouth and his jazz-coloured peacocks gathered about him. He traced out this line and that line of investigation—rivers running into the sand. They ran out from the thought of Levy, last seen at ten o'clock in Prince of Wales Road. They ran back from the picture of the grotesque dead man in Mr. Thipps's bathroom—they ran over the roof, and were lost—lost in the sand. Rivers running into the sand—rivers running underground, very far down—

Where Alph, the sacred river, ran
Through caverns measureless to man
Down to a sunless sea.

By leaning his head down, it seemed to Lord Peter that he could hear them, very faintly, lipping and gurgling somewhere in the darkness. But where? He felt quite sure that somebody had told him once, only he had forgotten.

He roused himself, threw a log on the fire, and picked up a book which the indefatigable Bunter, carrying on his daily fatigues amid the excitements of special duty, had brought from the Times Book Club. It happened to be Sir Julian Freke's "Physiological Bases of the Conscience," which he had seen reviewed two days before.

"This ought to send one to sleep," said Lord Peter; "if I can't leave these problems to my subconscious I'll be as limp as a rag tomorrow."

He opened the book slowly, and glanced carelessly through the preface.

"I wonder if that's true about Levy being ill," he thought, putting the book down; "it doesn't seem likely. And yet—Dash it all, I'll take my mind off it."

He read on resolutely for a little.

"I don't suppose Mother's kept up with the Levys much," was the next importunate train of thought. "Dad always hated self-made people and wouldn't have 'em at Denver. And old Gerald keeps up the tradition. I wonder if she knew Freke well in those days. She seems to get on with Milligan. I trust Mother's judgment a good deal. She was a brick about that bazaar business. I ought to have warned her. She said something once—"

He pursued an elusive memory for some minutes, till it vanished altogether with a mocking flicker of the tail. He returned to his reading.

Presently another thought crossed his mind aroused by a photograph of some experiment in surgery.

"If the evidence of Freke and that man Watts hadn't been so positive," he said to himself, "I should be inclined to look into the matter of those shreds of lint on the chimney."

He considered this, shook his head and read with determination.

Mind and matter were one thing, that was the theme of the physiologist. Matter could erupt, as it were, into ideas. You could carve passions in the brain with a knife. You could get rid of imagination with drugs and cure an outworn convention like a disease. "The knowledge of good and evil is an observed phenomenon, attendant upon a certain condition of the brain-cells, which is removable." That was one phrase; and again:

"Conscience in man may, in fact, be compared to the sting of a hive-bee, which, so far from conducing to the welfare of its possessor, cannot function, even in a single instance, without occasioning its death. The survival-value in each case is thus purely social; and if humanity ever passes from its present phase of social development into that of a higher individualism, as some of our philosophers have ventured to speculate, we may suppose that this interesting mental phenomenon may gradually cease to appear; just as the nerves and muscles which once controlled the movements of our ears and scalps have, in all save a few backward individuals, become atrophied and of interest only to the physiologist."

"By Jove!" thought Lord Peter, idly, "that's an ideal doctrine for the criminal. A man who believed that would never—"

And then it happened—the thing he had been half-unconsciously expecting. It happened suddenly, surely, as unmistakably as sunrise. He remembered—not one thing, nor another thing, nor a logical succession of things, but everything—the whole thing, perfect, complete, in all its dimensions as it were

and instantaneously; as if he stood outside the world and saw it
suspended in infinitely dimensional space. He no longer needed
to reason about it, or even to think about it. He knew it.

There is a game in which one is presented with a jumble of
letters and is required to make a word out of them, as thus:

COSSSSRI

The slow way of solving the problem is to try out all the per-
mutations and combinations in turn, throwing away impossible
conjunctions of letters, as:

SSSIRC

or

SCSRSO

Another way is to stare at the inco-ordinate elements until, by
no logical process that the conscious mind can detect, or under
some adventitious external stimulus, the combination

SCISSORS

presents itself with calm certainty. After that, one does not even
need to arrange the letters in order. The thing is done.

Even so, the scattered elements of two grotesque conun-
drums, flung higgledy-piggledy into Lord Peter's mind, resolved
themselves, unquestioned henceforward. A bump on the roof
of the end house—Levy in a welter of cold rain talking to a
prostitute in the Battersea Park Road—a single ruddy hair—
lint bandages—Inspector Sugg calling the great surgeon from
the dissecting-room of the hospital—Lady Levy with a nervous

attack—the smell of carbolic soap—the Duchess's voice—"not really an engagement, only a sort of understanding with her father"—shares in Peruvian Oil—the dark skin and curved, fleshy profile of the man in the bath—Dr. Grimbold giving evidence, "In my opinion, death did not occur for several days after the blow"—India-rubber gloves—even, faintly, the voice of Mr. Appledore, "He called on me, sir, with an anti-vivisectionist pamphlet"—all these things and many others rang together and made one sound, they swung together like bells in a steeple, with the deep tenor booming through the clamour:

"The knowledge of good and evil is a phenomenon of the brain, and is removable, removable, removable. The knowledge of good and evil is removable."

Lord Peter Wimsey was not a young man who habitually took himself very seriously, but this time he was frankly appalled. "It's impossible," said his reason, feebly; "*credo quia impossibile*," said his interior certainty with impervious self-satisfaction. "All right," said conscience, instantly allying itself with blind faith, "what are you going to do about it?"

Lord Peter got up and paced the room: "Good Lord!" he said. "Good Lord!" He took down "Who's Who" from the little shelf over the telephone and sought comfort in its pages.

FREKE, Sir Julian, Kt. *cr.* 1916; G.C.V.O. *cr.* 1919; K.C.V.O. 1917; K.C.B. 1918; M.D., F.R.C.P., F.R.C.S., Dr. en Méd. Paris; D. Sci. Cantab.; Knight of Grace of the Order of S. John of Jerusalem; Consulting Surgeon of St. Luke's Hospital, Battersea. *b.* Gryllingham, 16 March, 1872, *only son* of Edward Curzon Freke, Esq., of Gryll Court, Gryllingham. *Educ.* Harrow and Trinity Coll., Cambridge; Col. A.M.S.; late Member of the Advisory Board of the Army Medical Service. *Publications:* Some Notes on the Pathological Aspects of Genius, 1892; Statistical Contributions to the

Study of Infantile Paralysis in England and Wales, 1894; Functional Disturbances of the Nervous System, 1899; Cerebro-Spinal Diseases, 1904; The Borderland of Insanity, 1906; An Examination into the Treatment of Pauper Lunacy in the United Kingdom, 1906; Modern Developments in Psycho-Therapy: A Criticism, 1910; Criminal Lunacy, 1914; The Application of Psycho-Therapy to the Treatment of Shell-Shock, 1917; An Answer to Professor Freud, with a Description of Some Experiments Carried Out at the Base Hospital at Amiens, 1919; Structural Modifications Accompanying the More Important Neuroses, 1920. *Clubs:* White's; Oxford and Cambridge; Alpine, etc. *Recreations:* Chess, Mountaineering, Fishing. *Address:* 282, Harley Street and St. Luke's House, Prince of Wales Road, Battersea Park, S.W.II."

He flung the book away. "Confirmation!" he groaned. "As if I needed it!"

He sat down again and buried his face in his hands. He remembered quite suddenly how, years ago, he had stood before the breakfast table at Denver Castle—a small, peaky boy in blue knickers, with a thunderously beating heart. The family had not come down; there was a great silver urn with a spirit lamp under it, and an elaborate coffee-pot boiling in a glass dome. He had twitched the corner of the tablecloth—twitched it harder, and the urn moved ponderously forward and all the teaspoons rattled. He seized the tablecloth in a firm grip and pulled his hardest—he could feel now the delicate and awful thrill as the urn and the coffee machine and the whole of a Sèvres breakfast service had crashed down in one stupendous ruin—he remembered the horrified face of the butler, and the screams of a lady guest.

A log broke across and sank into a fluff of white ash. A belated motor-lorry rumbled past the window.

Mr. Bunter, sleeping the sleep of the true and faithful servant, was aroused in the small hours by a hoarse whisper, "Bunter!"

"Yes, my lord," said Bunter, sitting up and switching on the light.

"Put that light out, damn you!" said the voice. "Listen—over there—listen—can't you hear it?"

"It's nothing, my lord," said Mr. Bunter, hastily getting out of bed and catching hold of his master; "it's all right, you get to bed quick and I'll fetch you a drop of bromide. Why, you're all shivering—you've been sitting up too late."

"Hush! no, no—it's the water," said Lord Peter with chattering teeth; "it's up to their waists down there, poor devils. But listen! can't you hear it? Tap, tap, tap—they're mining us—but I don't know where—I can't hear—I can't. Listen, you! There it is again—we must find it—we must stop it.... Listen! Oh, my God! I can't hear—I can't hear anything for the noise of the guns. Can't they stop the guns?"

"Oh, dear!" said Mr. Bunter to himself. "No, no—it's all right, Major—don't you worry."

"But I hear it," protested Peter.

"So do I," said Mr. Bunter stoutly; "very good hearing, too, my lord. That's our own sappers at work in the communication trench. Don't you fret about that, sir."

Lord Peter grasped his wrist with a feverish hand.

"Our own sappers," he said; "sure of that?"

"Certain of it," said Mr. Bunter, cheerfully.

"They'll bring down the tower," said Lord Peter.

"To be sure they will," said Mr. Bunter, "and very nice, too. You just come and lay down a bit, sir—they've come to take over this section."

"You're sure it's safe to leave it?" said Lord Peter.

"Safe as houses, sir," said Mr. Bunter, tucking his master's arm under his and walking him off to his bedroom.

Lord Peter allowed himself to be dosed and put to bed without further resistance. Mr. Bunter, looking singularly un-Bunterlike in striped pyjamas, with his stiff black hair ruffled about his head, sat grimly watching the younger man's sharp cheekbones and the purple stains under his eyes.

"Thought we'd had the last of these attacks," he said. "Been overdoin' of himself. Asleep?" He peered at him anxiously. An affectionate note crept into his voice. "Bloody little fool!" said Sergeant Bunter.

IX

Mr. Parker, summoned the next morning to 110 Piccadilly, arrived to find the Dowager Duchess in possession. She greeted him charmingly.

"I am going to take this silly boy down to Denver for the week-end," she said, indicating Peter, who was writing and only acknowledged his friend's entrance with a brief nod. "He's been doing too much—running about to Salisbury and places and up till all hours of the night—you really shouldn't encourage him, Mr. Parker, it's very naughty of you—waking poor Bunter up in the middle of the night with scares about Germans, as if that wasn't all over years ago, and he hasn't had an attack for ages, but there! Nerves are such funny things, and Peter always did have nightmares when he was quite a little boy—though very often of course it was only a little pill he wanted; but he was so dreadfully bad in 1918, you know, and I suppose we can't expect to forget all about a great war in a year or two, and, really, I ought to be very thankful with both my boys safe. Still, I think a little peace and quiet at Denver won't do him any harm."

"Sorry you've been having a bad turn, old man," said Parker, vaguely sympathetic; "you're looking a bit seedy."

"Charles," said Lord Peter, in a voice entirely void of expression, "I am going away for a couple of days because I can be no use to you in London. What has got to be done for the moment can be much better done by you than by me. I want you to take this"—he folded up his writing and placed it in an envelope— "to Scotland Yard immediately and get it sent out to all the workhouses, infirmaries, police stations, Y.M.C.A.'s and so on in London. It is a description of Thipps's corpse as he was before he was shaved and cleaned up. I want to know whether any man answering to that description has been taken in anywhere, alive or dead, during the last fortnight. You will see Sir Andrew Mackenzie personally, and get the paper sent out at once, by his authority; you will tell him that you have solved the problems of the Levy murder and the Battersea mystery"—Mr. Parker made an astonished noise to which his friend paid no attention—"and you will ask him to have men in readiness with a warrant to arrest a very dangerous and important criminal at any moment on your information. When the replies to this paper come in, you will search for any mention of St. Luke's Hospital, or of any person connected with St. Luke's Hospital, and you will send for me at once.

"Meanwhile you will scrape acquaintance—I don't care how—with one of the students at St. Luke's. Don't march in there blowing about murders and police warrants, or you may find yourself in Queer Street. I shall come up to town as soon as I hear from you, and I shall expect to find a nice ingenuous Sawbones here to meet me." He grinned faintly.

"D'you mean you've got to the bottom of this thing?" asked Parker.

"Yes. I may be wrong. I hope I am, but I know I'm not."

"You won't tell me?"

"D'you know," said Peter, "honestly I'd rather not. I say I *may* be wrong—and I'd feel as if I'd libelled the Archbishop of Canterbury."

"Well, tell me—is it one mystery or two?"

"One."

"You talked of the Levy murder. Is Levy dead?"

"God—yes!" said Peter, with a strong shudder.

The Duchess looked up from where she was reading the *Tatler*.

"Peter," she said, "is that your ague coming on again? Whatever you two are chattering about, you'd better stop it at once if it excites you. Besides, it's about time to be off."

"All right, Mother," said Peter. He turned to Bunter, standing respectfully in the door with an overcoat and suitcase. "You understand what you have to do, don't you?" he said.

"Perfectly, thank you, my lord. The car is just arriving, your Grace."

"With Mrs. Thipps inside it," said the Duchess. "She'll be delighted to see you again, Peter. You remind her so of Mr. Thipps. Good-morning, Bunter."

"Good-morning, your Grace."

Parker accompanied them downstairs.

When they had gone he looked blankly at the paper in his hand—then, remembering that it was Saturday and there was need for haste, he hailed a taxi.

"Scotland Yard!" he cried.

Tuesday morning saw Lord Peter and a man in a velveteen jacket swishing merrily through seven acres of turnip-tops, streaked yellow with early frosts. A little way ahead, a sinuous undercurrent of excitement among the leaves proclaimed the unseen yet ever-near presence of one of the Duke of Denver's setter pups. Presently a partridge flew up with a noise like a police rattle, and Lord Peter accounted for it very creditably for a man who, a few nights before, had been listening to imaginary German sappers. The setter bounded foolishly through the turnips, and fetched back the dead bird.

"Good dog," said Lord Peter.

Encouraged by this, the dog gave a sudden ridiculous gambol and barked, its ear tossed inside out over its head.

"Heel," said the man in velveteen, violently. The animal sidled up, ashamed.

"Fool of a dog, that," said the man in velveteen; "can't keep quiet. Too nervous, my lord. One of old Black Lass's pups."

"Dear me," said Peter, "is the old dog still going?"

"No, my lord; we had to put her away in the spring."

Peter nodded. He always proclaimed that he hated the country and was thankful to have nothing to do with the family estates, but this morning he enjoyed the crisp air and the wet leaves washing darkly over his polished boots. At Denver things moved in an orderly way; no one died sudden and violent deaths except aged setters—and partridges, to be sure. He sniffed up the autumn smell with appreciation. There was a letter in his pocket which had come by the morning post, but he did not intend to read it just yet. Parker had not wired; there was no hurry.

He read it in the smoking-room after lunch. His brother was there, dozing over the *Times*—a good, clean Englishman, sturdy and conventional, rather like Henry VIII in his youth; Gerald, sixteenth Duke of Denver. The Duke considered his cadet rather degenerate, and not quite good form; he disliked his taste for police-court news.

The letter was from Mr. Bunter.

110, PICCADILLY,
W.I.

My Lord:

I write (Mr. Bunter had been carefully educated and knew that nothing is more vulgar than a careful avoidance of beginning a letter with the first person singular) *as your lordship directed, to inform you of the result of my investigations.*

I experienced no difficulty in becoming acquainted with Sir Julian Freke's man-servant. He belongs to the same club as the Hon. Frederick Arbuthnot's man, who is a friend of mine, and was very willing to introduce me. He took me to the club yesterday (Sunday) evening, and we dined with the man, whose name is John Cummings, and afterwards I invited Cummings to drinks and a cigar in the flat. Your lordship will excuse me doing this, knowing that it is not my habit, but it has always been my experience that the best way to gain a man's confidence is to let him suppose that one takes advantage of one's employer.

("I always suspected Bunter of being a student of human nature," commented Lord Peter.)

I gave him the best old port ("The deuce you did," said Lord Peter), *having heard you and Mr. Arbuthnot talk over it.* ("Hum!" said Lord Peter.)

Its effects were quite equal to my expectations as regards the principal matter in hand, but I very much regret to state that the man had so little understanding of what was offered to him that he smoked a cigar with it (one of your lordship's Villar Villars). You will understand that I made no comment on this at the time, but your lordship will sympathize with my feelings. May I take this opportunity of expressing my grateful appreciation of your lordship's excellent taste in food, drink and dress? It is, if I may say so, more than a pleasure—it is an education, to valet and buttle your lordship.

Lord Peter bowed his head gravely.

"What on earth are you doing, Peter, sittin' there noddin' an' grinnin' like a what-you-may-call-it?" demanded the Duke, coming suddenly out of a snooze. "Someone writin' pretty things to you, what?"

"Charming things," said Lord Peter.

The Duke eyed him doubtfully.

"Hope to goodness you don't go and marry a chorus beauty," he muttered inwardly, and returned to the *Times*.

Over dinner I had set myself to discover Cummings's tastes, and found them to run in the direction of the music-hall stage. During his first glass I drew him out in this direction, your lordship having kindly given me opportunities of seeing every performance in London, and I spoke more freely than I should consider becoming in the ordinary way in order to make myself pleasant to him. I may say that his views on women and the stage were such as I should have expected from a man who would smoke with your lordship's port.

With the second glass I introduced the subject of your lordship's inquiries. In order to save time I will write our conversation in the form of a dialogue, as nearly as possible as it actually took place.

CUMMINGS: *You seem to get many opportunities of seeing a bit of life, Mr. Bunter.*

BUNTER: *One can always make opportunities if one knows how.*

CUMMINGS: *Ah, it's very easy for you to talk, Mr. Bunter. You're not married, for one thing.*

BUNTER: *I know better than that, Mr. Cummings.*

CUMMINGS: *So do I—now, when it's too late. (He sighed heavily, and I filled up his glass.)*

BUNTER: *Does Mrs. Cummings live with you at Battersea?*

CUMMINGS: *Yes, her and me we do for my governor. Such a life! Not but what there's a char comes in by the day. But what's a char? I can tell you it's dull all by ourselves in that d—d Battersea suburb.*

BUNTER: *Not very convenient for the Halls, of course.*

CUMMINGS: *I believe you. It's all right for you, here in Piccadilly, right on the spot as you might say. And I daresay your governor's often out all night, eh?*

BUNTER: *Oh, frequently, Mr. Cummings.*

CUMMINGS: *And I daresay you take the opportunity to slip off yourself every so often, eh?*

BUNTER: *Well, what do you think, Mr. Cummings?*

CUMMINGS: *That's it; there you are! But what's a man to do with a nagging fool of a wife and a blasted scientific doctor for a governor, as sits up all night cutting up dead bodies and experimenting with frogs?*

BUNTER: *Surely he goes out sometimes.*

CUMMINGS: *Not often. And always back before twelve. And the way he goes on if he rings the bell and you ain't there. I give you my word, Mr. Bunter.*

BUNTER: *Temper?*

CUMMINGS: *No-o-o—but looking through you, nasty-like, as if you was on that operating table of his and he was going to cut you up. Nothing a man could rightly complain of, you understand, Mr. Bunter, just nasty looks. Not but what I will say he's very correct. Apologizes if he's been inconsiderate. But what's the good of that when he's been and gone and lost you your night's rest?*

BUNTER: *How does he do that? Keeps you up late, you mean?*

CUMMINGS: *Not him; far from it. House locked up and household to bed at half-past ten. That's his little rule. Not but what I'm glad enough to go as a rule, it's that dreary. Still, when I do go to bed I like to go to sleep.*

BUNTER: *What does he do? Walk about the house?*

CUMMINGS: *Doesn't he? All night. And in and out of the private door to the hospital.*

BUNTER: *You don't mean to say, Mr. Cummings, a great specialist like Sir Julian Freke does night work at the hospital?*

CUMMINGS: *No, no; he does his own work—research work, as you may say. Cuts people up. They say he's very clever. Could take you or me to pieces like a clock, Mr. Bunter, and put us together again.*

BUNTER: *Do you sleep in the basement, then, to hear him so plain?*

CUMMINGS: *No; our bedroom's at the top. But, Lord! what's that? He'll bang the door so you can hear him all over the house.*

BUNTER: *Ah, many's the time I've had to speak to Lord Peter about that. And talking all night. And baths.*

CUMMINGS: *Baths? You may well say that, Mr. Bunter. Baths? Me and my wife sleep next to the cistern-room. Noise fit to wake the dead. All hours. When d'you think he chose to have a bath, no later than last Monday night, Mr. Bunter?*

BUNTER: *I've known them to do it at two in the morning, Mr. Cummings.*

CUMMINGS: *Have you, now? Well, this was at three. Three o'clock in the morning we was waked up. I give you my word.*

BUNTER: *You don't say so, Mr. Cummings.*

CUMMINGS: *He cuts up diseases, you see, Mr. Bunter, and then he don't like to go to bed till he's washed the bacilluses off, if you understand me. Very natural, too, I daresay. But what I say is, the middle of the night's no time for a gentleman to be occupying his mind with diseases.*

BUNTER: *These great men have their own way of doing things.*

CUMMINGS: *Well, all I can say is, it isn't my way.*

(I could believe that, your lordship. Cummings has no signs of greatness about him, and his trousers are not what I would wish to see in a man of his profession.)

BUNTER: *Is he habitually as late as that, Mr. Cummings?*

CUMMINGS: *Well, no, Mr. Bunter, I will say, not as a general rule.*

He apologized, too, in the morning, and said he would have the cistern seen to—and very necessary, in my opinion, for the air gets into the pipes, and the groaning and screeching as goes on is something awful. Just like Niagara, if you follow me, Mr. Bunter, I give you my word.

BUNTER: *Well, that's as it should be, Mr. Cummings. One can put up with a great deal from a gentleman that has the manners to apologize. And, of course, sometimes they can't help themselves. A visitor will come in unexpectedly and keep them late, perhaps.*

CUMMINGS: *That's true enough, Mr. Bunter. Now I come to think of it, there was a gentleman come in on Monday evening. Not that he came late, but he stayed about an hour, and may have put Sir Julian behind hand.*

BUNTER: *Very likely. Let me give you some more port, Mr. Cummings. Or a little of Lord Peter's old brandy.*

CUMMINGS: *A little of the brandy, thank you, Mr. Bunter. I suppose you have the run of the cellar here. (He winked at me.)*

"Trust me for that," I said, and I fetched him the Napoleon. I assure your lordship it went to my heart to pour it out for a man like that. However, seeing we had got on the right tack, I felt it wouldn't be wasted.

"I'm sure I wish it was always gentlemen that come here at night," I said. (Your lordship will excuse me, I am sure, making such a suggestion.)

("Good God," said Lord Peter, "I wish Bunter was less thorough in his methods.")

CUMMINGS: *Oh, he's that sort, his lordship, is he? (He chuckled and poked me. I suppress a portion of his conversation here, which could not fail to be as offensive to your lordship as it was to myself.) He went on: No, it's none of that with Sir Julian. Very few visitors at night, and always gentlemen. And going early as a rule, like the one I mentioned.*

BUNTER: *Just as well. There's nothing I find more wearisome, Mr. Cummings, than sitting up to see visitors out.*

CUMMINGS: *Oh, I didn't see this one out. Sir Julian let him out himself at ten o'clock or thereabouts. I heard the gentleman shout "Good-night" and off he goes.*

BUNTER: *Does Sir Julian always do that?*

CUMMINGS: *Well, that depends. If he sees visitors downstairs, he lets them out himself: if he sees them upstairs in the library, he rings for me.*

BUNTER: *This was a downstairs visitor, then?*

CUMMINGS: *Oh, yes. Sir Julian opened the door to him, I remember. He happened to be working in the hall. Though now I come to think of it, they went up to the library afterwards. That's funny. I know they did, because I happened to go up to the hall with coals, and I heard them upstairs. Besides, Sir Julian rang for me in the library a few minutes later. Still, anyway, we heard him go at ten, or it may have been a bit before. He hadn't only stayed about three-quarters of an hour. However, as I was saying, there was Sir Julian banging in and out of the private door all night, and a bath at three in the morning, and up again for breakfast at eight—it beats me. If I had all his money, curse me if I'd go poking about with dead men in the middle of the night. I'd find something better to do with my time, eh, Mr. Bunter—*

I need not repeat any more of his conversation, as it became unpleasant and incoherent, and I could not bring him back to the events of Monday night. I was unable to get rid of him till three. He cried on my neck, and said I was the bird, and you were the governor for him. He said that Sir Julian would be greatly annoyed with him for coming home so late, but Sunday night was his night out and if anything was said about it he would give notice. I think he will be ill-advised to do so, as I feel he is not a man I could *conscientiously recommend if I were in Sir Julian Freke's place. I noticed that his boot-heels were slightly worn down.*

I should wish to add, as a tribute to the great merits of your lordship's cellar, that, although I was obliged to drink a somewhat large quantity both of the Cockburn '68 and the 1800 Napoleon I feel no headache or other ill effects this morning.

Trusting that your lordship is deriving real benefit from the country air, and that the little information I have been able to obtain will prove satisfactory, I remain,

   With respectful duty to all the family,

                                                    Obediently yours,
                                                    Mervyn Bunter.

"Y'know," said Lord Peter thoughtfully to himself, "I some-times think Mervyn Bunter's pullin' my leg. What is it, Soames?"

"A telegram, my lord."

"Parker," said Lord Peter, opening it. It said:

"Description recognised Chelsea Workhouse. Unknown vagrant injured street accident Wednesday week. Died work-house Monday. Delivered St. Luke's same evening by order Freke. Much puzzled. Parker."

"Hurray!" said Lord Peter, suddenly sparkling. "I'm glad I've puzzled Parker. Gives me confidence in myself. Makes me feel like Sherlock Holmes. 'Perfectly simple, Watson.' Dash it all, though! this is a beastly business. Still, it's puzzled Parker."

"What's the matter?" asked the Duke, getting up and yawning.

"Marching orders," said Peter, "back to town. Many thanks for your hospitality, old bird—I'm feelin' no end better. Ready to tackle Professor Moriarty or Leon Kestrel or any of 'em."

"I do wish you'd keep out of the police courts," grumbled the Duke. "It makes it so dashed awkward for me, havin' a brother makin' himself conspicuous."

"Sorry, Gerald," said the other; "I know I'm a beastly blot on the 'scutcheon."

"Why can't you marry and settle down and live quietly, doin' something useful?" said the Duke, unappeased.

"Because that was a wash-out as you perfectly well know," said Peter; "besides," he added cheerfully, "I'm bein' no end useful. You may come to want me yourself, you never know. When anybody comes blackmailin' you, Gerald, or your first deserted wife turns up unexpectedly from the West Indies, you'll realize the pull of havin' a private detective in the family. 'Delicate private business arranged with tact and discretion. Investigations undertaken. Divorce evidence a specialty. Every guarantee!' Come, now."

"Ass!" said Lord Denver, throwing the newspaper violently into his armchair. "When do you want the car?"

"Almost at once. I say, Jerry, I'm taking Mother up with me."

"Why should she be mixed up in it?"

"Well, I want her help."

"I call it most unsuitable," said the Duke.

The Dowager Duchess, however, made no objection.

"I used to know her quite well," she said, "when she was Christine Ford. Why, dear?"

"Because," said Lord Peter, "there's a terrible piece of news to be broken to her about her husband."

"Is he dead, dear?"

"Yes; and she will have to come and identify him."

"Poor Christine."

"Under very revolting circumstances, Mother."

"I'll come with you, dear."

"Thank you, Mother, you're a brick. D'you mind gettin' your things on straight away and comin' up with me? I'll tell you about it in the car."

X

Mr. Parker, a faithful though doubting Thomas, had duly secured his medical student: a large young man like an over-grown puppy, with innocent eyes and a freckled face. He sat on the Chesterfield before Lord Peter's library fire, bewildered in equal measure by his errand, his surroundings and the drink which he was absorbing. His palate, though untutored, was naturally a good one, and he realized that even to call this liquid a drink—the term ordinarily used by him to designate cheap whisky, post-war beer or a dubious glass of claret in a Soho restaurant—was a sacrilege; this was something outside normal experience: a genie in a bottle.

The man called Parker, whom he had happened to run across the evening before in the public-house at the corner of Prince of Wales Road, seemed to be a good sort. He had insisted on bringing him round to see this friend of his, who lived splendidly in Piccadilly. Parker was quite understandable; he put him down as a government servant, or perhaps something in the City. The friend was embarrassing; he was a lord, to begin with, and his clothes were a kind of rebuke to the world at large. He talked the most fatuous nonsense, certainly, but in a disconcerting way. He didn't dig into a joke and get all the fun out of it; he made it in passing, so to speak, and skipped away to some-

thing else before your retort was ready. He had a truly terrible
man-servant—the sort you read about in books—who froze the
marrow in your bones with silent criticism. Parker appeared to
bear up under the strain, and this made you think more highly
of Parker; he must be more habituated to the surroundings of
the great than you would think to look at him. You wondered
what the carpet had cost on which Parker was carelessly spilling cigar ash; your father was an upholsterer—Mr. Piggott, of
Piggott & Piggott, Liverpool—and you knew enough about car-
pets to know that you couldn't even guess at the price of this
one. When you moved your head on the bulging silk cushion
in the corner of the sofa, it made you wish you shaved more
often and more carefully. The sofa was a monster—but even so,
it hardly seemed big enough to contain you. This Lord Peter
was not very tall—in fact, he was rather a small man, but he
didn't look undersized. He looked right; he made you feel that
to be six-foot-three was rather vulgarly assertive; you felt like
Mother's new drawing-room curtains—all over great big blobs.
But everybody was very decent to you, and nobody said anything you couldn't understand, or sneered at you. There were
some frightfully deep-looking books on the shelves all round,
and you had looked into a great folio Dante which was lying on
the table, but your hosts were talking quite ordinarily and ratio-
nally about the sort of books you read yourself—clinking good
love stories and detective stories. You had read a lot of those,
and could give an opinion, and they listened to what you had to
say, though Lord Peter had a funny way of talking about books,
too, as if the author had confided in him beforehand, and told
him how the story was put together, and which bit was written
first. It reminded you of the way old Freke took a body to pieces.

"Thing I object to in detective stories," said Mr. Piggott, "is
the way fellows remember every bloomin' thing that's happened to 'em within the last six months. They're always ready

with their time of day and was it rainin' or not, and what were they doin' on such an' such a day. Reel it all off like a page of poetry. But one ain't like that in real life, d'you think so, Lord Peter?" Lord Peter smiled, and young Piggott, instantly embarrassed, appealed to his earlier acquaintance. "You know what I mean, Parker. Come now. One day's so like another, I'm sure I couldn't remember—well, I might remember yesterday, p'r'aps, but I couldn't be certain about what I was doin' last week if I was to be shot for it."

"No," said Parker, "and evidence given in police statements sounds just as impossible. But they don't really get it like that, you know. I mean, a man doesn't just say, 'Last Friday I went out at 10 a.m. to buy a mutton chop. As I was turning into Mortimer Street I noticed a girl of about twenty-two with black hair and brown eyes, wearing a green jumper, check skirt, Panama hat and black shoes, riding a Royal Sunbeam Cycle at about ten miles an hour turning the corner by the Church of St. Simon and St. Jude on the wrong side of the road riding towards the market place!' It amounts to that, of course, but it's really wormed out of him by a series of questions."

"And in short stories," said Lord Peter, "it has to be put in statement form, because the real conversation would be so long and twaddly and tedious, and nobody would have the patience to read it. Writers have to consider their readers, if any, y'see."

"Yes," said Mr. Piggott, "but I bet you most people would find it jolly difficult to remember, even if you asked 'em things. I should—of course, I know I'm a bit of a fool, but then, most people are, ain't they? You know what I mean. Witnesses ain't detectives, they're just average idiots like you and me."

"Quite so," said Lord Peter, smiling as the force of the last phrase sank into its unhappy perpetrator; "you mean, if I were to ask you in a general way what you were doin'—say, a week ago today, you wouldn't be able to tell me a thing about it offhand."

"No—I'm sure I shouldn't." He considered. "No. I was in at the Hospital as usual, I suppose, and, being Tuesday, there'd be a lecture on something or the other—dashed if I know what—and in the evening I went out with Tommy Pringle—no, that must have been Monday—or was it Wednesday? I tell you, I couldn't swear to anything."

"You do yourself an injustice," said Lord Peter gravely. "I'm sure, for instance, you recollect what work you were doing in the dissecting-room on that day, for example."

"Lord, no! not for certain. I mean, I daresay it might come back to me if I thought for a long time, but I wouldn't swear to it in a court of law."

"I'll bet you half-a-crown to sixpence," said Lord Peter, "that you'll remember within five minutes."

"I'm sure I can't."

"We'll see. Do you keep a notebook of the work you do when you dissect? Drawings or anything?"

"Oh, yes."

"Think of that. What's the last thing you did in it?"

"That's easy, because I only did it this morning. It was leg muscles."

"Yes. Who was the subject?"

"An old woman of sorts; died of pneumonia."

"Yes. Turn back the pages of your drawing book in your mind. What came before that?"

"Oh, some animals—still legs; I'm doing motor muscles at present. Yes. That was old Cunningham's demonstration on comparative anatomy. I did rather a good thing of a hare's legs and a frog's, and rudimentary legs on a snake."

"Yes. Which day does Mr. Cunningham lecture?"

"Friday."

"Friday; yes. Turn back again. What comes before that?"

Mr. Piggott shook his head.

"Do your drawings of legs begin on the right-hand page or the left-hand page? Can you see the first drawing?"

"Yes—yes—I can see the date written at the top. It's a section of a frog's hind leg, on the right-hand page."

"Yes. Think of the open book in your mind's eye. What is opposite to it?"

This demanded some mental concentration.

"Something round—coloured—oh, yes—it's a hand."

"Yes. You went on from the muscles of the hand and arm to leg- and foot-muscles?"

"Yes; that's right. I've got a set of drawings of arms."

"Yes. Did you make those on the Thursday?"

"No; I'm never in the dissecting-room on Thursday."

"On Wednesday, perhaps?"

"Yes; I must have made them on Wednesday. Yes; I did. I went in there after we'd seen those tetanus patients in the morning. I did them on Wednesday afternoon. I know I went back because I wanted to finish 'em. I worked rather hard—for me. That's why I remember."

"Yes; you went back to finish them. When had you begun them, then?"

"Why, the day before."

"The day before. That was Tuesday, wasn't it?"

"I've lost count—yes, the day before Wednesday—yes, Tuesday."

"Yes. Were they a man's arms or a woman's arms?"

"Oh, a man's arms."

"Yes; last Tuesday, a week ago today, you were dissecting a man's arms in the dissecting-room. Sixpence, please."

"By Jove!"

"Wait a moment. You know a lot more about it than that. You've no idea how much you know. You know what kind of man he was."

"Oh, I never saw him complete, you know. I got there a bit late that day, I remember. I'd asked for an arm specially, because I was rather weak in arms, and Watts—that's the attendant—had promised to save me one."

"Yes. You have arrived late and found your arm waiting for you. You are dissecting it—taking your scissors and slitting up the skin and pinning it back. Was it very young, fair skin?"

"Oh, no—no. Ordinary skin, I think—with dark hairs on it—yes, that was it."

"Yes. A lean, stringy arm, perhaps, with no extra fat anywhere?"

"Oh, no—I was rather annoyed about that. I wanted a good, muscular arm, but it was rather poorly developed and the fat got in my way."

"Yes; a sedentary man who didn't do much manual work."

"That's right."

"Yes. You dissected the hand, for instance, and made a drawing of it. You would have noticed any hard calluses."

"Oh, there was nothing of that sort."

"No. But should you say it was a young man's arm? Firm young flesh and limber joints?"

"No—no."

"No. Old and stringy, perhaps."

"No. Middle-aged—with rheumatism. I mean, there was a chalky deposit in the joints, and the fingers were a bit swollen."

"Yes. A man about fifty."

"About that."

"Yes. There were other students at work on the same body."

"Oh, yes."

"Yes. And they made all the usual sort of jokes about it."

"I expect so—oh, yes!"

"You can remember some of them. Who is your local funny man, so to speak?"

"Tommy Pringle."

"What was Tommy Pringle doing?"

"Can't remember."

"Whereabouts was Tommy Pringle working?"

"Over by the instrument cupboard—by sink C."

"Yes. Get a picture of Tommy Pringle in your mind's eye."

Piggott began to laugh.

"I remember now. Tommy Pringle said the old Sheeny—"

"Why did he call him a Sheeny?"

"I don't know. But I know he did."

"Perhaps he looked like it. Did you see his head?"

"No."

"Who had the head?"

"I don't know—oh, yes, I do, though. Old Freke bagged the head himself, and little Bouncible Binns was very cross about it, because he'd been promised a head to do with old Scrooger."

"I see. What was Sir Julian doing with the head?"

"He called us up and gave us a jaw on spinal haemorrhage and nervous lesions."

"Yes. Well, go back to Tommy Pringle."

Tommy Pringle's joke was repeated, not without some embarrassment.

"Quite so. Was that all?"

"No. The chap who was working with Tommy said that sort of thing came from over-feeding."

"I deduce that Tommy Pringle's partner was interested in the alimentary canal."

"Yes; and Tommy said, if he'd thought they'd feed you like that he'd go to the workhouse himself."

"Then the man was a pauper from the workhouse?"

"Well, he must have been, I suppose."

"Are workhouse paupers usually fat and well-fed?"

"Well, no—come to think of it, not as a rule."

"In fact, it struck Tommy Pringle and his friend that this was something a little out of the way in a workhouse subject?"

"Yes."

"And if the alimentary canal was so entertaining to these gentlemen, I imagine the subject had come by his death shortly after a full meal."

"Yes—oh, yes—he'd have had to, wouldn't he?"

"Well, I don't know," said Lord Peter. "That's in your department, you know. That would be your inference, from what they said."

"Oh, yes. Undoubtedly."

"Yes; you wouldn't, for example, expect them to make that observation if the patient had been ill for a long time and fed on slops."

"Of course not."

"Well, you see, you really know a lot about it. On Tuesday week you were dissecting the arm muscles of a rheumatic middle-aged Jew, of sedentary habits, who had died shortly after eating a heavy meal, of some injury producing spinal haemorrhage and nervous lesions, and so forth, and who was presumed to come from the workhouse?"

"Yes."

"And you could swear to those facts, if need were?"

"Well, if you put it that way, I suppose I could."

"Of course you could."

Mr. Piggott sat for some moments in contemplation.

"I say," he said at last, "I did know all that, didn't I?"

"Oh, yes—you knew it all right—like Socrates's slave."

"Who's he?"

"A person in a book I used to read as a boy."

"Oh—does he come in 'The Last Days of Pompeii'?"

"No—another book—I daresay you escaped it. It's rather dull."

"I never read much except Henty and Fenimore Cooper at school.... But—have I got rather an extra good memory, then?"

"You have a better memory than you credit yourself with."

"Then why can't I remember all the medical stuff? It all goes out of my head like a sieve."

"Well, why can't you?" said Lord Peter, standing on the hearthrug and smiling down at his guest.

"Well," said the young man, "the chaps who examine one don't ask the same sort of questions you do."

"No?"

"No—they leave you to remember all by yourself. And it's beastly hard. Nothing to catch hold of, don't you know? But, I say—how did you know about Tommy Pringle being the funny man and—"

"I didn't, till you told me."

"No; I know. But how did you know he'd be there if you did ask? I mean to say—I say," said Mr. Piggott, who was becoming mellowed by influences themselves not unconnected with the alimentary canal—"I say, are you rather clever, or am I rather stupid?"

"No, no," said Lord Peter, "it's me. I'm always askin' such stupid questions, everybody thinks I must mean somethin' by 'em."

This was too involved for Mr. Piggott.

"Never mind," said Parker, soothingly, "he's always like that. You mustn't take any notice. He can't help it. It's premature senile decay, often observed in the families of hereditary legislators. Go away, Wimsey, and play us the 'Beggar's Opera,' or something."

"That's good enough, isn't it?" said Lord Peter, when the happy Mr. Piggott had been despatched home after a really delightful evening.

"I'm afraid so," said Parker. "But it seems almost incredible."

"There's nothing incredible in human nature," said Lord

Peter; "at least, in educated human nature. Have you got that exhumation order?"

"I shall have it tomorrow. I thought of fixing up with the workhouse people for tomorrow afternoon. I shall have to go and see them first."

"Right you are; I'll let my mother know."

"I begin to feel like you, Wimsey, I don't like this job."

"I like it a deal better than I did."

"You are really certain we're not making a mistake?"

Lord Peter had strolled across to the window. The curtain was not perfectly drawn, and he stood gazing out through the gap into lighted Piccadilly. At this he turned round:

"If we are," he said, "we shall know tomorrow, and no harm will have been done. But I rather think you will receive a certain amount of confirmation on your way home. Look here, Parker, d'you know, if I were you I'd spend the night here. There's a spare bedroom; I can easily put you up."

Parker stared at him.

"Do you mean—I'm likely to be attacked?"

"I think it very likely indeed."

"Is there anybody in the street?"

"Not now; there was half-an-hour ago."

"When Piggott left?"

"Yes."

"I say—I hope the boy is in no danger."

"That's what I went down to see. I don't think so. Fact is, I don't suppose anybody would imagine we'd exactly made a confidant of Piggott. But I think you and I are in danger. You'll stay?"

"I'm damned if I will, Wimsey. Why should I run away?"

"Bosh!" said Peter. "You'd run away all right if you believed me, and why not? You don't believe me. In fact, you're still not certain I'm on the right tack. Go in peace, but don't say I didn't warn you."

"I won't; I'll dictate a message with my dying breath to say I was convinced."

"Well, don't walk—take a taxi."

"Very well, I'll do that."

"And don't let anybody else get into it."

"No."

It was a raw, unpleasant night. A taxi deposited a load of people returning from the theatre at the block of flats next door, and Parker secured it for himself. He was just giving the address to the driver, when a man came hastily running up from a side street. He was in evening dress and an overcoat. He rushed up, signalling frantically.

"Sir—sir!—dear me! why, it's Mr. Parker! How fortunate! If you would be so kind—summoned from the club—a sick friend—can't find a taxi—everybody going home from the theatre—if I might share your cab—you are returning to Bloomsbury? I want Russell Square—if I might presume—a matter of life and death."

He spoke in hurried gasps, as though he had been running violently and far. Parker promptly stepped out of the taxi.

"Delighted to be of service to you, Sir Julian," he said; "take my taxi. I am going down to Craven Street myself, but I'm in no hurry. Pray make use of the cab."

"It's extremely kind of you," said the surgeon. "I am ashamed—"

"That's all right," said Parker, cheerily. "I can wait." He assisted Freke into the taxi. "What number? 24 Russell Square, driver, and look sharp."

The taxi drove off. Parker remounted the stairs and rang Lord Peter's bell.

"Thanks, old man," he said. "I'll stop the night, after all."

"Come in," said Wimsey.

"Did you see that?" asked Parker.

"I saw something. What happened exactly?"

Parker told his story. "Frankly," he said, "I've been thinking you a bit mad, but now I'm not quite so sure of it."

Peter laughed.

"Blessed are they that have not seen and yet have believed. Bunter, Mr. Parker will stay the night."

"Look here, Wimsey, let's have another look at this business. Where's that letter?"

Lord Peter produced Bunter's essay in dialogue. Parker studied it for a short time in silence.

"You know, Wimsey, I'm as full of objections to this idea as an egg is of meat."

"So'm I, old son. That's why I want to dig up our Chelsea pauper. But trot out your objections."

"Well—"

"Well, look here, I don't pretend to be able to fill in all the blanks myself. But here we have two mysterious occurrences in one night, and a complete chain connecting the one with another through one particular person. It's beastly, but it's not unthinkable."

"Yes, I know all that. But there are one or two quite definite stumbling-blocks."

"Yes, I know. But, see here. On the one hand, Levy disappeared after being last seen looking for Prince of Wales Road at nine o'clock. At eight next morning a dead man, not unlike him in general outline, is discovered in a bath in Queen Caroline Mansions. Levy, by Freke's own admission, was going to see Freke. By information received from the Chelsea workhouse a dead man, answering to the description of the Battersea corpse in its natural state, was delivered that same day to Freke. We have Levy with a past, and no future, as it were; an unknown vagrant with a future (in the cemetery) and no past, and Freke stands between their future and their past."

"That looks all right—"

"Yes. Now, further: Freke has a motive for getting rid of Levy—an old jealousy."

"Very old—and not much of a motive."

"People have been known to do that sort of thing.* You're thinking that people don't keep up old jealousies for twenty years or so. Perhaps not. Not just primitive, brute jealousy. That means a word and a blow. But the thing that rankles is hurt vanity. That sticks. Humiliation. And we've all got a sore spot we don't like to have touched. I've got it. You've got it. Some blighter said hell knew no fury like a woman scorned. Stickin' it on to women, poor devils. Sex is every man's loco spot—you needn't fidget, you know it's true—he'll take a disappointment, but not a humiliation. I knew a man once who'd been turned down—not too charitably—by a girl he was engaged to. He spoke quite decently about her. I asked what had become of her. 'Oh,' he said, 'she married the other fellow.' And then burst out—couldn't help himself. 'Lord, yes!' he cried. 'To think of it—jilted for a Scotchman!' I don't know why he didn't like Scots, but that was

---

* Lord Peter was not without authority for his opinion: "With respect to the alleged motive, it is of great importance to see whether there was a motive for committing such a crime, or whether there was not, or whether there is an improbability of its having been committed so strong as not to be overpowered by positive evidence. But *if there be any motive which can be assigned, I am bound to tell you that the inadequacy of that motive is of little importance.* We know, from the experience of criminal courts, that atrocious crimes of this sort have been committed from very slight motives; *not merely from malice and revenge,* but to gain a small pecuniary advantage, and to drive off for a time pressing difficulties."— L. C. J. Campbell, summing up in Reg. v. Palmer, Shorthand Report, p. 308 C. C. C., May, 1856, Sess. Pa. 5. (Italics mine. D. L. S.)

what got him on the raw. Look at Freke. I've read his books. His attacks on his antagonists are savage. And he's a scientist. Yet he can't bear opposition, even in his work, which is where any first-class man is most sane and open-minded. Do you think he's a man to take a beating from any man on a side-issue? On a man's most sensitive side-issue? People are opinionated about side-issues, you know. I see red if anybody questions my judgment about a book. And Levy—who was nobody twenty years ago—romps in and carries off Freke's girl from under his nose. It isn't the girl Freke would bother about—it's having his aristocratic nose put out of joint by a little Jewish nobody.

"There's another thing. Freke's got another side-issue. He likes crime. In that criminology book of his he gloats over a hardened murderer. I've read it, and I've seen the admiration simply glaring out between the lines whenever he writes about a callous and successful criminal. He reserves his contempt for the victims or the penitents or the men who lose their heads and get found out. His heroes are Edmond de la Pommerais, who persuaded his mistress into becoming an accessory to her own murder, and George Joseph Smith of Brides-in-a-bath fame, who could make passionate love to his wife in the night and carry out his plot to murder her in the morning. After all, he thinks conscience is a sort of vermiform appendix. Chop it out and you'll feel all the better. Freke isn't troubled by the usual conscientious deterrent. Witness his own hand in his books. Now again. The man who went to Levy's house in his place knew the house: Freke knew the house; he was a red-haired man, smaller than Levy, but not much smaller, since he could wear his clothes without appearing ludicrous: you have seen Freke—you know his height—about five-foot-eleven, I suppose, and his auburn mane; he probably wore surgical gloves: Freke is a surgeon; he was a methodical and daring man: surgeons are obliged to be both daring and methodical. Now take the other side. The man who got hold of the Battersea corpse had to have access to dead bodies. Freke obviously had access to dead bodies. He had to be cool and quick and callous about handling a dead body. Surgeons are all that. He had to be a strong man to carry the body across the roofs and dump it in at Thipps's window. Freke is a powerful man and a member of the Alpine Club. He probably wore surgical gloves and he let the body down from the roof with a surgical bandage. This points to a surgeon again. He undoubtedly lived in the neighbourhood. Freke lives next door. The girl you interviewed heard a bump on the roof of the end house. That is the house next to Freke's. Every time we look at Freke, he leads somewhere, whereas Milligan and Thipps and Crimplesham and all the other people we've honoured with our suspicion simply led nowhere."

"Yes; but it's not quite so simple as you make out. What was Levy doing in that surreptitious way at Freke's on Monday night?"

"Well, you have Freke's explanation."

"Rot, Wimsey. You said yourself it wouldn't do."

"Excellent. It won't do. Therefore Freke was lying. Why should he lie about it, unless he had some object in hiding the truth?"

"Well, but why mention it at all?"

"Because Levy, contrary to all expectation, had been seen at the corner of the road. That was a nasty accident for Freke. He thought it best to be beforehand with an explanation—of sorts. He reckoned, of course, on nobody's ever connecting Levy with Battersea Park."

"Well, then, we come back to the first question: Why did Levy go there?"

"I don't know, but he was got there somehow. Why did Freke buy all those Peruvian Oil shares?"

"I don't know," said Parker in his turn.

"Anyway," went on Wimsey, "Freke expected him, and made arrangements to let him in himself, so that Cummings shouldn't see who the caller was."

"But the caller left again at ten."

"Oh, Charles! I did not expect this of you. This is the purest Suggery! Who saw him go? Somebody said 'Good-night' and walked away down the street. And you believe it was Levy because Freke didn't go out of his way to explain that it wasn't."

"D'you mean that Freke walked cheerfully out of the house to Park Lane, and left Levy behind—dead or alive—for Cummings to find?"

"We have Cummings's word that he did nothing of the sort. A few minutes after the steps walked away from the house, Freke rang the library bell and told Cummings to shut up for the night."

"Then—"

"Well—there's a side door to the house, I suppose—in fact, you know there is—Cummings said so—through the hospital."

"Yes—well, where was Levy?"

"Levy went up into the library and never came down. You've been in Freke's library. Where would you have put him?"

"In my bedroom next door."

"Then that's where he did put him."

"But suppose the man went in to turn down the bed?"

"Beds are turned down by the housekeeper, earlier than ten o'clock."

"Yes.... But Cummings heard Freke about the house all night."

"He heard him go in and out two or three times. He'd expect him to do that, anyway."

"Do you mean to say Freke got all that job finished before three in the morning?"

"Why not?"

"Quick work."

"Well, call it quick work. Besides, why three? Cummings never saw him again till he called him for eight o'clock breakfast."

"But he was having a bath at three."

"I don't say he didn't get back from Park Lane before three. But I don't suppose Cummings went and looked through the bathroom keyhole to see if he was in the bath."

Parker considered again.

"How about Crimplesham's pince-nez?" he asked.

"That is a bit mysterious," said Lord Peter.

"And why Thipps's bathroom?"

"Why, indeed? Pure accident, perhaps—or pure devilry."

"Do you think all this elaborate scheme could have been put together in a night, Wimsey?"

"Far from it. It was conceived as soon as that man who bore a superficial resemblance to Levy came into the workhouse. He had several days."

"I see."

"Freke gave himself away at the inquest. He and Grimbold disagreed about the length of the man's illness. If a small man (comparatively speaking) like Grimbold presumes to disagree with a man like Freke, it's because he is sure of his ground."

"Then—if your theory is sound—Freke made a mistake."

"Yes. A very slight one. He was guarding, with unnecessary caution, against starting a train of thought in the mind of anybody—say, the workhouse doctor. Up till then he'd been reckoning on the fact that people don't think a second time about anything (a body, say) that's once been accounted for."

"What made him lose his head?"

"A chain of unforeseen accidents. Levy's having been recognized—my mother's son having foolishly advertised in the *Times* his connection with the Battersea end of the mystery—Detective Parker (whose photograph has been a little promi-

nent in the illustrated press lately) seen sitting next door to the
Duchess of Denver at the inquest. His aim in life was to prevent the two ends of the problem from linking up. And there
were two of the links, literally side by side. Many criminals are
wrecked by over-caution."

Parker was silent.

XI

"A regular pea-souper, by Jove," said Lord Peter.

Parker grunted, and struggled irritably into an overcoat.

"It affords me, if I may say so, the greatest satisfaction," continued the noble lord, "that in a collaboration like ours all the uninteresting and disagreeable routine work is done by you."

Parker grunted again.

"Do you anticipate any difficulty about the warrant?" inquired Lord Peter.

Parker grunted a third time.

"I suppose you've seen to it that all this business is kept quiet?"

"Of course."

"You've muzzled the workhouse people?"

"Of course."

"And the police?"

"Yes."

"Because, if you haven't there'll probably be nobody to arrest."

"My dear Wimsey, do you think I'm a fool?"

"I had no such hope."

Parker grunted finally and departed.

Lord Peter settled down to a perusal of his Dante. It afforded him no solace. Lord Peter was hampered in his career as a private detective by a public-school education. Despite Parker's admonitions, he was not always able to discount it. His mind had been warped in its young growth by "Raffles" and "Sherlock Holmes," or the sentiments for which they stand. He belonged to a family which had never shot a fox.

"I am an amateur," said Lord Peter.

Nevertheless, while communing with Dante, he made up his mind.

In the afternoon he found himself in Harley Street. Sir Julian Freke might be consulted about one's nerves from two till four on Tuesdays and Fridays. Lord Peter rang the bell.

"Have you an appointment, sir?" inquired the man who opened the door.

"No," said Lord Peter, "but will you give Sir Julian my card? I think it possible he may see me without one."

He sat down in the beautiful room in which Sir Julian's patients awaited his healing counsel. It was full of people. Two or three fashionably dressed women were discussing shops and servants together, and teasing a toy griffon. A big, worried-looking man by himself in a corner looked at his watch twenty times a minute. Lord Peter knew him by sight. It was Wintrington, a millionaire, who had tried to kill himself a few months ago. He controlled the finances of five countries, but he could not control his nerves. The finances of five countries were in Sir Julian Freke's capable hands. By the fireplace sat a soldierly-looking young man, of about Lord Peter's own age. His face was prematurely lined and worn; he sat bolt upright, his restless eyes darting in the direction of every slightest sound. On the sofa was an elderly woman of modest appearance, with a young girl. The girl seemed listless and wretched; the woman's look showed deep affection, and anxiety tempered with a timid hope. Close beside Lord Peter was another younger woman, with a little girl, and Lord Peter noticed in both of them the broad cheekbones and beautiful grey, slanting eyes of the Slav. The child, moving restlessly about, trod on Lord Peter's patent-leather toe, and the mother admonished her in French before turning to apologize to Lord Peter.

"Mais je vous en prie, madame," said the young man, "it is nothing."

"She is nervous, pauvre petite," said the young woman.

"You are seeking advice for her?"

"Yes. He is wonderful, the doctor. Figure to yourself, monsieur, she cannot forget, poor child, the things she has seen." She leaned nearer, so that the child might not hear. "We have escaped—from starving Russia—six months ago. I dare not tell you—she has such quick ears, and then, the cries, the tremblings, the convulsions—they all begin again. We were skeletons when we arrived—mon Dieu!—but that is better now. See, she is thin, but she is not starved. She would be fatter but for the nerves that keep her from eating. We who are older, we forget—enfin, on apprend à ne pas y penser—but these children! When one is young, monsieur, tout ça impressionne trop."

Lord Peter, escaping from the thraldom of British good form, expressed himself in that language in which sympathy is not condemned to mutism.

"But she is much better, much better," said the mother, proudly; "the great doctor, he does marvels."

"C'est un homme précieux," said Lord Peter.

"Ah, monsieur, c'est un saint qui opère des miracles! Nous prions pour lui, Natasha et moi, tous les jours. N'est-ce pas, chérie? And consider, monsieur, that he does it all, ce grand homme, cet homme illustre, for nothing at all. When we come here, we have not even the clothes upon our backs—we are ruined, famished.

Et avec ça que nous sommes de bonne famille—mais hélas! monsieur, en Russie, comme vous savez, ça ne vous vaut que des insultes—des atrocités. Enfin! the great Sir Julian sees us, he says—'Madame, your little girl is very interesting to me. Say no more. I cure her for nothing—pour ses beaux yeux,' a-t-il ajouté en riant. Ah, monsieur, c'est un saint, un véritable saint! and Natasha is much, much better."

"Madame, je vous en félicite."

"And you, monsieur? You are young, well, strong—you also suffer? It is still the war, perhaps?"

"A little remains of shell-shock," said Lord Peter.

"Ah, yes. So many good, brave, young men—"

"Sir Julian can spare you a few minutes, my lord, if you will come in now," said the servant.

Lord Peter bowed to his neighbour, and walked across the waiting-room. As the door of the consulting-room closed behind him, he remembered having once gone, disguised, into the staff-room of a German officer. He experienced the same feeling—the feeling of being caught in a trap, and a mingling of bravado and shame.

He had seen Sir Julian Freke several times from a distance, but never close. Now, while carefully and quite truthfully detailing the circumstances of his recent nervous attack, he considered the man before him. A man taller than himself, with immense breadth of shoulder, and wonderful hands. A face beautiful, impassioned and inhuman; fanatical, compelling eyes, bright blue amid the ruddy bush of hair and beard. They were not the cool and kindly eyes of the family doctor, they were the brooding eyes of the inspired scientist, and they searched one through.

"Well," thought Lord Peter, "I shan't have to be explicit, anyhow."

"Yes," said Sir Julian, "yes. You had been working too hard. Puzzling your mind. Yes. More than that, perhaps—troubling your mind, shall we say?"

"I found myself faced with a very alarming contingency."

"Yes. Unexpectedly, perhaps."

"Very unexpected indeed."

"Yes. Following on a period of mental and physical strain."

"Well—perhaps. Nothing out of the way."

"Yes. The unexpected contingency was—personal to yourself?"

"It demanded an immediate decision as to my own actions yes, in that sense it was certainly personal."

"Quite so. You would have to assume some responsibility, no doubt."

"A very grave responsibility."

"Affecting others besides yourself?"

"Affecting one other person vitally, and a very great number indirectly."

"Yes. The time was night. You were sitting in the dark?"

"Not at first. I think I put the light out afterwards."

"Quite so—that action would naturally suggest itself to you. Were you warm?"

"I think the fire had died down. My man tells me that my teeth were chattering when I went in to him."

"Yes. You live in Piccadilly?"

"Yes."

"Heavy traffic sometimes goes past during the night, I expect."

"Oh, frequently."

"Just so. Now this decision you refer to—you had taken that decision."

"Yes."

"Your mind was made up?"

"Oh, yes."

"You had decided to take the action, whatever it was."

"Yes."

"Yes. It involved perhaps a period of inaction."

"Of comparative inaction—yes."

"Of suspense, shall we say?"

"Yes—of suspense, certainly."

"Possibly of some danger?"

"I don't know that that was in my mind at the time."

"No—it was a case in which you could not possibly consider
yourself."

"If you like to put it that way."

"Quite so. Yes. You had these attacks frequently in 1918?"

"Yes—I was very ill for some months."

"Quite. Since then they have recurred less frequently?"

"Much less frequently."

"Yes—when did the last occur?"

"About nine months ago."

"Under what circumstances?"

"I was being worried by certain family matters. It was a question of deciding about some investments, and I was largely
responsible."

"Yes. You were interested last year, I think, in some police
case?"

"Yes—in the recovery of Lord Attenbury's emerald necklace."

"That involved some severe mental exercise?"

"I suppose so. But I enjoyed it very much."

"Yes. Was the exertion of solving the problem attended by
any bad results physically?"

"None."

"No. You were interested, but not distressed."

"Exactly."

"Yes. You have been engaged in other investigations of the
kind?"

"Yes. Little ones."

"With bad results for your health?"

"Not a bit of it. On the contrary. I took up these cases as a sort of distraction. I had a bad knock just after the war, which didn't make matters any better for me, don't you know."

"Ah! you are not married?"

"No."

"No. Will you allow me to make an examination? Just come a little nearer to the light. I want to see your eyes. Whose advice have you had till now?"

"Sir James Hodges's."

"Ah! yes—he was a sad loss to the medical profession. A really great man—a true scientist. Yes. Thank you. Now I should like to try you with this little invention."

"What's it do?"

"Well—it tells me about your nervous reactions. Will you sit here?"

The examination that followed was purely medical. When it was concluded, Sir Julian said:

"Now, Lord Peter, I'll tell you about yourself in quite untechnical language—"

"Thanks," said Peter, "that's kind of you. I'm an awful fool about long words."

"Yes. Are you fond of private theatricals, Lord Peter?"

"Not particularly," said Peter, genuinely surprised. "Awful bore as a rule. Why?"

"I thought you might be," said the specialist, drily. "Well, now. You know quite well that the strain you put on your nerves during the war has left its mark on you. It has left what I may call old wounds in your brain. Sensations received by your nerve-endings sent messages to your brain, and produced minute physical changes there—changes we are only beginning to be able to detect, even with our most delicate instruments.

These changes in their turn set up sensations; or I should say, more accurately, that sensations are the names we give to these changes of tissue when we perceive them: we call them horror, fear, sense of responsibility and so on."

"Yes, I follow you."

"Very well. Now, if you stimulate those damaged places in your brain again, you run the risk of opening up the old wounds. I mean, that if you get nerve-sensations of any kind producing the reactions which we call horror, fear, and sense of responsibility, they may go on to make disturbance right along the old channel, and produce in their turn physical changes which you will call by the names you were accustomed to associate with them—dread of German mines, responsibility for the lives of your men, strained attention and the inability to distinguish small sounds through the overpowering noise of guns."

"I see."

"This effect would be increased by extraneous circumstances producing other familiar physical sensations—night, cold or the rattling of heavy traffic, for instance."

"Yes."

"Yes. The old wounds are nearly healed, but not quite. The ordinary exercise of your mental faculties has no bad effect. It is only when you excite the injured part of your brain."

"Yes, I see."

"Yes. You must avoid these occasions. You must learn to be irresponsible, Lord Peter."

"My friends say I'm only too irresponsible already."

"Very likely. A sensitive nervous temperament often appears so, owing to its mental nimbleness."

"Oh!"

"Yes. This particular responsibility you were speaking of still rests upon you?"

"Yes, it does."

"You have not yet completed the course of action on which you have decided?"

"Not yet."

"You feel bound to carry it through?"

"Oh, yes—I can't back out of it now."

"No. You are expecting further strain?"

"A certain amount."

"Do you expect it to last much longer?"

"Very little longer now."

"Ah! Your nerves are not all they should be."

"No?"

"No. Nothing to be alarmed about, but you must exercise care while undergoing this strain, and afterwards you should take a complete rest. How about a voyage in the Mediterranean or the South Seas or somewhere?"

"Thanks. I'll think about it."

"Meanwhile, to carry you over the immediate trouble I will give you something to strengthen your nerves. It will do you no permanent good, you understand, but it will tide you over the bad time. And I will give you a prescription."

"Thank you."

Sir Julian got up and went into a small surgery leading out of the consulting-room. Lord Peter watched him moving about— boiling something and writing. Presently he returned with a paper and a hypodermic syringe.

"Here is the prescription. And now, if you will just roll up your sleeve, I will deal with the necessity of the immediate moment."

Lord Peter obediently rolled up his sleeve. Sir Julian Freke selected a portion of his forearm and anointed it with iodine.

"What's that you're goin' to stick into me. Bugs?"

The surgeon laughed.

"Not exactly," he said. He pinched up a portion of flesh

between his finger and thumb. "You've had this kind of thing before, I expect."

"Oh, yes," said Lord Peter. He watched the cool fingers, fascinated, and the steady approach of the needle. "Yes—I've had it before—and, d'you know—I don't care frightfully about it."

He had brought up his right hand, and it closed over the surgeon's wrist like a vice.

The silence was like a shock. The blue eyes did not waver; they burned down steadily upon the heavy white lids below them. Then these slowly lifted; the grey eyes met the blue—coldly, steadily—and held them.

When lovers embrace, there seems no sound in the world but their own breathing. So the two men breathed face to face.

"As you like, of course, Lord Peter," said Sir Julian, courteously.

"Afraid I'm rather a silly ass," said Lord Peter, "but I never could abide these little gadgets. I had one once that went wrong and gave me a rotten bad time. They make me a bit nervous."

"In that case," replied Sir Julian, "it would certainly be better not to have the injection. It might rouse up just those sensations which we are desirous of avoiding. You will take the prescription, then, and do what you can to lessen the immediate strain as far as possible."

"Oh, yes—I'll take it easy, thanks," said Lord Peter. He rolled his sleeve down neatly. "I'm much obliged to you. If I have any further trouble I'll look in again."

"Do—do—" said Sir Julian, cheerfully. "Only make an appointment another time. I'm rather rushed these days. I hope your mother is quite well. I saw her the other day at that Battersea inquest. You should have been there. It would have interested you."

XII

The vile, raw fog tore your throat and ravaged your eyes. You could not see your feet. You stumbled in your walk over poor men's graves.

The feel of Parker's old trench-coat beneath your fingers was comforting. You had felt it in worse places. You clung on now for fear you should get separated. The dim people moving in front of you were like Brocken spectres.

"Take care, gentlemen," said a toneless voice out of the yellow darkness, "there's an open grave just hereabouts."

You bore away to the right, and floundered in a mass of freshly turned clay.

"Hold up, old man," said Parker.

"Where is Lady Levy?"

"In the mortuary; the Duchess of Denver is with her. Your mother is wonderful, Peter."

"Isn't she?" said Lord Peter.

A dim blue light carried by somebody ahead wavered and stood still.

"Here you are," said a voice.

Two Dantesque shapes with pitchforks loomed up.

"Have you finished?" asked somebody.

"Nearly done, sir." The demons fell to work again with the pitchforks—no, spades.

Somebody sneezed. Parker located the sneezer and introduced him.

"Mr. Levett represents the Home Secretary. Lord Peter Wimsey. We are sorry to drag you out on such a day, Mr. Levett."

"It's all in the day's work," said Mr. Levett, hoarsely. He was muffled to the eyes.

The sound of the spades for many minutes. An iron noise of tools thrown down. Demons stooping and straining.

A black-bearded spectre at your elbow. Introduced. The Master of the Workhouse.

"A very painful matter, Lord Peter. You will forgive me for hoping you and Mr. Parker may be mistaken."

"I should like to be able to hope so too."

Something heaving, straining, coming up out of the ground.

"Steady, men. This way. Can you see? Be careful of the graves—they lie pretty thick hereabouts. Are you ready?"

"Right you are, sir. You go on with the lantern. We can follow you."

Lumbering footsteps. Catch hold of Parker's trench-coat again. "That you, old man? Oh, I beg your pardon, Mr. Levett—thought you were Parker."

"Hullo, Wimsey—here you are."

More graves. A headstone shouldered crookedly aslant. A trip and jerk over the edge of the rough grass. The squeal of gravel under your feet.

"This way, gentlemen, mind the step."

The mortuary. Raw red brick and sizzling gas-jets. Two women in black, and Dr. Grimbold. The coffin laid on the table with a heavy thump.

"'Ave you got that there screw-driver, Bill? Thank 'ee. Be

keerful wi' the chisel now. Not much substance to these 'ere boards, sir."

Several long creaks. A sob. The Duchess's voice, kind but peremptory.

"Hush, Christine. You mustn't cry."

A mutter of voices. The lurching departure of the Dante demons—good, decent demons in corduroy.

Dr. Grimbold's voice—cool and detached as if in the consulting room.

"Now—have you got that lamp, Mr. Wingate? Thank you. Yes, here on the table, please. Be careful not to catch your elbow in the flex, Mr. Levett. It would be better, I think, if you came on this side. Yes—yes—thank you. That's excellent."

The sudden brilliant circle of an electric lamp over the table. Dr. Grimbold's beard and spectacles. Mr. Levett blowing his nose. Parker bending close. The Master of the Workhouse peering over him. The rest of the room in the enhanced dimness of the gas-jets and the fog.

A low murmur of voices. All heads bent over the work.

Dr. Grimbold again—beyond the circle of the lamplight.

"We don't want to distress you unnecessarily, Lady Levy. If you will just tell us what to look for—the—? Yes, yes, certainly—and—yes—stopped with gold? Yes—the lower jaw, the last but one on the right? Yes—no teeth missing—no—yes? What kind of a mole? Yes—just over the left breast? Oh, I beg your pardon, just under—yes—appendicitis? Yes—a long one—yes—in the middle? Yes, I quite understand—a scar on the arm? Yes, I don't know if we shall be able to find that—yes—any little constitutional weakness that might—? Oh, yes—arthritis—yes—thank you, Lady Levy—that's very clear. Don't come unless I ask you to. Now, Wingate."

A pause. A murmur. "Pulled out? After death, you think—

well, so do I. Where is Dr. Colegrove? You attended this man
in the workhouse? Yes. Do you recollect—? No? You're quite
certain about that? Yes—we mustn't make a mistake, you know.
Yes, but there are reasons why Sir Julian can't be present; I'm
asking *you*, Dr. Colegrove. Well, you're certain—that's all I want
to know. Just bring the light closer, Mr. Wingate, if you please.
These miserable shells let the damp in so quickly. Ah! what do
you make of this? Yes—yes—well, that's rather unmistakable,
isn't it? Who did the head? Oh, Freke—of course. I was going to
say they did good work at St. Luke's. Beautiful, isn't it, Dr. Colegrove? A wonderful surgeon—I saw him when he was at Guy's.
Oh, no, gave it up years ago. Nothing like keeping your hand
in. Ah—yes, undoubtedly that's it. Have you a towel handy, sir?
Thank you. Over the head, if you please—I think we might
have another here. Now, Lady Levy—I am going to ask you to
look at a scar, and see if you recognise it. I'm sure you are going
to help us by being very firm. Take your time—you won't see
anything more than you absolutely must."

"Lucy, don't leave me."

"No, dear."

A space cleared at the table. The lamplight on the Duchess's
white hair.

"Oh, yes—oh, yes! No, no—I couldn't be mistaken. There's
that funny little kink in it. I've seen it hundreds of times. Oh,
Lucy—Reuben!"

"Only a moment more, Lady Levy. The mole—"

"I—I think so—oh, yes, that is the very place."

"Yes. And the scar—was it three-cornered, just above the
elbow?"

"Yes, oh, yes."

"Is this it?"

"Yes—yes—"

"I must ask you definitely, Lady Levy. Do you, from these three marks identify the body as that of your husband?"

"Oh! I must, mustn't I? Nobody else could have them just the same in just those places? It is my husband. It is Reuben. Oh—"

"Thank you, Lady Levy. You have been very brave and very helpful."

"But—I don't understand yet. How did he come here? Who did this dreadful thing?"

"Hush, dear," said the Duchess; "the man is going to be punished."

"Oh, but—how cruel! Poor Reuben! Who could have wanted to hurt him? Can I see his face?"

"No, dear," said the Duchess. "That isn't possible. Come away—you mustn't distress the doctors and people."

"No—no—they've all been so kind. Oh, Lucy!"

"We'll go home, dear. You don't want us any more, Dr. Grimbold?"

"No, Duchess, thank you. We are very grateful to you and to Lady Levy for coming."

There was a pause, while the two women went out, Parker, collected and helpful, escorting them to their waiting car. Then Dr. Grimbold again:

"I think Lord Peter Wimsey ought to see—the correctness of his deductions—Lord Peter—very painful—you may wish to see—yes, I was uneasy at the inquest—yes—Lady Levy—remarkably clear evidence—yes—most shocking case—ah, here's Mr. Parker—you and Lord Peter Wimsey entirely justified—do I really understand—? Really? I can hardly believe it—so distinguished a man—as you say, when a great brain turns to crime—yes—look here! Marvellous work—marvellous—somewhat obscured by this time, of course—but the most beautiful sections—here, you see, the left hemisphere—and here—through the corpus striatum—here again—the very track of the damage done by the blow—wonderful—guessed it—saw the effect of the blow as he struck it, you know—ah, I should like to see *his* brain, Mr. Parker—and to think that—heavens, Lord Peter, you don't know what a blow you have struck at the whole profession—the whole civilized world! Oh, my dear sir! Can you ask me? My lips are sealed of course—all our lips are sealed."

The way back through the burial ground. Fog again, and the squeal of wet gravel.

"Are your men ready, Charles?"

"They have gone. I sent them off when I saw Lady Levy to the car."

"Who is with them?"

"Sugg."

"Sugg?"

"Yes—poor devil. They've had him up on the mat at head-quarters for bungling the case. All that evidence of Thipps's about the night club was corroborated, you know. That girl he gave the gin-and-bitters to was caught, and came and identified him, and they decided their case wasn't good enough, and let Thipps and the Horrocks girl go. Then they told Sugg he had overstepped his duty and ought to have been more careful. So he ought, but he can't help being a fool. I was sorry for him. It may do him some good to be in at the death. After all, Peter, you and I had special advantages."

"Yes. Well, it doesn't matter. Whoever goes won't get there in time. Sugg's as good as another."

But Sugg—an experience rare in his career—was in time.

Parker and Lord Peter were at 110 Piccadilly. Lord Peter was playing Bach and Parker was reading Origen when Sugg was announced.

"We've got our man, sir," said he.

"Good God!" said Peter. "Alive?"

"We were just in time, my lord. We rang the bell and marched straight up past his man to the library. He was sitting there doing some writing. When we came in, he made a grab for his hypodermic, but we were too quick for him, my lord. We didn't mean to let him slip through our hands, having got so far. We searched him thoroughly and marched him off."

"He is actually in gaol, then?"

"Oh, yes—safe enough—with two warders to see he doesn't make away with himself."

"You surprise me, Inspector. Have a drink."

"Thank you, my lord. I may say that I'm very grateful to you—this case was turning out a pretty bad egg for me. If I was rude to your lordship—"

"Oh, it's all right, Inspector," said Lord Peter, hastily. "I don't see how you could possibly have worked it out. I had the good luck to know something about it from other sources."

"That's what Freke says." Already the great surgeon was a common criminal in the inspector's eyes—a mere surname. "He was writing a full confession when we got hold of him, addressed to your lordship. The police will have to have it, of course, but seeing it's written for you, I brought it along for you to see first. Here it is."

He handed Lord Peter a bulky document.

"Thanks," said Peter. "Like to hear it, Charles?"

"Rather."

Accordingly Lord Peter read it aloud.

XIII

Dear Lord Peter—

When I was a young man I used to play chess with an old friend of my father's. He was a very bad, and a very slow, player, and he could never see when a checkmate was inevitable, but insisted on playing every move out. I never had any patience with that kind of attitude, and I will freely admit now that the game is yours. I must either stay at home and be hanged or escape abroad and live in an idle and insecure obscurity. I prefer to acknowledge defeat.

If you have read my book on "Criminal Lunacy," you will remember that I wrote: "In the majority of cases, the criminal betrays himself by some abnormality attendant upon this pathological condition of the nervous tissues. His mental instability shows itself in various forms: an overweening vanity, leading him to brag of his achievement; a disproportionate sense of the importance of the offence, resulting from the hallucination of religion, and driving him to confession; egomania, producing the sense of horror or conviction of sin, and driving him to headlong flight without covering his tracks; a reckless confidence, resulting in the neglect of the most ordinary precautions, as in the case of Henry Wainwright, who left a boy in charge of the murdered woman's remains while he went to call a cab, or on the other hand, a nervous distrust of apperceptions in the past, causing him to revisit the scene of the crime to assure himself that all traces have been as safely removed as his own judgment knows them to be. *I will not hesitate to assert that a perfectly sane man, not intimidated by religious or other delusions, could always render himself perfectly secure from detection, provided, that is, that the crime were sufficiently premeditated and that he were not pressed for time or thrown out in his calculations by purely fortuitous coincidence.*

You know as well as I do, how far I have made this assertion good in practice. The two accidents which betrayed me, I could not by any possibility have foreseen. The first was the chance recognition of Levy by the girl in the Battersea Park Road, which suggested a connection between the two problems. The second was that Thipps should have arranged to go down to Denver on the Tuesday morning, thus enabling your mother to get word of the matter through to you before the body was removed by the police and to suggest a motive for the murder out of what she knew of my previous personal history. If I had been able to destroy these two accidentally forged links of circumstance, I will venture to say that you would never have so much as suspected me, still less obtained sufficient evidence to convict.

Of all human emotions, except perhaps those of hunger and fear, the sexual appetite produces the most violent, and, under some circumstances, the most persistent reactions; I think, however, I am right in saying that at the time when I wrote my book, my original sensual impulse to kill Sir Reuben Levy had already become profoundly modified by my habits of thought. To the animal lust to slay and the primitive human desire for revenge, there was added the rational intention of substantiating my own theories for the satisfaction of myself and the world. If all had turned out as I had planned, I should have deposited a sealed account of my experiment with the Bank of England, instructing my executors to publish it after my death. Now that accident has spoiled the completeness of my demonstration, I entrust the account to you, whom it cannot fail to interest, with the request that you will make it known among scientific men, in justice to my professional reputation.

The really essential factors of success in any undertaking are money and opportunity, and as a rule, the man who can make the first can make the second. During my early career, though I was fairly well-off, I had not absolute command of circumstance. Accordingly I devoted myself to my profession, and contented myself with keeping up a friendly connection with Reuben Levy and his family. This enabled me to remain in touch with his fortunes and interests, so that, when the moment for action should arrive, I might know what weapons to use.

Meanwhile, I carefully studied criminology in fiction and fact—my work on "Criminal Lunacy" was a side-product of this activity—and saw how, in every murder, the real crux of the problem was the disposal of the body. As a doctor, the means of death were always ready to my hand, and I was not likely to make any error in that connection. Nor was I likely to betray myself on account of any illusory sense of wrongdoing. The sole difficulty would be that of destroying all connection between my personality and that of the corpse. You will remember that Michael Finsbury, in Stevenson's entertaining romance, observes: "What hangs people is the unfortunate circumstance of guilt." It became clear to me that the mere leaving about of a superfluous corpse could convict nobody, provided that nobody was guilty in connection with that particular corpse. *Thus the idea of substituting the one body for the other was early arrived at, though it was not till I obtained the practical direction of St. Luke's Hospital that I found myself perfectly unfettered in the choice and handling of dead bodies. From this period on, I kept a careful watch on all the material brought in for dissection.*

My opportunity did not present itself until the week before Sir Reuben's disappearance, when the medical officer at the Chelsea workhouse sent word to me that an unknown vagrant had been injured that morning by the fall of a piece of scaffolding, and was exhibiting some very interesting nervous and cerebral reactions. I went round and saw the case, and was immediately struck by the man's strong superficial resemblance to Sir Reuben. He had been heavily struck on the back of the neck, dislocating the fourth and fifth cervical vertebae and heavily bruising the spinal cord. It seemed highly unlikely that he could ever recover, either mentally or physically, and in any case there appeared to me to be no object in indefinitely prolonging so unprofitable an existence. He had obviously been able to support life until recently, as he was fairly well nourished, but the state of his feet and clothing showed that he was unemployed, and under present conditions he was likely to remain so. I decided that he would suit my purpose very well, and immediately put in train certain transactions in the City which I had already sketched out in my own mind. In the meantime, the reactions mentioned by the workhouse doctor were interesting, and I made careful studies of them, and arranged for the delivery of the body to the hospital when I should have completed my preparations.

On the Thursday and Friday of that week I made private arrangements with various brokers to buy the stock of certain Peruvian Oil-fields, which had gone down almost to waste-paper. This part of my experiment did not cost me very much, but I contrived to arouse considerable curiosity, and even a mild excitement. At this point I was of course careful not to let my name appear. The incidence of Saturday and Sunday gave me some anxiety lest my man should after all die before I was ready for him, but by the use of saline injections I contrived to keep him alive and, late on Sunday night, he even manifested disquieting symptoms of at any rate a partial recovery.

On Monday morning the market in Peruvians opened briskly. Rumours had evidently got about that somebody knew something, and this day I was not the only buyer in the market. I bought a couple of hundred more shares in my own name, and left the mat-

ter to take care of itself. At lunch time I made my arrangements to run into Levy accidentally at the corner of the Mansion House. He expressed (as I expected) his surprise at seeing me in that part of London. I simulated some embarrassment and suggested that we should lunch together. I dragged him to a place a bit off the usual beat, and there ordered a good wine and drank of it as much as he might suppose sufficient to induce a confidential mood. I asked him how things were going on 'Change. He said, "Oh, all right," but appeared a little doubtful, and asked me whether I did anything in that way. I said I had a little flutter occasionally, and that, as a matter of fact, I'd been put on to rather a good thing. I glanced round apprehensively at this point, and shifted my chair nearer to his.

"I suppose you don't know anything about Peruvian Oil, do you?" he said.

I started and looked round again, and leaning across to him, said, dropping my voice:

"Well, I do, as a matter of fact, but I don't want it to get about. I stand to make a good bit on it."

"But I thought the thing was hollow," he said; "it hasn't paid a dividend for umpteen years."

"No," I said, "it hasn't, but it's going to. I've got inside information." He looked a bit unconvinced, and I emptied off my glass, and edged right up to his ear.

"Look here," I said, "I'm not giving this away to everyone, but I don't mind doing you and Christine a good turn. You know, I've always kept a soft place in my heart for her, ever since the old days. You got in ahead of me that time, and now it's up to me to heap coals of fire on you both."

I was a little excited by this time, and he thought I was drunk.

"It's very kind of you, old man," he said, "but I'm a cautious bird, you know, always was. I'd like a bit of proof."

And he shrugged up his shoulders and looked like a pawnbroker.

"I'll give it to you," I said, "but it isn't safe here. Come round to my place tonight after dinner, and I'll show you the report."

"How d'you get hold of it?" said he.

"I'll tell you tonight," said I. "Come round after dinner—any time after nine, say."

"To Harley Street?" he asked, and I saw that he meant coming.

"No," I said, "to Battersea—Prince of Wales Road; I've got some work to do at the hospital. And look here," I said, "don't you let on to a soul that you're coming. I bought a couple of hundred shares today, in my own name, and people are sure to get wind of it. If we're known to be about together, someone'll twig something. In fact, it's anything but safe talking about it in this place."

"All right," he said, "I won't say a word to anybody. I'll turn up about nine o'clock. You're sure it's a sound thing?"

"It can't go wrong," I assured him. And I meant it.

We parted after that, and I went round to the workhouse. My man had died at about eleven o'clock. I had seen him just after breakfast, and was not surprised. I completed the usual formalities with the workhouse authorities, and arranged for his delivery at the hospital at about seven o'clock.

In the afternoon, as it was not one of my days to be in Harley Street, I looked up an old friend who lives close to Hyde Park, and found that he was just off to Brighton on some business or other. I had tea with him, and saw him off by the 5.35 from Victoria. On issuing from the barrier it occurred to me to purchase an evening paper, and I thoughtlessly turned my steps to the bookstall. The usual crowds were rushing to catch suburban trains home, and on moving away I found myself involved in a contrary stream of travellers coming up out of the Underground, or bolting from all sides for the 5.45 to Battersea Park and Wandsworth Common. I disengaged myself after some buffeting and went home in a taxi; and it was not till I was safely seated there that I discovered some-body's gold-rimmed pince-nez involved in the astrakhan collar of

*my overcoat. The time from 6.15 to seven I spent concocting some-
thing to look like a bogus report for Sir Reuben.*

*At seven I went through to the hospital, and found the work-
house van just delivering my subject at the side door. I had him
taken straight up to the theatre, and told the attendant, William
Watts, that I intended to work there that night. I told him I would
prepare the body myself—the injection of a preservative would
have been a most regrettable complication. I sent him about his
business, and then went home and had dinner. I told my man that I
should be working in the hospital that evening, and that he could go
to bed at 10.30 as usual, as I could not tell whether I should be late or
not. He is used to my erratic ways. I only keep two servants in the
Battersea house—the man-servant and his wife, who cooks for me.
The rougher domestic work is done by a charwoman, who sleeps
out. The servants' bedroom is at the top of the house, overlooking
Prince of Wales Road.*

*As soon as I had dined I established myself in the hall with
some papers. My man had cleared dinner by a quarter past eight,
and I told him to give me the syphon and tantalus; and sent him
downstairs. Levy rang the bell at twenty minutes past nine, and I
opened the door to him myself. My man appeared at the other end
of the hall, but I called to him that it was all right, and he went
away. Levy wore an overcoat with evening dress and carried an
umbrella. "Why, how wet you are!" I said. "How did you come?"
"By 'bus," he said, "and the fool of a conductor forgot to put me
down at the end of the road. It's pouring cats and dogs and pitch-
dark—I couldn't see where I was." I was glad he hadn't taken a
taxi, but I had rather reckoned on his not doing so. "Your little
economies will be the death of you one of these days," I said. I was
right there, but I hadn't reckoned on their being the death of me as
well. I say again, I could not have foreseen it.*

*I sat him down by the fire, and gave him a whisky. He was in
high spirits about some deal in Argentines he was bringing off the*

next day. We talked money for about a quarter of an hour and then he said:

"Well, how about this Peruvian mare's-nest of yours?"

"It's no mare's-nest," I said; "come and have a look at it."

I took him upstairs into the library, and switched on the centre light and the reading lamp on the writing table. I gave him a chair at the table with his back to the fire, and fetched the papers I had been faking, out of the safe. He took them, and began to read them, poking over them in his short-sighted way, while I mended the fire. As soon as I saw his head in a favourable position I struck him heavily with the poker, just over the fourth cervical. It was delicate work calculating the exact force necessary to kill him without breaking the skin, but my professional experience was useful to me. He gave one loud gasp, and tumbled forward on to the table quite noiselessly. I put the poker back, and examined him. His neck was broken, and he was quite dead. I carried him into my bedroom and undressed him. It was about ten minutes to ten when I had finished. I put him away under my bed, which had been turned down for the night, and cleared up the papers in the library. Then I went downstairs, took Levy's umbrella, and let myself out at the hall door, shouting "Good-night" loudly enough to be heard in the basement if the servants should be listening. I walked briskly away down the street, went in by the hospital side door, and returned to the house noiselessly by way of the private passage. It would have been awkward if anybody had seen me then, but I leaned over the back stairs and heard the cook and her husband still talking in the kitchen. I slipped back into the hall, replaced the umbrella in the stand, cleared up my papers there, went up into the library and rang the bell. When the man appeared I told him to lock up everything except the private door to the hospital. I waited in the library until he had done so, and about 10.30 I heard both servants go up to bed. I waited a quarter of an hour longer and then went through to the dissecting-room. I wheeled one of the stretcher tables

*through the passage to the house door, and then went to fetch Levy.
It was a nuisance having to get him downstairs, but I had not liked
to make away with him in any of the ground-floor rooms, in case
my servant should take a fancy to poke his head in during the few
minutes that I was out of the house, or while locking up. Besides,
that was a flea-bite to what I should have to do later. I put Levy
on the table, wheeled him across to the hospital and substituted
him for my interesting pauper. I was sorry to have to abandon the
idea of getting a look at the latter's brain, but I could not afford to
incur suspicion. It was still rather early, so I knocked down a few
minutes getting Levy ready for dissection. Then I put my pauper on
the table and trundled him over to the house. It was now five past
eleven, and I thought I might conclude that the servants were in
bed. I carried the body into my bedroom. He was rather heavy, but
less so than Levy, and my Alpine experience had taught me how to
handle bodies. It is as much a matter of knack as of strength, and I
am, in any case, a powerful man for my height. I put the body into
the bed—not that I expected anyone to look in during my absence,
but if they should they might just as well see me apparently asleep
in bed. I drew the clothes a little over his head, stripped, and put on
Levy's clothes, which were fortunately a little big for me everywhere,
not forgetting to take his spectacles, watch and other oddments. At
a little before half-past eleven I was in the road looking for a cab.
People were just beginning to come home from the theatre, and I
easily secured one at the corner of Prince of Wales Road. I told the
man to drive me to Hyde Park Corner. There I got out, tipped him
well, and asked him to pick me up again at the same place in an
hour's time. He assented with an understanding grin, and I walked
on up Park Lane. I had my own clothes with me in a suitcase,
and carried my own overcoat and Levy's umbrella. When I got to
No. 9A there were lights in some of the top windows. I was very
nearly too early, owing to the old man's having sent the servants to
the theatre. I waited about for a few minutes, and heard it strike the*

quarter past midnight. The lights were extinguished shortly after, and I let myself in with Levy's key.

It had been my original intention, when I thought over this plan of murder, to let Levy disappear from the study or the dining-room, leaving only a heap of clothes on the hearthrug. The accident of my having been able to secure Lady Levy's absence from London, however, made possible a solution more misleading, though less pleasantly fantastic. I turned on the hall light, hung up Levy's wet overcoat and placed his umbrella in the stand. I walked up noisily and heavily to the bedroom and turned off the light by the duplicate switch on the landing. I knew the house well enough, of course. There was no chance of my running into the man-servant. Old Levy was a simple old man, who liked doing things for himself. He gave his valet little work, and never required any attendance at night. In the bedroom I took off Levy's gloves and put on a surgical pair, so as to leave no tell-tale finger-prints. As I wished to convey the impression that Levy had gone to bed in the usual way, I simply went to bed. The surest and simplest method of making a thing appear to have been done is to do it. A bed that has been rumpled about with one's hands, for instance, never looks like a bed that has been slept in. I dared not use Levy's brush, of course, as my hair is not of his colour, but I did everything else. I supposed that a thoughtful old man like Levy would put his boots handy for his valet, and I ought to have deduced that he would fold up his clothes. That was a mistake, but not an important one. Remembering that well-thought-out little work of Mr. Bentley's, I had examined Levy's mouth for false teeth, but he had none. I did not forget, however, to wet his tooth-brush.

At one o'clock I got up and dressed in my own clothes by the light of my own pocket torch. I dared not turn on the bedroom lights, as there were light blinds to the windows. I put on my own boots and an old pair of goloshes outside the door. There was a thick Turkey carpet on the stairs and hall-floor, and I was not afraid of leav-

ing marks. I hesitated whether to chance the banging of the front door, but decided it would be safer to take the latchkey. (It is now in the Thames. I dropped it over Battersea Bridge the next day.) I slipped quietly down, and listened for a few minutes with my ear to the letter-box. I heard a constable tramp past. As soon as his steps had died away in the distance I stepped out and pulled the door gingerly to. It closed almost soundlessly, and I walked away to pick up my cab. I had an overcoat of much the same pattern as Levy's, and had taken the precaution to pack an opera hat in my suitcase. I hoped the man would not notice that I had no umbrella this time. Fortunately the rain had diminished for the moment to a sort of drizzle, and if he noticed anything he made no observation. I told him to stop at 50 Overstrand Mansions, and I paid him off there, and stood under the porch till he had driven away. Then I hurried round to my own side door and let myself in. It was about a quarter to two, and the harder part of my task still lay before me.

My first step was so to alter the appearance of my subject as to eliminate any immediate suggestion either of Levy or of the work-house vagrant. A fairly superficial alteration was all I considered necessary, since there was not likely to be any hue-and-cry after the pauper. He was fairly accounted for, and his deputy was at hand to represent him. Nor, if Levy was after all traced to my house, would it be difficult to show that the body in evidence was, as a matter of fact, not his. A clean shave and a little hair-oiling and manicuring seemed sufficient to suggest a distinct personality for my silent accomplice. His hands had been well washed in hospital, and though calloused, were not grimy. I was not able to do the work as thoroughly as I should have liked, because time was getting on. I was not sure how long it would take me to dispose of him, and moreover, I feared the onset of rigor mortis, which would make my task more difficult. When I had him barbered to my satisfaction, I fetched a strong sheet and a couple of wide roller bandages, and fastened him up carefully, padding him with cotton wool wherever the bandages might chafe or leave a bruise.

Now came the really ticklish part of the business. I had already decided in my own mind that the only way of conveying him from the house was by the roof. To go through the garden at the back in this soft wet weather was to leave a ruinous trail behind us. To carry a dead man down a suburban street in the middle of the night seemed outside the range of practical politics. On the roof, on the other hand, the rain, which would have betrayed me on the ground, would stand my friend.

To reach the roof, it was necessary to carry my burden to the top of the house, past my servants' room, and hoist him out through the trapdoor in the box-room roof. Had it merely been a question of going quietly up there myself, I should have had no fear of waking the servants, but to do so burdened by a heavy body was more difficult. It would be possible, provided that the man and his wife were soundly asleep, but if not, the lumbering tread on the narrow stair and the noise of opening the trap-door would be only too plainly audible. I tiptoed delicately up the stair and listened at their door. To my disgust I heard the man give a grunt and mutter something as he moved in his bed.

I looked at my watch. My preparations had taken nearly an hour, first and last, and I dared not be too late on the roof. I determined to take a bold step and, as it were, bluff out an alibi. I went without precaution against noise into the bathroom, turned on the hot and cold water taps to the full and pulled out the plug.

My household has often had occasion to complain of my habit of using the bath at irregular night hours. Not only does the rush of water into the cistern disturb any sleepers on the Prince of Wales Road side of the house, but my cistern is afflicted with peculiarly loud gurglings and thumpings, while frequently the pipes emit a loud groaning sound. To my delight, on this particular occasion, the cistern was in excellent form, honking, whistling and booming like a railway terminus. I gave the noise five minutes' start, and when I calculated that the sleepers would have finished cursing me and put their heads under the clothes to shut out the din, I reduced the flow of water to a small stream and left the bathroom, taking good care to leave the light burning and lock the door after me. Then I picked up my pauper and carried him upstairs as lightly as possible.

The box-room is a small attic on the side of the landing opposite to the servants' bedroom and the cistern-room. It has a trapdoor, reached by a short, wooden ladder. I set this up, hoisted up my pauper and climbed up after him. The water was still racing into the cistern, which was making a noise as though it were trying to digest an iron chain, and with the reduced flow in the bathroom the groaning of the pipes had risen almost to a hoot. I was not afraid of anybody hearing other noises. I pulled the ladder through on to the roof after me.

Between my house and the last house in Queen Caroline Mansions there is a space of only a few feet. Indeed, when the Mansions were put up, I believe there was some trouble about ancient lights, but I suppose the parties compromised somehow. Anyhow, my seven-foot ladder reached well across. I tied the body firmly to the ladder, and pushed it over till the far end was resting on the parapet of the opposite house. Then I took a short run across the cistern-room and the box-room roof, and landed easily on the other side, the parapet being happily both low and narrow.

The rest was simple. I carried my pauper along the flat roofs, intending to leave him, like the hunchback in the story, on someone's staircase or down a chimney. I had got about half-way along when I suddenly thought, "Why, this must be about little Thipps's place," and I remembered his silly face, and his silly chatter about vivisection. It occurred to me pleasantly how delightful it would be to deposit my parcel with him and see what he made of it. I lay down and peered over the parapet at the back. It was pitch-dark and pouring with rain again by this time, and I risked using my torch. That was the only incautious thing I did, and the odds against being seen from the houses opposite were long enough. One second's flash showed me what I had hardly dared to hope—an open window just below me.

I knew those flats well enough to be sure it was either the bathroom or the kitchen. I made a noose in a third bandage that I had brought with me, and made it fast under the arms of the corpse. I twisted it into a double rope, and secured the end to the iron stanchion of a chimney-stack. Then I dangled our friend over. I went down after him myself with the aid of a drainpipe and was soon hauling him in by Thipps's bathroom window.

By that time I had got a little conceited with myself, and spared a few minutes to lay him out prettily and make him shipshape. A sudden inspiration suggested that I should give him the pair of pince-nez which I had happened to pick up at Victoria. I came across them in my pocket while I was looking for a penknife to loosen a knot, and I saw what distinction they would lend his appearance, besides making it more misleading. I fixed them on him, effaced all traces of my presence as far as possible, and departed as I had come, going easily up between the drainpipe and the rope.

I walked quietly back, re-crossed my crevasse and carried in my ladder and sheet. My discreet accomplice greeted me with a reassuring gurgle and thump. I didn't make a sound on the stairs. Seeing that I had now been having a bath for about three-quarters of an hour, I turned the water off, and enabled my deserving domestics to get a little sleep. I also felt it was time I had a little myself.

First, however, I had to go over to the hospital and make all safe there. I took off Levy's head, and started to open up the face. In twenty minutes his own wife could not have recognised him. I returned, leaving my wet goloshes and mackintosh by the garden door. My trousers I dried by the gas stove in my bedroom, and

*brushed away all traces of mud and brickdust. My pauper's beard
I burned in the library.*

*I got a good two hours' sleep from five to seven, when my man
called me as usual. I apologized for having kept the water running
so long and so late, and added that I thought I would have the
cistern seen to.*

*I was interested to note that I was rather extra hungry at
breakfast, showing that my night's work had caused a certain
wear-and-tear of tissue. I went over afterwards to continue my
dissection. During the morning a peculiarly thick-headed police
inspector came to inquire whether a body had escaped from the
hospital. I had him brought to me where I was, and had the pleasure
of showing him the work I was doing on Sir Reuben Levy's head.
Afterwards I went round with him to Thipps's and was able to
satisfy myself that my pauper looked very convincing.*

*As soon as the Stock Exchange opened I telephoned my vari-
ous brokers, and by exercising a little care, was able to sell out the
greater part of my Peruvian stock on a rising market. Towards the
end of the day, however, buyers became rather unsettled as a result
of Levy's death, and in the end I did not make more than a few
hundreds by the transaction.*

*Trusting I have now made clear to you any point which you
may have found obscure, and with congratulations on the good
fortune and perspicacity which have enabled you to defeat me, I
remain, with kind remembrances to your mother,*

Yours very truly,
Julian Freke

POST-SCRIPTUM: *My will is made, leaving my money to St.
Luke's Hospital, and bequeathing my body to the same institution
for dissection. I feel sure that my brain will be of interest to the
scientific world. As I shall die by my own hand, I imagine that there*

may be a little difficulty about this. Will you do me the favour, if you can, of seeing the persons concerned in the inquest, and obtaining that the brain is not damaged by an unskilful practitioner at the post-mortem, and that the body is disposed of according to my wish?

By the way, it may be of interest to you to know that I appreciated your motive in calling this afternoon. It conveyed a warning, and I am acting upon it in spite of the disastrous consequences to myself. I was pleased to realize that you had not underestimated my nerve and intelligence, and refused the injection. Had you submitted to it, you would, of course, never have reached home alive. No trace would have been left in your body of the injection, which consisted of a harmless preparation of strychnine, mixed with an almost unknown poison, for which there is at present no recognised test, a concentrated solution of sn—

At this point the manuscript broke off.

"Well, that's all clear enough," said Parker.

"Isn't it queer?" said Lord Peter. "All that coolness, all those brains—and then he couldn't resist writing a confession to show how clever he was, even to keep his head out of the noose."

"And a very good thing for us," said Inspector Sugg, "but Lord bless you, sir, these criminals are all alike."

"Freke's epitaph," said Parker, when the inspector had departed. "What next, Peter?"

"I shall now give a dinner party," said Lord Peter, "to Mr. John P. Milligan and his secretary and to Messrs. Crimplesham and Wicks. I feel they deserve it for not having murdered Levy."

"Well, don't forget the Thippses," said Mr. Parker.

"On no account," said Lord Peter, "would I deprive myself of the pleasure of Mrs. Thipps's company. Bunter!"

"My lord?"

"The Napoleon brandy."

HB 07.28.2021 0930

THE WRIGHT SISTER

D0061514

THE
WRIGHT
SISTER

a novel

PATTY DANN

HARPER ● PERENNIAL

NEW YORK ● LONDON ● TORONTO ● SYDNEY ● NEW DELHI ● AUCKLAND

HARPER ● PERENNIAL

This book is a work of fiction. References to real people, events, establishments, organizations, or locales are intended only to provide a sense of authenticity and are used fictitiously. All other characters, and all incidents and dialogue, are drawn from the author's imagination and are not to be construed as real.

P.S.™ is a trademark of HarperCollins Publishers.

THE WRIGHT SISTER. Copyright © 2020 by Patty Dann. All rights reserved. Printed in the United States of America. No part of this book may be used or reproduced in any manner whatsoever without written permission except in the case of brief quotations embodied in critical articles and reviews. For information, address Harper-Collins Publishers, 195 Broadway, New York, NY 10007.

HarperCollins books may be purchased for educational, business, or sales promotional use. For information, please email the Special Markets Department at SPsales@harpercollins.com.

FIRST EDITION

Designed by Jen Overstreet

Library of Congress Cataloging-in-Publication Data has been applied for.

ISBN 978-0-06-299311-3

20 21 22 23 24 LSC 10 9 8 7 6 5 4 3 2

For my mother,
1925–2020

Preface

WINTER WINGS! WRIGHT SISTER WEDS AT 50!
November 21, 1926

NOVEMBER 21, 1926

The paper was incorrect. I was not fifty. On November 20, 1926, I was fifty-two when I got married for the first and only time to Harry Haskell. But my brother Orv, with whom I share a birthday, refused to attend the festivities. This was just yesterday, at 4:00 p.m. When Orv heard of my upcoming nuptials last year, he smashed the blue-and-white Limoges china pitcher full of daisies against the wall of our summerhouse on Lake Huron. Everyone in the world knows Orv as the Wright brother who has a mustache and wears zigzag socks, ones that I knit every year with the soft yarn from the sheep outside of Dayton he insists upon, because of his sensitive feet. The flowers scattered like an exploded bridal bouquet as the water and bits of china littered the floor.

It has occurred to me more than once that although Orv is brilliant, ingenious, extraordinary, and able to study the subtle arc of a seagull's wings and to create an invention that has changed the entire planet, unfortunately, he might also be insane. I do not say such a thing lightly or with any disrespect. I love Orv in what some say is an uncommon love. But I think all love is uncommon if it is worth its salt.

I am calling this diary my "marriage diary," as conjugal life is such a new adventure for me. I do not know how I will fare with this curious tie that binds. This diary is nothing fancy, just a worn, toffee-colored notebook I have saved from my Oberlin days. There's a nifty envelope inside the back cover where I keep some precious drawings of my scribbles and designs. I did have some French verbs in the first pages, but I have torn those out. My penmanship remains steady from my years as a schoolteacher. I still dot my i's precisely, and I can still do line after line of perfect o's, except when my fingers are cold. I am writing in the most beautiful heron-blue ink that Orv gave me as a Christmas gift just two

years ago, when my life seemed to be quite humdrum after years of living with the "Most Famous Brothers to Ever Leave the Earth." I keep the diary in a locked box with copies of letters I have begun to write to Orv, not that I imagine Harry or the housemaid would be interested.

I vow to take these new seasons of my life, fall and winter, and begin anew, to be bold where I have been timid and strong where I have hesitated. I have always been a woman of science and scholarly pursuits along with my work for the rights of women. But in my new life, I hope to be able to write some truths about another kind of Wrights: secrets both professional and personal, aspects that have been previously hidden. We discussed much in the Wright household, but there was much we did not say. It will not come easily to me to reveal what was for so long concealed, as I am the Reverend's daughter.

Have to go meet Harry's friends for drinks—more tomorrow.

KANSAS CITY, HERE I AM

I married Harry, a journalist for the Kansas City Star, *a smart and talky widower. We're head over heels for each other, even though his collar is often still wet from tears he sheds for his first wife, Isabel. I wore a cream-colored gown and new silk undergarments for our wedding at Oberlin College, from which we both graduated in the last decade of the nineteenth century. Harry was and still is fifty-two as well, but nobody has batted an eye at that.*

I'd bought the Limoges pitcher Orv smashed on our trip to Paris in 1908. Will, Orv, and I were there showing an admiring and amazed world our new invention. And Orv had picked those daisies for me when he took his morning bird-counting walk only hours before his violent display. He has not spoken a word to me since that horrible smashing last year, not by telegram, post, or telephone.

It was not I but Harry who ended up giving Orville news of our engagement, that day of his furious outburst, and since then he has remained living in the big house with every modern convenience in Dayton, Ohio, the house we had moved to with Father, a bishop in the United Brethren Church, after all the success and hoopla about the aeroplane. Now only Orv remains there with our housekeeper, capable Carrie Kayler, six hundred miles away from my Kansas City residence, as the crow flies. "Not a crow!" I hear Orv's voice shouting in my ear, even though he is stone silent. "I detest crows, sister. A red-winged blackbird is a much more interesting bird."

WRIGHT SISTER OVER THE MOON

I am over the moon about Harry, but I still imagine I hear Orv shouting at me in moments that should be serene, while I am in the bath or baking a batch of walnut brownies, his favorite, although he has become like a ghost in the tales that he and Will used to scare the dickens out of me with. When he was in a good mood, Orv called me Swes or Sterchens, from schwesterchen, *German for "little sister." I say called because our life together feels hidden in the past tense. Orv's voice could be as gentle as a cooing dove or as cruel as a squawking blue jay. The unpredictability of his moods made me walk around holding my breath. Not the way I was around the Reverend. That was more blind fear.*

It does not seem right to finally, shockingly, fall in love at this stage of life and lose the love of one's own brother. Truthfully, I have never heard of this happening to anybody, not anyone I have encountered or read about in novels, in English or in French. I have heard of people being disowned for some unspeakable sin, of course—for having a child out of wedlock, for committing adultery—but there is no sin (as sinful as I sometimes feel) in my marriage. Our love is not out of wedlock.

Tomorrow Harry is giving me a bicycle tour of our neighborhood.

PREACHER'S KID MARRIES PREACHER'S KID

Harry and I are both the grown children—very grown—of men of the cloth; we're PKs, as we say, as is Orv, of course.

Harry and Orv always got along before. I do not think Harry felt superior in any way because he went to college and my brothers did not. As he said, "Eli Whitney and Henry Ford started out as farm boys. They certainly could have taught us Oberliners a thing or two." And I do not think Orv felt superior to Harry because of the aeroplane. They were friends. There was no doubt about that. We had all known one another for years and were friends with Isabel as well.

First Husband, Second Wife

Does Harry have any flaws? We all do, of course. I would say the one thing I am beyond unaccustomed to is his mess of papers. I secretly and sometimes not so secretly refer to him as the "Paper Monster." If there is a surface—and there are: the kitchen table, the dining room table, our bed—it becomes instantly covered with newspapers and books the moment he enters the room. I am so used to Orv's neat way of doing everything, his cataloging and arranging, a trait that causes other people alarm but is so familiar to me. But this marriage business is all a fine howdy-do at this point. I've left the house of one man and gone to live with another. As Will used to say when we were sewing the wings, "We'll just have to see if this machine can fly."

Have to make pumpkin, apple, and pecan pies tonight. Must ask Orv to send me at least two of Mother's pie tins.

Dear Orv, Orv dear,

If this paper is stained, I cannot help myself, for I have been weeping on the typewriter. I just had my first Thanksgiving as Mrs. Harry Haskell, and I love Harry so, but there was a point during the dinner, with him and his son, and without you, when the maid spilled gravy in my lap, I believe on purpose, and I thought I would leap from the table. Being a second wife is not for the faint of heart.

We had our meal at noon, and by that I mean we were at the table at 11:45 in the morning, which of course is beyond ridiculous. I barely had recovered from breakfast. I love an evening meal, the way we always did, but it seems that the first Mrs. Haskell had a noon Thanksgiving dinner and that is that.

Harry's grown son is nice enough, a fine young man, as Mother would say, also a journalist, but there was not the joking or singing I am accustomed to, and there was a prayer before the meal, which felt familiar, but we all held hands, which of course we never did. I was holding Harry's lovely hand to my right and his son's to my left, and I just felt like I would start giggling, like we were about to play ring-around-the-rosy. My emotions are off-kilter, like someone has tossed me in a barrel over Niagara Falls.

Speaking of which, most of my mail seems to be forwarded to me here in Kansas City, but please send me anything that ends up in Dayton. Can you believe part of Kansas City is in Kansas and part in Missouri? Already there is something wrong here. I am in Missouri, which I have to remind myself daily. Some of the mail I've received is clearly for you as well, from people who have not caught up with my nuptial news. Yesterday I opened a letter from a gentleman, addressed to "The Wright Sister," inquiring whether we would both like to take a trip in a barrel over the falls.

"Dear Mr. Wright and His sister," he addressed it. I think "His" was capitalized as if you were royalty. I think it's the same crazed man who sent a similar invitation eight years ago, but I don't have my files to check. You could—they are in the tall filing cabinets in the study. They are chronological, except if there is a correspondence with one person, which will be in a separate folder marked in blue ink. It is strange not to be having this conversation with you face-to-face, not to laugh or fume about it together in the same room.

And you, my dearest brother? What did you do for Thanksgiving? Did you sit at the table with Carrie? I cannot imagine you having Thanksgiving alone. I made apple, pumpkin, and pecan pies, and the maid made some kind of dry raisin and nut bread I could not abide. You would have said, "Perhaps this was meant to be for gluing kites," as you did one time when a raspberry tart I had made failed. Please tell me everything. I am also heartsick that I did not vote in this recent election. I will have to register to vote here in Kansas City, but I do not yet have my sea legs. I don't know if I ever told you, but that first triumphant day, when I had the privilege of voting in 1920, while I was waiting in line to vote for our Ohio man Harding, a dreadful character came by and spit on my shoes! I was horrified. As if I didn't have the right to be there. I never told you because I was ashamed, but now that you and I are apart, in some sense I believe I want to confide in you more. I wonder why that would be. Perhaps Dr. Freud would have an opinion on that, although I know you are not a disciple.

I am obviously a bit blue, but a word from you would change my color.

Love,
Your only sister, K., who is a bit all over the map.

P.S. All those months when I still lived at home, yet knew I would be marrying Harry, it was like living with a specter, Orville Wright, an impossible specter, who would not say boo, I might add.

Harry Haskell Is a Rascal

I have been married for ten days. I have a hus-band. *I say that over and over like it's two words,* hus-band, hus-band. *Harry's lips turn down slightly whenever I talk about Orv, which is too much!*

I feel my life has been like an endless series of musical chairs, a game most people love as children, although it always set off a sentiment of excited dread in me, from the first time I played. Will and Orv would walk hurriedly around the chairs set up in a circle in the parlor, while I would play the piano, but if a friend was over and played, I would walk around the chairs as if I were going to meet my doom, because when the music stopped, the boys would shriek and grab for chairs, crashing fiercely into anyone in their path, including myself, as if I were but a piece of furniture. I do not yearn for a game of musical chairs just now. I plan to get involved with the women's movement here in Kansas City and make real change as I did in Dayton, but I have to get settled first. In my mind I hear the boys racing, racing around the parlor, grabbing at seats. I do not know why God insists on taking away the chairs. I know far too many chairs have been taken from people I have loved very much. I pray I have many years on this hallowed earth.

Tomorrow I'm going to get my Missouri library card! One must have priorities. And I am going to attend Isabel's book group. They are reading The Private Life of Helen of Troy, *which was published last year and which I have already read, but perhaps there will be a lively discussion.*

Dear Orv, Orv dear,

I hope this box of rock candy arrives intact. I let the strings stand in the sugar water from before the wedding so that I can hear you saying, "Stalactites! Stalagmites! Do you think I'm a caveman, sister?"

And while we, or should I say I, am on the subject of food, two nights ago, Harry did the wildest thing. He likes to cook outdoors! Something we certainly never did in Dayton. And even now in December. He says he does it year-round, which I have yet to see. There is no snow yet, but still, he was out there with his overcoat and gloves on and with a grill he had put over a fireplace out back, and he was making steaks. He marched in, bringing the cold with him. And then at the table I protested: "I can't eat this much, really!"

But I'm a changed woman. I was excited by the cold, and those steaks were the most delicious things I'd ever eaten. Father would certainly have given me his lecture on "untoward appetites."

I have a question for you. Have you ever been drunk? Even with this Prohibition, Harry does seem to drink a lot, and I have been joining him, not as much as he or the men at the office, but I quite like it. Gin. That's what I like, with some fizzy soda.

Carrie called and said you did not even want a turkey for Thanksgiving this year but insisted that the vegetable soup from the day before would suffice, and she said you barely ate that. I know she made a turkey, and it was there in the icebox, so I hope it did not go to waste.

I miss your homemade toffee and the mandolin that I used to complain about. I am sorry if I ever mocked you in any way.

I hope your hip is not causing too much pain these days. Please let Carrie know if you want me to visit. I shall be there in a flash. And I shall bake you whatever you please. The women here take such

pride in their baked goods. I do not object to their fancy cakes, but it is not what I value most in life.

In haste,
Your devoted and only sister, K., who is getting plump.

P.S. I'm sending you some postcards of the Hannibal Bridge, the railway bridge. They're very proud of it—the first railway bridge to cross the Missouri River! I know how you like bridges, and if Hannibal could cross the Alps on elephants, then you can make this journey!

P.P.S. Men like women to wrangle among ourselves, calling us suffragettes or suffragists or worse, but whatever the label, my boy, women have the vote now and I vote that you write me immediately.

WRIGHT SISTER TORN BETWEEN TWO MEN

Even though my union with Harry is so new, I hope to be as excited to see him each time he enters the room as I am now, and on until the middle of the twentieth century, until I am a truly old woman. "Winter Flight," indeed, as if I were a hundred years old, but I have not yet gone through the Change. I do not feel old. Maybe because I became "Sister" when I was so young, I always felt that I was old as a child and now am young as an adult when I am Katharine again. I once saw a freak like that at the Ohio State Fair, a child who looked like an old woman, with a wrinkled face and hands, dressed up, sitting on a rocking chair. Orv and Will used to talk about inventing a time machine. They believed without a doubt that someday it would be invented. The fact that I am married makes me think I am actually on such a machine, being born in the horse-and-buggy days in Dayton and now a married woman with an automobile, a Model T, in Kansas City.

True, I "never was a beauty," as I heard the Reverend say to the most inappropriate people—neighbors, a friend of his from seminary, and once to a woman's face that I cannot place. I do need stronger and stronger eyeglasses, and I am not doing handsprings as I did as a child, but I do not feel I am in the winter of my life. At our small wedding party, a woman friend of Harry and Isabel's looked me up and down and said with a feigned smile, "It is good for Harry to have companionship at this stage of life." I had to hold my hands tightly behind my back to keep from laughing out loud. Companionship! As if we were old dogs lying by the fire! There have been a few times we have lain by the fire, and we were not clothed. Perhaps I should have told this woman, "Madame, I

can assure you, we are more than companions," but I clenched my teeth and did not.

At Oberlin there was a girl who had a book of drawings she'd brought back from France, where she had worked as a summer tutor for a family with three children. The father was blind, and each summer he chose a different tutor because he did not want his wife getting "too attached" to the tutor, whether male or female. We laughed at all those drawings at the time, but now Harry and I do all of those positions—well, almost all. In that French book was a picture of some sort of acrobatics on the stairs, a complicated drawing that looked like one would require a trapeze installed in one's home, that I think neither of us would recover from at this point.

Right now, I am sitting up in my bed, our bed, which was once Isabel's, covered with white down comforters, looking out at a yard full of bare-limbed maple trees. I do take delight in the dance of sunlight on the trees, and if I squint, I can pretend I live in a tree house. Harry and I play a game of running up and down the stairs to greet each other. We whistle to each other, and the other always answers back, a conversation in song, as Harry says. Harry says that he and I are not human at all, but birds. Both Orv and Harry love birds, so I know Orv will be friendly again. We entertained Harry and Isabel at the house, for goodness' sakes. Will was the best whistler in our house, although I wouldn't say that to Orv's face. As close as those boys were, the competitive spirit was evident even in which boy dressed the quickest (it was also Will). My mind is darting all over the place, like the milkweed pods we used to blow on as children, as I try to find my bearings in this house. We all used to run up and down the stairs at home in Dayton. Once, Orv and Will fashioned a kind of pulley with a toboggan that banged horribly to send things up and down—not made for humans, although we had our go at that. The Reverend certainly never let us slide down the banister the way other children did, but once outside, we had complete sovereignty over that yard, which was full of the boys' clutter of bicycles and machines.

Many times, since I left Dayton, I have picked up the telephone and slowly dialed 0 for the operator to call Orv. I cannot control my longings and myself. And many times, I have heard the Dayton operator's voice

and I feel I am almost home, hearing that accent that of course a French-man would not hear as being Daytonian, but I know clear as day is not a Kansas City twang. "And what number would you like? And who is calling, please?" the operator always says, because people in Ohio are polite. I have rudely hung up on the kind operators each time. I don't think I have ever hung up on anyone in my life before, or slammed a door, or certainly thrown a vase. That is Orv's department.

But long-distance telephone calls are expensive. Sundays are the best, and station-to-station is cheaper, but then we have to pay if anyone answers. I usually call person-to-person and ask for Orv, and I don't have to pay unless he comes to the phone. Still, my longing is such that sometimes I call station-to-station and at least have a chat with Carrie, with hopes that she can unbend Orv's mind. Harry doesn't like the bills, but he knows it helps keep my sanity. As he says with a grin, "No man wants an addled bride." And I did bring some money of my own to this marriage.

I made a chart today, diagramming the Reverend's house at 7 Haw-thorn Street, then the big house, and now my house in KC, as they call it. Three homes, run by three men, and I have drawn a picture of each man, the Reverend, Orv, and now Harry, at the top sitting on the roofs of the houses. And then I drew a tightrope between the big house to the drawing of our house in Kansas City. Tomorrow I shall draw myself as well, walking the tightrope, carrying a parasol, walking very carefully.

Dear Orv,

Rejoice on this hallowed day. I feel close to you even though six hundred miles separate us. I had a delightful conversation with Carrie, who says you plan to be with us at some point in January of the New Year. I know you are not one for holidays, so any time in January will be fine. We shall keep the fires going to keep your sensitive feet warm. You are welcome to stay as long as you like (forever!). I shall begin making preparations.

In anticipation of your visit. Merry Christmas and happy 1927. May this year be full of clear skies!
K.

P.S. I have been thinking recently that Mother was never in an automobile, let alone an aeroplane, and to think Ford sold his first automobile just months before Kitty Hawk. Too much change, Orv, too much change.

P.P.S. Do you still think of yourself as part of the "Wright brothers"? I wish we could have had walk-and-talks with those other famous boys, like the Smith brothers from Quebec. I have a bowl of their cherry cough drops by my bedside. And then there was poor Vincent and his brother Theo. I wish I could have given Vincent some of these cough drops. I always felt I could have helped that boy. I was almost sixteen when he took his own life. I remember us all reading about it some years later when his paintings had become famous, and I cannot remember if it was you or Will who said, "Another poor minister's son."

Birthday Twins

To share the very same day of birth—August 19, in the heart of mid-western summer—although we are of course not really twins, is to share a soul. Surely Orv must still feel that in some part of his brain or being. We were told repeatedly as children by the Reverend, and twice by fortune-tellers we met on our American and European travels, that because we were born on the same day, then our bond is sacred. He was born in the small house at 7 Hawthorn in Dayton, and I was born on Orv's third birthday, in the same house, where the boys later raced their bicycles and tinkered with their inventions. Will had been born four years before Orv, but not on our birthday. He had one of his own. People in town just called them the "Bishop's Boys." We had two older brothers, Reuchlin and Lorin, but it felt like they were of another family and the public was not interested in them. There was a whole noisy world in that small house, as if we lived in a magnificent melon of music and laughter and an explosion of ideas, even with our weary sorrows. The Reverend was not an easy man to live with. Outside the house he was revered, as the word "reverend" suggests. Some men are different at home. I would not dare to utter that aloud if he were still alive, but I do feel free to write it here. As I try to make sense of this strange situation, I realize it is not true that I do not know a single person who was cut off from her family at her choice of husband. There was a girl at Oberlin, Mary, whose parents refused to speak to her because she married a man of the Jewish faith. I remember being so stunned at the time that a family could be so mean. This was in the 1890s, last century, as the young folks say, but still. I just couldn't believe one's own family wouldn't attend a wedding or even

speak to you again for finding love. It was I who consoled her and even attended the wedding. If our lives were a novel, one would say this was some kind of foreshadowing, but this is true life. Mary's wedding was in a very ornate dance hall. In fact, the ceremony itself had to be outside, because Jewish law said the vows had to be made under the sky! So we all marched outside after the sun set on Saturday and they got married under a canopy held up by some strong, handsome men. How wonderful to say one must get married under the sky. Will and Orv would have liked that, I should think, but I don't recall that they showed much interest when I told them at the time. Mary changed her name to Rachel and converted to her husband's faith. She spent hours poring over Hebrew texts in our house at college. I found it quite fascinating. And how we all loved the notion that she was supposed to make love with her husband on the Sabbath. I think the only surprising (I won't even say shocking) thing to me, a reverend's daughter, was that their Sabbath was on Saturday. The idea one is supposed to make love on a certain day was something I found quite titillating. I was happy to be there for my friend. Only one other member of our class was there, our friend the beautiful Sonya Rose, who is also Jewish, who left soon after because she was with child, but nobody from Mary/Rachel's family was there, not one soul.

Tomorrow night Harry is taking me to a jazz club, my first! Orv and I never went to such things, and of course the Reverend would not approve. "The sins of the father" is all I can say at the moment. The sounds in the house on 7 Hawthorn were music, laughter, and some screams. I could not identify all the sounds, the little murmurings, from the Reverend's room.

(I graciously resigned from Isabel's book group. I much prefer reading books on my own, without the chitchat. And there are only so many times one can listen to a woman look over her glasses and say, "Isabel was always such an important part of this gathering.")

19

SPINSTER NO MORE

It has been more than two months since I became Mrs. Harry Haskell and I cannot recall my last real conversation with Orv, nor can I remember the last time I held my beloved mother's hand. The ponds are frozen solid now, and Harry said this weekend we shall go ice-skating, which I've always loved!

There was nothing untoward or flirtatious when Harry first arrived on the island. After all, Orv had signed off on his visit. I wish I could recall, because there's even a chance that it was he who suggested to me that Harry visit us. It was not Orv who usually made social engagements, but life at the lake was different. In any event, no invitations were made unless Orv approved them, and he was as unpredictable as he was firm in his choices.

Orv had a system, as he did with most things. He liked to hear my suggestions at breakfast, so that if I proposed a guest come to the island over pancakes, which I might have done with Harry, then he always told me at dinner whether he approved. If he did, he would simply say, as he had done with Harry, "What day is Harry Haskell arriving?" and then I knew to make the invitation. Orv would also write it on an index card he would then catalog in his special filing system along with the previous years' calendars.

As the three of us walked the paths in the summer air, Orv mostly wanted to talk about birds, his birds, meaning the meticulous notebooks in which he recorded every bird he ever saw and the other ones full of his beautiful drawings of their wings along with his computations.

But on this day, at 3:30 p.m.—I know because I'd just checked the

clock in the hall—Orv was in the study reading his book of North American birds, writing in the margins as he always did, with the pencils he insisted I sharpen (although not too much, but just enough), when the kiss happened. Harry's lips pressed up through the cold mesh. That first kiss was the first time I felt shot through with sensations I had never known from a man's touch before. When I had gone up with Orv—that was what Orv called flying, "going up"—that was similar. Then too I felt the rush of the sky and the land pulling away from me at the same time, almost like the ocean pulling away as you stand on the sand. Going up and having Harry inside me are two very similar sensations.

Rocking the Boat

I am trying to figure out how I ended up in Kansas City! When I cannot sleep, which as I say is every night, I think of my husband's arms, the way they wrap around me in the morning, and then I reach for him and cannot believe he is still there. But I want to recall that first kiss, for it seems so recent.

We, Orv and I, had been spending summers at Lambert Island, "the island," as we called it. The other three seasons we were at the big house in Dayton. Carrie was always with us.

How did Harry and I tumble into love? How was it possible? I never saw my brothers fall in love with anything but their beloved machines. I had no experience in the ways of the heart, either a man's heart or my own. They say that widowed men often cannot live on their own, but I have not read the research on the effect of a sister leaving her brother to wed.

The Reverend never showed an inclination to remarry after Mother's death, although there were neighbors and parishioners delivering more covered dishes than we could have eaten, even with our icebox. But there were strange foods I had never seen before, women visiting, scenting our kitchen with unfamiliar perfumes.

A woman with unnaturally large eyes brought beef and noodle covered dishes every Sunday after services for several months. I saw the Reverend standing at the icebox once, red-faced, spooning the cold casserole, and his trousers were unbuttoned, but I silently withdrew up the stairs, and he did not see me. There were several nights, after the condolence callers had retreated, that I just scraped the food out back for the birds and raccoons.

I admit I was ill at ease, trying to imagine what Orv would say, when

Harry asked me to marry him. I was always "on my toes" with him, but it was a more heightened "on my toes"—ness than ever before. I do not recall that there was even a formal marriage proposal. Harry and I were out in a canoe on the lake one blowy afternoon, just the two of us, which did not happen much because Orv always seemed to be with us. I do not recall where Orv was. Harry was at the stern. I was at the bow, and at one point I paddled and feathered the way I had learned from Orv, and I turned to look at Harry and he was just sitting there grinning, with his paddle on his lap. That was the moment we both knew that we had to be together. In that moment I also knew Orv would be alarmed by any change in his daily life. He is someone who would have a fit if his polished left shoe was placed to the right of his right shoe in his closet.

Tomorrow morning, when Harry leaves for the paper, I am going to take a long walk in the snow.

WRIGHT SISTER OR MRS. HARRY HASKELL?

The six hundred miles between Dayton and Kansas City have sent Orv over the edge, but he was over the edge before that. I did not move to Kansas City right away. There were many months. He had time to adjust, although I am having trouble too, as I feel like an Ohio woman in my bones. The house is full of books and papers and passions that Harry shared with Isabel and now shares with me. There are still photographs of Isabel and Harry together throughout the house, a picture on the mantel of them with their son sitting on a pony when he was little. We both understand we cannot take away the stories of our lives before we wed. Harry came to me with his stories, and I came to him with mine, but sometimes the green-eyed demon attacks me, and I am overcome. When I watch Harry take off his shirt and hang it on the bedpost before we are together, or after lovemaking, when he is stroking my back, I want to scream, "Did you do this with your darling Isabel? Did you hang your shirt just so on the bedpost? Did you stroke her this way?" But I don't. I sigh and try to think of other things, like when I used to go up with Orv in the plane and he tied my skirt around my legs so it would not blow or get twisted, or when we were in Paris and it was not only my brothers who received invitations from royalty to go on boat rides on the Seine. The jealousy wells up and I put the pillow in front of my mouth so I do not scream at Harry. I know jealousy is a sin, and I know it is one of mine far too often for a woman with my education.

It was Orv himself who told me once when he was working on a bicycle in the shop, "Sister, life can never be equal. Wings must be equal. But love is not."

Where did Orv learn about love is what I would like to know.

We never discussed love with the Reverend. I do not know if he loved our beloved mother. I cannot recall the word "love" ever uttered in our home.

I think some of Orv's bad mood is because of his constant sense of shame about the war. Not that he caused it. It was the notion that this magnificent flying machine he created would be in any way a participant in violence. I sat with him in the movie theater and watched those newsreels. We both saw that boy who used to work in the pharmacy, now home, having to be wheeled in a wheelbarrow by his mother. I would study Orv's face and I could see his horror, and at times he would mutter that it was his aeroplane to blame, even though he knew trench warfare caused the most deaths. There was a boy who worked in the hardware store before the war, always cheerful, running up and down the aisles: "Mr. Wright, sir, how can I help you, sir?" And when he returned with one arm gone, he was back at the store but behind the counter with a dull look in his eyes, and he did not call Orv "sir" or anything at all.

And now I am dizzy. I think I drifted off. The one time I asked Harry if we could take down Isabel's photograph, he looked so sad, stricken almost, like a little boy I'd asked if I could take away his toy train, so I immediately took back my words. I know he misses her and their life terribly, and after all, they had a son together. Our passion does not create children. Our passion creates screams and flushed cheeks and tenderness. Once the boys started working on more than bicycles, I knew I never would become a mother. There was one moment I was at the kitchen sink, washing dishes after yet another dinner for our friends who had come over for a night of music and singing and arguing about whether man would ever fly. I'd made a pot roast and several peach pies with the lattice tops everyone preferred. I was scrubbing the baking pan and had gristle from the meat under my fingernails. I saw the boys out in the yard in the moonlight, trying to rig up some kind of tandem bicycle with wings, laughing and arguing as they did. I had the thought, almost like a ticker tape running across my brain: "These boys are my sons. These boys are my children."

I'm not sure what I would do with daughters. I know little of the complexities of braiding hair and fancy perfumes. I wear my hair up, simply. I have my hairpins, I have my mother's tortoiseshell brush. I do have my

lemon eau de toilette, but if I ever put on too much, Orv would sneeze and the Reverend would say, "You smell like a harlot." Also, I must wear my glasses. They are the last things I take off before I turn out the light, and I fumble for them in the morning on the nightstand. I have often not had time to take them off when Harry and I have made love, but he does not seem to care. The only time I don't feel plain is when I am in bed with Harry. Perhaps a woman in her fifties should not say that, but bluntness is part of who I am. The newspapers sometimes questioned whether I was too forthright for a woman, but if I were not, I do not know whether the boys would have gone up at all. Let me be honest. I know they would not have gone up. They each had a dreamy quality to them and needed to be taken care of. And there was more.

I find it interesting that Harry Jr. became a journalist like his father. Their family is certainly more orderly than ours, the son following in his father's footsteps. I cannot imagine any of my four brothers becoming men of the cloth. Harry and Isabel seemed to be a normal family, in the traditional sense, nothing that I was familiar with. I don't believe they would have abided the chaos we Wrights had in our house, all of us toiling away with such ferocity, with so many raised voices echoing off the walls.

Orville,

It is the fourth day of the second month, and you are not here. I polished the silver myself. I had baked three apple pies, with apples Harry and I had picked last fall. I had bought new bed linens for the guest bedroom. The pies have been eaten by hungry reporters at the paper. The silver gleams. Your bed is ready. I scrubbed the bathroom myself. I cleared off shelves for your books and bought fresh ink for "your" desk. I had put Harry's friends on notice that you were going to arrive and prepared a dinner of roast beef and mashed potatoes numerous times the way you like it, and green beans, and I made three loaves of lemon bread and your special brownies with walnuts. And then I canceled the party. Harry and I had a lonely feast, and I threw one of the lemon breads out the back door for the stray dogs, imagining it was at your face. Tonight I was so upset I started tidying like a madwoman the way I used to do at home (and you always have done). Harry was sitting by the fire reading one of his one million newspapers. As I bent to pick up a messy stack, he screamed, which he has never done before: "Stop, Katharine. I am not one of 'the boys.' I am a grown man who has lived quite well, thank you. I am reading my papers. Now just stop!"

In disappointment,
Your sleepless sister, K.

TRAVELING WITHOUT A COMPASS

The winds were far too strong for flying today. I do not pass a day without checking the wind. I did it before the aeroplane and I imagine I shall do it until the day I die.

Although I thought it would take Orv time to adjust to my moving out, I assumed that he and Harry would be fast friends. Their love of newspapers certainly should have been a bond. Newspapermen often seem as if part of the same sporting team, regardless of the fact that they are sometimes fighting fiercely for a story. But Harry and Orv never were working on the same story. In their early years Will and Orv helped the Reverend edit a journal called the Religious Telescope. *The boys used to laugh about the name behind the Reverend's back, calling it the "Tyrant's Telescope." Orv said, although not in earshot of the Reverend, "When I look through a telescope, I curse using the Lord's name when my eyelashes get in the way! Does that count as a religion?" No, neither boy would have crossed the Reverend to his face.*

Later, the boys began a paper of their own, West Side News. *They even went into business together as printers. Our house was full of all kinds of religious handouts, even though the boys were men of science not spirit, but none of us ever questioned the Reverend's religion and wrath. It is true, the boys never worked on a paper full of "hard news," as Harry calls it, but still, I would have thought they would be comrades because of their shared interests. I thought we would have wonderful meals together and continue to spend sumptuous summers at the lake. When I close my eyes, I am diving in that lake over and over again, with both men by my side. I am sweeping the floors of our cabin, and I can*

hear the screen door slam and the creaking bed where Harry and I first made love. There were no latches on the doors, so Orv could have come in at any moment, the way he sometimes did, bursting in on me half dressed, shaking his latest drawings at me.

We're having two couples for dinner tomorrow night, two reporters from the paper and their wives. I've told the housekeeper that I would be doing all the cooking and she could have the night off. You would have thought she was married to Harry!

THE BRAIN IS A DOODLE OF A THING

The brain is a "doodle of a thing," as Orv himself would say. Orv would certainly not be the first genius to be unfit for normal life. Or perhaps it has nothing to do with his extraordinary brain. It is possible it was all too much for him, my moving away from him, becoming a wife, and sharing a man's bed at this age. If a detective asked me to describe his reaction to the news, I would say horrified. What I am not sure of is whether he was horrified because he could imagine me being with a man or he couldn't imagine it. There's also the possibility his imagination is so vivid that he can imagine every detail of Harry and me as lovers, that he pictures what we do, and it disgusts him.

When I taught Latin at Steele High School in Dayton, I helped my brothers raise money for the flying machine project and I was always writing letters. I also gave speeches, but it was writing those letters, with my ink pen and the typing machine, that gave me the most pleasure, promoting our project, extolling the virtues of "the magical machine." I am also honored to be on the board of trustees of Oberlin, although I am not fulfilling my obligations at the moment, as I am trying to be a good bride. In fact, I have done more than that in my life, but right now I am trying to be Mrs. Harry Haskell as best as I can.

At our wedding party, even with all the chatter and clinking glasses, I overheard a Kansas City woman wearing far too much lavender perfume say to another, "You know they all knew one another at Oberlin. I imagine she had designs on him then." But that is incorrect. It is true that Isabel and I were friends at college. It is also true we were all friends, studying together, taking walks and heavenly bicycle rides. But I had no

designs on Harry then. I was not a siren seducing him by the water's edge. In fact, I was most excited by my studies. Isabel had twenty-two years with Harry before the cancer took her away. I am not sure how many women, young or otherwise, Harry courted or courted him before we wed. I have heard rumors. I know of two women who would have very much liked to be the second Mrs. Harry Haskell. Journalists are free with their charms, and Harry's ink-stained wrists are enough to lure many women. The Reverend once marched through the kitchen and said to me, while I was scouring a pot, "Men have their needs, Katharine. Men have their needs."

(I need to go into town as soon as possible to buy some new under-garments. In fact, I must remember to ask for lingerie instead.)

Dear Orv Wright,

Ice snapped the telephone wires outside the house, so I could not call even if I had wanted to. After not hearing from you all these months, I now have a formal invitation for you, dearest brother. March 8 is Harry's birthday, which falls on a Tuesday this year, even though I know your favorite day is Thursday. I remember when you learned the Dutch word *donderdag* and you kept shouting it around the house, *"Donderdag, donderdag."* And then the Reverend started screaming. I lose my train of thought. This is a birthday party invitation. I know you enjoy birthdays if they are not too lavish. You are a man of numbers. It will be a festive birthday—Harry will be fifty-three—but not out of hand. What I am trying to convey to you is I would like you to join us. I'm making several cakes, the coconut, which you used to call the "Angel's Dessert." There is even a market here that sells coconuts, and I have purchased one. If I don't injure myself cutting it, the cake will be as snowy white as you like it, and a chocolate mousse, which Harry says should be censored. I shall have his son and several men from the paper and their wives. I want to make a fresh start here, but certainly you could come, yes? You could take the train to Cincinnati and then to St. Louis before coming here. It is a long journey but an interesting one, and of course far too long for a Model T. You could stay for a few weeks in our guest room, which I would like you to think of as your room, Orv's room. I know Harry would love it. As for gifts, you know Harry's tastes. He loves birds almost as much as you do, and history.

I will prepare the whole birthday dinner if I can keep the maid at bay. I must convey to her that I am the "lady of the house." I see you smiling at that one.

Please let me know as soon as possible.

Hopefully,
Katharine

ORVILLE HAS MAGNOLIA MADEMOISELLE

I wanted to ask Orv several times about the women in his life, but I never had the courage. Perhaps I shouldn't say courage. I was not frightened of him the way I was with the Reverend. It was more of an awareness that there were aspects of Orv's being that should not be touched. There was one woman who smelled of rose blossoms and chardonnay in France who seemed like more than an adoring fan, and I know they went out for pastries one morning because he came back with crumbs on his lapel, which he swatted away with his hat. But I have no knowledge of whether he and that particular woman shared more than croissants. It was I who sorted through the letters at 7 Hawthorn. Some letters arrived at the house, but when there was a large amount, which was often, I went to the post office to pick up the bundles. The postmistress, who was my friend, handed me a stack tied in that rough twine I miss and said, "It seems that Miss Magnolia has a particular interest in your Orville." It did seem to be the case, because once she passed along a parcel of mail the scent of sticky-sweet, slightly artificial magnolias filled the air. When I got home, Orville was standing at the front door like a petulant child, and before I could put my hat on the side table, he snatched the whole bundle from me, as if I were holding fresh flowers in my hands. He ran off to his study, in that forceful way of his, sneezing to beat the band.

At this new stage of my life I am trying not to fret about things so much. I do long for friendship of my own sex. I do not prefer les filles *in a romantic way, but sometimes my husband and brother wear me down. Isabel liked to go on long walk-and-talks. If it weren't getting dark, I would love to go for one more walk today, but now the snow is falling*

lightly, and I can hear the squirrels running across the roof, and I still don't feel I know my way around. I do not want to have the headline WRIGHT BROTHERS' SISTER LOSES WAY IN SNOW.

I must learn to not take things so personally. The maid refuses to call me Mrs. Haskell, instead calling me Miss Katharine, and I want to scream at her, but I try to maintain my composure.

I must focus on what is good, because my mind can be pulled like the wind to dreary spots. One of the most wonderful privileges was to finally be able to vote in 1920. To think, Harding and Coolidge both came around to agreeing the "fairer" sex should be able to vote. But there was that Night of Terror in 1917 that still chills me, although I only heard about it the next day. A good friend of mine from Oberlin was one of the suffragists arrested while picketing outside the White House. The guards at the prison twisted their arms and tied the women to the bars of the cells. The sacrifices women have made!

I know what a privileged life I have had, full of education and travel, and I also know to have such pleasure at my age is rare. I want to ask other women if they make love with their husbands as frequently as Harry and I do, but I do not know whom to ask. My monthly occasionally leaves a stain on the sheets, which I hurriedly wash out myself, before the maid can see. Once, when I was hanging sheets on the line, she asked what I was doing and I said, "I just like to help out. You do so much work," and you could see the horror she felt that I had stained the sheets.

On the subject of sheets, Mother once sighed as we were hanging the laundry on the line. "We live in a house of men," she said. "There is a dampness that is a part of their lives that we must accept."

At the end of last century, which seems so long ago now, we opened the Wright Cycle Shop. Will wanted to call it "Wright Cycle Right!" But Orv thought that was ridiculous and prevailed. Perhaps that was the happiest time for them. Hard to believe now that the bicycle was then such a new invention. When the mailman rides up on his bicycle here in Kansas City, I think he almost looks quaint with his cap, as he says, "Good morning, Mrs. Haskell."

I find that men have an easier time accepting that I am the new Mrs. Haskell. I catch myself thinking: If we had stopped with the bicycle—

just had the bicycle shop and worked on handlebars and wheels—where would we humans be today?

And now is it destiny that if I was to marry at all, that I was to be married to the son of a reverend? Perhaps it is in my veins—the rules, the discipline, and the sin. It was not so subtly suggested, in a publication I shall not name, that my beloved Harry married me for the sole reason that I am "a good story." In fact, I have those most beautiful and intimate letters between us when we were courting that I shall not divulge to the world, even when I read such attacks.

Once, I sent Harry a letter when we were courting, written in royal-blue ink. In the moisture of the summer heat, my hand blotted the ink as I signed my name. Next to it I wrote, Please excuse the smudge. Consider it as a kiss.

I am still shocked I was so bold. I was never forward with a man before. And I was only once bold with the Reverend.

The one and fiercely startling time I let myself snap at him was when he stepped over me, as I was on my knees scrubbing the kitchen floor. I muttered, "Is this why I got an Oberlin education?" to which he replied, not so gently pushing me with his shoe, "You are the girl. Of course it is your job."

I have bequeathed all my not-so-worldly belongings to Orv when I leave this earth. I think that is right. I do not think Harry would object.

When I talked about the ends of our lives, while we were sitting by the fire in Dayton, Orv jumped up and said, "Sister, if you talk about bequeathing one more time, I shall have to throttle you."

Even so, when I see Orv, I shall need to clarify that I bequeath everything to him, whether I'm throttled or not.

Dear Orv,

Harry's birthday was yesterday, and I would say it was a success. You were missed, but it was not your party, not your day, so I will not dwell on your absence. I know Harry loves me although he does miss Isabel. So we were both missing loved ones. At one point I saw him staring out the window after he'd blown out his candles on the coconut cake and I wanted to ask him what he wished for, but I did not.

Love,
Your sister

P.S. Do you remember when Mother used to stir a big bucket of soap bubbles in the yard with that screwdriver we used on the wings? And that giant wand you and Will made? "Bubbles for Paul Bunyan," you said, as we watched those bubbles go up to the sky.

WRIGHT SISTER WRITES HER HEAD OFF

I cannot control myself from writing letters that I usually post myself. But sometimes my dear Harry does it for me when he has time. When he does, he bows as if he were onstage when he takes my letters and says, "Would the madame have me do any other errands this morn?"

And then he adds, "Now who could you possibly be corresponding with?"

And then he tickles me.

Last time this happened, distinct words of the Reverend came to me after all these years. I was at his feet, polishing his shoes while they were on him, as he had to leave quickly, which seemed to happen more than one would think. I believe Mother was still alive, and he said to me or to himself, "A man of faith must keep a table between himself and his parishioners."

I have a cigar box full of beautiful stamps that I keep in the drawer next to the bed, and I choose carefully each time I send one to Orv. Although I took so few treasures with me, I couldn't imagine leaving my blessed box of stamps, including ones from Haiti and Morocco that both have beautiful pictures of aeroplanes.

When we were children and used to play the game what-would-you-take-with-you-if-there-was-a-fire? Will would always laugh and say, "Myself," and Orv would look to the ceiling and say, "Now that depends upon where the fire started," and then launch into explanations of lift and draft and his latest scientific theories.

I always said, "My stamps," even when I was a child, but I also said the one photo of Mother, which I have in the cigar box with the stamps.

I look like her, same dark hair and serious face. We used to use a wonderful sled that she built herself when I was little. Her father was a carriage maker, and I often think that is where we got our abilities to make things, from our mother. She should be the one to have headlines in the newspapers, THE WRIGHT BROTHERS' MOTHER, but there are no headlines about the Reverend's wife. And once, when we were out hanging laundry, and I was staring up at her and the sheets on the line and the sky and birds, she said, "Katharine Wright, you must never let them know it, but you are the smartest child I have, smarter than all four boys."

Mother died on July 4, and ever since I was fourteen years old, starting with that day, I cannot abide that holiday. That is not true. I love fireworks, but when I watched them with Orv at the lake house, sitting shoulder to shoulder on the dock, we both felt a surge of great joy and great sorrow. There was a girl at Oberlin from Portugal, which seemed so exotic, although now that I've been to Europe perhaps less so. She would teach us beautiful words in Portuguese. I do not remember many, for French is my other language, but I roll the word *saudade* around in my mouth often. It is this feeling of sorrow and joy, remembered joy, which I now feel for Orv, and for fireworks.

When I was little, Mother made sturdy paper dolls with an array of outfits with little tabs to be folded over them on the shoulders. Boy dolls and girl dolls, and there were all kinds of clothes she had painted with watercolors—railroad engineers, presidents in top hats, and my favorite, a ship's captain in a blue-and-gold uniform. None of the clothes were girls' clothes though. We never thought twice about that, as Will, Orv, and I played with them on the floor of the kitchen as she cooked.

They're on a shelf in the big house in Dayton. Must ask Orv to send them.

Orv,

I wish I could have shared with you Mr. Lindbergh's triumph as he lifted off into the Long Island sky just a few days ago. Isn't it terribly exciting, or are you a little bit jealous? I am jealous! I wanted to be there with you on that field, wishing him well. But also a part of me wanted to be up there with him—or that you, Will, and I could have done this brave flight all together. And I do find it quite unbelievable that he was able to fly in the rain; true it was light, but rain was never our friend.

Are you saving all the newspapers? I am copying out the best lines, as I always have, although Harry says that I'm "very last century."

"I first saw the lights of Paris a little before 10:00 p.m., or 5:00 p.m. New York time, and a few minutes later I was circling the Eiffel Tower at an altitude of about 4,000 feet." —Charles Lindbergh

And this after traveling more than 3,600 miles in thirty-three and a half hours. I would like to be in Paris again. Not that Kansas City doesn't have its charms. Here there are also endless stories about a local man, not a gentleman, and certainly not a flier, named Tom Pendergast, a mob boss! I hesitate to even write his name down, because Harry says he is known to shoot people on their own doorstep if he suspects they are onto him. But everybody is onto him. The whole city seems to be at his beck and call.

And prostitutes. Harry said he interviews them all the time. He says, "Kansas City is a wide-open place, where sin is the name of the game, as wide open as the Wild West."

Yours,
Your sister, Katharine—that's the name of my game.

P.S. I have a proposition for you, Mr. Wrong. I have done the calculations. Jeisyville, Illinois, is precisely halfway between Dayton and Kansas City and, as you would point out, also precisely halfway between Kansas City and Dayton. I am happy to meet you there to discuss what ails you. Surely peculiar incidents and subsequent decisions occurring over thirty years ago in our home could not be the reason for your obstinance. Surely you have matured.

Lucky Lindy

The sky was clear as a bell today, so it was fitting that I read about Lindbergh receiving the Distinguished Flying Cross from Coolidge! I wish we had received that. I try not to get caught up in coveting such honors. In fact, when les frères *Wright were the toast of the town, of the world, it was often too much for me. And yet, as the sages know, as soon as the spotlight is removed, one hungers for more. I can imagine Orv huffing and puffing about the news. I have heard from Carrie that Lindbergh has planned to visit him. And now it is I who am jealous. I do think jealousy might be the death of me.*

I think my moving to Kansas City has made some things come into focus. First, I wish I had spoken up more as the "Wright sister," and second, I admit, yes, once there was a moment when I was serving Harry and Isabel a pot roast in Dayton—it was a full house and I had spent hours preparing the meal and polishing silver. There was a moment then, yes, but nothing more. Isabel was charming. Harry was charming. We've established that. I admit I did notice Harry's wrists then, the way they emerged from his cuffs. I don't know why. I am saying that now, in retrospect, but I did flush at the sight of his wrists and perhaps, yes, also the nape of his neck. So yes, if a reporter were to ask, not that one would now, I did experience a hint of desire those years ago.

Speaking of dear Harry, he has posed an important but seemingly unanswerable question to me, which is "Why do you persist on writing to your brother when he does not respond? If anyone else did that you would say to heck [although he did not say 'heck'] with him!"

Why indeed. What is it about siblings that we have such a desire

to be glued to them for life, even if they behave atrociously? I am not a biologist. Perhaps that would be a good experiment—to study the effects on a person when a friend does not respond versus a sibling. I do know that Orv would say, "Clear the decks, sister!" if someone treated him this way.

Solo Flight

It is so stifling hot that when Harry was at work, I pulled off my under-garments and just wore a cotton dress. I even played Harry's phonograph record of Louis Armstrong and his "Wild Man Blues" and danced in front of the mirror. I am sending birthday greetings to Orv, who is fifty-six today. I am fifty-three. Mother lived to fifty-eight, so I think it is important to dance before it is too late. Harry is taking me to a jazz club on the river this weekend.

I would very much like to imagine Orv is saying happy birthday back to me, or rushing to the post office to send off a belated book as a gift or even some new kind of gadget for the bicycle that can hold a compass and a mileage calculator. I have not gotten the mail today, so perhaps there is a card or a tidily wrapped parcel with an origami peacock on the top. Mother always said imagining is an important attribute.

This is our first birthday not celebrated together and our first birthday without a shared birthday cake. And the first in years that it has not been at the lake. Nine months a married lady and no word from Dayton. Al-though of course those two birthdays he had before I was born, I imagine Mother made a cake just for him. I wonder if he had one for his third birthday, while I was being born. I never asked Mother that. I should have. Knowing her she would have made arrangements.

This past Saturday, I went into town to get a new bathing cap, and the young clerk asked if I really should be seen in public in a bathing costume, and then she said, "At your age." Only moments later, in that same store, I heard two young girls talking about how if you don't bob your hair, you're a dinosaur. I'm afraid I am a dinosaur, but one that

loves to swim. Swimming is the one thing that soothes my restless bones. Now we swim in the river, and there is a public pool that has the most dreadful chemical smell. I still have the urge to swim the English Channel. How is it that I was stronger at swimming than both boys? Harry talks often about Electric Park, which had so many tantalizing rides and "the best pool around," he claims, until the fire of 1925 destroyed most of it. Every so often he was assigned what he calls "puff pieces" about the park. But I don't want any electric park. I want to swim in our lake.

Last night when I could not sleep—because of the heat, I would say, although I always seem to have some excuse—I drew my dressing gown around me and reached for the divine Eveready flashlight Orv gave me for my last birthday. I tiptoed out of the bedroom, down the stairs, and into the study, where I shined my nifty light on the bookshelves and took the U.S. and Canadian atlas off the shelf. The moment I opened the book to Ohio, I traced my finger around the state as if it were my lover. And then I turned to Lake Huron and I could not find our island, but I touched the outline of the water just the same. It's possible it was my nighttime madness or simple exhaustion, but I thought I could see tiny black terns flying around the study. The afternoon Orv first spied one with his binoculars was one of the rare times I saw him jump for joy or jump at all. I wish I had a photograph of that. ORVILLE WRIGHT JUMPS!

I sat in the study in the heat and switched on the electric fan. I sat there perspiring, missing Orv and our dear lake.

But then Harry came down, and we sat there perspiring together and more!

WOMAN FOUND LIVING IN BATHTUB

I would like to go on record that along with being in bed with Harry, I am currently only comfortable at night sitting in the cool empty tub. I've been reading some curious old articles in the Star, *from the messy stacks Harry insists on saving. (I even had the thought of throwing away all his stacks of paper while he was downtown one day. But I think he would come home and hurl me out the window, which perhaps would not be a bad thing.) In my straightening I did read one article about "Pet Night," in which children won prizes for showing the largest, smallest, and most peculiar-looking pup. Another contest was for boys to make the best wood carving, and the winner got bathing trunks.*

I know for Orv, our lake is the only place to swim as well. I believe that lake was the first place we ever had a "real vacation." Of course, we traveled for work, but we never really did take a vacation, the way people here are always talking about going on vacation or "on holiday," which feels like a foreign term to me.

*In my heart I am at Cliff House, although I still like to call it "the cottage," looking down at the rough water with that wild wind. And that little train track we concocted. I try to explain to people how we used to carry supplies up and that time we even tried to carry guests all the way to the house, but I think I need a photograph. No, I think Harry and I need to return, that would be the solution. I have the clipping with the pictures of us cutting a ribbon at a restaurant in Cleveland and that ridiculous headline—*THE WRIGHTS, FROM SKY TO LAND!—*but I could use more photographs to make this house my home.*

I am missing Will these days too. How he loved our combined birth-

day parties. *I don't think we ever complimented him enough, but he was quite a good baker. He once confided in me that had he not been an inventor he would have been a baker. I can imagine the Reverend's response to having a baker for a son. He would have not loved that. His son, in the kitchen.*

I asked Carrie to send my aprons, which just arrived today—and they smell of cinnamon and apples and home!

The Telephone Temptress

It is so hot I am sitting stark naked in the bathtub. I love the cool porcelain on my skin. Harry sleeps like a rock and he snores a bit, which I am still not accustomed to, but then I am not used to sharing a bed with anyone. I think I like sharing a bed when we make love, more than when we are sleeping. I don't know if other women feel that way, and I am certainly not going to ask.

Harry was peeved with me today. When he walked in, which was admittedly a time he is rarely home, 2:00 p.m., I was talking on the telephone under the stairs. I had just dialed the operator and she said, "Who is calling, please?" and when he appeared next to me, I didn't know what to do. I didn't want to be rude to the operator and there was a chance Orv would actually pick up the phone, so I stayed on the telephone, even when Harry kissed me on the cheek. He obviously wanted me to hang up, but I did not, so he stomped up the stairs and slammed the door of our bedroom behind him.

After speaking with the operator and she did ring the big house in Dayton, nobody picked up, not Carrie or Orv or anyone else. I waited for eighteen rings, which was my custom. I thought this would always be sufficient, even if Orv was deep in a book or taking a nap, which he rarely did, or if there was a chance he was taking a bath, which he did only at 9:09 every night, or if he was standing by the phone wanting to pick it up but lacked the courage. In any event, before the nineteenth ring I thanked the operator and hung up.

When I went upstairs, I knocked on our bedroom door, which seemed a ridiculous thing to do on one's own bedroom door, but when

nobody answered I went in and Harry was taking a nap, or at least pretending to nap, facing away from me with his eyes tightly shut, and I left him alone. I returned downstairs and called the operator again. I feel I have become hooked to the telephone like a morphine addict.

Dear Orv, Orv dear,

There was such a fierce thunderstorm today that I could not stop thinking, "I hope Orv is not flying today," which of course you are not. But while most women are concerned with getting the clothes off the line in this weather, which I still am, I am also always thinking of people trapped in flying machines as lightning pierces the air.

On another note, I'm determined to concoct a way to send you my deviled eggs through the mail. "A risky endeavor, but the reward would be great!" as you would say. I think we should invent a refrigerated envelope that can be sent through the mail, but I think it might be easier to send you live hens. Would one be able to send deviled eggs via carrier pigeon? Of course, to do that I would have to obtain a pigeon—and then you would have to care for the bird first. I would have to pick him up from Dayton, take him to my new home in Kansas City, and make sure he then would fly back to you in Dayton.

I can hear you on that long-ago day, just as we put on our goggles, just before we went up. You shouted into the breeze, "I don't want to be a mere carrier pigeon! I want to build a machine that goes two ways!"

Instead of my deviled eggs (which you know you are missing), I could attach one of my letters, which would fly directly to you without risk of mashed eggs being dropped on an unsuspecting farmer along the way. But alas, I have been doing research and those dear birds cannot be trained to fly more than one hundred miles, and Dayton is six times that. Perhaps you could invent some kind of relay race for carrier pigeons, my boy. I have complete faith in you. Until then, I will use the old-fashioned postal service.

With affection,
K.

P.S. A friend from Oberlin has just been in Amherst, Massachusetts, and she says the town is abuzz with talk about Emily Dickinson's brother having been the lover of the woman who has brought Dickinson's poems to light. What my friend says is that nobody bothered Emily's brother, but it was this woman, Mabel, who was shunned.

Will that ever change?

A WOMAN'S PLACE

I picked three baskets of strawberries today and now my fingers are stained with a combination of ink and strawberry juice.

And now I am thinking often of my friend Lucy, whom I did not speak up for when I should have, who was not thrown from a horse but whose husband took his hand to her. She kept a wooden stool in her room at Oberlin, and once I saw her carrying it out of her room, down the hall. As she was leaving, I inquired where she was going. "My fiancé's mother is visiting," she said quietly. "I'm meeting her at the railroad station. She does not have long legs."

I often think of Lucy, placing the wooden stool down on the platform as the train pulled in, reaching up one arm to help her mother-in-law-to-be step off the train and the other to carry her bag. I never knew where the fiancé with the harsh hand was at this time. I think often of Lucy, who was not thrown off a horse ever, carrying that wooden stool.

I had thought that all would be right with the world when we got the vote, but the lingering verbal lashings of the Reverend ricochet through my dreams.

This afternoon I went downtown and joined the Women's League and met some smart women, so I am not totally lost.

Dear Orville,

I received a letter that alarmed me. It had quite a circuitous journey, with the original letter sent to Oberlin, to my attention, which they forwarded to me from Ohio.

It was from a young woman named Rochelle, who claims she is the daughter of my classmate—you know beautiful Sonya, the Jewish girl who left college because she was with child. We all thought she had ended the pregnancy, but here was this young woman writing to me, and she was, or is, asking for money.

I want to tell you more about Rochelle. A few days after I received the letter from Rochelle, she showed up at the back door, in a silvery flapper dress and broken-down shoes. I did not check, but I believe she was not wearing undergarments. She asked for food and she smelled not a little of alcohol. She is staggeringly beautiful, not a description I would use often, and there is something about her dark eyes that makes you feel as if you should take care of her, put your arms around her. And she has enormous breasts, not something I usually speak of either. We sat at the kitchen table. I shooed out the disapproving maid (whom I now refer to as Mrs. Crossbottom), and we sat there as she ate two full plates of the noodle and cheese dish I had made the day before. You know the one you like with the extra cheese in large chunks. (Mrs. Crossbottom of course had told me this was not healthy for "Mr. Haskell," but he seems quite healthy in all departments.) Rochelle told me about going to France in 1918, to help the troops—when General Pershing asked women to "provide amusement and moral welfare." I fear she provided more amusement than moral welfare, and she still feels that selling her body "is what the Lord put me on the earth to do." She told me this after I said I would try to help her, perhaps get her a job at the library. She is not

a dull girl, but her eyes became vacant when I suggested this. She asked me several times between very quick mouthfuls of noodles and cheese whether I wanted to attend a séance with her and communicate with anyone. I quickly said I had no such interest, but she said I should think about it. I do not know why the occult has gained such popularity, and I must say it makes me uncomfortable.

On another note, did you get my parcel of gingerbread, with extra slices of ginger the way you like it?

I long to be in France today with our French friends, but the tomatoes are ripe here, and Harry and I spent the morning barefoot in the garden! We brought a saltshaker out there and stood like animals eating tomatoes and shaking salt. But you never liked to have bare feet, I know so well. Even those photographs of you at Kitty Hawk, so proper with your shoes polished and tightly laced!

Do you need more zigzag stockings? I will continue to knit them and send them every month, but please let me know if you need more. I know how you wear them to shreds from all that pacing around. Carrie says that you are pacing more than before, which I hardly think possible. Sometimes she thinks you are barely sleeping two hours at night, with all your back and forth. Mint tea with lemon would help your nerves. I know you are not fond of it, but too much agitation is not good for anyone. Do you have any new inventions up your sleeve? I have always felt so honored that you tell me first and that you always listened to mine.

Lovingly,
Swes

P.S. I'm glad I took one of the bicycles with me. Knowing you built it gives me pleasure. A man took a picture of me riding the other day. If you see a photograph in the papers with the headline THE WRIGHT BROTHERS' SISTER RIDES OFF INTO THE SUNSET, you'll know why.

One Man, Two Wives

Isabel and Harry were occasionally our guests at home in Dayton when we were young. But I was far too involved with the boys, raising money, traveling with them around the world, to honestly ever think of men in an amorous way. And the Reverend was clear that this was not in the stars for me.

I told Harry that I would like to paint a picture of him and me holding hands with each other, but then on either side, he would be holding hands with Isabel and I would be holding hands with Orv. Harry said, "Be my guest," and shook his head. I have not embarked on such a painting, but I did bring my watercolors with me as well as my drafting pens.

When Harry returns from visiting Isabel's grave at the cemetery, he leaves his gardening tools and muddy boots at the kitchen door. He has invited me to go with him, and if I were a better woman I would have, but I am not.

Perhaps Harry will plant flowers for me someday. Although I would like to be laid to rest in Woodland Cemetery, with Mother and the Reverend and Will. Dayton should be my final resting place. But sometimes I don't want to be near the Reverend ever again.

Crazed Woman Longs for Baby

I still long for a baby. I well understand that at my age that is absurd, although I did read in one of the tabloids I saw at the pharmacy that a woman gave birth at fifty-seven! So perhaps anything is possible.

I love Harry, and when he handed me Isabel's key to the front door, on the chain with the little silver rose on a stem, I know it was difficult for him, but nobody forced his hand.

I have the freedom to write, as finally we do have the freedom to vote. Many people still treat me like a child—Mrs. Crossbottom, for instance. If I make a simple slip of the tongue calling the modern refrigerator the icebox, she chastises me as if I am a fool. I wish to tell her what it is to be at the birth of the invention of manned flight, but I hold my tongue and say, "Yes, of course, refrigerator."

My hands are far more often smudged with carbon paper than most women's and perhaps more than Harry would like, but as he has ink in his veins, he never complains. Once, after we had made love in the afternoon rain—this was before we were married—with the shutters wide open and only the screens protecting us from all of nature, I screamed out first in delight and then again when I saw the sheets stained with purplish ink, when I thought I had some terrible disease.

I'm assuming Orville has read the letters, but only God knows. How can one not open a letter addressed to oneself? Carrie keeps in touch with me by post and telephone. I understand Mrs. Crossbottom here is not my confidante, and I am as polite as I can be to her. I understand that she is the one who changes the sheets and she is used to working for Isabel, so there is nothing I can do. She has been "with the family" for a long time.

I do not know if Harry and Isabel continued to make love toward the end of their marriage, and of course I would never ask. But the look the maid gives me when she carries our sheets to the laundry room is not kind.

I feel remarkably lucky that my stepson, dare I say that word, does not despise me or think of me as a wicked stepmother. In fact, today he said he was happy his father had found love again.

AGITATED WOMAN SEEKS SOLACE

Apparently when Harry Jr. was just a two-year-old, when Harry came home from work he would eagerly ask, "What's the news, Papa?"

Harry Jr. is extremely well educated. He graduated from Harvard in 1924 and is cultured in a way I do not think is common for a man. He almost seems European to me, yes, that is what I would say about him: a sweet young man, a lover of music and the arts.

The Kansas City Star is the religion of the house. Definitely our religion now. We do not say prayers every day the way we did in the Reverend's home, although I do silently before each meal, including one for Orv to not be insane. Harry Jr. was at our wedding and even asked me to dance, which I did, with everyone watching. I am certainly glad there were no newsreels of that! I tried not to step on the poor young man's feet, and I had to remind myself that his father and I had a marriage license and we were not doing anything illegal. As we danced to "Sleepy Time Gal" I had to say over and over to myself, "I did not kill Isabel; I did not kill Isabel."

Harry was in the class of 1896, two years ahead of me, although he is just a few months older than I am. I had things to attend to at home. There were always things for me to attend to at home, the Reverend made certain of that. Mother had died in 1889. And as he told me repeatedly, "Girls who are free with their charms will meet their match with the devil."

Thank goodness I am younger than Harry by a few months, because the ladies in Kansas City would have words about that if I were a minute older than he. I can barely tolerate the chatter as it is, even though it is

not as if we just bumped into each other at the corner grocery store. I shall always feel privileged to have attended Oberlin, the first men's college to allow women and the first college to allow Negroes. Just as we all studied together, on music nights we sang and played instruments together. Harry was always very modern about rights for women, and he was outspoken about racial injustice. A group of us would go for endless walk-and-talks through the Ohio fields. We'd say, "Let's go for a walk-and-talk," as if it were one word, and there was always a smart and lively group who joined in. I replay those animated arguments about politics and the future of our nation as I sit in the empty tub. We would quote lines of William Wordsworth and Walt Whitman as if we knew them personally. The men and women would walk arm in arm, so confident and excited about the new century. We all believed there would be a thrilling time ahead. We had no idea there would be a horrifying war. Those walk-and-talks formed me as much as life with the boys shaped me at home. The "W Boys," we called those brilliant poets. Now when I am agitated about Orv and feel I should be home in Dayton caring for him, I recite the poem "I Wandered Lonely as a Cloud."

I am writing this in very small print now, for it seems ungrateful to say this less than a year into my marital state, but I am weary of being the Wright brothers' sister and I am weary of being Mrs. Harry Haskell. I feel wings growing from my heart. I must make a name for myself.

How?

FIRST KISS AT FIFTY

Although my first kiss with Harry was indeed through the screen door at Lambert Island up in Georgian Bay, Orv might say Lambert Island's great claim to fame was the "hot-potato incident," not because I kissed my future husband there. It is true that on cold summer nights there, I would try all kinds of things to warm the bed for Orv. Hot rocks and, yes, hot potatoes. The potatoes work well, if you put them in the fire for a while—and then of course the next morning you can cook them further and scramble them with eggs. But on the night of the hot-potato incident, I had become distracted by my reading. In fact, I was rereading Madame Bovary *in French from my college days, and the timer did go off— one of the ones Orv had devised with the bell that sounded a bit like a rooster if your imagination was very keen. The short version of it is that I wrapped the potato in a towel, placed it at the foot of Orv's bed, and he woke up "covered in mashed potatoes," as he said, which wasn't precisely true, but there was laundry to be done, by me.*

Lambert Island is where Orv and I were happiest, with its simple cottages and boathouses, and no young men from the press with their large cameras, banging on our door. The peace of the lake, and the birds, and that cool northern air are idyllic. Once, on one of our walks by the lake, bundled up with two wool sweaters each and our binoculars around our necks, Orv said, "I hope the birds do not mind sharing the sky with us, sister. I hope we have not created a kind of hell in their sky."

The most important feature of our magical island was that Orv rarely had one of his spells there, until he threw the vase. If he was restless, as he was in the hot-potato incident, he would take the rowboat out for a

vigorous row, or pace on the front porch, or arrange and rearrange the cans in the pantry, but not much more. Although there was no question, he was worse after Will died in 1912. We all were. How could we not? (Our older brother Reuchlin died in 1920, but it felt like he had left the family years before, and although it now seems wrong, we did not cry.)

One morning up at the lake I was awakened by screams, which I later learned was because of a contraption Orv was working on, a device. It was supposed to make ice, but he never could get it to work. The kitchen floor in the cottage was often full of puddles from his attempts. On this morning I thought he was having some kind of attack, appendicitis, or he had been injured.

I threw on my robe and ran to the kitchen. And there he was, yanking the ice machine and cursing, which he did on rare occasions, definitely more so since the Reverend had died. I shouted at him, but he did not respond, which was not uncommon, and when he finally yanked the contraption off the floor, he insisted on dragging it out of the house, still not speaking to me. I ran after him, as the geese lifted off the lake in the fog. When he got to the dock, he dragged the contraption out to the end, then hurled it into the water. I caught up with him, and there we stood, watching it sink, and neither of us saying a word.

I then pulled him by the hand, and we walked silently back up to the kitchen, where I made him stack after stack of pancakes, which he drenched in syrup from the cans that Canadian guests always seemed to bring.

I made breakfast for Harry this morning, and there was a moment, when I placed a spatula piled with pancakes on his plate and he looked up at me, that I thought, "This is the happiest I have ever been."

FOOLISH PRESS

If Will had lived, how would things have been different?

Frequently the press got them confused, although Orv usually sported a mustache and Will was clean-shaven. Orv said that was why he wore his jazzy socks, "to help the foolish press." I do not recall when he first requested that I knit him a pair. I never questioned the task. I never questioned a lot of things. I have one sock done now for another pair. Perhaps I should send him the one. He always can use a spare.

The Reverend was the most stoic of us when Will died. I do not know what Mother would have done if she had lost Will while she was alive. The Reverend was the only one among us who did not cry. I served him his tea that night after dinner, and all he said was "The Lord taketh away."

CORRESPONDENCE LEADS TO CONJUGAL LIFE

When Harry's wife died—first wife, I must always remember to say about Isabel—I did send a condolence letter to him. We were taught to send condolence notes as children by our mother and so it was. I kept a bottle of black ink and a box of thick cards on my desk for such too-frequent occasions. I took the ink and stationery with me here to Kansas City with my stamps.

Harry did respond to my condolence note, but our correspondence was as chaste as the wing of a lark, until that cool afternoon when he visited the island. Writing to Harry after the death of Isabel was the proper thing to do. I never intended more. It was beyond my wildest dreams to think that I would ever marry Harry, that I would touch him naked. I was not fond of the word "spinster," but that was what I was called for years, when the press did not make the mistake of calling me Orv's wife! I grew to accept the title of spinster. It is true I did much of the sewing of those wings, but I was never a spinner on a spinning wheel. I am quite competent in sewing, although it is not one of my greatest attributes. Indeed, I would much prefer to be known for work for women's rights. And let us be honest, Orv and Will were always better seamstresses than I. And, as history continues to surprise us, they turned out to be the spinsters.

I was accustomed to the boys' ways and never scolded them for their quirks. There was once something in the French press about neither of the boys speaking a word at a dinner in their honor but went on to say that they both "made themselves known." I forget the French expression for that, but it was crystal clear what they were saying. I always knew that it was my task to make conversation wherever we traveled. Orville once said I was their "front man."

THE OTHER WRIGHT BROTHERS

The one brother I might contact if the ship went down is Lorin. He is not a soul mate, but neither he nor his wife and children have scorned me. I sometimes wonder why Reuchlin and Lorin left the nest so easily and married at expected ages, while Will and Orv never did.

I must get books for Lorin's children next time we visit. An empty-handed aunt is of no use.

Dear Orville,

I must ask you a question. As you see I ask you questions from afar I would not dare have asked if we were at home together. Here goes, as the kids say. Were you angry that I was the one who went to college? It is curious, I admit, and I do think the Reverend would have sent you if you had wanted to. If Will had been able to go to Yale as planned and not been horribly injured on the ice, perhaps you would have been accustomed to being without him at a younger age, but then perhaps you would have never gone up.

I was thinking of the one time you took the Reverend up and he was so excited, but he was also frightened, I could tell that. Afterward he was very quiet, almost humbled, if I may say. I could see he was a scared man, scared for his own safety but also for yours. We rarely saw that protective side, but that day I did. We never spoke of that flight. Did you talk? Did you feel forced to take him up? We were all concerned we might lose one another.

I'm not sure why you and Will were one little unit, and Lorin and Reuchlin were another. I wonder if Mother ever spoke of those tiny twins, Otis and Ida, who died in infancy, before you were born. It is Carrie who told me about them once while we were picking bits of silk out of the corn. Maybe it's just something women speak of. We were sitting on the back steps. We had shucked a dozen ears. I had corn silk in my hair, and Carrie reached over to take a strand from my braids, and she started to cry. I had never seen her cry, and when I asked her why, she kept shaking her head, but when I asked her again, she said quietly, "On account of the twins." But that was that. "We have more corn. You know how the boys can eat" is all she said. It is hard to imagine I could have had a sister in that house. Now that I think of it, everybody in the family had a partner—even the twins—except for me. Now that Reuchlin is gone, I regret I was not

kinder to his wife, but Lulu seemed so different from us with those hats. We never were really around people like that, but there are women who enjoy shopping as if it were a profession. I don't mind going into the shops when I need something, but in truth I find more amusement in a hardware store than in one of the ladies' boutiques. I do like the post office as well, but if I never had to go into a clothing store, I would dance a jig.

Should we have handled the finances differently with Reuchlin? I know he was not comfortable with the $50,000 he inherited from Wilbur in 1912. He always believed that because he had not helped with the invention then he should not receive any monetary gain. Reuchlin always said he did not want charity. When you come to visit, we could visit his grave. You know he's buried not far from here. I have visited a few times and left flowers, but I should go more often. When I die, I would like to be scattered from an aeroplane. Does that sound too modern? Some of the flappers I've met talk about all sorts of ways they want to be buried. One woman I read about in the *Star* was said to be buried with her goldfinches! Would you like to be buried with birds? I can't bear to think of you being buried at all. I need to be near you, I think in Dayton, in our family plot.

Forgive my mood today, but sometimes I am overtaken with emotions. Perhaps it is all this activity I am having with Harry. I recommend it though, I do, Orville—yes, even at our age. Do I shock you? In Ohio I feel women were making so much progress. I was so excited about the prospect of sitting on a jury. And here in Missouri we do not have that right. I wish I could go home for that. I fear I will never be a true citizen of Missouri. Did you know it's called the "Show Me State"? I imagine you do, because you know the names of everything, but do you know why? In 1899, Representative Willard D. Vandiver said, "Frothy eloquence neither convinces nor satisfies me. I'm from Missouri. You've got to show me." Of course, though it did not secede, it was also a slave state. We must never forget that.

Yours truly,
Your sister, a proud suffragist

THE WRIGHT BROTHERS' MOTHER

The sky today was perfect for flying—no clouds and, of course, a breeze, but not too much, and I had the desire to leap into a plane and fly back to teaching Latin to those high school girls. I would say they helped shape my world as much as Oberlin. I loved when there were winter breaks on sunny days, when the headmistress blew her whistle and we would all, teachers and students, burst out into the snow. We teachers tried to be grown-up, but we would play hide-and-seek with the girls, crouching behind the big sugar maples in our long dark skirts and coats against the white, white snow. We would all grab the wooden toboggans leaned up at the side of the chapel for the girls to hurl down the snowy hill. Many nights after sledding, I'd fall into my cold sheets and listen to the clatter of deer hooves on the steps of the back porch. And when I missed Mother, I would take out my copy of Little Women *that she read to me when I was young.*

Our mother was born in 1831 in Virginia and then moved with her family to Union County, Indiana, the following year, and she studied literature at Hartsville College. I know she wanted to be more than a wife and mother. She was an educated woman. I never had time to ask if she had suitors other than the Reverend. People say her skill with a hammer and nail and all things mechanical came from her father. She did say he let her work in his shop, side by side as if she were a boy.

But what I really want to ask is "Mother dearest, how did the Reverend, your husband, treat you? Did you enjoy your lovemaking with him?" but of course I never did and shall never know. But what does echo and prove to be so true is what she told me once, when she was braiding my hair on the kitchen steps. It was late March. The geese were honking as they returned after their winter travels.

"*Katharine Wright*," she said, yanking on my hair, "*some of the best ideas are the simplest. Remember that.*"

Mother treated me like the inventor I was, even from a time now long ago. One winter day a man came to interview me after classes. He had waited for me all day, lurking outside the schoolyard, and when I finished my last Latin lesson, there he was at the classroom door.

"*Are you the Wright brothers' sister?*" *he asked. It was the first time anyone had called me that. Perhaps that was when my life changed forever.*

"*And what is it like to be the Wright brothers' sister?*" *he asked, taking his pencil from his hatband.*

"*My brothers are hard workers*" *is all I could muster up to say. My head was a tumble of thoughts, but that is what was in the paper the next day:* WRIGHT SISTER SAYS WRIGHT BROTHERS ARE HARD WORKERS.

Life has come to feel like swimming in Lake Huron, where you pass from ice-cold water to a patch of warm water, and then before you know it, you're in cold water again.

I am reading a book by the psychoanalyst Carl Jung. He said, "Thoroughly unprepared we take the step into the afternoon of life . . . But we cannot live the afternoon of life according to the programme of life's morning—for what was great in the morning will be little at evening, and what in the morning was true will at evening have become a lie."

I think he is a wise if peculiar man, as all wise men are, and that no matter how smooth or raggedy the arcs of our lives are, we are all trying to leave our mark, just like those girls' toboggans left tracks in the snow.

I think if a journalist knocked on my door and asked what it was like to be the Wright brothers' sister now, I would add a few things, not about Orv not saying boo to me. I could not bear for that to be the headline, WRIGHT BROTHER REFUSES TO TALK TO WRIGHT SISTER. *No, but I would have other things to add besides the fact that they were hard workers. There are other facts I would add. Things were said and done thirty-five years ago, when we were not technically children, but because Orv, Will, and I were late bloomers, we were like children. The Reverend was, of course, not a child, but grief can be a shocking master.*

On another note, about the sky, I wish I were as comfortable with the

nighttime sky as I am when the day breaks. Right this minute I could walk outside in my dressing gown and stare up at the summer night sky, but it is not the stars that guide me. I am much more confident when the sun is blazing through the clouds. Someday I shall learn the constellations though. Orv and Will knew them all.

SEPTEMBER STORMS

It is 2:00 a.m., and a raging thunderstorm is clapping down on us with jagged lightning zigzagging the sky like Orv's socks, but Harry is sleeping through it.

I think thunderstorms are one of the few times I actually pray for people who are in the air.

I think of Mother in storms as well, when we used to run outside and grab the clothes off the line, even in the middle of the night. Mother did not believe it was bad luck to leave clothes out overnight, but Mrs. Crossbottom wouldn't dream of it. As she told me with great authority, "People steal all kinds of things these days." Yesterday I suggested that we could lock up each item on the line. Predictably, she was not amused.

Once, in Dayton, when Mother was still alive, a deluge hit us on an August day, and quickly all of us, even the Reverend and the boys, were out there grabbing clothes off the line. We all got drenched, and when we came in and threw the soaked clothes in a heap on the kitchen table, I could see the Reverend look at Mother's breasts through her wet dress. I saw her blush, and she said to me, "Katharine, please wring out these clothes. Your father and I have something to discuss upstairs."

It has occurred to me, just at this moment, as I sit naked in the tub in Kansas City and the storm bangs and flashes all around, that possibly my parents did not go up to discuss anything but went up the stairs to make love.

Dearest Orville,

I want to tell you to be careful with your finances. As precise as you can be in some areas, we both know you can be scatterbrained. I feel as if an arm has been removed, by not being able to look at the books. Who is doing that now?

I am not wasting ink on telling you something for my amusement. I am writing this because I sense something is wrong in the world, Orville. You know how you and Will teased me about having premonitions. You are correct, I have made errors. I predicted people would have telephones in their automobiles and that it would be possible to walk on the moon, neither of which has occurred, but financially I have not steered you wrong. You always said, "All the world needs is a suitable breeze," but things are more complicated than that, and I believe America is spinning out of control. A breeze is not the solution, Orville Wright, a breeze will solve nothing.

With concern,
Your worried sister

Censored

I know this is not something I would normally talk about, but nothing is normal anymore. Blame it on the humidity. I am perspiring as I sit naked in the tub.

I was straightening out my closet, trying to find some comfortable clothes in this heat, and I came across a brown paper parcel. I brought it down, it smelled faintly of lemon soap, and I checked to make sure Mrs. Crossbottom wasn't around. This was when Harry was downtown. I opened the package, and there were lace underthings! There was a brassiere that was most provocative, with a flower on each nipple (excuse the smudges but my hand is shaking as I write that word). And then there was a sort of girdle with garters, but also very lacy and provocative. I knew they were Isabel's. I've seen enough photographs to know they were her size, which is not unlike mine. But they had not been worn, that was clear.

And then, forgive me, I shut the door quietly but firmly and locked it, and took off all of my clothes and laid them on the bed. Then I put on the underthings, which were a bit tight, and I looked at myself in the mirror. I had never done such a thing.

I think I shall wear them for Harry.

WRIGHT SISTER BECOMES WRIGHT MOTHER

There is a possibility that if our mother hadn't died of tuberculosis when I was fourteen, things would have been different. How is one to know? Orv always grew impatient with me if I asked such questions. In fact, I never did mention Mother to him, because I knew how upset he would get, but he didn't like if I posed the question of "what if?" unless it was about something scientific. Then he was in "all hog," as Will would say. I confess I was sometimes jealous of Will and Orv's closeness. In a way they had a marriage, and then when Will died, I was there for Orv, perhaps too much so. But matters of the heart? It wasn't that Orv would normally hurl a vase of flowers against the wall or even speak about things fraught with emotion, more that, instead of having a civil conversation, he would get a glazed look in his eyes and respond with "Sister, do we still have any of that apple cobbler?" The most emotional he got was when he said, "Sister, do you think that flying is an affliction?"

Had our dear mother lived, I certainly would not have taken care of the Reverend and the boys the way I did. In fact, it was when our mother died that I stopped being Katharine around the house and became "Sister." They couldn't call me "Mother," so "Sister" would have to do. I now had a role. I was in charge in a way for which I was not prepared, taking on a job I did not want to do.

As for marriage, I simply did not believe it was in the cards for me. Would Mother have wanted me to go to Oberlin? The Reverend was oddly forward thinking about women when it came to education. I did have a suitor, more than that, at Oberlin. I was engaged briefly when I was there, but the young man played football and baseball and talked

incessantly of that. His lips did brush my cheek, although perhaps *brush* is an overstatement. He really was not the sort of person for me, and we drifted apart. My roommate said he was "too much of the world" for me, meaning he did not read poetry. But the fact was I had the boys to take care of at home and the Reverend's demands were clear. I could have wed at a "normal" time and had children. But here I am, in Kansas City, a newlywed in my fifties.

One family story goes like this: when I was only a few weeks old, Orv picked me up from the cradle and insisted on trying to sit me on his chair at the dining table. He threw a fit when I rolled off onto the floor. Family lore also insists I did not land on my head and was not damaged in any way, which is comforting. This occurred when my mother was alive, so it seems Orv was always protective of me, or at least had some sort of special feelings for me.

September 26, 1927

Dear Orv,

I picked the very last valiant raspberries today, not many, but later I shall make some jam. As I knit your socks, I am sitting here on the cozy embroidered armchair by the fireplace in our study. Of course, there is no need for a fire, but I do have my feet up on a footstool. I don't think I've ever sat this way before. What would the Reverend have thought? I know what he would have said. "Sloth is not becoming to you, Katharine Wright." The fact that I am knitting would not matter to him. Harry is home from downtown, sitting on his chair on the other side of the fireplace, reading about the Civil War, which now is beginning to feel further away from our lives. I have seen that look in his eyes before and know not to push him. In that way he is like you. As you boys and Father are the only men I have shared a home with, I do not know if this is normal. All I know is that when you are upset, it is best to leave you to stew.

Just now he looked up from his book and said, "All those young boys, all those young boys."

I recall you said those exact words during the Great War. I wish you could be here to discuss your thoughts with Harry. A hundred times you've said if it were not for the aeroplane so many would not have suffered. But as always, I don't think you should take it all on your shoulders. I had a friend, a girl at Oberlin, a woman now— she's moved to California with her husband, who is a pilot, and he is teaching her to go up on her own. She said she would have enlisted if she could have, but I don't feel that way. I don't feel it is in women's nature to fight. To fly, yes, but not to kill.

If you came for dinner tonight, you and Harry could talk into the evening and I would not disturb you. I see you rolling your eyes and tapping your pencil on your mustache. It is true, I would put

forth my views, but I would allow you men to find your friendship again.

Even though Harry is a journalist, he is not immune to the horror of war or the horror of a young Negro man being hanged from a tree. It is not only men, though they are doing this too, Orv. It is women, and we are doing nothing.

The Battle of Antietam is what Harry is most obsessed with these days. I have just learned to use that word. I realize you have your obsessions too, although I know you might throw a heavy object at me if I used such a word. But Harry is reading everything he can get his hands on about the battle. To think all those boys just faced one another in a cornfield and 23,000 were injured or died in one single day. If you boys had gone off to war, I do not know what I would have done. Just now Harry read to me how an order from General Robert E. Lee had been left wrapped around three cigars in a field near Antietam, which changed the course of the Civil War. I think General Lee was supposed to have written it in his own hand, but maybe it was an aide. Should I send you a note wrapped around three cigars?

Love,
Your sister, who cannot stand the smell of cigars (although it is one of the smells of Harry I love, along with his pine shaving lotion)!

P.S. Today I was at the pharmacy and a woman passed me and said, "It's snowing down south!" and it took me a while to realize she meant my slip was showing. I turned bright red, I'm sure!

Pardon, pardon, pardon, s'il vous plaît—we are having rhubarb pie tonight if that will entice you.

MISIDENTIFIED WOMAN

Thank the good Lord there was a breeze today, a perfect day for flying. Perhaps it is being intimate with Harry, although I have never used that word before, but Harry has made me freer in all kinds of ways. If you asked any number of people who observed Orv and me when we were younger—and we were constantly observed by the press from all around the world as well as folks in town—they would say Orv and I were like son and mother, even though I am three years his junior. And several times, as we got older, and stood patiently for photos on dusty fields and even at the White House with photographers shouting at us to smile, they would assume something odder. I would nudge Orv and mutter to him to look less serious, and the following day it would be written, by otherwise intelligent journalists, that we were husband and wife. I do not make such things up. I have all the clippings carefully filed in boxes in Dayton. I did not take many belongings with me when I left Ohio. In some ways I admit I feel like a runaway bride, although this is not my choice. If Orv had approved of my marriage, we could have gotten married in the backyard behind the big house or, better yet, up at the lake, on the dock on Lake Huron. No, he should have been at the wedding. There is no excuse. I would much prefer to be back and forth to Dayton, staying over there after making the journey, continuing to participate in some of my work—the rights of women, the rights of children—and I do miss being the Wright brothers' sister.

Dear Orville Wright, inventor of three-axis control, which allows the pilot to steer the aeroplane and maintain equilibrium,

Attention, attention, to the world-famous man who alphabetizes dairy products in the icebox. Attention, attention, this is your sister calling.

Harry has gone to watch baseball—the Blues is the name of the team. I thought I'd go through life as a canceled stamp, but here I am married to a man who loves baseball. I'm afraid I don't know whom the Blues are playing though. Perhaps they are playing the Yellows. I know you don't care, but I'm trying to. Sometimes he goes to watch the Monarchs, which is a team in the Negro League. I have slowly, very slowly, learned the rules—and some of the terms. Ducks on the pond. That's when there is a player on every base. How do you like them apples?

When did you first realize that Harry Haskell had gone from being a friend from college to a gentleman caller? Was it when I put rosewater on my wrists, and you had a sneezing fit? You said, "Lord have mercy on my wanton sister!" I assumed you were just teasing. The rosewater had been a gift from Harry. Of course, the Reverend would not have approved. "Ornamentation leads to temptation, and the tempted shall be punished"—how many times did he tell us that? "There is no need to embellish for one's own glory."

It seems I shall rot in hell. But perhaps you will join me there, although I do not think there are many places to park a flying machine.

I sometimes even wear a lipstick called "Raspberry Splash," a color the young girl at the pharmacy chose for me, although I tend to lick it off. Here, look at the marks on the bottom of the page where I've kissed it—I am showing you the color, nothing more, although I have become more affectionate. I would not mind giving you a hug.

I think I'm mainly a tomboy, don't you? I look like a clown with lipstick, but at my age a little color on my face helps. The young salesgirl at the dress shop that sells flapper dresses said, "Are you looking for something for your daughter, or perhaps your granddaughter?" Sigh.

I think I can say with certainty that the Reverend approved of nothing I did but homemaking. But on my grave, be sure to put that I organized the women's march in Dayton in 1914.

Those things you did not object to. Nor the Reverend. How strange he believed women should get an education and was for the women's vote when many men were not, but then told me not to marry. When I got engaged the first time, at Oberlin, Father did not speak to me for three weeks. And when I ended the relationship, which I always said was my "narrow escape," he said, "I suppose you would not have made a good wife anyway." Although I was stung by his words, I also felt a bolt of freedom, as if I'd been shot out of a cannon at the county fair.

I would have preferred to be like Julia Morgan, the first woman architect in California, although I believe she never wed. To design buildings I know is not like designing aeroplanes, but I have faith I could do it. I continue to write my ideas in notebooks, which I would love to show you. My latest idea is for a footbridge across Kansas City, one that swings, that will make the Hannibal Bridge seem old-fashioned. I think you will like it. I have enclosed my drawings. Along the bridge, there would be places to sit and even cafés, like in Paris, and stands for bicycles, but all above the city, so it won't interfere with the automobile traffic below, and you would need to wear special ropes to attach you to the bridge—because of the wind, of course. I've called it the Wright Bridge—do you like it? But no automobiles or trains or even aeroplanes! And we could serve snow ice cream. Yes, the snow could be brought down from Canada, in freezing containers. Just add cream and sugar the way we did in heavy snows as children, and even colors—blue snow, blue made from crushed pansy petals, could be served at the landing stations. What do you say, Orv, blue ice cream?

I often imagine what my life would be like if I had been born a boy, if there had been five Wright brothers instead of four. I would have been Cyril, that's what Mother told me, instead of Katharine.

Perhaps the Reverend sent me to Oberlin so he could give me the illusion of being a modern woman, when in fact I was an educated servant to him. I did rise up in the company. But that was for those outside the home. The other day Harry said preachers can be the most dangerous people in society.

"Hitch yourself to a star and you remain a wagon," the Reverend used to say, from behind his newspaper. Of course, you and Wilbur were stars. You know that. The world knows that. At various times as a child I wanted to be an anthropologist or an actress or even an American Joan of Arc. I dreamed. I dreamed as much as you boys.

The Reverend said, "Loss is the Lord's way of teaching us virtue and strength," but I disagree. When I graduated from Oberlin College in '98 and took that position at Steele High School, of course, as is still their policy, they did not allow us women teachers to be married. Thank heavens Carrie stayed with us all those years. She says you are still not eating well and spend hour upon hour with your bird books. I hear she has to lure you to the dinner table as if you were a small child. She could tell the world what went on in our house. She remembers it all.

Humbly,
Katharine Wright Haskell

P.S. Our brother Lorin said he visited you and you definitely had lost weight. He said that not only would you not speak to me but that you refused to talk about me. Is this true?

Dear brother,

Do you have those letters I constantly wrote to you, when you boys began spending time away from home out in North Carolina on the beach and later in Europe? I thought I could reach across the country, and then the Atlantic Ocean, to hold your hand and give you all the news about our Dayton life. Are those letters still organized chronologically? I apologize if I sometimes scolded you when you didn't regularly correspond. I know I could be such a schoolmarm, warning you of "distractions" when in Europe. I know I still am. I think I should have encouraged you to be more distracted. We never spoke of things of a personal nature during those days of constant writing and talking, in that remarkable time when we convinced the U.S. Signal Corps to allow you to test the Flyer. Orv, I think it was right you were the pilot for the demonstrations, but honestly, I wish it had been me who had flown that historic day. You know I have the ability to be a good aviator. I just need some lessons. You know it's in our Wright blood.

I believe that in future generations they will think of going up as common as riding a horse. As I look out the window and see yet another young man barely walking with a crutch, I think of how dangerous your life has been, even without having gone to war. After that one week of breaking all those records with the flights, I had premonitions. I was not entirely surprised when I got the telegram. I have it with me. September 17, 1908. When the propeller broke and sent the aeroplane out of control . . . Lieutenant Thomas Selfridge's death is a nightmare I continue to have. I liked Thomas. We all did. I tried to prepare myself for such an event, but I was not prepared. I thought I would die myself. I would have gladly given up my life for his and not to have you injured so violently.

I must hurry to the post office to mail this. I will write tomorrow.

In haste,
K.

P.S. I will post this tomorrow because there is suddenly a rainstorm. The silver maple leaves are pressed up flat against the screen, giving off the most beautiful scent.

Katharine Wright Shoots Maid

I was talking to Mrs. Crossbottom about Will, which I should not do. I should not confide a single thought to that woman. When I said we believe dearest Will died of eating oysters, she asked what month he died. First of all, I don't think that is the proper response when you are speaking about a loved one's death. Wouldn't "I'm so sorry about your loss" or a shake of the head with a sorrowful face be more appropriate? But when I said, "May 30, 1912," the horrid woman said, "I did not ask the day or the year, simply the month. Everyone knows the danger of eating oysters in a month without the letter R in it. Everyone knows that."

I wish I could have fired her on the spot, but I cannot. I wish I could have thrown a vase of flowers at her, a violent and wild smashing. Was she accusing me of killing Will? Or that he died from his own stupidity? One thing Will was not was stupid. Nor am I.

I do many things to keep my hands from being idle here. I still love sweeping and raking, to soothe my muddled brain. One of my favorite things at home was to be out in the yard while the boys were working on their contraptions. And because of the boys I have indoor-outdoor thermometers in the windows, very similar to the nifty ones they fashioned when they were young. And then I have brought with me a few of the drawings of my inventions as well.

Last night, as I sat in the study with the atlas, I thought of the wretched boy who hit Will with his hockey stick out on the frozen pond. I wonder what makes a boy do that and for him to become a murderer, a real murderer, and our boys to go forward to change the course of history.

One never knows the power of human character. But Orv's brilliance does not justify his abandoning me. It feels like a murder to my soul.

The Reverend always said that we Wrights had an obligation to society but also to family. He once suggested we sign an "oath of allegiance to the family," although that was one of the threats he did not follow through on. Orv used to say, "Batten down the hatches, sister," if I worried too much, but I think the man should seriously batten down his own hatches at this point.

Censored

I never saw Orv sneak a kiss with a woman behind the stairs. I never came upon him holding hands strolling down the street. Nor did I ever hear him say, "That woman has lovely gams," or anything of that sort. I should add this was the same for Will. Once the boys and I were walking along the Seine in Paris, and suddenly a man who claimed he was a journalist, although he looked more like some kind of a street performer with a striped shirt and beret, walked up behind us and said in my ear, "Vos frères préfèrent-ils les hommes?"

I don't know if the boys heard, and their French was minimal at best, but I understood completely what he said. I was so shocked I said back to the man, "Les hommes?" and shook my head, and he vanished. I admit I was startled. But then again, if hommes prefer hommes, c'est la vie.

The day Mother died, I felt a darkening net thrown over me. I could see out of the net, but a net I could not escape from, as if I had stepped into a new and peculiar garment of adulthood. Although I acted outwardly with strength, part of my spirit was smashed, and it was not until the moment Harry kissed me through the screen door on the porch that I felt completely whole. "Whole" is not the proper word. More as if my wings were aligned. Yes, I felt aligned.

I wish Orv and Will could have experienced that. Orv still has time!

My dear mute brother,

This is a continuation from September 29's letter—so now I am mailing two on the same day. This morning I had to go to an appointment to have my eyes examined. I say "had to," but I must say I love the feel of having someone touch my forehead and around my eyes. The optician is a most gentle man, with the most sensual (do you mind I use that word? I have been reading Tolstoy's *War and Peace* and I find that his words are sensual) hands. And when the optician asks about you, I answer as if we were in constant communication. In fact, I lied and said we spoke daily on the telephone, right before dinner, to share every detail of our days. As I left his shop today, the little bell above the door rang and he said, "When you speak to Mr. Wright today, please tell him that he is my hero, even more than Charles Lindbergh." I smiled sweetly and said, "Of course, certainly, I will telephone him as soon as I return home."

And last time he asked how much I had helped with our flying machine, and I just smiled. I do have memories of being no more than five years old, as usual with Mother hanging clothes, clothespins in her mouth. I would stand clinging to her skirts, looking up at a lone hawk or a flock of jays, already watching their wings, trying to figure out how they stayed up there. But if it is attention I want, I was born in the wrong body. There are times I have not spoken up in my life, and for that I am forever sorry.

My friend Lucy, who died so young, just a year after graduation when she was "thrown from a horse," had confided in me months before that her husband used to beat her about the face with a wooden spoon and more. When I saw her bruised eye, she said I must never breathe a word. She did not use that word, "beat," that time. She said something else, which was more demure. She could not bring herself

to say out loud all that he actually had done to her. All she whispered into my ear was "He took his hand to me."

I asked her a few more questions, but she sat there with a bowed head, like a nun, as if she had struck him instead of the other way around.

I fault myself for not breathing a word. I know she was not thrown from a horse.

I vow to become more honest at this stage of my life.

Speaking of honesty, one of Harry's colleagues at the office came for dinner last night. He has never married. He was most flirtatious, but not in a way that bothers Harry, saying that I added "sparkle" to the house; it just makes me feel less freakish in this place. He makes me feel it is normal to marry at fifty-two, but he would make you feel that it is just as normal not to marry. He is a modern man. I do not know whether he has girlfriends or prefers men. Last night he asked me if I agreed with Freud that what one sees in childhood leaves stains for the rest of your life. I was surprised at that word, but that's what he said. Stains. Perhaps we should all speak up about such stains. There are things we need to talk about, Orv.

Yours,
Sister

INDECENT WIFE

It still feels like summer even though it is October, and I am sitting naked in the bathtub at 3:00 a.m. I can't stop thinking about Reuchlin. He often reminds me of a copy of a painting I have seen of the Brontë sisters with their brother, Branwell, just a faint image, almost floating away. Reuchlin seemed to have fallen from another family tree. He did not get along with the Reverend and cared not a whit about aeroplanes. It's possible the Reverend screamed most at Reuchlin, but Reuchlin was not cowed. The morning the Reverend found a book lying open, upside down, on the kitchen table, instead of primly closed with a bookmark, he screamed, "A book spread like that is indecent, Reuchlin!" and took the ruler to him. Soon after I heard Reuchlin mutter, "'Decency' is not a word that man knows much about."

I believe Reuchlin was lucky to get out and marry and have four children, although the rest of us did not know what to make of his Lulu. Reuchlin might not have had an interest in flying machines, but he had a normal life. I like to think Reuchlin would have approved of our marriage and he and Mother would be appalled by Orv's behavior. I had worried over what to wear to her funeral, knowing I had to wear black even though it was high summer, in that Ohio heat. I wore a shawl of Mother's I found in the back of her closet, perhaps as a shield.

In the carriage after the service, the Reverend grabbed my arm so hard I feared he would break my wrist if I resisted. My mind might be confused about other things, but I know his exact words were "You are Mother now, Katharine Wright. You are our Mother now."

I know if he were alive today, he would have insisted that I should

stay and care for him and Orv. Would I have the courage to contradict his will?

I am constantly startled by people's interpretations of the love between Harry and me, which is quite simply and wonderfully love. I do not think people would have whispered at any age if Orv had found his true love. Wilbur used to call Orville "Bubs" and Orville called Wilbur "Ullam." Once I made the grave error of calling for Bubs and Ullam to come to the dining table. Monsieur Ullam (Wilbur) just laughed it off, but Monsieur Bubs (Orville) came up behind me and pulled on my ear so hard it stung for a week.

Today I was at the library and the librarian seemed a nice enough woman. We chatted about which Brontë we preferred (I, of course, voted for Charlotte, and she claimed Emily), and I had the thought that this would be a fine place to spend several hours a week, but after I had checked out two French novels, I saw her whispering behind her hand to another woman. I heard the word "improper." I do have excellent ears. I wish the librarian could see me now, naked in the tub. My nakedness is not something I've ever been proud of or ever really experienced before now. Before Kansas City, I would get dressed immediately when I woke, hurry to cover myself and that was that. Looking glasses were not featured in our home. Honestly, I never looked at myself naked in a full-length mirror until I met Harry. Here there is a full-length mirror on the back of the bathroom door.

And my breasts, which have never nursed a baby, now give me so much pleasure. There never was a mention of my face or shape in the newspapers, or what style of dress I wore in any publication in any country in the world.

In every language on this fair planet, the boys were known as the Wright brothers, "Les frères Wright!" *as the French liked to announce, whenever we appeared in public or they were written about in the French papers. But few people could remember which was which or who was who. My breasts were certainly nobody's concern.*

Before I was married, I copied out my new name, Katharine (Katharine with an a) Wright Haskell, on a notebook up at the lake, and after the smashing of the vase, I found that sheet of paper, torn into tiny bits in the wastebasket.

I admit that as jubilantly in love as I am, this move has made my mind askew. As Mother said faintly, as she was losing her wits before she died that dreadful day in 1889, "How many years ago was this?" At first I did not understand what she was saying. I put my ear closer to her lips as she lay upstairs at 7 Hawthorn. "How many years ago was this?" she murmured.

She was speaking of the moment, in the present tense, as she was leaving us and the earthly world behind, but in fact, what does time matter?

Time matters when the milk goes sour. I must tell Mrs. Crossbottom we need to order fewer bottles from the milkman.

Dear Orville,

I have a confession to make. You know how sensitive I've always been to lavender (I can barely write the word without getting a headache) and how so many women use it in sachets, but you know better than most how it makes me instantly seasick on land. I thank you for being a good nurse several times.

Do you remember the time that lady in Spain sent you a letter professing her love for you—I think it was you; perhaps it was to Will or even both of you—and she had sprayed the envelope with lavender perfume? I almost passed out in the post office when I went to retrieve all your mail from your adoring fans.

This morning I had another incident, not one I am proud of, but which I want to confide in you. I opened the bottom drawer of my bureau to retrieve my heavy sweater, the heather-green one I knitted especially for cold nights up at the lake, and I got a strong waft of lavender. I had never smelled it before in the bedroom, so I knelt down and reached in the back of the drawer and there was a small lavender sachet. It must have been Isabel's—unless Harry had another lady visitor before me . . .

I immediately snatched it, stood up, and threw it out the window as if it were a hand grenade that was going to explode. Perhaps the sparrows will use it to build a nest. Wouldn't it serve me right if they built one right outside my window and the scent blew right back in?

On a more serious note, I do understand that when Will died so young your heart was broken. But mine was too. I saw a man at the post office with a tattoo on his arm of a date (not the dreaded Wednesday, May 29, 1912); he looked so weary with grief I had the strong suspicion that the tattoo was of a lost loved one. I had sympathy for him, and I imagined a hot needle digging into my own flesh

with Will's death date. You must think I have lost my senses, but this marriage business has made my imagination experience a fierce craziness I have not known before.

What I am trying to say is, I understand more than ever why you are always melancholy now on Wednesdays. Perhaps my marrying Harry felt like another loss, but I am not dead. If you cannot abide Harry, even though I do not understand it, I could see you on my own. Harry is a modern man. I picture you so clearly with all those newspapers from around the world piled precisely like narrow clouds, and all those perfectly arranged books on the shelves with your volumes about birds, bicycles, and aeroplanes. I can also see you at Will's deathbed, all of us there, the family, a few friends, unwilling to admit it, and you saying over and over, "He will recover. He must get well," like a small child. We all felt that, Orv. That headline is tattooed in my mind. MAN WHO FIRST CONQUERED THE AIR AND LED THE WAY IN THE AERONAUTIC MARVELS OF THE LAST DECADE SUCCUMBS TO TYPHOID.

This is not a time for our hearts to be broken once again. Rather to rejoice, yes? That our family is yet bigger again? I know I would rejoice if you found the love of your life. I swear I would.

I sometimes wake up with a start at 3:15 in the morning and Harry must soothe me, that precise time our beloved Will passed away. But to fall in love and marry is not the same as typhoid.

In truth,
Katharine

KATHARINE WRIGHT TAKES EMERGENCY LEAVE

Carrie says Orv has intentions of visiting this fall. She said she thought he might enjoy the rail journey, but I am not clear if she thought he would enjoy it or if he actually said he would enjoy it, but as Emily Dickinson wrote, "I dwell in possibility."

I am thinking tonight of Orv's crash almost twenty years ago. Perhaps if Lieutenant Selfridge had not been so heavy. He was the heaviest person to have flown at that point, and the first to die in an aeroplane crash. His weight should not have affected the propeller, but we will never know for sure.

I would have taken a hot-air balloon to be by Orv's side. Instead, I took those endless train rides to that dreadful army hospital in Virginia. When I arrived, I do not think I sat at a table to eat for those seven weeks. I know that it was always after midnight when I would return to my room. I would fall over onto the bed, fully dressed, like a large doll. I barely bathed. Orv's broken ribs and that nasty broken leg—they made me feel that my own ribs and leg were broken. I could not return to teaching after that. Emergency leave simply became my life.

Sometimes when I am blue, as I am now, I make myself remember something happy, like when we dragged the Ping-Pong table outside at the lake house and we would play in the sunlight. I'd love to see those photographs. And when we played eight games and then we chased each other around the table like children and ran into the lake fully clothed.

Censored

There are times when I have worn out my fingers writing letters to Orv on the typewriter and I am smudged with typewriter ink, and the other days when I switch to the fountain pen, because I am upstairs, and I have no idea if Orv cares either way. I want to be a modern woman and have equal rights, but then part of me would be happy to be back in our bicycle shop with the boys.

On another subject, when I hear the screen door bang shut in the kitchen, I know it is my Harry come back from the cemetery with his muddy trowel and gardening gloves. I know he's been planting again and weeding around Isabel's grave. It is these times that I splash my face with water and pinch my cheeks extra hard, willing him to love me as much as Isabel. As I hear him climb the stairs, I want to greet him with all my body. He pulls off his shirt so quickly and hangs it on the bedpost, and we are immediately with each other like ruffians.

We had received an unusual wedding gift—we did not receive many and they were not large, as Harry of course had a whole household, rather a whole lifetime, of items, so we were in no need of a new toasting machine. But we did get a most thoughtful gift from Jean-Louis from his vineyards. Our lunch with the boys and Jean-Louis outside in that court-yard is on the list I am compiling of the happiest meals of my life. He sent a case of his fine wine, which I have only begun to drink a bit, and quite enjoy, but also several bottles of the most delicious olive oil from his vineyards that I use to prepare salad dressing, when Mrs. Crossbottom does not interfere.

One day Harry brought one of the smaller bottles upstairs and put it

on the bed stand, and soon he poured a tiny bit into his palm and rubbed it on my breasts. And then we were rubbing it on each other, every part, as we made love. The olive oil bottle is now in the bathroom, in the medicine cabinet. I do not know what Mrs. Crossbottom will do if she finds it. Smash it to bits? But she should not be snooping around. I know Carrie would have simply brought it downstairs and put it in the pantry, where she believed it belonged, and Carrie would not have uttered a word.

Dear brother,

I feel as if I should have kept one foot on base. Is that the base-ball expression? I imagine I should be asking Harry that question and not you, but I simply must know what is happening in Dayton. We are waiting on pins and needles for your autumnal visit. I hear from my women friends about progress in the cause, but I care also about your cause, ours, about the tiniest details of our home and the smallest and most precise details of your latest drawings. I want to hear the chiming of the clocks, you lining up your newspapers and measuring the stacks with your ruler, then smacking each stack if it was the proper height. I want to hear the sound of you organizing your papers in that special way, with the special paper clips you've fashioned, in the shape of an aeroplane.

Are you warm enough? Even though it is still early October, there can be a chill. And in the evenings, when your work is done, do you sit by the fire the way we used to and read? I loved reading to you, even when you insisted; I read you the newest edition of *Birds of North America* and showed you each picture like a schoolchild. Harry wears sheepskin slippers when he gets home. I think you would love them. I know, I know, you insist on wearing your perfectly pol-ished shoes until you go to bed. Sometimes I would sneak into the doorway and watch you, standing on one leg and carefully untying one shoe, then placing it neatly by your bed. Then repeating on your other leg. And then bending down to retie them and line them up! I've never known anyone else to tie their shoes once they are off. I can assure you, Harry not only does not tie his shoes after he takes them off, but inevitably the left is where the right should be, and the right is where the left should be. One would think that 50 percent of the time this would not be the case, but perhaps I could send you

some photographs of the crooked way his shoes are aligned, or not aligned, although I think the evidence might not be good for your nerves.

Harry and I read to each other as well, although not bird books. He likes American and European books of history, and I keep my American and French novels for myself. We both enjoy Wordsworth, and often before we turn out the light, we say to each other, "I wandered lonely as a cloud . . ." And many nights we are in each other's arms. Does that strike you as odd for a couple of our age? It is true that in certain positions our bones crackle and we laugh, but we laugh together. Because you are not writing back, I feel free to write about our lovemaking. I hope you are not shocked. But perhaps I want to shock you after what you have done to me.

Lovingly,
Sister

P.S. You know you have always said I had such good ears I would have been a good spy. Today, as I was standing in line, I saw two women ahead of me who were old friends of Isabel's. We smiled and gave our polite greetings, bowing our heads slightly, but then one of them leaned into the other and said what of course she thought I couldn't hear—but I did. She said, "Why would he take a spinster bride?"

BABY BORN TO GRANDMOTHER

I got such a scare, or should I say thrill. My monthly was two weeks late, and I had the remarkable and jubilant sense that I was with child, that I was carrying new life. I know, my goal in life is not to be written up in Ripley's Believe It or Not!, *but the thought that out of our lovemaking a human baby could be created is beyond astounding to me, more astounding than being able to fly. I so long to carry a child inside me and give birth. But then, of course, after two weeks, I realized I was not with child. I am not a fool. And I realize the Change will soon be here. I have nobody in the world to tell. I have not told a soul my outlandish imaginings.*

Dear Orv, Orv dear,

Are my letters tied with a ribbon by your bed or stored in a box on a shelf in the linen closet, or have they not even gotten that far? Perhaps you have instructed the postman to return to sender, but if that is the case, I have not received them. Carrie insists that she hands you every letter, and she is a person I trust with all my heart. I can just hear you instructing Carrie, "Take them away, feed them to the wolves. Scatter them to the winds. Do not disturb me for I am having a spell."

Carrie says you are slamming the door to your study with increased frequency.

Tuesday I was speaking to her on the telephone, and I know you were right there. I could hear you tapping your pencil on the staircase the way you do. For one extraordinary moment I believed you would come to the telephone the way a normal person would when someone called. I actually heard you talking, although I could not make out what you said, after I heard Carrie asking you, begging you, to talk to me, but then you screamed, "She is making me ill! I am having a spell!" I heard you march away on those hardwood floors, and then I heard one of your famous door-slamming charades.

Perhaps you are so angry that you throw my letters in the fire as soon as they arrive. I know Carrie does not want to cause you any further distress, but I also know she has no desire to cause me pain. She was honest when I told her the news that I intended to wed. It did not destroy her world. She said she would miss me but that I deserved to live. Her exact words were that I should "have a spin at the dance."

Before she died, Mother told me, as I stood on a stool in the kitchen and she brushed my hair, "Clarity, clarity, clarity. That is

what is most important in life—in work and in the home." And you know? I agree with her. I believe that the way "things" are between us now makes things extremely unclear and this muddiness is causing us both to have spells. I am deeply and desperately in love with my husband, Orv, but you are causing undue distress. Yes, undue.

Sometimes I think if I make clear how much I am grateful for all you have given me it will help. A million thanks, I then send. Thank you for taking me to France with you boys and to Germany. You know the list: going to the White House, the parades . . . Sometimes I wander into the kitchen and stand in front of the sink, gazing out into the yard, and think of the glorious things we did together. It is I who am wandering lonely as a cloud. I did love joining you in Pau in 1909. I loved the parties; I loved the food. The first time I had a croissant I thought I would cry.

You boys were always so shy, but when you bit into your first croissant and said, "I believe the interior of these delights would be just the thing for designing a new wing," that whole room laughed and cheered in French, and I saw that you enjoyed the attention.

People asked me all the time whether you had a special girl—a *fille*—back in America who was waiting for you. I know French newspapers were fascinated by what they saw as the "human side" of us. In some ways I think I could have stayed living there. My French is quite good, if I may say so. I loved their attention to daily life, and although they treated you as heroes, they made me feel more human, if that makes sense. There was that woman who left her perfumed handkerchief in your hotel room. I never asked you whether she had left anything else there as well, but when I went in to tidy up, the sheets were rumpled, and I know you are not one for naps. The Reverend did not allow us such indolence during the day. Early to bed and early to rise.

Perhaps we were closest when we were sewing the wings. What a lark, trying to make wings of silk, but let's be clear: a lark would have known better. There's the one photo of Will at the sewing machine in one of the albums. I would so like to be seated by you in the front room, turning the pages of the albums together. Although you

wouldn't permit me to take an album, I did sneak one photograph from Kitty Hawk. It sits on my dresser—Isabel's and my dresser—next to a very faint photograph of Mother. And the strong muslin scent of the wings stays with me. I also can smell when you boys came back from Kitty Hawk with all that laundry that reeked of the salt air. With the sand that had accumulated in the steamer trunks we could have made a whole beach in the backyard in Dayton.

The morning the Reverend found a few grains of sand on the kitchen table at breakfast, I thought he was going to kill us all. Almost as bad as when he railed against us about those piles of silk. "Inventions are one thing, but waste is another," he scolded. He never liked all the "stuff" of the inventions. But I am thankful for all of it.

And I will be ever thankful to the French for including me in the Légion d'honneur.

In anticipation,
Your devoted sister

Orv!

News alert: Harry is married to the *Kansas City Star*—she is his real lover, although I have no doubt of our love. And I am feeling more comfortable with Harry Jr. I know it is not easy to lose a mother, at any age. I recently confided that to him, that I understood, and I could see a tear in his eye. We were at the dining table, just the two of us, about to eat one of Mrs. Crossbottom's dreadful zucchini concoctions that taste like watery pudding. His father had not yet come home from downtown. He is a dear boy, really young man now. And I know what it's like to be a young man in his twenties, after living with you boys. He is musical and does seem wistful when I play the piano. I know he is thinking of his mother, but he has never shown any objection that his father had married again. He acts very kindly to me, his stepmother, although that word has never been said aloud by anyone. The other day I made up a batch of my chocolate toffee cookies, and the next day I found some of the cookies in the trash bin, but I have a feeling it was Mrs. Crossbottom, not Harry Jr.

I had never been down to the paper and I asked Harry if he could give me a tour. He said he would be delighted to, so I went yesterday. I had awoken in the morning, riding a blue wave of melancholia—perhaps because it was a Wednesday—but when I appeared at his desk and Harry blushed, my spirits lifted. He jumped up and guided me around the office. At each desk we passed, all the men stood up and nodded, even those with green eyeshades on, then quickly returned to hunching over their desks, clacking away at their typing machines. I do find those garters on their sleeves most lovely. I imagine someday there will be women reporters, but when? Judging from the cloud of cigar smoke in that room, it could be many years before those cigar boys let us in.

Most interesting was the linotype machine room. The sound of those machines was louder than a locomotive. Have you ever heard it? Harry had told me before, but I had forgotten, that all the linotype workers were deaf, and it was startling to observe them the moment we stepped into that room. In contrast to the painfully loud machines, the men looked like they were doing an intricate dance with their hands to communicate. They weren't deaf because the machines made them so, but that is why they were hired! They can concentrate amid all that noise. Isn't that curious? I took a course in sign language at Oberlin, but these men's hands flew faster than hummingbird wings, and I understood nothing. When you visit us, not only will you have your own quarters and as much privacy as you need, but I do think you would enjoy a tour of the *Star*. You and Harry could take in a baseball game and, if you're willing, jazz along the Missouri River.

I've always wanted to ask you how you felt after the Reverend died, just three years after we moved to the big house. I did not see you shed a tear. I know he could be strict, and all that went on, but when you wake in the morning do you expect to hear his voice calling us downstairs to prayers? I cannot say I miss him. Rather, I miss our family's life at 7 Hawthorn. I do not miss the screech of the photographers shouting questions about how much money we have as we were walking down the street, or those flashbulbs that nearly blinded us during the wild evening in Paris when we went to the opera, but I miss much of what was.

Lovingly,
Sister

P.S. Have you been reading news of this most dreadful tornado in St. Louis—72 dead and 550 people injured? I have been charting the daily winds here, and I think our next task is to create an aeroplane to survive such force.

WOMAN OF THE HOUSE

Harry drinks so much Coca-Cola it drives me mad. The Reverend never let us drink soda pop, and I agree with him on that one. Although once, after Mother had died, I saw him in town drinking a soda pop outside the post office. He had sent me on some errands, and I came around the corner and saw him there like some kind of teenage boy with a straw in his mouth. I was so shocked, I retraced my tracks, and when I returned to the post office, he did not have the Coca-Cola bottle in his hand, just the straw hanging out of his mouth like a cigarette, in a not very reverendly sort of way. He said, "Tardiness is not becoming, Sister," and that was that, as if it were I who had transgressed.

MOLLUSKS AND THE MOON

Last night I made Orv's favorite meal for Harry. I am fairly certain it would be ill advised to tell such things to a husband, although I have no experience and have not spoken to other women about this. I made beef stew, tomatoes and basil from our garden, baked potatoes with gobs of whipped butter, and then I made Orv's favorite apple cobbler. Harry is a rational man. He does not understand why Orv does not speak to us, but he, unlike me, simply accepts it. "Humans are complicated beings," he has said on more than one occasion when I start one of my tirades, and then he often snaps his newspaper and holds it in front of his face the way men do and keeps on reading.

Today I shall make the chicken and corn dish both boys enjoyed so much. Once, after two portions of my apple cobbler, Orv put down his fork and said, "Sister, I believe that one day if we fly to the moon, your apple cobbler should be served!"

At which point Will said, "Yes, and you could eat it with a piece of cheese from the surface of the moon!"

I felt our giggling would never stop, until Orv stood up from the table and swished his napkin from his lap and said so seriously, "Young man, the moon is not made of green cheese or any kind of cheese, and someday I will prove it to you!"

I loved when Orv called Will "young man."

I have a confession to make. The smell of Scotch makes me want to pull Harry by the hand and race upstairs to our bedroom. I think there is much to learn from teetotalers, and yet, people who enjoy liquor seem to weather the struggles of daily life with a bit more gaiety. I am, of

course, speaking of liquor in moderation. I think a stiff drink might calm Orv as much as when I endlessly read to him from the Encyclopedia of Mollusks *that he frequently insisted upon. Not that a mollusk fact isn't soothing once in a while . . .*

The view from the first time I went up, after Orv tied back my hair, scolding me that it could get caught in the wings . . . I loved it all. Perhaps I should become one of those skywriting aviators. I know Orv would not approve, saying it is "making the commercial out of the sublime," but I would write to him in the sky above Dayton: COME VISIT, ORV! DON'T BE A THICKHEAD!

Orv once told me, while sitting in his "thinking chair" in the den, that going up made him think God "knew what he was doing when he chose where he would perch." Just now I had the image of a carnival worker who uses one of those mallets to hit the thing—what is that thing?—that speeds the puck up to the top and rings a bell. That sudden soaring is how I felt the first time Orv took me up.

KATHARINE WRIGHT STEPS OUT SOLO

Today I took a magnificent bicycle ride and sat for an hour reading Wordsworth under the shade of a copper beech. Orv, Will, and I rarely agreed on anything, but the copper beech, especially in autumn, is and will always be our favorite tree.

But now it is night, and once again I am sitting in the bathtub. It's a grand tub, my favorite place in this house, but it is not enough. I am not sure about this "till death do us part." I have left my suffragist soul back in Ohio, the way Peter Pan lost his shadow, and I am determined to regain it.

Orville,

Did I tell you about the eighty-year-old twins I often see at the post office? They dress identically. I have no idea which is which, but they are so friendly to me and call me "Mrs. Wright Brothers' Sister," which I find most amusing. I think they know I feel like I'm a twinless twin without you.

   And of course I know you felt like a twinless twin without Will. We Wrights all have active imaginations—from Mother's side of the family—and I want you to know I don't want you to be ashamed of any of your imaginings.

Love,
Katharine

P.S. Lorin visited with his wife last week. They say they have visited you and wanted to know if I wanted to go with them next time, and they did not have kind words about our estrangement, precisely your abandonment of me. Curiously, I found myself coming to your defense, as I have always done in the past. I want you to know that, always.

P.P.S. I am not getting all the mail forwarded, so I am not keeping up on the latest legal wrangling. Please advise.

FULL DISCLOSURE!

It is pouring rain to beat the band. I hope Orv remembers to wear his galoshes, although he doesn't like putting them over his shined shoes.

Sometimes I wake up in the morning and, as I put on my spectacles, I imagine Harry as a young man with bright eyes and I'm a young woman with firm breasts, but what I see is Harry, a somewhat fit man in his fifties, grabbing for his spectacles at the same time. When I was director of the Young Women's League in Dayton, nobody would have pointed to me and said, "That woman who still looks like a schoolteacher will marry when she is more than a half century old."

For all those times the boys and I talked about the press as if they were the enemy . . . to think that now I share the sheets with one of them. The press are not the enemy, they are just an extremely curious lot. In some ways they are like inventors, like explorers, always pushing to see what is around the bend. Harry gets jolly and talks more than usual when he drinks, and while he becomes more affectionate with me, he also tells me stories about his life before, and sometimes it is too much.

I think perhaps it is the journalist's mind—"Full disclosure," he calls it. The facts, always the facts. For instance, we were sitting at the table looking out at the bird feeder at dusk, and we heard the geese flying south for the winter, and he said, "I remember when Junior [that's what he called his son] was young and the geese passed, and he would run around the yard flapping his arms, saying, 'I want to go with them! I want to go with them,' and Isabel and I laughed and laughed."

I wanted to cry out, "And Orv and Will did that as well, but they did really fly!" I confess I did once mutter that under my breath, as I've

heard that story several times, but I don't tend to make a practice of it. It would not help our union. I think I still have some very old-fashioned ways. I learned as a child that men don't want to hear about other men.

As I am writing I am smelling the peppermint scent of Mother's hair, because Harry uses the very same shampooing soap! I can see Mother standing in the front yard picking Queen Anne's lace and black-eyed Susans for the table. I must have been ten years old.

And I can see her when she took me inside and sat me down at the kitchen table, which she often did when she had something serious to say. She had been teaching me to make biscuits, those ones Orv likes with extra butter and dill.

"Katharine Wright," she said. "Katharine Wright, you must never beat a man in anything. They don't like it, and it is not seemly, even though girls are frequently better at things than boys. That Elizabeth Painter who lives down the road has been beating her brother in badminton, and her mother is not pleased."

There was another thing she told me after the biscuits were in the oven and I'd brushed all the dough and crumbs from the table and swept the floor and washed the dishes. We sat at the kitchen table again and she said, "Now, Katharine Wright, as you are my only daughter, you will be in charge if I leave this earth early. You know the Reverend is not an easy man."

Did she know she would leave us so young?

I'm sorry, I'm meandering here, but although I try to keep some thoughts to myself with Harry, I have gotten it in my head to purchase one of those Sears kit houses, which could be built with no memories of Isabel. You simply send a check and a truck arrives with all the wood and nails and even young men to put it together! Of course, Harry would never do such a thing, but I like the idea of a kit arriving as if it were some kind of dollhouse, but human size and starting fresh. Perhaps someday there will be kit aeroplanes from Sears as well, and not just ones for children!

Yesterday we visited friends of Harry's, very bohemian. When they asked if I wanted a drink, they brought me lemonade in a jelly jar! And when one of them had to go to the toilet, they'd wink and say, "Have to go iron my shoelaces!"

CENSORED

Last night I thought I'd lost my marbles.

I was in the same lovely claw-footed bathtub where I am now, but I was bathing in hot, soapy water. I was staring at the tiny hexagonal white tiles on the floor, with black lines that are so hard to clean, the exact tiles as we have in our bathroom in the big house in Dayton. First, I was daydreaming of when Orv and Will built the tandem, and we'd take turns on it riding down the street, Orv in the front, steering like a mad scientist. They even fashioned that map stand, because Orv said, "A proper cyclist needs to have a map at all times. Maps and globes are man's greatest gifts," to which I always added and still add, "And women's too." Orv also said it would be a good project to mount a globe on the handlebars. I have never seen that.

And then, while I was in the bathtub, I was recalling Harry washing my hair outside in the yard this past summer. I bent over in front of him. It was so hot, and he sprayed me with the cool water from the garden hose. He washed my hair with his peppermint shampooing soap out in the sunlight, and there I was out in the garden, bent over, smelling like Mother. I was looking through my half-closed eyes, careful not to get soap in them, and it was almost as if there were stained glass between the branches of the maple trees, the way the colors lit up. The cardinals were dashing around in their red coats, and I thought I could never be happier.

But then, after the tandem bicycle thought and the washing my hair in the yard thought, there was Harry J. Haskell, really standing next to me, in the bathroom, fully clothed by the tub, without knocking! I was looking up at him, perhaps the way a child would, and he took the bar of soap from my hand and began to wash my breasts.

Dear Orv, Orv dear,

I long to tell you what marriage is really like. Of course I can't tell you about all marriages, but my marriage is like a dance, where my partner holds me close as we dance around the room, then at times spins me out so our hands barely touch, and I twirl and twirl, not knowing if I will ever manage to get back to him, but then I do, so far I always do, but it's more unpredictable than any dance steps I know. I can feel so close to Harry, and then . . . and then . . . I feel I will leave him forever.

Yours truly,
K.

P.S. Perhaps marriage is like having a permanent houseguest, although in this case it is I who is the houseguest!

P.P.S. Harry asked me if I thought you and Will just forgot to find women to marry.

College Woman Worries About Hair

Yesterday, before Harry got home, I was looking in the mirror and I saw so many gray hairs that I pulled them out with tweezers and threw them out the window to help the wrens weave their nest. Sonya says I should use a hair dye and that women cannot afford to have gray hair. That's what she said. I think I can afford it. And Harry has not mentioned it. He even says sometimes I am beautiful! But with these women with bobbed blond hair and I with my hair in a bun that birds can use to make nests, do I have a chance?

Dear Orville,

I am shaking. Harry hasn't spoken to me all day. He had to "cover" another lynching outside the city line. When he came home, he walked upstairs, then immediately downstairs, and went out back and got sick in the garden.

I shudder, although this country does not need another shuddering woman. I would like my legacy to be more than a sister to you boys, as proud as I am of our work, but I want to be a soldier against evil, like Emmeline Pankhurst. She said, "Trust in God. She will provide." But she also emphasized, "Deeds not words."

The same year you boys first went up, she founded the Women's Social and Political Union, but of course you had other things on your mind at the time.

Rochelle has written to me again and she is with child, and I have been giving her money, from my account. This is what I am doing. She told me yesterday that her baby's father is a Negro man she loves very much. She is due in two months, although she is not the most reliable source for anything. She came here last week, when Harry was downtown, looking so swollen and tired. I do not need to tell him about what funds I use. I shall cover the hospital.

The Reverend always said that mankind was essentially evil. Do you remember that one time he said that? And you said quietly, "Perish the thought that Father Wright is not always right."

The Reverend raised his hand to strike, but he did not strike that time.

Yours truly,
Your sister, K.

WOMAN WALKS ALONE

Yesterday I took a magnificent autumn trek and walked 5.8 miles, according to the pedometer Orv and Will made for me years ago. As I was returning home, with my knees a bit weary, I passed a young man with tattered clothes, begging in the middle of the street just around the corner. I beckoned to him, because I didn't want him to get hit by an automobile. As I dropped a coin in his cup, I looked into his eyes, and I could imagine him when he was a baby, in a tiny baby outfit, clean and warm, somewhere in America. The man smiled at me, tipped his scruffy hat, and said, "May I present myself. I am Theodore," and he gave a little bow, tipping forward with a graceful bend of his waist.

I said, "I am Katharine with an a," and in that moment, as I bent my head to him, I felt a sensation strong as the Canadian lake wind, a rushing through me, and I knew that soon I was going to align my wings.

At Oberlin we learned about Christine de Pisan, who lived from 1364 to "sometime after 1429"—that's what our professor told us. Supposedly she was the first female to earn her living by the pen. Harry has asked me if I want to write a book about Orv and Will, but I know if I did, I would lose Orv's trust completely, if that hasn't already happened, because I would have to tell the truth, the whole truth, so help me God.

We were at a cocktail party yesterday when a woman came right up to me, not a flapper, but a woman with her hair up the way I wear mine, and also spectacles. I thought she might talk about a novel she had just read, so I extended my hand eagerly.

But she did not recommend a novel, although she was an educated woman. What she said, although softly, was as distinct and dramatic as if it were written in the sky.

"Dear," she said, "are you acquainted with A Midsummer Night's Dream, by William Shakespeare?"

"Yes, of course," I said in earnest. "Of course I love that play. We read all of Shakespeare at Oberlin. It was required."

And then she leaned in closer, and for a moment I thought, at last, I had a new friend.

"Of course," I repeated. "As Titania sleeps, Oberon sprinkles magic love juice in her eyes so that when she wakes up, she will fall in love with the first creature she sees. When Titania wakes up she sets her eyes on Bottom, who has been recently transformed into a donkey."

This new woman, who turned out not to be a friend, then said, "Well, we in the book club believe that Harry was Titania after dear Isabel died. And you, my dear, are the donkey."

I did not throw my cocktail—a gin and tonic—at her, although I longed to, and perhaps Orv would have if he were here. I just laughed. Something has shifted within me. These women can no longer hurt me. Later that night, when I told Harry in bed, he laughed as well, held me close, and said, "Well, a fine-looking donkey, if I say so myself!"

Harry has a beautiful copper-colored globe in his study, the kind of globe we have at home, where we traced our flights and our imagined flights as we spun it around. And once, when Orv was waiting for my strawberry-rhubarb pie to cool, he marched over to the globe, spun it, and shouted, "If that pie isn't ready soon, I think I shall eat the world!"

Right now, the air is filled with that beautiful scent of burning leaves. I disliked how the Reverend would make us rake and rake them until our arms ached, but I loved the smell of the smoke and the rough burlap we picked them up with. I loved when Will told me to lie down on the burlap and then Orv piled leaves on top of me. It was not an intelligent thing to do, as the leaves were a bit wet, and I was the one who had to launder my clothes of course, but that feeling of the burlap beneath me and the leaves on top of me, looking up at the blue October sky, with the boys singing one of their crazy songs about the moon . . . it was the cat's meow, as the kids say.

Dear Orv,

For one's one-year anniversary a gift of paper is expected, so you would have been the perfect gentleman if you could have written me a letter, rather than silence for over a year. But Carrie says you are thinking of making a surprise visit. I would like nothing more. I would race down the stairs to greet you! No, I would meet you at the railroad station, anywhere. Just say the word, or don't say a word—just appear like a rabbit in a magician's act.

Looking forward,
Katharine Wright Haskell

P.S. Harry gave me the most beautiful bamboo rake as a gift. Sometimes he understands me perfectly. He knows I don't want jewelry. He knows how I love to rake leaves (but not being told to rake leaves by other people!).

P.P.S. I am missing so many people. Sometimes I don't think we thanked Amos Root enough. Harry thinks it's crazy that *Gleanings in Bee Culture* got the scoop on our first flight in 1905. But you boys trusted him. In a way you were not unlike that man, with your shared love of bees, bikes, and aeroplanes. Sometimes when I cannot sleep, I sneak out of bed and read from the few clippings I took with me. We had several copies of that article, and I thought I could steal one away, about you "Ohio boys" and your first successful trip of an airship, without a balloon to sustain it . . .

   We did it, Orv, yes, we did.

NOVEMBER 30, 1927

LIFE ON EARTH

Here I am sitting comfortably, albeit in an empty bathtub, and I can't stop thinking about the international news. One of the reporters from the Star *was in Japan and reported on the Tango earthquake, with 2,956 people killed and 7,806 injured. I have little to complain about.*

Orville Wright, please do not tell a soul, but the former governor of the state, Governor Hadley, died, though he was not an old man, only fifty-five, and I do not care a hoot. Who cares, you say? I second the motion. Everyone is talking about it as if he were President Lincoln. Harry is, of course, "covering the story."

Love,
Your insensitive sister

P.S. When he died, Governor Hadley was chancellor of Washington University in St. Louis, though he visited Kansas City, his hometown, quite often. I met him and Mrs. Hadley at a social function. She seems to be a good woman, comfortable with all the social life that goes along with being married to such a man!

Beware Sewing Implements

I am sitting shivering in my flannel nightgown and robe in the empty tub. Harry didn't come back until after midnight last night. He tried not to disturb me, but I was fully awake as he tiptoed in, took off his glasses, and laid them on the nightstand by the bed.

Covering stories might drive me to drink even more than I am. This obsession with Governor Hadley's death is beyond me. That was why Harry was gone from 8:00 a.m. until after midnight. What did Governor Hadley invent? And all the papers clamoring around, waiting to see what will happen to the state. MISSOURI POLITICS BORES THE WRIGHT BROTHERS' SISTER!—and the newspapers can quote me.

I did something in my anger after breakfast with those scissors, yes. Keep me from scissors, apparently, for that is my weapon. At breakfast Harry said, "Katharine dear, do you think we should invest in a new toaster?" And I wanted to scream at him, how he could stay out so late without a care in the world. And did he really think talking about the possibility of a new toasting machine would appease me? I don't care a whit about toasting machines at this point, although I usually do enjoy a good piece of toast covered with thick butter and fresh berries. As soon as he left for work, I picked up a cigar that lay resting, not yet smoked, on his desk in the study. I slid the paper band off the cigar and on to my wedding finger, next to my ring. Then I grabbed the scissors and cut up the cigar. It's true. Then I took the remains into the kitchen and mashed it into the jug of old potato peels and onion skins under the sink. I better find something to do here in KC!

WRIGHT SISTER LUSTS FOR AUTOMOBILE

Forgive me for I have sinned. I lust after the Model A that Ford has just created. Harry says I have lost my marbles. It includes a safety-glass windshield, four-wheel brakes, and hydraulic shock absorbers. And it comes in four different colors. I think I would like one for each season. Perhaps I am more like the ladies of the Flower Arranging Society than I have imagined. Just four hundred thousand vehicles sold in the first two weeks after its debut!

Dear Orv, Orv dear,

Happy 1928, brother. May you have clear skies. (Although I some-times think you deserve a good hailstorm!)

I have not written for some time. I must tell you why. I am trying not to write until I see you, but you are making that extremely dif-ficult. Is that a fair assessment of the situation? And don't you dare say, "Sister, your wings are not aligned."

I have also not written because Rochelle gave birth to her baby, a beautiful little boy, with dark eyes and skin. She has been with many men, Jews and Negroes, and she said she does not keep count. When she talks to me about her men, it is as if she's in a trance. I cannot help that I feel so protective of her. I've been taking care of the baby several hours a day. I simply informed Mrs. Cross-bottom that I would be doing this, and remarkably, she has not said a word to me about it, and it turns out that she is a master at settling him down. She taught me how to rub his ears to get him to sleep and a wonderful technique of rocking him while rubbing his back, with your hand just so. Rochelle named the baby Psalm, isn't that lovely? I am in love. It all comes quite naturally to me. I love to give him a bottle, but we have not gone outside because it is so cold. I'm not sure where Rochelle goes. I know she loves the child, although when she comes back, she smells of alcohol. The other day I rocked Psalm in my arms and whispered, "Here you are, little boy. You are my lost child. And someday you shall meet your uncle Orv!"

I am enjoying that Mrs. Crossbottom is not cross about some-thing. And there are moments when the two of us are in the kitchen taking turns rocking Psalm and I wish Mother could be here too.

Sonya has not had contact with her daughter in years but has begun coming over to see her grandson, but she seems ill at ease around Psalm. Sonya is not happy in her marriage at all. It is true that Rochelle leaves the baby with me often enough for Sonya to be jealous, but Sonya does not say that. She does not use the old-fashioned term "ill repute." Rather she says the girl has "fallen in with some rough characters." As I sit cooing with Psalm, Sonya tells me of all the times Rochelle has written for money. I have not told Sonya that I gave her daughter money. I am quite confused.

I long so for a child of my own, and Psalm fills an empty well for me. Do you think I am batty?

And it causes my mind to go all over the map yet again.

Perhaps I am more like you boys than I should be. I do still prefer the smudges of carbon paper on my brow to the makeup the ladies are wearing now. I have been called a bluestocking, and one paper said, "Katharine Wright [although they spelled my name *Katherine*, with an *e*] could run for president if she chose, but thankfully she will not choose."

As excited am I by the vote, I am confused by all the new fashions. Harry has teased me and said I should get a flapper dress. One day when I was not caring for Psalm, Sonya came with me to the shop—"20s," it's called. I tried on a dress with shimmery spangles, but by the time I had managed to zip myself up I was exhausted, and I refused to go out of the dressing room. The salesgirl, who was wearing sheer stockings and a flapper dress herself, kept saying to me, "Please, ma'am, come out. You'll be the toast of the town!" As if I were not fully a woman if I did not have a jazzy dress, but as quickly as I could, which was not quickly in the least, I managed to pull off that flapper dress and put on my sensible clothes.

Sonya purchased the gaudy number she had tried on and made small talk with the salesgirl, who carefully wrapped it up in gold paper. I confess I wanted to run screaming out of the store.

And when finally, mercifully, we left the store, I felt hollow, as if I had entered into a kingdom where I did not belong. But where do

I belong, where do *we* belong, Orv? If I had not left Dayton, if I had not left you, then what?

Forgive me, for I almost forgot to wish you a healthy and robust New Year.

Bewildered,
K.

Married Woman on the Loose

Harry and I had a terrible fight. He said I would have to choose between Orv and him. It was one more time when I couldn't help myself and was tidying up his precious newspapers. What human being needs to keep newspapers for over six months? (At least Orv has his organized.) Is the concept of old news too much to ask? I was joking with him, because there's someone who's opened up a restaurant and cooks barbecue outdoors in newspaper like it's the latest craze. I told Harry if he isn't careful, I was going to scoop up all his newspapers and barbecue them, with no meat at all. I was kidding but not kidding. In any event, Harry grabbed my wrist as I reached for a newspaper and screamed, "You must stop, do you hear me? I can't take it anymore!"

And then he jumped up and ran out of the house. I imagine he went "downtown," as he calls it, although who knows. Perhaps he has a woman who doesn't mind a mess of newspapers, or perhaps enjoys them. Perhaps they make love in a messy pile of papers! At this point I don't care.

I had to get away from this ghost house. While Harry was downtown, I rang Sonya Rose to help me escape. I packed a bagful of my warmest clothes and bundled up for the cold. It wasn't two hours before she was tooting the horn of her Model T and I was in my heavy overcoat and winter boots and we were running away.

I am in Ohio now.

Dear Orv, Orv dear,

I am not being entirely honest with you about all that has to do
with Sonya Rose. I went on a driving trip with her. In my first vision
of the trip I thought I needed to get away from the cold and we left
Rochelle and dear Psalm, and Harry . . . We had wanted to drive
all the way to Florida. But then I completely changed my mind and
packed my warmest clothes and dressed in my winter boots and
heavy coat and two scarves. I did have to get away. I realized I was
getting too close to that baby and I was becoming confused.

So we did not go to Florida at all, despite the mean weather. In
fact, we drove home, to Dayton. All I wanted to do was end up on
the Hawthorn Street of our youth, but that would be going back too
far in time. I wanted to end up at the big house, where you are now,
and walk in the door and say, "Orville Wright, what is going on in
that cockeyed mind of yours?"

We did get back to Dayton, can you believe it? We took turns
driving on those endless snowy roads. And we were lucky we were
not killed. I felt like Shackleton with his frozen toes, exploring the
Antarctic. Did you see us out the window? We were driving Sonya
Rose's new black 1927 Model T. Actually, at the time we drove past
the house, she was driving, and I was ready to leap out the automobile door while we were moving! There was a man I did not recognize shoveling the path. The wind was fierce and biting, and the
snow was spinning around. I had such a longing to walk up the steps
and into the house, such a longing I cannot tell you. But when Sonya
Rose stopped the car, I suddenly screamed, "No! Keep driving! Keep
driving!" and I shut my eyes and sang "I've Been Working on the
Railroad" until we made it out of the neighborhood.

That night we stayed in a rooming house in Dayton on the far

side of town. Nobody recognized me, because I wore my hair down in a braid inside and I kept my hood up as much as possible as we traveled.

In some ways those days "on the road" are a blur, but in other ways, they are as vivid as the time I went up with you.

I shall not tell you all we did in those days and nights away from both you and Harry. I will tell you that we went to a sauna, yes; it was off the beaten path, in Indiana of all places. There was a sort of community, a spiritual community. I know. Please don't laugh. Sonya had been there before. They had their own filling station. They took us in, because we were so cold, and fed us a casserole—of what I am not sure, which perhaps normally I would have not thought about, but it tasted like ambrosia. They do not believe in killing animals, but I swear there was chicken in it, but what do I know? And there was even a woman who knew more about automobiles than I did.

The sauna was a cedar building, and it was full of naked women baking themselves. I never saw so many kinds of breasts. I will admit Sonya is introducing me to all sorts of interesting people I never had met before. I stayed up all night more than once, and I drank quite a bit. The only times before I stayed up until daybreak were with you, when we sat on the dock at the lake, looking at the stars and watching the sunrise and listening to your beloved loons. Sonya's friends are writers and dancers and singers and performers (including a contortionist)—not a scientist or inventor or journalist in the bunch! You can see why I did not sleep.

Now that we're back in Kansas City, my mind is twisted up and I say to myself, "You have to get your fin wet."

I keep thinking about those women. You men swim naked in the public pools, but we have to wear our heavy wool swimming costumes. In my dreams my hair is always wet. In truth, yesterday, when it was hovering near zero, I did go swimming at the indoor public pool, and when I returned home my hair was frozen in icicles. When Mrs. Crossbottom saw me, she said, "You'll catch your death," but did not seem overly concerned.

Next time I go to the lake, which I plan to next summer, I intend

to skinny-dip. I want to feel the water change from warm to cold on my flesh. You do not have to partake, but that is what I intend to do.

When we drove up to the house in Dayton, Orv, even though the front yard was heavy with snow, all I could think of was swimming with you.

On a more serious note, someone Harry works with wants to interview me. Harry says he is pretty convinced that I helped more than I have ever admitted with the plans for the Flyer. He said he wanted to talk to me about who precisely came up with the movable rudder. I have never told anyone, Orv. I have never told a soul.

K.

HOME SWEET HOME

I think I shall knit Orv a striped sweater. They're quite the fashion now in France, although I have never seen him wear anything with stripes. WRIGHT BROTHER WEARS STRIPES! I could even knit him a zigzag sweater to match his socks!

I wish I could have gotten a glimpse of Orv. Next time I shall knock on the door until he opens it, even if I have to sleep in the front yard. Or at least until Carrie lets me in. There was smoke coming out of the chimney, so I know Orv had built a fire with those wonderful pinyon branches that young man always sends Orv from New Mexico. I know how blowy it can get in there.

I have some yarn I bought with Sonya on our driving tour. We stopped at the farm where I always got wool for Orv's socks, and the farmer's wife came out to greet us. At first she did not recognize me, but when I took off my goggles and hood, she said, "The Wright brothers' sister is here! The Wright brothers' sister is here!" and I had to laugh, because she made us feel so welcome. She ushered Sonya and me in and helped us pull off our wet clothes, and we sat by their fire as she served us a hearty chicken and barley soup. Real chicken! She even insisted that we stay the night, and we did, up a ladder in the loft. I thought I might not be able to get back down, but I did.

I was happy to be back in Harry's arms after running away, but I don't feel I belong in Kansas City, in Isabel's house, and I can feel he is still angry at me for leaving. Mrs. Crossbottom sniffed at me, when he wasn't in the kitchen: "Aren't you a bit old for such high jinks?"

I almost had the courage to tell Harry that I cannot continue living

here, but I know how much this house means to him. I want to be with him, but I want to move. At Oberlin I felt I did belong, always, not that there wasn't the drama of love and love lost with the boys, but we did not focus on such things as fashion. We went to prayers, we went to classes, we went for long walk-and-talks about philosophy and spirituality. I don't recall anyone talking about dresses or patent leather dancing shoes. I did have one friend, Charlotte Anne, who had grown up on a farm and was brilliant at Latin and literature. She brought her sewing machine with her and would sit at it with her bobbins and all while reciting Shakespeare. We sat behind her as if she were backward onstage, and if she wasn't quoting the Bard, we all would chat and sing, while she was sewing clothes for her pig back home. Yes, I said pig.

FORBIDDEN FRUITS

Harry recently surprised me when he brought home a copy of Lady Chatterley's Lover. *He took it out of a brown paper sack. "Ta-da," he said, "the forbidden fruit." The book is banned in England, because of all the scandalous language, but the* Kansas City Star *is a modern newspaper and all kinds of things are sent to the paper. Books arrive from around the world. Harry winked and said, "We Americans are not prudes."*

I know Orv doesn't read such books. There is not a mention of wingspan or draft or speed or torque. There are no accounts of bird migration or wind velocity, but forgive me, I cannot put it down. And even though I'm reading it at home, I have taken off the dust jacket for fear that Mrs. Crossbottom or the postman or even someone other than Harry will see me reading it. You would think I have a pistol under the covers, it feels so fraught and quivering with danger. I suppose I've picked up the word "quivering" from what I just read. I should cross that out, just "fraught with danger" will suffice, although it is even a thrill to pen the word "quivering."

In the bedroom, I think I can say my desire is burgeoning, even at this age, something I did not know existed, except in novels. Is "burgeoning" even the correct word? It feels like that, like I am learning how to find as much excitement as I did when we went up in our machine. And it is not only in the bedroom when I have these feelings. I will be sitting in the bathtub, as I am now, or answering some letters about the great Wright brothers, or even, dare I say it, when I am driving in the automobile. After I'm tangled up in Harry's arms and legs, I feel I shall need nothing more ever again in my life, for those minutes we lie entwined after.

This morning I awoke thinking of when Orv and I took that trip to Florida, just the two of us, and we stayed with people—what was their name?—who kept saying, "You'll like our food. We've got swamp offerings. Gator tails. And frog legs."

Swamp offerings!

And both of us went to bed hungry that night.

I hope Orv has been wearing the trousers I lined with flannel. I am not doing much sewing these days, but I've met a woman here who could make him a pair.

I wonder if Orv is still a virgin. Forgive me, Lord, but I've been drinking some Scotch while Harry is off on a story. I cannot control my impertinence and curiosity.

I wish to be less of a schoolmarm, with my hair in a bun and my librarian glasses, but I can't bear to bob my hair. When we finally do meet again, I can't stand the thought that Orv might not recognize me. I do think there was some kind of chemical reaction between Harry and me, and since Orv and Will did all those studies in the shop with the magnets, I thought Orv might understand. Perhaps it is all a matter of science and engineering.

I almost broke the news to Orv that day on the lake, when it was Harry who was out for a walk by himself. I had told Harry that this was going to be the day I told my brother.

Orv and I were sitting on the porch, looking out at the trees, and just as I was about to tell him that I had found love, he began speaking. Although in my ears it sounded like preaching. I had practiced saying, "You know how Harry and I have become friends. It has turned into something deeper than that, and I hope you will be happy for us."

I thought Orv might say, "I had thought so for a while," or "When do you intend to wed? How can I help with the arrangements? Would you like to get married at the house or perhaps here at the lake? I will start working on a toast right now. And what would you two like as a wedding gift?"

But I didn't say anything, and Orv did not respond, because just at the moment I was about to speak, he said, "Sister, look at those kestrels circling around each other," and indeed we saw two small falcons fly by.

So I asked Harry that night, after we had been on that very same porch and there had been unbuttonings. I asked him if he would break the news to Orv, gently, almost as if he were asking permission, as if Orv were the Reverend. But why did Orv throw that vase against the wall? What grown man throws a vase full of water and freshly cut flowers? And then he ripped up the coleus plant Mother had potted before she died, and those leaves and the dirt and ceramic crashed to the floor! Who does that?

And I was the one on my knees sweeping up afterward, of course.

Maybe he thought Harry did have to ask his permission, as if Orv were the Reverend in the family.

Dear Orv, Orv dear,

I am listening to Al Jolson singing "All Alone" on the phonograph. The aeroplane and the phonograph, the two best inventions in the world, that is something we have always agreed upon. So perhaps that makes the sandwich number three.

I am wearing my wedding shoes today, in the house, of course, a pair of soft beige kid leather shoes that I love. They're easy to button, slightly pointed. Did you see our photograph in the papers?

Today I went to the post office with a purpose, to have a long talk with the postmistress, to see if my mail had been misdirected in any way. She is a modern woman in that her hair is bobbed, but she is old-fashioned in that she cares about the way stamps are put on an envelope, just as you do. Do you remember when you screamed at Will because he had put a stamp on an envelope with a slight tilt? Agnes is her name, and she is one of the few women whom I consider a friend here, and she has had such loss from the war—one son dead and the other missing a leg. But she said the hardest part is he has lost his mind. She even said she could handle it if he were just missing a leg. "Crutches are nothing," she said. "But when your own son, your remaining son, looks at you and screams, 'I think there's a man with a knife hiding in the pantry,' each time I try to make him some dinner, it makes a mother weep."

I don't know what to say to her. I have never been a mother, but I just say how sorry I am. But then she asked me, directly to my face, if I thought there would have been the Great War without the aeroplane. Of course, you and I know it wasn't better when the boys were looking at one another in the eye as they did in the Civil War, but something has been unleashed now, so I had to tell her honestly, I did not know. It's so different from when we were flying in those

just-beginning days. To think when we went up, we used to sing our songs above the propellers, like it was a walk in the park. "By the Light of the Silvery Moon," that was the best, yes? The two of us shouting into the wind, as simple as do-si-do.

But let me talk more about something that makes you happy, like when we used to study the hummingbirds when we were young. Those endless discussions we had in the parlor, how they have to eat twice their body weight each day to survive. And you said you would eat twice your body weight if I made you apple pie every day! Do you still have those charts of the thousands of miles of routes they fly from Mexico each year? And those wings . . . that was the first time you talked about flying.

Humbly yours,
Sterchens

RESPECTABLE WOMAN TURNS GREEN

I am having a case of jealousy again, and this time not about Isabel, who of course suffered greatly at the end of her life. I actually wish I could confide in Isabel right now! But there is a woman down at the paper who brings Harry fruit every day. She is the telephone operator at the Star. *As I said, it will be a long hop, skip, and a jump before they allow women journalists there, but I saw her at a party, she has her hair dyed red like a kind of parrot in a short bob, and she said, "Harry gets so hungry in the afternoon. I am always sure I have an apple or pear to bring him, and I cut it up for him when he's on deadline. You know he likes his fruit peeled."*

My mother once told me, at her pulpit, the clothesline, "If you ever feel jealousy toward someone, you must invite them over to the house, Katharine. Feed them a meal and you'll lose all that silly jealousy."

At the time, I had no idea what Mother was talking about, but that is exactly what I shall do.

The next time we have people over, this fruit woman will be number one on the guest list!

Dear Orville,

After all those years of fast bicycles and sleek gliders and the excitement of the flying machines, the bending and banging, the thinking and tinkering, it was so sad to see it all turn into lawsuits and
lawyers. It was especially sad that Wilbur did not live to see it all
resolved. It was wonderful to get all that money that meant so much
to our family and was so well deserved, but I know that what really
drove all of us was that the Wright brothers (and sister) should get
credit for coming up with the idea of how to control a flying machine before anyone else did. Does it really matter if the entire wing
is warped or only a part of it is hinged? Of course not! We Wrights
in Dayton, Ohio, figured that out. As a result, the world is a different
place.

But the aeroplanes today look so different from the ones you
built, with their engines and propellers in the front and those long
sleek bodies stretching out behind. We put the "elevator" in the front
and the rudders out back, and now they are always part of one tail
unit. Why didn't we think of that? Our pilots were so exposed. But
all the more thrilling, is what I say. Still, all of that, cockpits and the
rest, came about because of what *we* worked out.

I just wonder what else all of us might have come up with, had
the Reverend been different, had the lawyers not come to dominate
our lives, taking over so much of our minds that we were steered
away from the important work of watching birds, creating new designs, and building engines.

K.

Dear Orv, Orv dear,

Two women from Isabel's old book group have influenza, and I fear they will not make it. Although I do not feel any closeness to these women, I certainly do want them to enjoy good health.

Are you keeping warm? There is a wonderful yarn store here with the most beautiful hues, and I was able to purchase a turquoise blend of silk and wool I think you will enjoy in your stockings.

When the woman in the store asked whom I was knitting for, I murmured that it was for you, and she said, "I assume you are knitting for your poor husband as well," which in fact I am not, because "poor" Harry has enough socks to last a lifetime and likes to purchase them from the department store.

It is true that I am Christian, although we don't know how good a Christian I am, and though I am intrigued by the followers of the Koran and the Jewish people, and studied both religions at college, I think all those hymns we sang from birth have been permanently stamped into my brain. I think it is those hymns I will sing as I pass to the next life.

But still, I do think that there should be more tolerance for different peoples, and I know you do too.

With the whole country screaming about Prohibition, I would say I certainly am opposed to it at this point. I believe I shall vote for Al Smith, and I am not upset one bit that he is a Catholic.

Some of my fondest memories are when Will was still alive, and we stayed up talking in the parlor. And he was folding all that origami. You both were so good at it. You would sit there by the fire, folding and folding. I thought it was wasteful—if you didn't get it right you threw the papers into the fire—but you did not give a hoot about that. I still have a white paper crane you folded before you

went to Kitty Hawk the first time. You said, "We can't be as graceful as this crane, sister, but if you promise to be here with blueberry pancakes when we return, I'll make you proud."

And you did. And I think I made two dozen pancakes that you ate until your lips were stained dark with the blueberries. I was telling Harry last night about Will's very complex scheme, complete with diagrams, on how you boys would fly to every country in the world, and that you would take a child up from every country, and then those children would grow up and talk about the Going Up Project.

He did not roll his eyes, as you did, but I thought it was an excellent idea. I have no idea where we put those diagrams and the drawings I did of children with their goggles and their hair flying in the wind.

I do not really have anything of Will's except for two handkerchiefs I took from his drawer when I left. I use them and wash and iron them when Mrs. Crossbottom has her day off. And when I weep and wipe my eyes with those cloths, I think of him. To die young is a crime, but I am relieved he did not see the Great War.

When I last saw the boy with one arm who works in the hardware store in Dayton, I felt he was angry at us for starting something terrible, but we had no idea. The night we got the reports from Europe about the strategic bombing, you kept muttering, "Strategic? Strategic?" with such disdain. "What human strategy is this, killing people from zeppelins and aeroplanes?"

Wearily,
Sister

Dearest Orville,

I came across the list of full moons that Mother had written out for us and made us memorize. I keep it in my Bible at the Twenty-Third Psalm. When I see her penmanship, I place my hand on the words and I am with her. You were the best of us at memorizing. I don't remember it all, but I do know that February has the Snow Moon, or Hunger Moon, so perhaps you'll visit at the Crow Moon?

Although we never made it to the moon, whatever you think, I do not believe by going up we flew too close to the sun. I believe aeroplanes were going to be invented, and we were the ones to do it. We did do it, of course, so we can't look back.

Looking back is your problem, I believe. I know you've always gone through your spells. Katy, bar the door, as you might have another fit if you read this: you were an impossible boy to be around. And that constant counting and stacking of your books. I do know I was the only one you wanted to wash your socks, and I always did, inside out, then ironed them. I never told any of the ladies I worked with on the vote that I ironed your socks, then laid them individually on your bed, with the toes facing east, toward the Atlantic. I knew you had to fold them in your special way yourself and line them up in the drawer. Paying attention to all those things I had to do for you, and the things you insisted on doing your way, by yourself, became second nature to me. And who does those things now?

You could drag out the printing press you boys built—I think it was from a part of a bicycle and scrap metal. I know it's in the attic at the big house now. Did it involve a bicycle or is my memory failing? Why don't you start a newspaper of news from Dayton and hand-deliver it?

Perhaps we were happiest then, printing that newspaper, *West*

Side News, about the neighborhood animals that escaped and those poems. You did like your poetry.

Harry wrote a beautiful story yesterday. There was a mining accident, and he was sent to write about it and interview some of the widows. He went to the cemetery in the deep snow, and he said how silent and stoic everyone was as the minister was speaking. He said the flurries fell like feathers and that every step he took was covered in a soft gray ash. The whole village was covered in ash. Of course, it's a very sad story, but I think that image is beautiful too.

I shan't ask you for Harry's birthday celebration this year. It will be a small gathering. The Lenten roses look like they might bloom early this year!

Missing you,
Sister

FIRST WOMAN ON THE MOON

I was holding the tin bucket of clothespins up for Mother when she was hanging laundry on a March day like today, with everything achingly ready to burst green. I was looking up at the sky when I winced, because she pinched me on the back with a clothespin. It did not hurt too much, but my eyes stung.

"Katharine Wright," she said, "when I was a child, I was helping my father in his shop, and I told him, 'I believe we will go to the moon someday.' He said, 'The moon is not for men to stand on, Susan, not to stand on at all.'"

And then my mother said to me, right after she pinched me on the back with a clothespin, "But, Katharine, I believe you and the boys will go there someday."

We both laughed, but there was something in her tone, as she went back to hanging clothes. I held out the bucket of clothespins to her, and she gave me a look I will never forget. "You and the boys have work to do on this earth. This will be your mission in life," she said.

Harry has just returned home from planting. He always is particularly subdued after his visits to the cemetery, and I let him take a few hours to come back to me. He folds his gardening gloves over the handle of the shovel at the kitchen door as neatly as Orv folds his socks. That is the only neat thing he does. He doesn't tell me where he's been, but of course I know. It's not that he lies. He is just extremely silent. I saw him load up the car with impatiens. I like that he plants flowers at Isabel's grave.

Dear Master Orville Wright,

The star magnolias are in bloom, exploding white! Have they bloomed in Dayton yet¿

There's a boy who delivers the *Star*, the newspaper not the tree. I know, it's funny we get it delivered, when Harry writes for it, but we do. A bit like coals to Newcastle. But the delivery boy comes by on his bicycle and it lands on the porch with a thump. He knocked on the door once while Harry was downtown and I answered. The boy was extremely polite, tipped his hat and said, "Would you like to contribute to the boys' baseball league, Mrs. Haskell¿" and then he paused and said, "Or Mrs. Haskell, sort of." I tried not to giggle. Now when we are teasing each other, Harry sometimes calls me "Mrs. Haskell, sort of." Such is the lot of a second wife!

Love and laughter,
Katharine

P.S. Do you recall when we were in Europe and King Alfonso wanted Wilbur to take him up for a flight, but the king's mother wouldn't give him permission¿

Orville Wright!

I think you are the most selfish man in the world, and that's quite a feat. How dare you not respond after us being so close all our lives?

Last night I was dreaming of canoeing on Lake Huron with you and Scipio, who was sitting proudly up front in the bow with me, his ears perked up, scouting for birds or even fish! I looked up in my dreams book to see what the new brain doctors think dreaming of dogs represents, and it says, "When a person dreams of dogs he is dreaming of fidelity or someone who is loyal or in some instances disloyal." It is entirely possible the dog in the dream is you (but perhaps not!). I also dreamed of the fireflies flickering through the trees up at the lake in summer, like Christmas lights, so high up. But there was nothing in the book about dreaming of fireflies.

The hydrangeas are bursting blue, as you say!

Your only sister,
Katharine

Orville,

Harry has built the sweetest bird feeder, shaped like a little house and covered with birdseed and straw. I think you would approve of the design and the construction. It is similar to the ones you used to build. It is now hanging on the sugar maple outside our bedroom window, but getting it there was a hoot. I was holding on to his waist as he leaned out the window to find a suitable branch, and when he backed up afterward, we tumbled onto the bed like in one of those Charlie Chaplin movies.

I keep trying to read more of Dr. Sigmund Freud, trying to figure you out, but after reading the last article I actually tossed it into the fireplace! You would have been proud of me.

Dr. Freud—I can't imagine he's a real doctor—was talking about young girls wanting to be lying in bed with their fathers and boys having similar thoughts about their mothers, and I really thought it was vile. If you read him, which I doubt you would, you would say, "Sister, he is full of beans, that one, he's just Dr. Beans."

But on the subject of obsession, when Harry broke the news to you, now that would have been an American newspaper headline!

SURVIVING WRIGHT BROTHER KILLS SISTER AND LOVE INTEREST!

Lord knows what the English would have done with it.

LOVE NEST TRIANGLE CAUSES WRIGHT SIBLING MURDER!

I thought that if you had thrown a vase filled with those summer flowers you had tenderly picked, that it was very possible you would throw something else. I know you did not possess a pistol, but at this point I'm not clear what you might have done. I know you're not a violent man. You possess a violent temper, yes, but I don't think you would willingly hurt another human being physically. I remember so clearly when we read the headline 16 MILLION DEAD IN GREAT

WAR. We were sitting at the dining room table. Just you and me. As always, I know you and I both thought but did not say out loud, "We miss our Will, but I don't think he would have survived this."

If Will had not missed the whole thing by some years and the Reverend had not died the year before it began, would we have tried to do anything about it? We certainly weren't pacifists; we did nothing to oppose it. My only marching has been for the women's vote.

I can still see you sitting there at the kitchen table during the war, with your head down in your arms on the newspaper on the table. I could see your shoulders shaking, like a small child's.

Even if the aeroplanes were responsible for only a small percentage of the deaths, we did try to sell them to the military—in America and all over Europe. And look what our customers did . . .

And then, without finishing your dinner, you got up from the table and moved like a sleepwalker into your study. I went to pick up the paper and it was damp from your tears, as if the print had come alive, rivers of ink, weeping for all the boys. I cleaned up the dishes, put away the uneaten food, and you did not say another word to me that evening. It was Carrie's day off. When I went to see how you were, I stood in the doorway of the study. There was no fire going, even though it was cold, and those tiny origami paper cranes were scattered on the floor around you. You were absorbed, making another one, so I cleared my throat.

"Orv?" I said. "Orv, it's not your fault."

And you shook your head and cried some more. When I walked toward you to comfort you, you waved me away and I withdrew.

I heard you wandering the house that night in your pajamas and polished shoes. I always heard you, Orv.

Humbly,
Sister K.

P.S. I suddenly remember Mother taking the three of us ice-skating. It might have been the first time, because she held my hands criss-

cross with hers, and I skated with my double-runners by her side. What was curious was the look on your face as you turned around and skated backward in front of Mother and me. As cold as it was that day, your face was laughing and laughing in a way I've never seen since—your white teeth the same bright whiteness of snow falling on the frozen pond.

Dear Orv, Orv dear,

I have not written in some time because I have been writing in my journal, which I intend to burn someday. I have been spending more time with Sonya Rose. I would enclose a photograph, but she says she prefers to be photographed naked, and that I would not send you, and that I do not possess! I think the postal clerk would open the letter and lock me up.

For me, one of the most sacred days of my life was August 26, 1920, when women got the vote, another Thursday, yes, as you would say, the 239th day of the year. I had marched and asked hundreds of men and women to sign petitions, but Sonya Rose says I should be bolder in my life now. She says that simply marching is not enough, that I must do more. "Think boldly. Live boldly," she says to me whenever she greets me and whenever we part. And last night she took my hand and I think wanted more than friendship, but that I cannot do. I don't think she is wrong, for I know there are women like that. She believes women and men should be free to love everyone. I think I agree, although I can hear the Reverend's screams as I write this.

Sometimes when I am in the kitchen, I will look for the rolling pin, which I did bring with me, but I forget I'm not back home. I am searching in my mind in the house on Hawthorn Street. I can remember every stair and shelf and closet. And then my imaginings take me to the big house, where you are now, and I am standing at the kitchen table, packing cans to be sent overseas to the boys, when Hoover asked for that. We did our part—those Meatless Tuesdays. I dutifully made that corn-and-cheese casserole and every-vegetable-I-could-think-of casserole. But we could have done more. Meatless Tuesdays did not save any of those poor souls.

I miss the lake house this time of year, and all that bicycle riding on the island. I still think the most perfect form of transportation is the bicycle. You always used to say that. Do you still? You and Will used to ride with arms out like wings. Reporters have asked me if I recall when you first had the thought of flying. I always thought that was too intimate a question, but I do wish I had a photograph of you, racing each other on the bicycles, arms outstretched, ready to take off.

Confused,
K.

P.S. There is to be a World Conference of Spiritual Science and Its Practical Applications in London from July 20 to August 1. Rochelle appeared with baby Psalm and wants her mother and me to attend. I am hesitant to mention it, because I know you think séances and otherworldly interests are opposed to modern science. I am a skeptic as well, but I am also a curious person. We were raised that way. Curiosity is what bonds us. Would you accompany me? Harry thinks it's "beyond frivolous." You can quote me on this one. Please consider it. It would be good to get away. We could sail from New York. Please let me know as soon as possible so I can make arrangements. What I would really like to do is go on the *Île de France*—shall I send you pictures? It's a beautiful ship. We could go visit our friends in France first and then go to the conference in London! Please confirm!

P.P.S. I've found another advertisement for "The Magnificent Ships!—largest, fastest American liners offer you every shipboard comfort and luxury. Spacious interiors—furnished and decorated to create the atmosphere of a well-planned home. Staterooms—really bedrooms and living rooms combined. Broad decks. Famous food. We know what Americans want!"

P.P.P.S. The Republican National Convention was here, as I imagine you have read, and I am quite shocked Coolidge announced he

would not run again. Hoover it is. I must say there is still a part of me that every time I think of Hoover, I think of our old vacuum cleaner in Dayton, which I used frequently. We have one here, but Mrs. Crossbottom guards it with her life. Yes, I know Herbert Hoover did not invent the machine. Inventions are our department.

June 28, 1928

Wright Sister Is Real Wizard!

I drank two gin fizzes tonight, if truth be told. If truth be told, indeed. I did help the boys with the plans for Kitty Hawk, if truth be told. I did more than help. I drew the plans on that parchment both of them preferred, with the ink they treated like mother's milk. It had come to me one night when I could not sleep. It was all about the lift. They had not been able to figure it out. The journalists whom we accused of being crazy when they suggested I had helped were not crazy at all. They were correct on this one, even if years later they were not correct about my age at my marriage. They were correct that the plane would never have taken off without my design. I did the drawing in two hours—well, perhaps three—with all angles of the rudders, the movable rudders, yes. I had the picture in my head so clearly, as if it were on a moving-picture screen. Was it from watching the gulls? I cannot say. It was a burst. That was all. I burst my vision onto the paper that enabled the plane to fly. Then late that night I had put the drawing on Orv's desk and the next day the drawing was gone. We never spoke about it. Not Orv to me or Will to me. I do not know what those crazy boys said to each other. Did Will pretend he had the idea or did Orv? Or did they thank me secretly, standing over my bed at night and saying, "Thank you, dear Katharine, for inventing the movable rudder?"

I do not know. It was just the way we did things. If truth be told.

I have been wanting to say this truth out loud for many years now. I still have not said it out loud. I have simply written it here, in my marriage diary of all places.

I wonder, if the boys had just stuck with the bicycle shop, where would we all be now? Would Will be alive? Would the boys be married? Would I?

I just this moment called you and you picked up the phone! You said, "Orville Wright speaking," and I said, "Orv, Orv, how are you?" I don't know why I am telling you, for it just happened, and your memory is good. And when you heard my voice you did not simply hang up. Instead, you said, "Hold the wire! Hold the wire!" so I can say I heard your voice, if that is something to be thrilled about.

Rather than speaking to me, I heard you scream for Carrie, but she didn't come, and then you hung up. Orv, you are not well in the head.

Harry and I went on the most heavenly bicycle ride on Saturday. I packed a picnic, and we rode out to the fields past farm after farm to what Harry calls "France in Missouri." I'm not sure I would say that, but it is beautiful, and he loves my egg salad sandwiches as much as you do. Yes, there is no doubt that sandwiches, perhaps egg salad sandwiches in particular, should be on the list of best inventions.

I also made one of my "visiting lemon cakes." I used eight lemons and more sweet butter than is called for, and after it was baked, I wrapped it in a tea towel, one that apparently Isabel embroidered.

I'm always surprised how good it is. Although it was Will who once said, "And if the people you visit don't like it, they could build a wall outside their house with that cake!" I remember chasing him around the kitchen for that one, or was it you?

Harry has a habit that reminds me of you.

Sometimes in the evenings when he's worked on a particularly hard story, he sits in the study next to the large globe and spins it with one hand as he holds his glasses in his other hand. Do you still do that?

What will you do for the Fourth this year? Will you be at the lake? I know how cold it can be there, even in summer, so remem-

ber to bring extra socks! As you said to that reporter, "It is true I have not flown to Antarctica, nor would I wish to, but I have spent many summers on Lake Huron, so I am well aware of freezing temperatures."

Your loving sister

P.S. And now I've been asked to join yet another flower-arranging club. How is this possible? Sometimes I think I was born in the wrong body. Of course I love flowers, but how many clubs does one need to arrange flowers? In truth, I think you arranged the flowers best in our house, Orv, although you certainly didn't need to join a club for it! SOS. Please save me.

P.P.S. I am eager to go to London in July, so please consider it. And now that there are transatlantic phone calls being made, we could even try calling London on the telephone to make arrangements!

Reporter Uncovers Truth!

Last week I did something I had not done before, and I am concerned about my mental state. Once again it involved scissors—not injuring Mrs. Crossbottom, although that might have been more satisfying, but Isabel's favorite tablecloth. At previous times, whenever I saw Mrs. Crossbottom ironing it, she would sigh and say, "Mrs. Haskell," and give an artificial smile to me, because we both knew she meant Isabel. "Mrs. Haskell so loved this cloth. I believe it was a wedding gift."

It was beige lace, pretty enough, although nothing to write home about, but last Thursday, when Mrs. Crossbottom had her day off, I took that special tablecloth from the bottom of the sideboard in the dining room. I grabbed it, took it upstairs, snatched up Harry's special scissors for clipping his sacred newspapers, and cut the tablecloth into pieces. I then stuffed the bits into a large canvas bag Harry and I have used when we go for picnics. I put the bag into my bicycle basket and went for a very long ride. I will simply say that when I returned home the bag was in the basket, but the bag was empty. Perhaps the birds can use the bits of cloth.

I am, indeed, a sinner.

And on another note, one of the pushy reporters who works with Harry appeared at the door today while Harry was at work. I did not let him over the threshold, but he was rather insistent and said, "I know the truth, Mrs. Haskell. You must write your story. You must correct the story. It will come out eventually, you know. I hear there are drawings of the movable rudder that you might have in your possession."

I just shut the door on him. This rumor has swirled from the first flight. But it is odd for him to come so soon after I confided in my marriage diary. But I sincerely do not believe Harry or Mrs. Crossbottom has found it.

Idiot Orville,

We do not seem to be at the World Conference of Spiritual Science and Its Practical Applications, do we? Or as you and Will liked to say, "Do we Dewey decimal system." And Sonya Rose bowed out as well. I should have gone on my own. Instead, I am here in Kansas City. Sonya caused a scene yesterday when we went to lunch. The waiter handed us each a menu without prices! It was fancy, the way some restaurants are for no reason, and I thought maybe the place was trying to put on airs, some kind of Roaring Twenties trend. I mean I knew this was Kansas City, not Paris, but I thought they were trying.

Sonya Rose knew immediately that this was not the case. She knew, as she often does, what the situation was, and she was not pleased. She slammed her menu down on the table and declared loudly, "Ladies' menus! We want the same menus as the gentlemen! We are quite capable of reading the prices! Please give us the gentlemen's menus."

I had never heard of ladies' menus, although it's true that after the Reverend died and we were bold enough to go out for sodas in Dayton, they would give me a straw and you boys had to (heaven forbid!) coarsely drink from the rim of the tall glasses. The waiter always said, "Straws for the lady," although I have no idea why. Perhaps it helps our lips for kissing. I just laughed out loud. I haven't sipped a soda with you in too long!

I wanted to quiet down Sonya Rose, because I don't like to make a scene, but then I realized she was correct. After all, it was I who ran our business for all those years, and more. I am quite capable of reading sandwich prices. And it's not as if there was a gentleman with us who was going to pay. So, what were they thinking? If we can read a ballot, we can read a menu.

On another note, I am concerned about all this Roaring Twenties talk. As you know, I am intrigued by some of the modern advancements (fascinated by, and I have been studying designs of new underwater boats), but the Reverend would say, "Pride goeth before a fall," and that the fall of Rome came at times like these.

When we did get the menu, I did see that my cheese sandwich was 25 cents, which seems steep. And globally—I know you used to mock me for using that word—but globally, I do think people are buying stocks too easily now. The company has suffered far too much with all the lawsuits. So you be careful, Orv. We have made financial errors in the past, but on this one I believe I am correct.

But then Sonya began talking, as she does, about how Rochelle is not married and she is concerned about how baby Psalm will be treated, Jewish and Negro, with an unmarried mother. I don't like it when Sonya talks that way about her own daughter. I do not like these family disagreements. If I had the chance to talk to Mother one more time, I doubt I would argue with her. I told Sonya that if she is saying she is worried about how the world will treat baby Psalm, I understand, but if it is her own prejudice she is talking about, I will put my foot down. The child is a child of God. When, over our "ladies' lunch," I pointed out she was not married when she gave birth to Rochelle, she simply nodded and gave a kind of sniff.

It is imperative that I talk to you, because now I am worried about the situation with Rochelle. I am very concerned about the choices she is making. This young girl, who was born in a field near the college, thinks so little of herself that, as she has confided in me, even though she is a mother herself now, selling her body is the only way she can survive.

Respectfully,
Your only sister

July 31, 1928

Orville Wright,

Did you give the World Conference of Spiritual Science and Its Practical Applications a second thought, or a first one?

I must learn to be more independent. I should have booked passage from New York and taken the ship myself, but you two men have me caught in a tightrope between you both, and I did not. I spoke to Carrie on the telephone yesterday, and she said you are working on a new device, meaning she found many drawings on your desk, that looked like balloons hanging off the back of an aeroplane, but she was not sure what it would be used for. Weather, she surmised. I have to say, for the first time in my life I am not interested. I am going out with Rochelle now, and her sweet baby. I said I would take them for a drive.

Sincerely,
K.H.

Dear Orv, Orv dear,

Something has happened. I hesitate to tell you though. Last week I met Gertrude Caroline Ederle, yes, the first woman to swim the Channel. I almost expected her to be wearing a bathing costume and covered in Vaseline, but there she was at a Rotary meeting wearing a summer dress and sensible shoes.

She is shy and a bit deaf, which I'd wrongly assumed came from all that swimming. I felt instantly at ease with her, a woman not quite comfortable with fame. I even teased her and called her "Queen of the Waves," as they refer to her in the papers. Not long after we met, she took both my hands in hers—and hers are quite rough, certainly not from flower arranging—and said, "Come swim with me sometime, won't you?" Perhaps she says that to everyone when she greets them, but it put a smile on my face, a much-needed smile.

But that is not why I am writing to you. I am writing to you because you are my best friend, my confidant. If I mail this before I finish, I shall continue tomorrow.

Yesterday morning, after Harry left for the office, the doorbell rang. I did not have any appointments. I was upstairs reading. I often read upstairs, to have peace and quiet away from our Mrs. Crossbottom. I'm reading a most interesting book about Gertrude, which Harry kindly brought home from the office. In any event, the doorbell interrupted me; I believe I was reading about how Gertrude had measles when she was a child and that was why she was deaf, not from the swimming, although I still think the miles of cold water didn't help. The doorbell rang again. I put down my book and went to see who was there.

The postman had left a postcard from Rochelle. It was a photograph of the Hannibal Bridge. When I turned the card over, I read, *I*

need money now!! Immediately. For Psalm, in enormous and messy pen-manship. I am at a loss as to what to do.

I have some money in a savings account, which I am happy to give her, but I am distressed to think of what she needs it for.

Your sister,
Katharine

ISLAND ROMANCE

I cannot stop thinking about that summer afternoon up at the lake, when suddenly Harry was on the porch steps, and I was inside. It was a magnificent Canadian day, with the pinesap wind blowing in from the Arctic. Orv always said had he been to the island before he flew, he might never have left the ground. Harry had been staying with us for a few days. He had always been a talky man, even as a boy at Oberlin, but perhaps more so during these walks. Grief is an unpredictable visitor and can make one mentally ill, I believe. So the three of us took walks at dawn and at the end of the day to watch the sunset, and on two days even after lunch. There was a restless quality to the conversations.

I believe the atmosphere was what we used to call "full of churn" when we were talking about the wind. But it was not wind that was caus-ing the churn.

Harry did not talk about Isabel. And neither Orville nor I brought her up. I must add that Orville rarely initiated conversation at all, so it would have been me, but it didn't seem natural to do so. Instead, we talked of the events of the day, about President Coolidge, and the plans to carve giant likenesses of the presidents on Mount Rushmore. Looking back, it was not just the restlessness I recall, but it was clear even then it was not a completely peaceful trio, because I would stand between the men at the start of the walk, and as we continued Orv kept moving to get between Harry and me, the way the ducks nudge one another on the lake. Harry once asked if it was possible Orv felt abandoned by him, that it was their lost bond that he was so miffed

about. It's possible, but Orv also did things like that. He liked to stand or walk where he wanted to be, and he might even quietly push someone out of his way if he was not pleased with the "configuration," as he used to explain if anyone questioned him, although few people ever did.

Dear Orv, Orv dear,

I dearly miss the lake at this time, and the fireflies, as I miss you and Mother, all in one great and sorrowful cloud of yearning. I am recalling when you were ten years old and I was seven and you would wander into my room in the middle of the night because you couldn't sleep.

"Tell me something to dream about, sister," you would say, sitting on my bed.

Never mind that you woke me up from a deep sleep or that I was ashamed for you to see me in my bedclothes.

I would let you sit there, and I would stroke your hand as I listed lemon meringue pie, strawberry-rhubarb pie, carrot cake with walnuts, banana pudding, and all your favorite desserts, including each of the ingredients and their precise amounts, and you would calm down. Occasionally you would call out if I missed one tiny detail: "How much vanilla?" or "How many times do you stir that?"

If that wasn't enough, I'd tell you stories about Mother singing to us as she sewed and making us memorize the presidents as we sat on the floor by her machine. And you'd mumble in your half sleep, "Tyler, Polk, Taylor, Fillmore, Pierce." And if still that wasn't enough, I'd quietly sing you "Row, Row, Row Your Boat." Finally, you would say to me, "What on earth am I doing here, sister?" and I'd lead you back to your bed, tucking you in quietly so as not to wake Will.

Does all that attention to you mean nothing?

I am sorry to say I don't have memories of the Reverend teaching anything but Scripture. Or some kind of admonition, as in "make haste slowly," when he felt I was not being attentive enough with my chores, particularly washing dishes for all of you if Carrie wasn't

there. I detest washing dishes, if anyone is interested in knowing. I think we missed our calling with the aeroplane business. I do think an electric dishwasher would have been the way to go, and certainly the way to my heart! I've heard the Germans are working on it, but not soon enough in my book. "Step right up, folks, and see the amazing Wright brothers and sister and their dishwashing machine!" You have never explained properly why you think it's acceptable not to rinse dishes after they've been washed. How many times I rinsed them off after you set them soapy in the drainer! But you are an excellent dish drier, I shall give you that.

I wonder what would have happened if I'd married my college sweetheart. I dread to think. I thought I loved him briefly, the way he would leap up when I entered the room, and he did have a pleasant-enough smile, but then I could never have been a teacher because, of course, teachers were not allowed to marry. I would never have traveled with you boys to Europe for all the flying demonstrations. Perhaps I would have a child, though I might never have tasted champagne along the Seine. Yes, I would never have my Harry. My life would not have been my life.

Yours truly,
Sister

P.S. Last night when I couldn't sleep, I tried to remember everything about when we were in France, and what came to mind was that little town where everyone, men and women, was buying a sweet perfume from a large glass container at the grocery store. Everyone stood there with their own bottles. I loved that and still have the little bottle of the stuff you bought for me. We did not come prepared with a bottle, but they had small ones for sale. In my haste I left it on my dresser at home. I hope you have not dumped the contents or, worse, smashed it against the wall. Carrie has made no mention of it, but she says you wander into my room at strange hours.

Dear Orv, Orv dear,

Harry is downtown, and I am listening to the phonograph, to one of our Irving Berlin records. I think I shall wear this one out, which would not please Harry. I believe Irving Berlin is a genius the way he talks about blue skies smiling, although I imagine he has his quirks as well. I think all you brilliant boys do!

I never told the press, after all their pestering, and not even Harry, about all your quirks. I never told anyone about how you counted all your steps each day and how you insisted not only that I keep everything in the pantry alphabetized, but if there were two identical tins, let's say of green beans, I would have to place them precisely on top of each other, or how once you screamed at me because the tin of sugar was to the right of the jar of tomato sauce I'd canned. How could I have been so foolish to put *T* before *S*? I have never told people all that.

Yours,
Sister

P.S. Do you think I should bob my hair?

Dear childish man,

Are you up at the lake? It is horridly hot here in Kansas City and the ceiling fan is not enough. I tie my hair up or pile it on top of my head, and in some ways, I think my neck would be even hotter with short hair.

You must know that when you sent that first telegram from Kitty Hawk and said you'd be home for Christmas and that you'd been fifty-seven seconds up in the air, I believed it, even if others doubted, including that man who said fifty-seven minutes would have been more impressive. The Reverend held up the telegram like a flag. I think you should know he was truly proud of you boys, although I know he did not express it to you. I also want to add that though I was not with you on the sands physically, I was with you spiritually at Kitty Hawk, more than you will ever know.

Lovingly,
Your sister

VIVID, JOYOUS, BRAVE

I did something bold today in this prickly heat. I drove to the cemetery, with my bare legs sticking to the seat—no stockings, just a cotton dress and underwear—to Mount Washington Cemetery, where Isabel is buried. Yes, I went to her grave. I had not been acting well. I had become unhinged. I had to go. I have not told Harry, but I know in my heart that I still care for Isabel as I always did, as a friend, and that it is a gift she has given me to have this time with Harry now. I wept when I read what Harry had written on her stone. VIVID, JOYOUS, BRAVE. I saw Harry's flowers, the impatiens he had planted, and they were wilting. I asked the groundskeeper for a watering can, and he filled it up and I watered those flowers, and they lifted their heads almost immediately.

I whispered to Isabel, "I am glad you got to vote, but sorry you did not get to vote more. I am sorry I have now taken your bed."

I must always remember what Harry had written on her stone. Vivid. Joyous. Brave. I must learn from Isabel. In my weak times I will learn from her.

Dear Orv, Orv dear,

Harry went to meet with the husband of a woman who was lynched.
I am saying this: a woman was lynched.

When he came back and we sat at the dining room table, he did
not say a word during our whole evening meal. He did not look me
in the eye. And then he pushed away his dessert and slid his chair
hard from the table. As he left the room he muttered, "I think we
need another Civil War."

Sister Katharine

Dear Orv,

Will you be back from the lake soon? Who is trimming your mustache these days? The first time you asked me to do your "ablutions," as you called it, you demanded, rather than asked: "Sister, help with my ablutions." You spoke, as I used to teach my students, in the imperative case. I was scared to hold the razor and scissors so close to your face, and it did not help that you were so particular . . . that never helped.

Once you said, "Don't worry, sister, if your hand slips, you know where my goggles are, you can steer the plane!"

And that was when we were sitting in the backyard on a hot Ohio day, with the laundry flying like sails before us.

Your devoted sister

P.S. I think you are one tough customer—that's an expression Harry uses, and I think it applies well to you.

Dear brother,

This is a list of what I would like you to bring me or send me from the big house.

1. Two drawings of seagulls, the ones you did at Kitty Hawk.
2. One photo of you and Will and me, the three of us in France, the one in front of the Eiffel Tower (not the one where your eyes are closed and not the one where you look like you swallowed some salty sardines).
3. One box of clippings of you boys, and while you're at it there's one box specifically from France, when we visited the vineyard—with the picture of the women stomping grapes and you looking like you would faint.
4. The sheet music I left on the piano from when I tried to sing Irving Berlin to you to coax you into talking to me—the day you pushed me off the piano bench.
5. The two summer straw hats I take to the lake, perhaps there are three. Please leave one up at the lake.
6. The hatbox with Mother's braid in it, which is on the top shelf of my bedroom closet.
7. My measuring cups. But ask Carrie first. If she insists she needs them, she is welcome to them. I do not want to cause more trouble.
8. The mixing bowl with the faded flowers that was Mother's. This one I long for when I make lemon bread.
9. The little bottle of perfume from France that is on my bureau.
10. You.

   I can see you reading this letter by the fire, and I hope you don't just toss it into the flames!

I am at my breaking point. I don't know if you know that expression, but I am not referring to pencils.

Your sister

P.S. I am thinking of that night when it felt like we both shouted at once, "Wing warping! Wing warping!" and you and Will ran out of the house without your coats in the cold, like troubled children, flapping your arms.

P.P.S. I also keep thinking about Gertrude Ederle. I realize she became the first woman to swim the English Channel the same year I got married. In some ways I think marriage is as daunting as the English Channel. Maybe I should have attempted to do that rather than to marry. Maybe it would have been easier, and more people would have cheered! I would have covered myself in sheep grease, olive oil, and Vaseline, as she did. I'd have to purchase the sheep grease, but otherwise I'm ready to go.

I long to swim in the cold lake one more time—no, not one more time, many more times.

LOST, NOW FOUND

This is the second time I am in the bathtub today. This afternoon I took a hot bath to clean off all the dust from my expedition. And now at 3:00 a.m. I am sitting in the empty and dry bathtub wearing my dressing gown and wool socks. I am in a trance. Each day Harry has left for the paper downtown, I have so often felt at a loss, like I have no purpose, but now I do. I love him dearly, even if I am not exactly what he was looking for in the wife department. But today I have become myself. I no longer feel like a placeholder, which I have told him I have felt in the past.

Today, September 12, 1928, in the year of Our Lord, in the year of Oh Lord! I have done what I was meant to do in this world. I went flying. And I also went on the back of a motorcycle.

But the motorcycle is beside the point. I knew last week I was going up, but I did not tell a soul. Sonya had telephoned and asked if I wanted to go out to the airstrip, because she had a friend who gave flying lessons. I reacted the way other women would have said yes to a fancy dance.

There are women fliers, Blanche Scott, Harriet Quimby, Bessie Coleman . . . I would like Katharine Wright to be on the list with them.

I am exhausted and stiff from sitting in this empty tub and from flying. I wore trousers I had purchased on our escape journey to Dayton (they are rough and wool and perfect for flying) and a leather jacket Sonya lent me. But the most exciting thing is I was not wearing a girdle, and tomorrow I shall throw away all my girdles. If I wear stockings, I shall simply wear a garter belt. I wore cotton underwear along with a cotton brassiere! Freedom! And I brought my camera with me, which hung around my neck.

I shrieked when Sonya invited me, and I shrieked again this morning when Sonya picked me up on her new motorcycle, with a camera hanging on a strap around her neck, and there I was with my arms around her waist on the way to the airfield outside of town. And those chilling words the Reverend spoke soon after Mother died—"Cultivate modest feminine manners and control your temper, for temper is a hard master"—were left in the dust.

After a wild ride out of town, with me hanging on for dear life, we ended up out on the field right next to the most magnificent flying machine. The plane was made in Kansas, and it's called a Stearman. I am in love with Stearman, so perhaps I am having an affair. Standing by it, patting the wing, was a tall and gangling young woman named Flo, with straight dark hair cropped in a bob. She wore fire-red lipstick like a flapper girl, and she was wearing a one-piece flying suit. I had barely climbed off the back of the motorcycle when she reached out her hand and shook mine hard. She said, "Wright Sister Finally Learns to Fly."

She handed me a pair of goggles that I strapped on. Then she helped me climb into the plane and got in after me. All the while she was talking and talking, giving me all sorts of instructions that felt like a familiar lullaby to me. She made me repeat every sentence she said after her, while I was itching to get up into the air. She could see my excitement and said, "Hold your horses, sister," more than once.

I had to control myself from screaming, "When are we going to go up?"

But finally, finally, we were. We were racing down the runway, and then and then we were lifting off. I felt the wind and smelled the fuel, and I laughed out loud, as the earth fell away. I felt that rushing, rushing and quivering, when I was up in that aeroplane and looked down at the sunlit autumn fields and houses and roads. I rode as a passenger, as it was my first lesson, but Flo let me put my hand on the stick twice. We flew for one half of an hour, and although Flo landed a bit bumpily, she did it. There is no question in my addled mind. I should not say addled. I feel clear as a bell. I will take as many hours as needed until I can fly solo.

When we landed, Sonya was waving from her motorcycle like the Queen of England. Then I posed smiling in the breeze in front of the Stearman like it was my prize horse, while she took several shots.

As we walked away from the machine, covered in dust, Sonya proposed to Flo an arrangement. She posed that if I tutor Flo in French, because she wants to move to France to be with her fiancé and be a flying instructor there, then it will be an even exchange.

At first Flo was silent and took out a piece of gum, popped it into her mouth, and chewed very slowly. She offered me a piece, and I accepted, but frankly I would have eaten a live toad at that point.

Flo finally put out her hand to shake mine again.

"A deal," she said.

I cannot wait to go up again, although Flo calls it "taking off." I will insist that she teach me how to take off and land, the whole kit and caboodle, as Orv would say. No secrets now.

Sonya has another friend with a darkroom, and I can't wait to develop the pictures myself.

When we parted, she slapped me on the back and said, "I think you're part bird. Yes, Birdwoman Wright."

I do not know when I will tell Harry or Orv.

October 15, 1928

Dear Orv,

Harry brought me a new phonograph record by Buddy DeSylva, Lew Brown, and Ray Henderson. I'd love to listen to it with you. Aren't the lyrics to "The Best Things in Life Are Free" great? Or "swell," as Harry likes to say? They say the moon belongs to us, yes indeed!

You would have loved our ladies' literary society at Oberlin, Litterae Laborum Solamen (LLS). "Literature is a solace from troubles"! Although I imagine you would say going up in our flying machine provided you with that.

K.

P.S. We started a group at Oberlin called the Order of the Empty Hearts—perhaps we should have included you.

P.P.S. Harry just brought home a Steinite seven-tube radio. He is of two minds about the radio. He loves to hear music, but he is afraid the news reports will put newspapers out of business.

Dear Orv,

Well, it seems people in this country really do not like Catholics, and so Hoover it shall be. I was proud to vote. Although I longed to ask what you thought of what he said when he accepted the Republican nomination in August. "We in America today are nearer to the final triumph over poverty than ever before in the history of any land." I do not think so, Orville Wright. I do not think so at all.

Honorably,
Katharine W. Haskell

Day after Second Wedding Anniversary

Harry took me to see Charlie Chaplin in The Circus*! It was a grand movie. It first played at the start of the year and he saw it with men from the office. Thankfully when it appeared again, he invited me! I screeched when he was in the cage with the lion. Harry just laughed. I had a great time and longed to share it with Orv. This great joy and sorrow make me feel pulled apart. Perhaps I should be in the circus myself: "Lady pulled apart, live in the big tent . . ."*

Dear Mr. Wright,

Mr. and Mrs. Harry Haskell request your presence for Christmas Eve meal and a two-week stay of the holidays and a celebration of the glorious New Year.

RSVP by December 15.

Sincerely,
Sister

Dear Mr. Orville Wright,

I cannot help but wish you a merry Christmas and a happy 1929, and also, as is our Wright tradition, I must say may you have clear skies.

Finally, I have my wits about me. If you do not respond by telephone, Harry and I are going to visit you, not now, but in the spring, when the roads are clear and the weather is "sweet," as you would say. And this time we're going to march right up to the door. And not just a visit in the spring. No, I told Harry that I will not be spending another birthday apart from my brother. We will be joining you up at the lake for a week in August as well. I do not know if Harry will be able to get off from work, and of course it depends on the news of the day—the cucumber days of August, as our European friends say—but you and I shall be together, for your fifty-eighth birthday and my fifty-fifth. This will be the tradition. I am taking command of this ridiculous situation.

Ridiculously yours,
The Wright brothers' sister

P.S. I am determined to be a leader here as I was in Dayton, but I am hesitant to toot my own horn. You watch, Orville Wright, soon you shall be reading about the Wright sister!

P.P.S. Although it is winter, I am thinking of how we like to lie in the sun like turtles on the dock. Next summer, *mon frère*, next summer!

I was looking through Harry's set of encyclopedias and there's a whole section on the Wright brothers. It reads: "To solve the control reversal problem, the Wright brothers made the rudder movable, so its position could be coordinated with the wing-warping."

That is what it says. But that is incorrect. That is what I did. Not the Wright brothers. The Wright brothers' sister. The Wright sister. That's what I solved.

Dear Orv, Orv dear,

Harry bought me the most magnificent camera, a brand-new Rollei-
flex, as a Christmas gift. Would you like one as a late Christmas
present?

He has taken a number of pictures of me seated on the bed without my glasses! And I have taken some of him. I shall send you pictures, not those of course, but in the springtime when I go up again. I
haven't told you, but I've been taking flying lessons. Yes. The camera
is a wonderful design. I will be able to simply look down into it and
see the whole world.

I am so cold right now though, so there is no flying around. I cannot even bear to go outside. For some reason the fire at home seemed
warmer, or at least I knew how to warm myself up. I feel like I am
living in an icebox except when I am in Harry's arms.

I have been calling you repeatedly on the telephone. Even if you
just picked up the phone and shouted, "Hold the wire," as you did
last time, I feel we would be making progress. But in this case, that
ringing feels like I am there with you as it rings. Do you sit by the
phone? Do you pretend you don't know who it is? And that time
you picked up the phone and I said, "Dearest Orv," and without saying a word you hung up—unconscionable. I think that is the only
word I can use.

I confess I have some photographs of you taken with that camera you built for me, and I have always known you would not like
them, but I shall never show a soul.

Sincerely yours,
Swes

TRUTH BE TOLD

I have been reading the letters of Vincent van Gogh to his brother Theo. He seems to capture the beauty of the sky even though he never flew.

I longed to have a child since I was five years old. One August morning I was helping Mother make raspberry jam, and the whole kitchen seemed to be pink. She wiped her hands on her apron and said, "Someday you will be doing this with your daughter," and even then I did not quite believe her. It is good to be an aunt to Lorin's children, but still it is not the same. We rarely see them. They are busy with their own lives. If the Reverend wasn't always after me to have "modest feminine manners," perhaps I would have been braver, but my brave time is now. And I have even tried cigarettes, with a cigarette holder!

I do think he was strict with the boys, but they were expected to go out into the world, or at least have a name in the world, if not be fully in it.

The year after Mother died, fourteen years before the boys made history, I think the boys and I were all in a trance for a few weeks about our loss. But then there was the incident, and the boys were certainly in a trance after that. Reuchlin and Lorin were out of the house, but Orv (almost eighteen) and Will (twenty-two) were still home, years before Kitty Hawk. We were all doing what we had to do, what was expected of us. We were an obedient flock.

And then our world changed for the three of us, the afternoon Orv, Will, and I had all gone inside and saw what the Reverend was doing in his study. Grief can make you act improperly, even a reverend, I suppose, but after what we saw, we three stood pale, outside in the hot summer sun. At first Orv and Will and I stood looking stricken around the bicycle the boys had been working on. Then Orv and Will started wrestling

with each other on the ground in a way I had never seen them do before. I pulled them apart, and suddenly Will was hammering so hard on a piece of metal I thought he was going to kill someone. Now Orv was screaming at him to stop. Will pushed Orv away, and then I was there with both of them, and the sheets were blowing on the line like it was a normal day, but it was not.

And it was because of what we had all seen. The Reverend was often working in his study, and we always knocked before we entered, but—and this point is a blur—but one of the boys, or both, bumped against the door as we were going back outside with our lemonade. There was the Reverend, naked—his flesh looked so white—on top of a woman in all her pink flesh, on the floor when the boys tumbled in. When all three of us fell into the door. If I had to diagram it, I'm not sure I could do it justice, but there was no doubt the sight was such a shock. I believe the Reverend was wearing his shoes, naked except for his shoes.

But it was those strange sounds from both of them, not little murmurings, but animal groans—from both of them? Of that I am not sure, but the sounds stayed with me for so many years. The Reverend did not practice what he preached.

Only now at fifty-four do I know what those sounds are. But then we were horrified. We could all see the Reverend's face, with his eyes shut like he was not long to this world. We slammed the door shut and ran out to the yard. That's what we kept saying out in the yard, "like he was dying." We started trying to guess who it was.

"Her breasts were young," gasped Will.

"There was a strange smell," said Orv.

It was certainly the first time I heard my brothers say the word "breasts," which was said more in that yard with the bicycle than ever before or since by the boys. We could not figure out who she was, but then we did not talk about it again after we made the pact. Not speaking about it was part of the pact.

It was like wind shear, which can happen at any altitude. I never heard of it happening inside a house, but it did that day, that fast change of wind, vertical or horizontal, that can cause a crash. Wind shear happened at 7 Hawthorn on that day.

It went so long not being spoken about that sometimes I wondered if it actually happened, if I had just made it up. But I know it did happen, so I am finally speaking about it now, or at least writing it in my marriage diary. Even though we vowed never to tell anyone what the pact entailed.

It was Will's idea to get the needle. Orv ordered me to go back inside and get a large needle from Mother's sewing basket, one of the ones we later used for sewing the muslin wings. And matches.

I hurried into the kitchen, covering my ears for fear of hearing more sounds.

When I returned to the yard with the needle, Orv commanded, "Burn the needle."

I held the needle as Will struck the match against the flint at the corner of the house, then passed the end of the needle through the flame.

Will forced Orv and me to prick our fingers; all of us in that July heat, with our fingers bleeding, rubbing and rubbing them together. First Will and Orv rubbed their bloody fingers with each other and then they rubbed mine. There was blood dripping on the bicycle and also on my dress, which I had to scrub later with lemon juice that stung my finger, and then I had to wash my dress twice.

Orv was the one who said quietly and harshly in a voice I had never heard before, "We will make a pact. None of us shall ever marry. None of us shall ever do what that man did. None of us shall sully our mother's name. From this day forth that man is the Reverend."

And then he said we all had to hold up our bloody hands to the sky and say amen, which we did, waving our hands up to the blue sky in the heat.

It was I who went inside again, dripping blood as I went. The boys did not go inside until I called them for dinner. I got rags from the bag of torn linens from under the sink we used for cleaning and wrapping wounds. I brought makeshift bandages back outside for the three of us.

All day we walked around with our fingers swathed in stained rags like red flags.

But the four of us, including the Reverend, were at our places at the dinner table that night as if it were a normal day. If it had been a play,

we were all in our proper places. The director would not have had to rep-rimand us, but nothing was the same again.

The Reverend did not question our bandaged fingers, and of course we did not say a word to him. It was Carrie's day off that day. It was I who served the meal, a tomato and beef stew that we all pushed around our plates. There was no dessert served or asked for that night.

CENSORED

I have been thinking more of the boys seeing the Reverend that way, on that woman. Now, of course, after what I have done with Harry, a widower, I understand it differently. I long to know who the woman was, and yet I do not ever want to know.

Dear Orv, Orv dear,

When I was a member of LLS—you remember, the ladies' literary society at school, Litterae Laborum Solamen, "literature is a solace from troubles" . . . you mocked me, and I would like you to apologize for that.

I think I need to make zigzag socks for myself, as I am freezing.

Shiveringly yours,
Sister

I've caught a ridiculous cold, Orv, and I feel a bit feverish. I keep thinking of my friend Margaret—you liked her—and that trip we took to the St. Louis Exposition. It feels long ago, for the centennial of the Louisiana Purchase, all ancient history now. That was the first time I had an ice-cream cone and pink fairy floss, as we called it then, and I am missing her. I keep thinking that if I hadn't insisted that we try "every new-fangled food," she might not have fallen ill. I miss her terribly. I am upstairs in bed now. I miss everyone terribly.

Love,
Katharine

I am listening to Helen Kane singing "I Wanna Be Loved by You." I do not know where Rochelle is, and where is that baby? Where is baby Psalm?

Please visit soon.
K.

Orv,

I cannot stop coughing. I long to use the camera out in the snow. Right now, it sits by my bed like a patient friend. The Reverend always told us that if we were good brethren here, we would have no problem in the hereafter. Al Jolson's "When the Red, Red Robin Comes Bob, Bob, Bobbin' Along" is in my head.

Do you know, dear Orv, that with so many people flying these days, that some married couples think it is wise to take separate flights, so that if there were a crash, their children would not lose both their parents. But you and I, we were never blessed with children, so that does not apply. If you don't think it is too macabre to say, I should not mind dying with you, and doing so after a magnificent flight, or in the midst of a magnificent flight, simply "flying off into the sunset" would be just fine.

K.

February 23, 1929

Dear Orv, Orv dear,

Did you like being called *L'homme oiseau*, "Bird Man"? I think they called Will that more than you, but then we all started using it. I am thinking a lot about the one time we swam naked in a pond in Dayton. I cannot remember how old we were, only that we had always done that, like slippery fish, and then suddenly, one time we seemed to be too old.

CONFUSED

There was a flapper at the jazz club, and she came right up to me and kissed me on the lips, and when she pulled away, she said, "There's more where that came from, sister!"

I am getting confused.

I was thinking again about when Dr. Russel, the Reverend's friend, came to visit at 7 Hawthorn Street and he grabbed at my breasts. If there was one time I wanted to throw a vase, that was it, at his head, and sometimes I wish I had screamed out instead of silently going to the kitchen afterward and doing chores as if it were a normal evening. It was not. I do not like handsy men.

I long to be back as director of the Young Women's League of Dayton, although I am no longer a young woman.

Dear Orv, Orv dear,

A Winter's Tale

I beseech thee, I am not able to write much. My fingers are cold. I am wearing gloves, which make it cumbersome to write. I am cold inside my bones. Is that possible?

In France, remember how we almost died—when our passenger train collided with a freight train—how strange it would have been if we died in a railroad accident rather than an aeroplane. I am trying to recall all that we have done. It is the only way I can realign my wings.

I took French lessons while you boys flew. I met King Edward VII of England and King Alfonso XIII of Spain. And the balloon ride to a mountain.

Lovingly,
Swes

PRAYERS

A tragedy has happened. Rochelle jumped off the Hannibal Bridge with baby Psalm in her arms. The river was full of sharp shards of ice, and they probably died instantly in the freezing water. They say they will wait until spring to find the bodies. I cannot breathe. Harry was the one who told me. He had stayed late at work, to write the story and I think for fear of telling me. Sonya telephoned weeping and said she does not know where she is going. I am coughing and coughing.

Mainly I am crazy with grief, the way we were when Will died. This young girl, she really was like a daughter, and that baby . . . I loved that baby. I would have cared for him. My thoughts are like bats flying around.

I think I am losing my mind now. I am reaching for baby Psalm. I want to hold him close. I want to rub Psalm's baby ears.

I have lost my appetite. I need to get away. Maybe Orv could visit, and we could all drive together to Canada and then take the boat to Lambert Island for our birthdays this summer. Orv once said he wanted to be buried there, or even walk the plank from one of the canoes.

At night I hear baby Psalm crying. I hear my dear friend Frances from school, how she sang when we used to hike together. Identifying trees without their leaves—just by their bark. I have long woolen underwear on, and Harry keeps saying, "Dearest one, just get better. That is all I ask."

I imagine he would prefer not to be a widower again. People might think there was something fishy going on here. JOURNALIST KILLS SECOND WIFE!

I found some notes from Isabel, they were stuck at the back of the second drawer in her bureau, our bureau, and although I was shocked, it made me feel closer to her. She too got lonely, and I have come to believe that all women get lonely. I want to tell her about baby Psalm. I understand that loneliness is simply part of the river of our lives, and I want to thank her for sharing her husband. I imagine Orv would say he is lonely too, although he would not say that out loud. Isabel's notes are written in a girlish handwriting on thick cream cards with her initials on them, I.H. Isabel Haskell. I miss H. when he is downtown, *she writes.* What can possibly always be so important!

Rather than feeling jealous, I feel a great kindred spirit with her.

I am weary now.

FEBRUARY?

When Harry got home, I was sitting up in bed covered in a pile of comforters. I heard his automobile door slam, but then he did not come in the house immediately and I feared he was out in the snow, pacing around the outside of the house like he was on some kind of Aborigine walkabout. I heard him walk up the stairs, and then he was there, my dear man with a pile of newspapers in his hands. He traipsed snow all the way into our bedroom and dumped the papers on his chair in the corner. I know he is scared, and I want to comfort him. I don't know if he can hold in his head the thought of two wives who have died. I cannot stop coughing.

Then, as he stood by the bed, he took his cold hands and rubbed them together before he touched me. "Katharine dear, I want to hold you, but my hands are so cold."

I took his hands in mine as I lay in bed. "Harry, I have been to your Isabel's grave. Last summer. The impatiens needed watering. I watered them."

Harry looked startled, and I said, "Harry Haskell, I saw what is written."

Harry knelt down by my bed and kissed my hands.

"I understand," I said. "Vivid. Joyous. Brave," I recited, as he stroked my forehead. "I want to hold that baby boy."

February ₹, 1929 (my calendar is downstairs),
written upstairs by hand . . .

Dear Orville Wright!

Please come for Harry's fifty-fifth birthday on March 8. Don't be late!

K.

P.S. I saw you wrapped in silk from the wings and just your underclothes. Of course, you were wearing your polished shoes. I saw you that day, in your room, before you went to sleep. You were smiling, doing some kind of two-step.

Are you coming? I wonder if Harry will marry again.

Do you remember when Harry, my Harry, came to interview us in Washington after we returned from Europe? I did feel a flicker then—I admit it. Once when he helped me with my math lessons at Oberlin, our hands had touched as they lay on the composition book.

P.S. Harry and I are to set sail on March 9 to Italy and Greece. It will mean I miss four flying lessons, but I will race to the airfield as soon as I am back. I am beside myself with grief and coughing. I am trying to remember everything. When the three of us went to Italy in 1909, King Victor Emmanuel III—or was it IV?—showed us how to eat spaghetti without dropping a strand.

February 4, 1929

Dear Orv, Orv dear,

    I don't know what day it is . . . I'm so blue . . .

    Orville, do you recall the photo that was taken when we went to the White House and met President Taft? I wore a white dress, and people said you and I looked like bride and groom. Do you still have that photo? I long to see it again. The Reverend talked from the pulpit about women voting, and that march down Main Street in 1914 was one of my happiest days, with you and the Reverend by my side.

I am dizzy. It's just you and me and Lorin left. Please come visit. It is pneumonia. We have to cancel our voyage to Italy and Greece . . . If you come, we can dance together in silks from wings at the club . . .

Who pushed the door open, when the Reverend was with the woman, was it you or Will? I can't keep the story straight. I can't keep anything straight. Still, I want to tell you love is not like that, Orv. Love can be pure. The word "pact" comes from the Latin word for "peace"—we must make a new pact.

THE LEAVING PART

I am leaving. "It is the way of nature," as Will said once when the three of us were looking at a blackbird in the shed, one that had been caught and dragged in by one of the cats. The poor bird lay on its side on the dirt floor. It's the way of nature. I was seven, so Orv must have been ten and Will fourteen. Will was right. It's the way of nature.

Where am I? What state? I miss Ohio. Why is Kansas City mainly in Missouri? Shouldn't it be in Kansas?

I hear a strong wind outside, too strong for flying.

Orv once said, "I like a state that begins and ends with the same vowel!"

March is so beautiful—Sap Moon, Crow Moon, Lenten Moon.

I try not to let Harry know that I am dying, and he does the same for me. I am certain that he does know, but I think he does not want to admit it. I understand it is too hard for him. I can see in his eyes that combination of fear and sadness. He has been here before and does not want to go back again. I wish I could keep him from making that visit. But I can't. I am too weak. I am too cold.

One regret I have is, I was not able to continue reading to Orv at night. After the Reverend died, I read to him bedtime stories, but what comforted him most was his list of birds. The birds from Kitty Hawk did the trick: kestrels, black-bellied plovers, great blue herons, mallards, and his favorites, the piping plovers.

I would love to see Orv before it comes, even with the way he has behaved. Deaths have so defined our lives. How different they would have been if Mother had not died when she did, if Tom Selfridge had not died,

if Wilbur had not died. And then Isabel. If she had not died, I would never have married Harry. And Rochelle and baby Psalm. I should have helped Rochelle more.

How can I miss April? Grass Moon, Egg Moon, Pink Moon. And our birthday month, Green Corn Moon and Grain Moon.

I did make a copy of the movable rudder I designed, of the drawing I placed on Orv's desk so many years ago. I always made copies of my drawings. We all did. There is a folded copy of the rudder plans in the envelope at the back of my marriage diary. I don't know what Will and Orv did with my original drawing. I had put it on Orv's desk late one night and it was gone by daybreak the next morning. A woman has needs. A woman has needs.

But now, so that Orv might remember me, I am writing a list of all the words for flying he might not know and might find amusing. I think he should start flying again. When I learn to fly solo, I shall fly to Dayton and pick him up. He would think that is a fine howdy-do.

aviate
buzz
climb
control
cross
dart
dash
dive
drift
flat-hat
fleet
flit
float
flutter
glide
hop
hover
maneuver

mount
operate
pilot
reach
rush
sail
seagull
shoot
skim
soar
speed
swoop
take a hop
take wing
whisk
whoosh
wing
zip
zoom

Whatever word one uses, I am going up now forever and I am flying solo now. Clear skies. I wish I could take a picture and show Orv the view, and our mother. I hope Orv has enough socks.

I am not able to get out of bed, so now I am writing in my mind, not my right mind, but here for a few more moments, or is it days? I hear Harry making telephone calls to Lorin in the hallway downstairs, imploring him to contact Orv. There is a screaming in his voice when he says the word "bleak." And now he is begging him to call Orv to make the journey to visit me, now before I take off.

I can see Carrie packing him a tin of biscuits and a Thermos of apple juice. Orv loves his traveling case. She is helping him pack for the journey. He will come.

I can see him standing in his bedroom at 7 Hawthorn, holding the pale green ceramic vase he had brought home for me from Kitty Hawk. Yes, he will bring that as a gift. And stay here, the guest room is made up, and in two months there will be forsythia and then the roses. He will fill the vase and set it on the kitchen table here in KC. I will make him French toast while Harry is at the paper.

I can see Orville sitting up the entire way on the train, with his traveling case flat on his knees, barely looking out at the snowy fields, not eating a bite of biscuit or sipping juice, just folding endless origami cranes.

I hear the doorbell downstairs. Is it Orv? I know he is in his suit. I hear Harry asking him to come in, but I do not hear my brother speak. There is someone climbing the steps now. We used to make flour-and-water paste with my mother in the bucket in the yard. It was such strong paste for paper and projects we fastened together. But that paste was not strong enough after the wind shear.

I can see Harry pointing Orv upstairs to the bedroom. I hear Harry's singsong voice—"Harry Haskell, Kansas City Star"—but I do not hear Orv's voice. My mind is tangled. I hear Orv climbing the stairs slowly, his bad hip preventing him from moving as fast as he would like. I want to rush to him and hold his arm. The bedroom door is shut, and I imagine he puts up his hand to knock but realizes that is foolish. Orv opens the door slowly, and quietly enters the bedroom that smells of rose-water and rubbing alcohol and death.

I smell him now, his licorice candies, as I lie under several white comforters. Where are my glasses? I want to see Orv. I think his hat is off, close to his chest.

I feel him reaching out to touch my arm. The room is silent now except for stray squirrels scrambling on the roof and my breath. Such a struggle to draw in air. Orv is with me, at my bedside that way, for minutes, for hours.

Someone else is here. Harry, I think, is now sitting on the chair in the corner. The room is dim as the sun goes down, eclipsing my sight. There is no turbulence. There is no wind shear. I draw in a breath and let it out.

I can hear the men far away, and I feel Orv placing paper cranes on my chest.

Is the doctor here? I am hungry for air. I cannot draw in another breath.

And now Orv stands and says to Harry, "I am sorry for your loss."

"I am sorry for yours," Harry replies.

I believe I hear the men speaking, but I am not in my right state of mind.

"I want to give you this," Harry says, handing Orv my locked box from the closet and a key that hangs on a ribbon.

"Thank you," I can hear Orv say.

I long to touch baby Psalm's little ears again. That always helped him sleep.

I am writing, with my finger in the air in invisible ink, one last letter to Orv, or I am trying to.

Dear Orv,

I am by your side on the long and horrible train ride back to Dayton, as you open the box with my marriage diary and the copies of the letters.

Listen to me, brother, I broke our pact to never marry, but I am not sorry that I did break it. I love Harry. Are you listening, Orv⸮ I also wish you had broken it and found love.

Over the three years I wrote to you, is it true you took each letter Carrie handed you⸮ Is it true you always thanked her kindly, even when two envelopes arrived on the same day⸮ I know when you were alone you read each one carefully, but then always tossed them into the fire. A sister knows.

Now, on the train, we are together, shivering, as you read each one again, mouthing the words silently to yourself as if in prayer. You are sitting so stiffly in your seat, reading every word, in the cold and noisy railcar as it makes the rattling journey east.

And then you read my marriage diary. You reach for Carrie's biscuits, eating and reading, scattering crumbs on the words I had written, thoughts and emotions you had never known before. By the end of the journey, your hands are stained a deep black purple from the carbon, which still clings to the letters.

When you arrive in Dayton, cold and frail, Carrie meets you at the front door. She cannot see me by your side as you clutch the box with the diary and letters as if it were a beloved toy.

That night, after Carrie insists, you eat some chicken and carrot soup, but you keep the box next to you on the dining table. You do not eat enough. You eat so slowly, no more than a half a bowl of

soup, then stand stiffly, lifting the box and carrying it into the study, where you build a fire. I see how you kneel down and set the box on the hearth, then slowly place small sticks in the fireplace and light a match.

At first, it seems you want to burn the copies of the letters and rip out the pages of the marriage diary and throw them into the fire. But you do not. You stand and walk over to the filing cabinet that I always kept so organized. You open the top drawer.

First you take out four custard-colored folders and lay them on your desk. You label each one of them in your neat hand in heron-blue ink.

K LETTERS: NOVEMBER 20, 1926–NOVEMBER 19, 1927

K LETTERS: NOVEMBER 20, 1927–NOVEMBER 19, 1928

K LETTERS: NOVEMBER 20, 1928–FEBRUARY 1929

The last folder you label MARRIAGE DIARY. You methodically place the letters and the diary in the proper folders. Then you place the folders back in the filing cabinet and close the top drawer.

I see that hesitation before you bend down and open the bottom drawer. If I could scream I would have, because now you take out a folder, labeled KATHARINE IN KANSAS CITY, of letters you had never mailed to me. I see the stack of envelopes, sealed and addressed to Mrs. Harry Haskell, but you had never stuck on stamps. And then you walk back to the fireplace.

I am kneeling by the fire with you as you place the stack of letters on the hearth. One by one, taking each letter you'd written from its envelope. Without reading a word, you fold each letter into a paper aeroplane. As you kneel, I believe you feel something that you have only felt rarely before, first when Will died, and later, thinking about all the young boys in the Great War, but also when years ago you had gone up and the buckle of the strap on your goggles failed. You had to take off your goggles and face the harsh wind without them. I am here, close by your side, as you fly all the paper aeroplanes into the fire, as a tear runs down your cheek.

Katharine Wright Haskell died on March 3, 1929, at fifty-four, five days before Harry's fifty-fifth birthday.

Lorin died in 1939 at the age of seventy-seven.

Orville died in 1948 at seventy-six.

Will, Katharine, Orv, and Lorin are buried in the family plot with their parents in Dayton. Reuchlin is buried in Kansas City.

In 1931, Harry Haskell married for the third time, to Agnes Lee Hadley, the former wife of the governor of Missouri.

Harry Haskell died in 1952 at seventy-eight.

When the astronauts landed on the moon in 1969, they brought with them small pieces of muslin fabric from the wings and two pieces of the propeller from the Wright Flyer that first took off at Kitty Hawk in 1903.

Acknowledgments

Great thanks to Jill Lipton, whose keen eye and wit were key in imagining this story. Thanks also to Kate Ginna, Mary Rae, and Carol Weston for their careful readings and apt suggestions.

As always, thank you to my agent and friend, Malaga Baldi, who has supported me through thick and thin.

I am extremely fortunate to have the wise and wonderful editor Sara Nelson, whose sage edits transformed the manuscript into a book.

Mary Gaule's support and attention (and patience) are a writer's dream.

I could not have written this tale without my husband, Michael Hill, who endured years of my musings about the Wrights, read several drafts of the story, listened to it read aloud, and even went on our honeymoon to Kitty Hawk.

About the author

About the book

Read on

Insights,
Interviews
& More...

Meet Patty Dann

PATTY DANN HAS PUBLISHED THREE novels, *Mermaids, Starfish*, and *Sweet & Crazy*. Her work has been translated into French, German, Italian, Portuguese, Dutch, Chinese, Korean, and Japanese. *Mermaids* was made into a movie starring Cher, Winona Ryder, and Christina Ricci.

Her articles have appeared in the *New York Times, Boston Globe, Chicago Tribune, Philadelphia Inquirer, Christian Science Monitor, O, The Oprah Magazine, Oregon Quarterly, Redbook, More, Forbes Woman, Poets & Writers, The Writer's Handbook, Dirt:The Quirks, Habits, and Passions of Keeping House*, and *This I Believe: On Motherhood*.

New York magazine named Dann one of the "Great Teachers of NYC." She earned an MFA in writing from Columbia University and a BA in Art History from the University of Oregon. She taught at the Fairfield County Writers' Studio, Sarah Lawrence Writing Institute, and the West Side YMCA in NYC.

Dann is married to journalist Michael Hill and has one son and two stepsons. ∾

Behind the Book

I'D ALWAYS BEEN DRAWN TO THE brilliant and dapper Wright brothers, but only five years ago did I learn they had a younger sister, Katharine. When a friend sent me a postcard of her wearing a delightful hat and long dress standing with "the boys" in their suits and polished shoes at the White House in 1909, I was entranced.

I tacked the postcard on the wall above my desk and, I confess, I googled the Wright brothers' sister. I was surprised to read that Katharine got married at fifty-two and was shocked that Orville refused to speak to her ever again. That night I went to sleep with the Wright siblings on my mind.

At three a.m. I got up and returned to my desk. I sat in my nightgown and began writing an imaginary letter from Katharine to Orville, trying to make sense of what had happened. The language did not seem foreign to me. Three of my grandparents were born in the 1890s. Phrases like "hold your horses" and "bee's knees" come more readily to my mind then some newfangled expressions.

When I was a child, my mother wrote a column about nearby attractions, often about historical sites, for our local ▸

Behind the Book *(continued)*

newspaper. I would follow her around with a little notebook and pencil and make up my own stories about what I had observed. I was seven years old when we went to a colonial reenactment where women in muslin clothes and wooden clogs were churning butter. My mother bent down and said to me, "The key to a good story is to imagine walking in another person's shoes," and I imagined having wooden soles.

In my young mind I took her counsel literally and from then on, I have imagined what it is like to wear other people's shoes. I did this with the Wright brothers' tightly laced formal oxfords and with Katharine's 1926 wedding pumps, as well.

In the years since I first learned about Katharine Wright, while I taught, swam, even cleaned the bathtub, I imagined being

Katharine. I thought of her finding great love at fifty-two, moving six hundred miles away from Dayton, Ohio, to Kansas City, Missouri, and the pain of losing the close relationship she had with Orville.

After I began writing the letters, I realized that some of what I had written seemed too intimate to send to Orville, so I began what I call Katharine's "marriage diary" that I folded into the book.

As I wrote the book, although it takes place in the 1920s, the themes threading through seem universal—how it is not uncommon to lose people after a new marriage or another joyful event, and how adult siblings are always entwined, no matter what the circumstances or geographic distance.

I continued to write the letters that dealt with Katharine's personal joy and sorrow and I became increasingly fascinated with what the invention of the airplane had wrought for the world—the great freedom of flight and the new possibilities for war.

I've had the privilege of talking with authors who have written many historical novels and they almost always do an enormous amount of research. I did not. After I began writing the letters, I would stop at certain points and read about the events of the day or other books on the Wrights. It took my sage editors to point out that I could not have Katharine wanting a car that was not yet invented or vote in an election before it actually occurred. I never looked at existing letters. I did not go libraries or Oberlin College, which both Katharine and Harry graduated from. I did not travel to Dayton and Kansas City while I was writing this book.

While I sat at my desk in New York City, imagining being at Katharine's desk in Kansas City in the 1920s, I realized the book would be published exactly one hundred years after women got to vote for president in the United States for the first time.

I hesitated at times in my writing, for I have always been a bit in awe of the Wrights. I mean no disrespect to the Wright family, the Haskell family, or to either family's descendants. The book is simply an imagining of what I might do if I found great love and lost great love at the same time. ∽

Further Reading

THERE ARE TWO BOOKS THAT GIVE Katharine her long overdue attention.

- *The Wright Sister: Katharine Wright and Her Famous Brothers* by Richard Maurer is a biography.

- *Maiden Flight: A Novel* by Harry Haskell, grandson (and keeper of his name) of Harry Haskell, who married Katharine Wright. This book is an ingenious creation using biographical primary sources as well as imagined material, creating three first-person accounts by the author's grandfather, Orville Wright, and Katharine, the woman in the middle.

BOOKS ABOUT THE WRIGHT BROTHERS

- *The Wright Brothers* by David McCullough

- *The Wright Brothers: How They Invented the Airplane* by Russell Freedman

- *Wilbur and Orville: A Biography of the Wright Brothers* by Fred Howard

- *Hidden Images of the Wright Brothers at Kitty Hawk* by Larry E. Tise

- *The Wright Brothers* by Fred C. Kelly

Discover great authors, exclusive offers, and more at hc.com.